ST
WA

AR

RS™

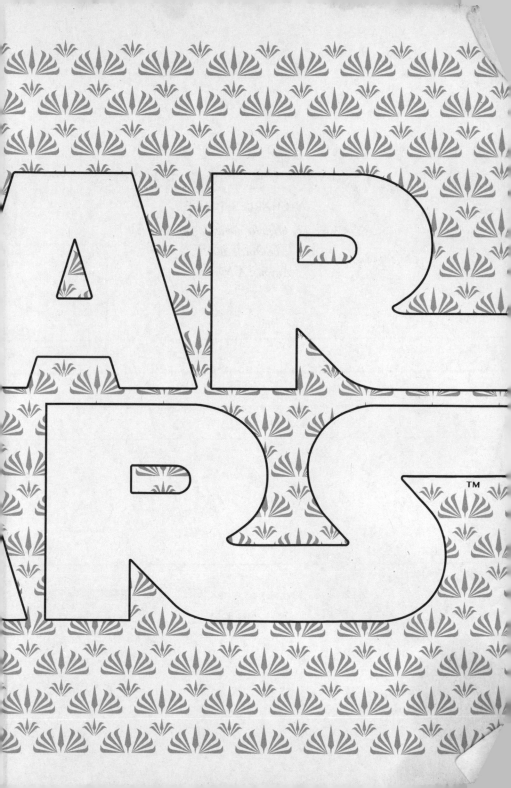

BY CHARLES SOULE

Star Wars: The High Republic: Light of the Jedi

The Oracle Year

Anyone: A Novel

STAR WARS
THE HIGH REPUBLIC

LIGHT OF THE JEDI

The galaxy is at peace, ruled by the glorious REPUBLIC and protected by the noble and wise JEDI KNIGHTS.

As a symbol of all that is good, the Republic is about to launch STARLIGHT BEACON into the far reaches of the Outer Rim. This new space station will serve as a ray of hope for all to see.

But just as a magnificent renaissance spreads throughout the Republic so does a frightening new adversary. Now the guardians of peace and justice must face a threat to themselves, the galaxy, and the Force itself. . . .

STAR WARS
THE HIGH REPUBLIC

LIGHT OF THE JEDI

Charles Soule

DEL REY
NEW YORK

Star Wars: Light of the Jedi is a work of fiction.
Names, places, and incidents either are products of the author's imagination or are used fictitiously. Any resemblance to actual events, locales, or persons, living or dead, is entirely coincidental.

2021 Del Rey Trade Paperback Edition

Published in the United States by Del Rey, an imprint of Random House, a division of Penguin Random House LLC, New York.

DEL REY is a registered trademark and the CIRCLE colophon is a trademark of Penguin Random House LLC.

Originally published in hardcover in the United States by Del Rey, an imprint of Random House, a division of Penguin Random House LLC, in 2021.

LIBRARY OF CONGRESS CATALOGING-IN-PUBLICATION DATA
Names: Soule, Charles, author.
Title: Light of the Jedi / Charles Soule.
Other titles: At head of title: Star Wars
Description: New York: Del Rey Books, [2020]
Identifiers: LCCN 2020030118 (print) | LCCN 2020030119 (ebook) | ISBN 9780593157732 (trade paperback; acid-free paper) | ISBN 9780593157725 (ebook)
Subjects: LCSH: Star Wars fiction. | GSAFD: Science fiction.
Classification: LCC PS3619.O8766 L54 2020 (print) | LCC PS3619.O8766 (ebook) | DDC 813/.6—dc23
LC record available at https://lccn.loc.gov/2020030118
LC ebook record available at https://lccn.loc.gov/2020030119

Printed in the United States of America

randomhousebooks.com

2 4 6 8 9 7 5 3 1

For Hannah, Sam, Chris, and Jay,
who love *Star Wars* as much as I do

THE STAR WARS NOVELS TIMELINE

THE HIGH REPUBLIC

Light of the Jedi
The Rising Storm

Dooku: Jedi Lost
Master and Apprentice

I THE PHANTOM MENACE

II ATTACK OF THE CLONES

Thrawn Ascendancy: Chaos Rising
Thrawn Ascendancy: The Greater Good
Dark Disciple: A Clone Wars Novel

III REVENGE OF THE SITH

Catalyst: A Rogue One Novel
Lords of the Sith
Tarkin

SOLO

Thrawn
A New Dawn: A Rebels Novel
Thrawn: Alliances
Thrawn: Treason

ROGUE ONE

IV A NEW HOPE

Battlefront II: Inferno Squad
Heir to the Jedi
Doctor Aphra
Battlefront: Twilight Company

V THE EMPIRE STRIKES BACK

VI RETURN OF THE JEDI

The Alphabet Squadron Trilogy
The Aftermath Trilogy
Last Shot

Bloodline
Phasma
Canto Bight

VII THE FORCE AWAKENS

VIII THE LAST JEDI

Resistance Reborn
Galaxy's Edge: Black Spire

IX THE RISE OF SKYWALKER

A long time ago in a galaxy far, far away. . . .

STAR WARS
THE HIGH REPUBLIC

LIGHT OF THE JEDI

The Force is with the galaxy.

It is the time of the High Republic: a peaceful union of like-minded worlds where all voices are heard, and governance is achieved through consensus, not coercion or fear. It is an era of ambition, of culture, of inclusion, of Great Works. Visionary Chancellor Lina Soh leads the Republic from the elegant city-world of Coruscant, located near the bright center of the Galactic Core.

But beyond the Core and its many peaceful Colonies, there is the Rim—Inner, Mid, and finally, at the border of what is known: the Outer Rim. These worlds are filled with opportunity for those brave enough to travel the few well-mapped hyperspace lanes leading to them, though there is danger as well. The Outer Rim is a haven for anyone seeking to escape the laws of the Republic, and is filled with predators of every type.

Chancellor Soh has pledged to bring the Outer Rim worlds into the embrace of the Republic through ambitious outreach programs such as the Starlight Beacon. But until it is brought online, order and justice are maintained on the galactic frontier by Jedi Knights, guardians of peace who have mastered incredible abilities stemming from a mysterious energy field known as the Force. The Jedi work closely with the Republic, and have agreed to establish outposts in the Outer Rim to help any who might require aid.

The Jedi of the frontier can be the only resource for people with nowhere else to turn. Though the outposts operate independently and without direct assistance from the great Jedi Temple on Coruscant, they act as an effective deterrent to those who would do evil in the dark.

Few can stand against the Knights of the Jedi Order.

But there are always those who will try…

PART ONE

The Great Disaster

CHAPTER ONE

HYPERSPACE. THE *LEGACY RUN.*
3 hours to impact.

All is well.

Captain Hedda Casset reviewed the readouts and displays built into her command chair for the second time. She always went over them at least twice. She had more than four decades of flying behind her, and figured the double check was a large part of the reason she'd survived all that time. The second look confirmed everything she'd seen in the first.

"All is well," she said, out loud this time, announcing it to her bridge crew. "Time for my rounds. Lieutenant Bowman, you have the bridge."

"Acknowledged, Captain," her first officer replied, standing from his own seat in preparation to occupy hers until she returned from her evening constitutional.

Not every long-haul freighter captain ran their ship like a military vessel. Hedda had seen starships with stained floors and leaking pipes and cracks in their cockpit viewports, lapses that speared her to her very soul. But Hedda Casset began her career as a fighter pilot with the

Malastare–Sullust Joint Task Force, keeping order in their little sector on the border of the Mid Rim. She'd started out flying an Incom Z-24, the single-seat fighter everyone just called a Buzzbug. Mostly security missions, hunting down pirates and the like. Eventually, though, she rose to command a heavy cruiser, one of the largest vessels in the fleet. A good career, doing good work.

She'd left Mallust JTF with distinction and moved on to a job captaining merchant vessels for the Byne Guild—her version of a relaxed retirement. But thirty-plus years in the military meant order and discipline weren't just in her blood—they *were* her blood. So every ship she flew now was run like it was about to fight a decisive battle against a Hutt armada, even if it was just carrying a load of ogrut hides from world A to world B. This ship, the *Legacy Run,* was no exception.

Hedda stood, accepting and returning Lieutenant Jary Bowman's snapped salute. She stretched, feeling the bones of her spine crackle and crunch. Too many years on patrol in tiny cockpits, too many high-g maneuvers—sometimes in combat, sometimes just because it made her feel alive.

The real problem, though, she thought, tucking a stray strand of gray hair behind one ear, *is too many years.*

She left the bridge, departing the precise machine of her command deck and walking along a compact corridor into the larger, more chaotic world of the *Legacy Run.* The ship was a Kaniff Yards Class A modular freight transport, more than twice as old as Hedda herself. That put the craft a bit past her ideal operational life, but well within safe parameters if she was well maintained and regularly serviced—which she was. Her captain saw to that.

The *Run* was a mixed-use ship, rated for both cargo and passengers—hence "modular" in its designation. Most of the vessel's structure was taken up by a single gigantic compartment, shaped like a long, triangular prism, with engineering aft, the bridge fore, and the rest of the space allotted for cargo. Hollow boom arms protruded from the central "spine" at regular intervals, to which additional smaller modules could be attached. The ship could hold up to 144 of these, each customizable, to handle every kind of cargo the galaxy had to offer.

Hedda liked that the ship could haul just about anything. It meant you never knew what you were going to get, what weird challenges you might face from one job to the next. She had flown the ship once when half the cargo space in the primary compartment was reconfigured into a huge water tank, to carry a gigantic saberfish from the storm seas on Tibrin to the private aquarium of a countess on Abregado-rae. Hedda and her crew had gotten the beast there safely—not an easy gig. Even harder, though, was getting the creature back to Tibrin three cycles later, when the blasted thing got sick because the countess's people had no idea how to take care of it. She gave the woman credit, though—she paid full freight to send the saberfish home. A lot of people, nobles especially, would have just let it die.

This particular trip, in comparison, was as simple as they came. The *Legacy Run*'s cargo sections were about 80 percent filled with settlers heading to the Outer Rim from overpopulated Core and Colony worlds, seeking new lives, new opportunities, new skies. She could relate to that. Hedda Casset had been restless all her life. She had a feeling she'd die that way, too, looking out a viewport, hoping her eyes would land on something she'd never seen before.

Because this was a transport run, most of the ship's modules were basic passenger configurations, with open seating that converted into beds that were, in theory, comfortable enough to sleep in. Sanitary facilities, storage, a few holoscreens, small galleys, and that was it. For settlers willing to pay for the increased comfort and convenience, some had droid-operated auto-canteens and private sleeping compartments, but not many. These people were frugal. If they'd had credits to begin with, they probably wouldn't be heading to the Outer Rim to scrape out a future. The dark edge of the galaxy was a place of challenges both exciting and deadly. More deadly than exciting, in truth.

Even the road to get out here is tricky, Hedda thought, her gaze drawn by the swirl of hyperspace outside the large porthole she happened to be passing. She snapped her eyes away, knowing she could end up standing there for twenty minutes if she let herself get sucked in. You couldn't trust hyperspace. It was useful, sure, it got you from here to there, it was the key to the expansion of the Republic out from the Core, but no one really understood it. If your navidroid miscalculated the coordinates, even a little, you could end up off the marked route, the main road through whatever hyperspace actually was, and then you'd be on a dark path leading to who knew where. It happened even in the well-traveled hyperlanes near the galactic center, and out here, where the prospectors had barely mapped out any routes . . . well, you had to watch yourself.

She put her concerns out of her mind and continued on her way. The truth was, the *Legacy Run* was currently speeding along the best-traveled, best-known route to the Outer Rim worlds. Ships moved through this hyperlane constantly, in both directions. Nothing to worry about.

But then, more than nine thousand souls aboard this ship were depending on Captain Hedda Casset to get them safely to their destination. She worried. It was her job.

Hedda exited the corridor and entered the central hull, emerging in a large, circular space, an open spot necessitated by the ship's structure that had been repurposed as a sort of unofficial common area. A group of children kicked a ball around as adults stood and chatted nearby; all just enjoying a little break from the cramped confines of the modules where they spent most of their time. The space wasn't fancy, just a bare junction spot where several short corridors met—but it was clean. The ship employed—at its captain's insistence—an automated maintenance crew that kept its interiors neat and sanitary. One of the custodial droids was spidering its way along a wall at that very moment, performing one of the endless tasks required on a ship the size of the *Run.*

She took a moment to take stock of this group—twenty people or so, all ages, from a number of worlds. Humans, of course, but also a few four-armed, fur-covered Ardennians, a family of Givin with their distinctive triangular eyes, and even a Lannik with its pinched face, topknot, and huge, pointed ears protruding from the side of its head—you didn't see many of those around. But no matter their planet of origin, they were all just ordinary beings, biding time until their new lives could begin.

One of the kids looked up.

"Captain Casset!" the boy said, a human, olive-skinned with red hair. She knew him.

"Hello, Serj," Hedda said. "What's the good word? Everything all right here?"

The other children stopped their game and clustered around her.

"Could use some new holos," Serj said. "We've watched everything in the system."

"All we got is all we got," Hedda replied. "And stop trying to slice into the archive to see the age-restricted titles. You think I don't know? This is my ship. I know everything that happens on the *Legacy Run.*"

She leaned forward.

"Everything."

Serj blushed and looked toward his friends, who had also, suddenly, found very interesting things to look at on the absolutely uninteresting floor, ceiling, and walls of the chamber.

"Don't worry about it," she said, straightening. "I get it. This is a pretty boring ride. You won't believe me, but in not too long, when your parents have you plowing fields or building fences or fighting off rancors, you'll be dreaming of the time you spent on this ship. Just relax and enjoy."

Serj rolled his eyes and returned to whatever improvised ball game he and the other kids had devised.

Hedda grinned and moved through the room, nodding and chatting as she went. People. Probably some good, some bad, but for the next few days, her people. She loved these runs. No matter what eventually happened in the lives of these folks, they were heading to the

Rim to make their dreams come true. She was part of that, and it made her feel good.

Chancellor Soh's Republic wasn't perfect—no government was or ever could be—but it was a system that gave people room to dream. No, even better. It encouraged dreams, big and small. The Republic had its flaws, but really, things could be a hell of a lot worse.

Hedda's rounds took over an hour—she made her way through the passenger compartments, but also checked on a shipment of supercooled liquid Tibanna to make sure the volatile stuff was properly locked down (it was), inspected the engines (all good), investigated the status of repairs to the ship's environmental recirculation systems (in progress and proceeding nicely), and made sure fuel reserves were still more than adequate for the rest of the journey with a comfortable margin besides (they were).

The *Legacy Run* was exactly as she wanted it to be. A tiny, well-maintained world in the wilderness, a warm bubble of safety holding back the void. She couldn't vouch for what was waiting for these settlers once they dispersed into the Outer Rim, but she would make sure they got there safe and sound to find out.

Hedda returned to the bridge, where Lieutenant Bowman all but leapt to his feet the moment he saw her enter.

"Captain on the bridge," he said, and the other officers sat up straighter.

"Thank you, Jary," Hedda said as her second stepped aside and returned to his post.

Hedda settled into her command chair, automatically checking the displays, scanning for anything out of the ordinary.

All is well, she thought.

KTANG. KTANG. KTANG. KTANG. An alarm, loud and insistent. The bridge lighting flipped into its emergency configuration—bathing everything in red. Through the front viewport, the swirls of hyperspace looked off, somehow. Maybe it was the emergency lighting, but they had a . . . reddish tinge. They looked . . . sickly.

Hedda felt her pulse quicken. Her mind snapped into combat mode without thinking.

"Report!" she barked out, her eyes whipping along her own set of screens to find the source of the alarm.

"Alarm generated by the navicomp, Captain," called out her navigator, Cadet Kalwar, a young Quermian. "There's something in the hyperlane. Dead ahead. Big. Impact in ten seconds."

The cadet's voice held steady, and Hedda was proud of him. He probably wasn't that much older than Serj.

She knew this situation was impossible. The hyperlanes were empty. That was the whole point. She couldn't rattle off all the science involved, but she did know that lightspeed collisions in established lanes simply could not happen. It was "mathematically absurd," to hear the engineers talk about it.

Hedda had been flying in deep space long enough to know that impossible things happened all the time, every damn day. She also knew that ten seconds was no time at all at speeds like the *Legacy Run* was traveling.

You can't trust hyperspace, she thought.

Hedda Casset tapped two buttons on her command console.

"Brace yourselves," she said, her voice calm. "I'm taking control."

Two piloting sticks snapped up out from the armrests of her captain's chair, and Hedda grasped them, one in each hand.

She spared the time for one breath, and then she flew.

The *Legacy Run* was not an Incom Z-24 Buzzbug, or even one of the new Republic Longbeams. It had been in service for well over a century. It was a freighter at the end of—if not beyond—its operational life span, loaded to capacity, with engines designed for slow, gradual acceleration and deceleration, and docking with spaceports and orbital loading facilities. It maneuvered like a moon.

The *Legacy Run* was no warship. Not even close. But Hedda flew it like one.

She saw the obstacle in their path with her fighter pilot's eye and instincts, saw it advancing at incredible velocity, large enough that both her ship and whatever the thing was would be disintegrated into atoms, just dust drifting forever through the hyperlanes. There was no time to avoid it. The ship could not make the turn. There was no room, and there was no time.

But Captain Hedda Casset was at the helm, and she would not fail her ship.

The tiniest tweak of the left control stick, and a larger rotation of the right, and the *Legacy Run* moved. More than it wanted to, but not less than its captain believed it could. The huge freighter slipped past the obstacle in their path, the thing shooting by their hull so close Hedda was sure she felt it ruffle her hair despite the many layers of metal and shielding between them.

But they were alive. No impact. The ship was alive.

Turbulence, and Hedda fought it, feeling her way through the jagged bumps and ripples, closing her eyes, not needing to see to fly. The ship groaned, its frame complaining.

"You can do it, old gal," she said, out loud. "We're a couple of cranky old ladies and that's for sure, but we've both got a lot of life to live. I've taken damn good care of you, and you know it. I won't let you down if you won't let me down."

Hedda did not fail her ship.

It failed her.

The groan of overstressed metal became a scream. The vibrations of the ship's passage through space took on a new timbre Hedda had felt too many times before. It was the feeling of a ship that had moved beyond its limits, whether from taking too much damage in a firefight or, as here, just being asked to perform a maneuver that was more than it could give.

The *Legacy Run* was tearing itself apart. At most, it had seconds left.

Hedda opened her eyes. She released the control sticks and tapped out commands on her console, activating the bulkhead shielding that separated each cargo module in the instance of a disaster, thinking that perhaps it might give some of the people aboard a chance. She thought about Serj and his friends, playing in the common area, and how emergency doors had just slammed down at the entrance to each passenger module, possibly trapping them in a zone that was about to become vacuum. She hoped the children had gone to their families when the alarms sounded.

She didn't know.

She just didn't know.

Hedda locked eyes with her first officer, who was staring at her, knowing what was about to happen. He saluted.

"Captain," Lieutenant Bowman said, "it's been an—"

The bridge ripped open.

Hedda Casset died, not knowing if she had saved anyone at all.

CHAPTER TWO

THE OUTER RIM. HETZAL SYSTEM.
2.5 hours to impact.

Scantech (third-class) Merven Getter was *ready.* Ready to clock out for the day, ready to get the shuttle back to the inner system, ready to hit the cantina a few streets away from the spaceport on the Rooted Moon where Sella worked tending bar, ready to see if today was the day he might find the courage to ask her out. She was Twi'lek, and he was Mirialan, but what difference did that make? *We are all the Republic.* Chancellor Soh's big slogan—but people believed it. Actually, Merven thought he did, too. Attitudes were evolving. The possibilities were endless.

And maybe, one of those possibilities revolved around a scantech (third-class) staffed on a monitoring station far out on the ecliptic of the Hetzal system, itself pretty blasted far out on the Rim, sadly distant from the bright lights and interesting worlds of the Republic Core. Perhaps that scantech (third-class), who spent his days staring at holoscreens, logging starship traffic in and out of the system, could actually catch the eye of the lovely scarlet-skinned woman who served him up a mug of the local ale, three or four nights a week. Sella usually stayed around to chat with him for a while, circling back as other customers drifted in and out of her little tavern. She seemed to find his stories about life on the far edge of the system inexplicably interesting.

Merven didn't get why she was so fascinated. Sometimes ships showed up in-system, popping in from hyperspace and appearing on his screens, and other times ships left . . . at which point their little icons disappeared from his screens. Nothing interesting ever happened—flight plans were logged ahead of time, so he usually knew what was coming or going. Merven was responsible for making sure those flight plans were followed, and not much else. On the off chance something unusual occurred, his job was just to notify people significantly more important than he was.

Scantech (third-class) Merven Getter spent his days watching people go places. He, in contrast, stayed still.

But maybe not today. He thought about Sella. He thought about her smile, the way she decorated her lekku with those intricate lacings she told him she designed herself, the way she stopped whatever she was doing to pour him his mug of ale the moment he walked in, without him even having to ask for it.

Yeah. He was going to ask her to dinner. Tonight. He'd been saving up, and he knew a place not too far from the cantina. Not so far from his place, either, but that was getting ahead of himself.

He just had to get through his blasted shift.

Merven glanced over at his colleague, Scantech (second-class) Vel Carann. He wanted to ask her if he could check out a little early that day, take the shuttle back to the Rooted Moon. She was reading something on a datapad, her eyes rapt. Probably one of the Jedi romances she was always obsessed with. Merven didn't get it. He'd read a few—they were all set at outposts on the far Republic frontiers, full of unrequited love and longing glances . . . the only action was the lightsaber battles that were clearly a substitute for what the characters really wanted to do. Vel wasn't supposed to be reading personal material on company time, but if he called her out on it, she'd just tap the screen and switch it to a technical manual and insist she wasn't doing anything wrong. The trouble was, she was second-class, and he was third-class, which meant that as long as he did his job, she thought she didn't have to do hers.

Nah. Not even worth asking for an early sign-off time. Not from Vel. He could get through the rest of his shift. Not long now, and—

Something appeared on one of his screens.

"Huh," Merven said.

That was odd. Nothing was scheduled to enter the system for another twenty minutes or so.

Something else appeared. A number of somethings. Ten.

"What the—?" Merven said.

"Problem, Getter?" Vel asked, not glancing up from her screen.

"I'm not sure," he said. "Got a bunch of unscheduled entries to the system, and they're not decelerating."

"Wait . . . what?" Vel said, setting down her datascreen and finally looking at her own monitors. "Oh, that is odd."

More icons popped up on Merven's screens, too many to count at a glance.

"Is this . . . do you think it's . . . asteroids, maybe?" Vel said, her voice unsteady.

"At that velocity? From hyperspace? I dunno. Run an analysis," Merven said. "See if you can figure out what they are."

Silence from Vel's station.

Merven glanced up.

"I . . . don't know how," she said. "After the latest upgrade, I never bothered to learn the systems. You seemed to have it all under control, and I'm really here to supervise, you know, and—"

"Fine," he said, utterly unsurprised. "Can you track trajectories, at least? That subroutine's been the same for like two years."

"Yeah," Vel said. "I can do that."

Merven turned back to his screens and started typing commands across his keypads.

There were now forty-two anomalies in-system, all moving at a velocity near lightspeed. Incredibly fast, in other words, much quicker than safety regulations allowed. If they were in fact ships, whoever was piloting them was in for a massive fine. But Merven didn't think they were ships. They were too small, for one thing, and didn't have drive signatures.

Asteroids, maybe? Space rocks, somehow thrown into the system? Some kind of weird space storm, or a comet swarm? It couldn't be an attack, that much he knew. The Republic was at peace, and looked like it was going to stay that way. Everyone was happy, living their lives. The Republic worked.

Besides, the Hetzal system didn't have anything worth attacking. It was just an ordinary set of planets, the primeworld and its two inhabited moons—the Fruited and the Rooted—with a deep focus on agricultural production. It had some gas giants and frozen balls of rock, but really it was just a lot of farmers and all the things they grew. Merven knew it was important, that Hetzal exported food all over the Outer Rim, and some of its output even found its way to the inner systems. There was that bacta stuff he'd been reading about, too, some kind of miracle replacement for juvan they were trying to grow on the primeworld, supposed to revolutionize medicine if they could ever figure out how to farm it in volume . . . but still, it was all just plants. It was hard to get excited about plants.

As far as he was concerned, Hetzal's biggest claim to fame was that it was the homeworld of a famous gill-singer named Illoria Daze, who could vibrate her vocal apparatus in such a way as to sing melodies in six-part harmony. That, in combination with a uniquely appealing wit and rags-to-riches backstory, had made her famous across the Republic. But Illoria wasn't even here. She lived on Alderaan now, with the fancy people.

Hetzal had nothing of any real value. None of this made sense.

Another rash of objects appeared on his screens, so many now that it was overloading his computer's ability to track them. He zoomed out the resolution, shifting to a system-wide view, making a clearer picture. Merven could see that the things, whatever they might be, were not restricting themselves to entering the system from the safety of the hyperspace access zone. They were popping up everywhere, and some were getting awfully close to—

"Oh no," Vel said.

"I see it, too," Merven said. He didn't even have to run a trajectory analysis.

The anomalies were headed sunward, and many of them were on intercept courses with the inhabited worlds and their orbital stations. The things weren't slowing down, either. Not at all. At near-lightspeed, it didn't matter whether they were asteroids, or ships, or frothy bubbles of fizz-candy. Whatever they hit would just . . . go.

As he watched, one of the objects smashed through an uncrewed communications satellite. Both the anomaly and the satellite vanished from his screen, and the galaxy got itself a little more space dust.

Hetzal Prime was big enough that it could endure a few impacts like that and survive as a planetary body. Even the two inhabited moons might be able to take a couple of hits. But anything living on them . . .

Sella was on the Rooted Moon right now.

"We have to get out of here," he said. "We're right in the target zone, and more of these things are appearing every second. We have to get to the shuttle."

"I agree," Vel said, some semblance of command returning to her voice. "But we need to send a system-wide alert first. We have to."

Merven closed his eyes for a moment, then opened them again.

"You're right. Of course."

"The computer needs authorization codes from both of us to activate the system-wide alarm," Vel said. "We'll do it on my signal."

She tapped a few commands on her keypad. Merven did the same, then waited for her nod. She gave it, and he typed in his code.

A soft, chiming alarm rang through the operations deck as the message went out. Merven knew that a similar sound was now being heard across the Hetzal system, from the cockpits of garbage scows all the way to the minister's palace on the primeworld. Forty billion people just looked up in fear. One of them was a lovely scarlet-skinned Twi'lek probably wondering whether her favorite Mirialan was going to come by the tavern that evening.

Merven stood up.

"We've done our job. Shuttle time. We can send a message explaining what's happening on the way."

Vel nodded and levered herself up out of her seat.

"Yeah. Let's get out of—"

One of the objects leapt out of hyperspace, so near, and moving so fast, that in astronomical terms it was on them the moment it appeared.

A gout of flame, and the anomaly vanished, along with the monitoring station, its two scantechs, and all their goals, fears, skills, hopes, and dreams; the kinetic energy of the object atomizing everything it touched in less than an instant.

CHAPTER THREE

AGUIRRE CITY, HETZAL PRIME.

2 hours to impact.

"Is this real?" Minister Ecka asked as the chimes rang through his office—consistent, insistent, impossible to ignore. Which, he supposed, was the point.

"Seems so," Counselor Daan answered, tucking a curl of hair behind his ear. "The alert originated from a monitoring station at the far edge of the system. It came in at the highest priority level, and it hit system-wide. Every computer linked to the main processing core is sounding the same alarm."

"But what's causing it?" the minister asked. "There was no message attached?"

"No," Daan replied. "We've repeatedly asked for clarification, but there's been no response. We believe . . . the monitoring station was destroyed."

Minister Ecka thought for a moment. He rotated his chair away from his advisers, the old wood creaking a little beneath his weight. He looked out through the broad picture window that made up the wall behind his desk. As far as he could see: the golden fields of Hetzal, all the way to the horizon. The world—the whole system, really—believed in using every bit of available space to grow, create, to cultivate. Buildings were roofed with cropland, rivers and lakes were used to grow helpful algae and waterweeds, towers were terraced, with fruit vines spilling from their sides. Harvester droids floated among them, plucking ripe fruits—whatever was in season. Right now, that would be honeyfruit, kingberries, and ice melons. In a month, it would be something else. On Hetzal, something was always in season.

He loved this view. The most peaceful in the galaxy, he believed. Everything just so. Productive and correct.

Now, with the alarm chimes ringing in his ears, it didn't look like that anymore. Now it all just looked . . . fragile.

"Something's happening out there," another adviser said, a Devaronian woman named Zaffa.

Ecka had known her for a long time, and this was the first time he'd ever heard her sound worried. She was staring down at a datascreen, frowning.

"A mining rig out in midsystem just went down," Zaffa said. "The satellite network's starting to show holes, too. It's like something's taking out our facilities, one by one."

"And we still don't have any images? This is madness," Ecka declared.

He pointed at his security chief, a portly middle-aged human.

"Borta, why don't your people know what's happening?"

Borta frowned. "Minister, respectfully, you know why. Your recent cuts have reduced Hetzal's security division to a tenth of its former size. We're working on it, but we can't bring much to bear."

"Is it some sort of natural anomaly? It can't be . . . we're not under attack, are we?"

"At this point, we don't know. What's happening is consistent with some sort of enemy infiltration, but we're not seeing drive signatures, and the locations being hit are pretty random. We do still have some orbital defense platforms out there, and they're all intact. If it's an attack, they should be targeting our ability to strike back, but they're not."

The chimes sounded again, and Ecka spun his chair and pointed at Counselor Daan, who cringed back.

"Will you turn off that blasted alarm? I can't think!"

Daan pulled himself up, standing a little straighter, and tapped a control on his datascreen. The chimes, blessedly, ceased.

Another adviser spoke up—a slim young man with red hair and extremely pale skin, Keven Tarr. The Ministry of Technology had sent him over. Ecka didn't have much use for tech that wasn't related to agricultural yields. In his heart, he was still a farmer—but he knew Tarr was supposed to be very smart. Probably wouldn't be long until the boy moved on, found himself a job in some more sophisticated part of the galaxy. It was the way of things on a world like Hetzal. Not everyone stayed.

"I think I can show you what's going on, Minister," Tarr said.

The man had long fingers for a human, and they danced over his datapad.

"Let me give the data to the droid—it can project the information so we can all see."

He tapped a few last commands, then unreeled a connection wire from his datapad and plugged it into the access port on the squat, hexagonal comms droid waiting in the corner of the room. It rolled forward, its single green eye lighting up as it moved.

From that eye, the machine projected an image on the large white wall in the minister's office reserved for the purpose. Normally, presentations on the vidwall would be concerned with crop yields or pest eradication programs. Now, though, it displayed the entire Hetzal system, all its worlds and stations and satellites and platforms and vessels.

And something else.

To Minister Ecka, it looked like a field overrun with a swarm of all-consuming insects. Hundreds of tiny lights moved through his system at what had to be tremendous speed, all in the same direction:

sunward. More particularly, planetward. Toward Hetzal Prime and the moons Fruited and Rooted not so far away, not to mention all those stations, satellites, platforms, vessels . . . many of which had people on them.

"What are they?" he asked.

"Unknown," Tarr responded. "I got this image by linking together signals from the surviving satellites and monitoring stations, but they're going down quickly, and we're losing sensor capacity as they do. Whatever these anomalies are, they're moving at near-lightspeed, and it's very difficult to track them. And, of course, whenever thcy hit something, it's . . ."

"Not good," General Borta finished for him.

"Apocalyptic, I was going to say," Tarr said. "I'm tracking a good number on impact paths with the primeworld."

"Is there nothing to be done?" Ecka said, looking at Borta. "Can we . . . shoot them down?"

Borta gave him a helpless look. "Once, maybe, we'd have had a chance. At least some. But system defense hasn't been a priority here for . . . a long time."

The accusation hung in the air, but Ecka did not indulge it. He had made decisions that seemed correct at the time, with the best information he had. They were at peace! Everywhere was at peace. Why waste money that could help people in other ways? In any case, no looking back. It was time for another decision. The best he could make.

He did not hesitate. When the crops were burning, you couldn't hesitate. As bad as things might be, the longer you waited, the worse they tended to get.

"Give the evacuation order. System-wide. Then send a message to Coruscant. Let them know what's happening. They won't be able to get anyone here in time, but at least they'll know."

Counselor Zaffa looked at him, her eyes hooded.

"I don't know if we can actually implement that order effectively, Minister," she said. "We don't have enough ships here for planetary evacuations, and if these things are really moving close to lightspeed, there isn't much time until—"

"I understand, Counselor Zaffa," Ecka said, his voice steady now. "But even if the order saves just one person, then one person will be saved."

Zaffa nodded, and tapped her datascreen.

"It's done," she said. "System-wide evac in progress."

The group watched the projection on the wall, fritzes of static lancing through it now. Tarr's makeshift network was losing capacity as more satellites met fiery ends, but the message was still clear. It was like a massive gun had been fired at the Hetzal system, and there was nothing they could do to save themselves.

"You should probably all try to find yourselves a way offworld," Ecka said. "I imagine the starships we do have will be very full quite quickly."

No one moved.

"What will you do, Minister?" Counselor Daan asked.

Ecka turned back to his window, looking out at the fields, golden to the horizon. It was all so peaceful. Impossible to believe anything bad could ever happen here.

"I think I'll stay," he said. "Broadcast to the people, maybe, try to keep folks calm. Someone has to look after the harvest."

Across Hetzal Prime and the broad expanses of its two inhabited moons, the message of Minister Ecka traveled rapidly, appearing on datapads and holoscreens, broadcast across all communication channels, saying, in essence: *Nowhere is safe. Get as far away as you can.*

Explanation was limited, which caused speculation. What was happening? Some kind of accident? What disaster could be so huge in scope that an entire system needed to be evacuated?

Some people ignored the warning. False alarms had happened

before, and sometimes slicers pulled pranks or showed off by breaking into emergency alert computer systems. True, nothing had ever happened on this scale, but really, that made it easier to dismiss the whole thing. After all, the entire system in danger? It just wasn't possible.

Those people stayed in their homes, at their workplaces. They turned off their screens and got back to their lives, because it was better than the alternative. And if they glanced to the skies from time to time, and saw starships heading up and out . . . well, they told themselves the people in those ships were fools, easily spooked.

Others, elsewhere, froze. They wanted to find safety but had no idea how. Not everyone had access to a way offworld. In fact, most did not. Hetzal was a system of farmers, people who lived close to the land. If they traveled anywhere else in the Republic, it was for a special occasion, a once-in-a-lifetime experience. Now, being told to find a way to space on a moment's notice . . . how? How could they possibly do such a thing?

But some people in Hetzal did have starships, or lived in the cities where space travel was more common. They found their children, gathered their treasures, and raced to the spaceports, hoping they would be the first to arrive, the first to book passage. They, inevitably, were not. They were greeted by crowds, queues, ticket prices spiking to unattainable levels for all but the wealthiest, thanks to unscrupulous opportunists. Tension rose. Fights broke out, and while Hetzal did have a security force to calm these squabbles, these officers also eyed the skies and wondered if they would spend their last moments alive trying to help other people to safety. A noble end, if so . . . but a desirable one? The security officers were people, too, with families of their own.

Order began to break down.

On the Rooted Moon, a kind trader decided to open the doors of the starship he used to transport the exceedingly fresh produce of the moon to the voracious worlds of the Outer Rim. He offered space to all who could possibly fit, and though his pilot told him the vessel was old, and the engines were a bit past their prime, the trader did not care. This was a moment for magnanimity and hope, and by the light he would save as many as he could.

The ship, holding 582 people, including the trader and his own family, managed to take off from its landing pad, once the pilot pushed its engines to maximum. It just needed to escape the moon's gravity well. Once they were in space, everything would get easier. They could get away, to safety.

The vessel achieved most of a kilometer before the overtaxed engines exploded. The fireball rained down over those left behind, and they were not sure whether they were lucky or not, considering they still had no idea what was coming for them. Minister Ecka's message did not say.

A variant on that message was sent out from Hetzal to any other systems or ships that might hear it: *We are in desperate trouble. Send aid if you can.*

It was picked up by receivers in the other worlds of the Outer Rim—Ab Dalis, Mon Cala, Eriadu, and many more, spreading outward via the Republic's relay system, and then inward to the planets of the Mid and Inner Rims, the Colonies region, and even the shining Core. Virtually everyone who heard it wanted to do something to help—but what? It was clear that whatever was happening in Hetzal would be over well before they could arrive.

But ships were sent anyway—mostly medical aid vessels, in the hope they might be able to offer treatment to injured citizens of Hetzal.

If any survived.

"Get to your nearest offworld transport facility," Minister Ecka said to a cam droid recording his words and image and broadcasting them across the system. "We will send ships to pick up people who don't have other ways to leave the planet. It might take time, but stay calm and peaceful. You have my word, we will come for you. We are all of the same crop. Hearty stock. We will survive this the way we have survived harsh winters and dry summers, by pulling together.

"We are all Hetzal. We are all the Republic," he said.

He raised a hand, and the cam droid ceased transmitting. This was the fourth message he had sent since the emergency began, and he hoped his communications were doing some good. Reports suggested they were not—riots were beginning at spaceports on all three inhabited worlds—but what else could he do? He broadcast his messages from his office in Aguirre City, demonstrating that he had not abandoned his people even though he surely could. A show of solidarity. Not much, but something.

Around him, the rest of his staff coordinated their own attempts to assist in whatever way they could. General Borta worked with his meager security fleet to both keep order and ferry people offplanet. With the help of Counselor Daan, they had organized a number of the huge crop freighters currently in transit to act as relay points, ordering them to dump their cargo and clear all space for incoming refugees. Each could hold tens of thousands of people. Not comfortably, of course, but this was not a situation where comfort mattered.

Smaller ships were ferrying Hetzalians up to the cargo vessels, offloading their people then rushing back to pick up more. It was an imperfect system, but it was what they had been able to arrange on no notice. There was no plan for something like this.

Minister Ecka blamed himself for that—but how could he have known? This wasn't supposed to happen. It was impossible, whatever it was. He was just a farmer, after all, and—

No, he thought, suddenly ashamed of himself. He was Minister Zeffren Ecka, leader of the whole blasted system. It didn't matter if he couldn't have anticipated this disaster—it was happening, and he needed to do everything he could.

As he considered that thought, he looked over at Keven Tarr, who had never stopped running his little network, trying to keep information flowing. The young man was now working with three separate datapads and a number of comms droids projecting various displays on the walls, pulling in as much data as he could about the scope of the disaster that continued to wreak havoc in the system. He still had no real answers, other than to continually confirm that Hetzal was being savaged by whatever was afflicting the system. Satellites, arrays, stations . . . smashed apart by the storm of death that had come calling. It was like the seasonal chewfly swarms that used to plague the Fruited Moon until they had been genetically modified out of existence.

If the swarm came, there was nothing you could do. You hunkered down, survived, and sowed your fields again once it was all done.

Ecka watched as Keven Tarr wiped sweat from his eyes, then looked back at his main datapad, the one he had propped up on the little side table he was using as a desk.

Tarr's eyes widened, and his fingers froze, hovering over the screen.

"Minister," he said. "I'm . . . I'm getting a signal."

"What signal?" Ecka said.

"I'll just . . . I'll just put it through," Tarr said, and there was an odd note in his voice, of surprise, or just something unexpected.

Words crackled into the air, one of the technician's comms droids broadcasting the message out into Minister Ecka's office. A woman's voice. Just a few words, but they brought with them, yes . . . the one thing most needed at that moment.

"This is Jedi Master Avar Kriss. Help is on the way."

That one thing.

Hope.

CHAPTER FOUR

REPUBLIC *EMISSARY*-CLASS CRUISER
THIRD HORIZON.
90 minutes to impact.

A vessel appeared in the Hetzal system, leaping out of hyperspace and rapidly slowing as it returned to conventional speeds. It was deeply sunward, and the gravity wells it needed to navigate would rip a lesser ship apart, or even this one, if its bridge crew did not represent the best the Republic had to offer.

The ship was the *Third Horizon,* and it was beautiful. The ship's surfaces rippled along its frame like waves on a silver sea, tapering to a point, with towers and crenellations along its length, like a fortress laid on its side, all wings and spires and spirals. It spoke of ambition. It spoke of optimism. It spoke of a thing made beautiful because it could be, with little consideration given to cost or effort.

The *Third Horizon* was a work of art, symbolic of the great Republic of worlds it represented.

Smaller vessels began rolling off berths on the ship's hull, peeling away like flower petals in a breeze, darting specks of silver and gold. These were the craft of the Jedi Order, their Vectors. As the Jedi and Republic worked as one, so did the great ship and its Jedi contingent.

Larger ships exited the *Third Horizon*'s hangars as well, the Republic's workhorses: Longbeams. Versatile vessels, each able to perform duties in combat, search and rescue, transport, and anything else their crews might require.

The Vectors were configured as single- or dual-passenger craft, for not all Jedi traveled alone. Some brought their Padawans with them, so they might learn what lessons their Masters had to teach. The Longbeams could be flown by as few as three crew, but could comfortably carry up to twenty-four—soldiers, diplomats, medics, techs—whatever was needed.

The smaller vessels spun out into the system, accelerating away from the *Third Horizon* with purpose. Each with a destination, each with a goal. Each with lives to save.

On the bridge of the *Third Horizon*, a woman, human, stood alone. Activity churned all around her, in the arched spaces and alcoves of the bridge, as officers and navigators and specialists began to coordinate the effort to save the Hetzal system from destruction. The woman's name: Avar Kriss, and for most of her three decades or so, a member of the Jedi Order. As a child, she came to the great Temple on Coruscant, that school and embassy and monastery and reminder of the Force connecting every living thing. She was a youngling first, and as her studies advanced, a Padawan, then a Jedi Knight, and finally . . .

. . . a Master.

This operation was hers. An admiral named Kronara was in command of the *Third Horizon*—itself part of the small peacekeeping fleet maintained by the Republic Defense Coalition—but he had ceded control of the effort to save Hetzal to the Jedi. There was no conflict or discussion about the decision. The Republic had its strengths, and the Jedi had theirs, and each used them to support and benefit the other.

Avar Kriss studied the Hetzal system, projected on the flat silver display wall in the bridge by a purpose-built comms droid hovering before it. The images were a composite gathered from in-system sources as well as the *Third Horizon*'s sensors. In green, the worlds, ships, space stations, and satellites of Hetzal. Her own assets—the Vectors, Longbeams, and the *Third Horizon* itself—were blue. The bits of hot death moving through the system at incredible speed, source and nature as yet unknown, were red. As she watched, new scarlet motes appeared on the display. Whatever was happening here, it was not yet over.

The Jedi reached to her shoulder, where a long white cape was secured by a golden buckle made in the shape of her Order's symbol—a living sunrise. This was ceremonial clothing, appropriate for the joint Jedi–Republic conclave the *Third Horizon* had attended at the just now completed, galaxy-changing space station called Starlight Beacon. Now, though, considering the task at hand, the ornamental garments were a distraction. Avar tapped the buckle and the cape released. It slipped to the ground in a puddle of fabric, revealing a simpler white tunic beneath, ornamented in gold. At her hip, in a white sheath, a metal cylinder, a single piece of sleek silver-white electrum, like the handle of a tool without the tool itself. Along its length, a spiraling incised line of bright-green seastone, serving as both grip and ornament, running up to a crossguard at one end. A weapon, with which she was skilled—but she would not need it today. The Jedi's lightsabers would not save Hetzal. It would be the Jedi themselves.

Avar sank to the ground, settling herself, legs crossed. Her shoulder-length yellow hair, seemingly on its own, moved back and away from her face. It folded itself into a complex knot, a mandala, the creation of which was itself an aid to focus. She closed her eyes.

The Jedi Master slowed her breathing, reaching out to the Force that surrounded her, suffused her. Slowly, she rose, ceasing once she floated a meter above the deck.

Around the bridge, the crew of the *Third Horizon* took notice. They nodded, or smiled faintly, or simply felt hope bloom, before returning to their urgent tasks.

Avar Kriss did not notice. There was only the Force, and what it told her, and what she must do.

She began.

CHAPTER FIVE

HETZAL PRIME. IN ORBIT.

80 minutes to impact.

Bell Zettifar felt the first licks of atmosphere touch the craft. Their Vector didn't have a name, not officially—all the ships were basically the same, and in theory interchangeable among their Jedi operators—but he and his master always used the same one, with the scoring along the wings from an ion storm they'd once flown through. The pattern looked like little starbursts, and so Bell—only in his mind, never spoken aloud—called their ship the *Nova.*

The Vectors were as minimally designed as a starship could be. Little shielding, almost no weaponry, very little computer assistance. Their capabilities were defined by their pilots. The Jedi *were* the shielding, the weaponry, the minds that calculated what the vessel could achieve and where it could go. Vectors were small, nimble. A fleet of them together was a sight to behold, the Jedi inside coordinating their movements via the Force, achieving a level of precision no droid or ordinary pilot could match.

They looked like a flock of birds, or perhaps fallen leaves swirling in a gust of wind, all drawn in the same direction, linked together by some invisible connection . . . some Force. Bell had seen an exhibition on Coruscant once, as part of the Temple's outreach programs. Three hundred Vectors moving together, gold and silver darts shining in the sun above Senate Plaza. They split apart and wove into braids and whipped past one another at incredible, impossible speed. The most beautiful thing he'd ever seen. People called it a Drift. A Drift of Vectors.

But now the *Nova* was flying alone, with just two Jedi aboard. Him, Jedi apprentice Bell Zettifar, and up ahead in the pilot's seat, his master, Loden Greatstorm. The Jedi contingent aboard the *Third Horizon* had split up, Vectors heading to locations all over the system. There were too many tasks to be accomplished, and too little time.

Their destination was the largest inhabited planetary body, Hetzal Prime. Their assignment, vague but crucial: help.

Bell glanced out the viewport to see the curve of the world below—green and gold and blue. A beautiful place, at least from this height. Down on the surface, he suspected things might be different. Drive signatures from starships could be seen all the way to the horizon, a mass exodus of vessels heading offworld. The *Nova* and a few other Vectors and Republic Longbeams he could see here and there were the only ships heading inward to the planet.

"Entering the upper atmosphere, Bell," Loden said, not turning. "You ready?"

"You know I love this part, Master," Bell said.

Greatstorm chuckled. The ship dived, or fell, it was hard to tell the difference. A roar filtered in from outside as space transitioned to atmosphere. The precision-manufactured leading edges of the Vector's wings sliced the air as finely as any blade, but even they encountered some resistance.

The *Nova* tore its way through the highest levels of Hetzal Prime's atmosphere—no, not tore. Loden Greatstorm was too fine a pilot for that. Some Jedi used their Vectors that way, but not him. He wove the craft, sliding through the air currents, riding them down, letting the ship become just another part of the interplay of gravity and wind above the planet's surface. The ship wanted to fall, and Greatstorm let it. It was exhilarating, deadly, unsurvivable, and the Vector was designed to transmit every last vibration and shimmy to the Jedi inside, so they could let the Force guide them to the best response. Bell clenched his hands into fists. His face stretched into a grin.

"Spectacular," he said, without thinking. His master laughed.

"Nothing to it, Bell," Loden said. "I just pointed us at the planet. Gravity's handling the rest."

A long, gliding curve, smooth like the bend of a river, and then the *Nova* straightened out, now close enough to the planet's surface that Bell could make out buildings, vehicles, and other smaller features below. It looked so peaceful. No indication of the disaster-in-progress in the system. Nothing but the increasing number of ships launching from the surface.

"Where should we put down?" Bell said. "Did Master Kriss tell you?"

"It was left to our discretion," Greatstorm replied, glancing to one side, his profile dark, craggy, mountainlike, his Twi'lek lekku sweeping back from his skull. His eyes tracked the drive trails from the ongoing planetary evacuation. "We help any way we can."

"But it's a whole planet. How will we know where to . . ."

"You tell me, kid," Loden said. "Find me somewhere to go."

"Training?" Bell asked.

"Training."

Loden Greatstorm's philosophy as a teacher was very simple: If Bell was theoretically capable of something, even if Loden could do it ten times as fast and a hundred times more skillfully, then Bell would end up doing that thing, not Loden. "If I do everything, no one learns anything," his master was fond of saying.

Loden didn't have to do everything, but Bell would have been fine if, occasionally, he did *something.* Being the apprentice to the great Greatstorm was an endless gauntlet of impossible tasks. He had been training at the Jedi Temple for fifteen of his eighteen years, and it had never been easy, but being Loden's Padawan was on an entirely different level. Every day, without exception, pushed him to his limits. Any personal time Bell ever got was spent desperately collapsing into the deepest sleep of his life until it all began again. But . . . he was learning. He was better now than he was even six months ago, at everything.

Bell knew what his master wanted him to do. Another impossible task—but he was a Jedi, or getting there, and through the Force all things were possible.

He closed his eyes and opened his spirit, and there it was, the small light within him that never stopped burning. Always at least a candle flame, and sometimes, if he concentrated, it could surge up into a blaze. A few times, he'd felt as bright as the sun, so much light pouring through him he was afraid he might go blind. Honestly, though, it didn't matter. From spark to inferno—any connection to the Force chased away the shadows.

Bell delved into the light within himself, feeling for the connection points to other life, other repositories of the Force on the planet below. Very near to him, he felt a source of great power and energy. It was currently banked, like coals in a fire, but enormous reservoirs of strength were clearly available if needed. This was his master, Loden. Bell pushed on past him. He was looking for something else.

There. Like a long-distance holo coming into focus when the signal finally gained enough strength, the Force web connecting the minds and spirits of Hetzal Prime's billions snapped into Bell's mind. It wasn't an entirely clear picture; more like impressions, a map of emotional zones, not so different from the patchwork of cropland flashing along far below the *Nova.*

Mostly, what he sensed was panic and fear—emotions the Jedi worked very hard to purge from themselves. According to the teachings, a true Jedi's only contact with fear was supposed to be sensing it in other beings; a common enough experience. Bell had felt those reflected emotions many times, but always alongside love and hope and surprise and many shades of joy; the spectrum of feelings inherent in all beings.

Well, usually. On Hetzal Prime, at this moment, it pretty much was just panic and fear.

Bell wasn't surprised. He'd heard the evacuation order: *"System-scale disaster in progress. All beings are immediately ordered to depart the Hetzal system by any available means, and remain at a minimum safe distance."* No explanation, no warning, and the math had to be obvious to everyone. Billions of people, and clearly not enough starships to evacuate all of them. Who wouldn't panic?

On a world seething with that sort of negative energy, it was hard to think of what two Jedi would be able to accomplish. But Loden Greatstorm had set Bell a task, and so he continued to reach out, seeking a place they could help.

Something . . . a knot of tension, coiled, dense . . . a conflict, a question, a feeling of things not being as they should, a sense of injustice.

Bell opened his eyes.

"East," he said.

If there was injustice out there, well . . . they would bring justice. The Jedi *were* justice.

The *Nova* banked, accelerating smoothly under Loden's control. Bell's master did let him fly occasionally—the ship could be controlled from either seat—but the Vectors required almost as much skill to handle as a lightsaber. Under the circumstances, Bell was happy to let Loden take the lead.

Instead he served as navigator, using his still-strong connection to the Force to guide their Vector toward the area of intense conflict he had sensed, calling out directions to Loden, fine-tuning the ship's path.

"We should be directly above it," Bell said. "Whatever it is."

"I see it," Loden said, his voice clipped, tight. Ordinarily, his words carried a smile, even when delivering a brutal critique of Bell's Jedi scholarship. Not now. Whatever Bell was sensing, he knew Master

Greatstorm could feel it, too, and probably on a more intense level. Down on the surface, just below where the Vector circled, people were going to die. Maybe already had.

Loden banked the ship again as he flew in a tight circle, giving them both a clear look at the ground through the transparisteel of the *Nova*'s cockpit bubble.

A hundred meters below was a compound of some kind, walled. Large, but not enormous—probably the home of a wealthy individual or family rather than a government facility. A huge crush of people surrounded the walls, focused around the gates. A single glance gave Bell the reason.

Docked inside the compound was a large starship. It looked like a pleasure yacht, big enough to comfortably hold twenty or thirty passengers plus crew. And if the passengers didn't care about comfort, the yacht could probably cram in ten times that many people. The ship had to be visible from ground level—its hull protruded above the compound walls, and the people crowding the gates clearly thought it was their only way offworld.

Armed guards posted on the walls at all sides seemed to feel differently. As Bell watched, a blaster bolt shot into the air from near the gate—a warning shot, thankfully, but it was clear that the time for warnings was rapidly coming to an end. The tension in the crowd was mounting, and you didn't need to be a Jedi to tell.

"Why aren't they letting the people in?" Bell asked. "That ship could get plenty of them to safety."

"Let's find out," Loden said.

He flipped a toggle switch on his control panel. The cockpit bubble slid smoothly back, vanishing into the *Nova*'s hull. Loden turned back, smiling, the wind whipping past them both, sending Loden's lekku and Bell's dreadlocks streaming out from their heads.

"See you down there," he said. "Remember. Gravity does most of the work."

Then he jumped out.

CHAPTER SIX

HETZAL SYSTEM. REPUBLIC LONGBEAM *AURORA IX*.
75 minutes to impact.

"You sure about this, Captain?" Petty Officer Innamin said, pointing at his screen, which displayed the rough path of one of the hyperspace anomalies as it sped toward the center of the system. "We need to shoot this thing down before it kills someone. Maybe a lot of someones. The problem is that our targeting computers can't calculate the trajectory. The anomaly's moving too fast. At best, I'd say we'd have a one-in-three chance of hitting the target."

Captain Bright shook his head, his tentacles rustling against his shoulders. He knew he should probably reprimand Innamin for questioning his orders. The kid did it all the time—he was young for a human, little more than two decades old, and as a rule thought he knew better. Bright usually let him get away with it. Life was too short, and the ships they flew were, on balance, too small to bring unnecessary tension into the mix. A thoughtful question from time to time wasn't exactly insubordination.

One in three, he thought. He didn't know exactly what he'd expected.

Just . . . better than one-in-three odds that they could actually accomplish their mission.

The Longbeam, call sign *Aurora IX*, was state-of-the-art, a brand-new design from the Republic shipyards on Hosnian Prime. It wasn't a warship *per se*, but it was no pushover, either. The vessel had distributed processors that could handle multiple target firing solutions and prepare a spread of blasterfire, missiles, and defensive countermeasures in a single salvo. Not too hard on the eyes, either. Bright thought it looked like one of the hammerfish he used to hunt back home on Glee Anselm—a thick, blunt skull tapering into a single elegant, sinuous tailfin. It was a tough, beautiful beast, no doubt about it. On the other hand, their target, one of the mysterious objects racing through the Hetzal system, was moving at a velocity near lightspeed. It had whipped out of hyperspace like a red-hot pellet fired from a slugthrower. The *Aurora IX* might be state-of-the-art, but that didn't mean the ship could work miracles.

Miracles were for the Jedi.

And they were, apparently, otherwise occupied at the moment.

"Fire six missiles," Bright ordered.

Innamin hesitated.

"That's our full complement, sir. Are you sure—"

Bright nodded. He gestured at Innamin's cockpit display. A red threat indicator—the projectile—on a collision path with a larger green disk, representing a solar collection station equidistant from all three of the Hetzal system's suns. The thing was still some distance away but moving closer with every moment.

"The anomaly is headed straight for that solar array. The data we got from Hetzal Prime says the station has seven crew aboard. We can't get there in time to evacuate before it gets hit, but our missiles can. If we have a one-in-three chance at shooting the object down, then sending six doubles our chances. Still not perfect odds, but—"

The final member of his crew, Ensign Peeples, buzzed his proboscis as if he was about to speak, but Bright waved him off, continuing without stopping.

"Yes, Peeples, I know that math is off. I'm mostly worried about a different equation: If we fire six missiles, we might save seven people. Let's see what we can do."

The *Aurora IX*'s targeting systems chugged along, not seeming quite so state-of-the-art now as the deadly red dot crept closer to people trapped on a solar farm with no way to escape. The Longbeam zoomed toward the array at its own top speed, narrowing the distance its weapons had to travel, sort of an interesting problem of trajectory and acceleration and physics, something that awakened Bright's own three-dimensional instincts built on much of a life lived underwater. He shook his head again, rustling the cloud of thick green tentacles that emerged from the back of his skull, angry at himself for getting distracted when people out there were praying for their lives.

The missiles fired, six quick *whmphs* transmitted through the ship's hull, and the *Aurora IX* was down to lasers only. The weapons shot away, leaving thin trails of smoke behind to mark their path. They were out of visual range in an instant, accelerating to their max velocity in seconds.

"Missiles away," Innamin said.

Now it was up to that fancy distributed processor, and whether it had successfully transmitted effective firing solutions to the missiles. Maybe all six would hit. It wasn't impossible.

The deck crew looked as one at the display screen tracking the six missiles, the fast-moving anomaly, their own ship, and the solar array that was rapidly becoming the collision point for all nine objects.

The first of the missiles blinked out on the screen. Nothing else changed.

"Missile one is a miss," Innamin said, unnecessarily.

Two more missiles vanished. Bright held up a hand before Innamin could speak again.

"We can all see, Petty Officer," he said.

Two more misses. Leaving one. All else remained unchanged.

The last missile vanished from the display, nowhere near the incoming anomaly. A communal sigh of despair washed across the bridge.

"Blasters?" Bright asked, knowing the answer.

"I'm sorry, sir," Ensign Peeples said, his voice a high-pitched, reedy whine. "Even the best gunner in the universe couldn't make that shot, and I would guess I'm barely in the top ten."

Bright sighed. Peeples's species had a radically unique understanding of humor—not the jokes themselves, which were often decent enough, but the appropriate moment to deploy them.

"Thank you, Ensign," Bright said.

The solar array was now visible in the viewscreen—a large, spindly structure, like one of the feather corals back in Bright's homesea. Hundreds of long arms arranged in a spiral spinning out from a central sphere in which the crew lived and worked. Each of those arms fitted with collection eyes along its length, blinking and rotating slowly as they drank in the light of the three suns that gave Hetzal Prime and its satellite worlds their uniquely long growing seasons. The array fed the sunlight back to the cropworlds, storing and beaming it down through proprietary technology that was the pride of the system.

The array was beautiful. Bright had never seen anything quite like it. It looked grown—and maybe it was. Supposedly every crop in the galaxy could grow somewhere on the worlds of Hetzal. Perhaps that extended to space stations.

Then, a bright streak, too fast to process even with eyes as capable as Bright's large, dark orbs, designed by evolution to pick out details in the lightless depths of the seas of Glee Anselm. In an instant the solar array was destroyed. One moment it was intact, performing its function. The next, it was ablaze, half the collection arms shattered, drifting slowly away into space.

The central sphere remained, though flames washed across its outer hull, the muted dance of fire in zero gravity. As Bright watched, the array's exterior lighting blinked, flickered, and went out.

Bright put a hand to his forehead. He blinked, too. Once, slowly.

Then he turned to his crew.

"We don't know for sure that the people aboard that station are dead," he said, looking at his crew's solemn faces.

"I would like to try to attempt a rescue, but that"—here he pointed out the viewscreen at the wrecked, burning array, getting larger as the *Aurora IX* approached—"could collapse at any moment. Or explode. Or implode. I don't know. The point is, if we're docked when it goes, we're dead, too."

Bright tapped one of his tentacles with a fingertip.

"I'm Nautolan, a fact of which I'm sure you're both aware. Green skin, big black eyes, what else would I be? What you might not know is that these tentacles of mine let me pick up pheromones from other beings, which I translate into an understanding of their emotional states. That's how I know you two . . . are terrified."

Peeples opened his mouth, then, somehow, miraculously, thought better of making a joke and closed it again.

"I get that you're scared," Bright went on, "but we have a duty. I know it, and you both know it, too. We need to do this."

Innamin and Peeples looked at each other, then back at their captain.

"We're all the Republic, right?" Innamin said.

Bright nodded. He smiled, showing his teeth.

"Indeed we are, Petty Officer."

He pointed at Peeples.

"Ensign, take us in."

CHAPTER SEVEN

HETZAL SYSTEM. ABOVE THE FRUITED MOON.
70 minutes to impact.

Three Jedi Vectors and a Republic Longbeam whipped through space, slingshotting around the orange-and-green sphere that was the Fruited Moon of Hetzal, legendary throughout the galaxy for its bounty. Four billion people resided there, farming and growing and living their lives. All would be dead in less than thirty minutes if the four Jedi and two Republic officers could not destroy or somehow divert the object headed directly for the moon.

The anomaly was on the larger side, bigger than the Longbeam, and on a collision course with the moon's primary landmass. Due to its velocity, a significant portion of the moon's outer layer would be instantly vaporized on impact, surging into the atmosphere. Then would come the heat, the flames, scouring the surface clean of all life, plant and animal and sentient alike.

That's assuming the whole blasted moon doesn't just shatter when the anomaly hits, Te'Ami thought as she banked her ship smoothly, following a precise curve with the other two Vectors piloted by her Jedi colleagues, performing the maneuver as much through her connection to the Force as her hands on the control sticks.

Total destruction of the Fruited Moon wasn't impossible. The amount of energy transferred upon the object's impact would fall like a hammerblow on the little planetoid. Worlds seemed unbreakable when you were standing on them, but Te'Ami had seen things in her day . . . the galaxy didn't care *what* you thought couldn't be broken. It would break things just to show you it could.

The little fleet was moving at incredible velocity, headed directly for the anomaly. Master Kriss back on the *Third Horizon* had designated this as a high-priority mission, which Te'Ami understood. Four billion people—a high priority indeed.

She could feel Avar at the back of her mind—not in words, more of a sense of the woman's presence. Master Kriss had a skill set rare among the Jedi: She could detect the natural bonds between Force-users and strengthen them, use them as almost a sort of communications network. It was inexact, best for transmitting sensations, locations, but it was still a useful ability, particularly in a scenario when a hundred Jedi were all trying to save a system at once.

Not just useful, though. It was comforting. She was not alone. None of them were. Fail or succeed, the Jedi were in this together.

But we will not fail, Te'Ami thought. She reached out a long, green finger and flipped one of the finely wrought switches on her console. Her comm toggled open.

"Republic Longbeam, it's time. I need you to transfer your weapons systems to my control," she said.

"Acknowledged," came the reply from the Longbeam, spoken by its pilot, Joss Adren. His wife, Pikka, was in the copilot's seat. Te'Ami didn't know them personally—only that they weren't part of the *Third Horizon*'s crew, and had volunteered their help immediately when the cruiser dropped into the system and the scale of the disaster became clear. Admiral Kronara assigned them a Longbeam—better to put another ship out there to help instead of leaving it sitting idle in its hangar. The little bit of non-task-oriented chatter on the way out to the Fruited Moon had suggested Joss and Pikka were contractors of some kind—workers on the Starlight Beacon hitching a ride back to the Core now that their job was done.

They seemed like good people. Te'Ami hoped they were skilled as well. This would not be easy.

An amber light flashed on Te'Ami's display, then went steady.

"Weapons are under your control," Joss said.

"Thank you," she said, then flipped another few switches before quickly moving her hands back to the sticks. Vectors could be tricky craft—the fluid responsiveness of the controls meant they could accomplish incredible maneuvers, but only if significant focus could be maintained.

"All right, my friends," she said. "Are we ready?"

The replies came in across the Jedi-only channel.

The low voice of Mikkel Sutmani rumbled from her speakers, immediately translated into Basic via the onboard systems. "Good to go," he said. Mikkel. The steadiest Ithorian she had ever met. He never said much, but the job always got done.

"We're ready as well," said Nib Assek, the third and final Jedi Knight in their little squadron. Her Padawan, Burryaga Agaburry, didn't say anything. No surprise there. He was a young Wookiee, and spoke only Shyriiwook, though he understood Basic. Nib spoke his language well—she had learned it specifically to take him on as her apprentice. It wasn't easy for a human throat to re-create the warbling growls and whines that composed Wookiee speech, but she had made the effort. Te'Ami and Mikkel, though, could not understand a word Burryaga said.

Regardless, if Nib Assek said she and her Padawan were ready, they were.

"Reach out," Te'Ami said. "We'll do it together. As one."

She stretched out her senses through the Force, seeking the deadly meteor—or whatever it was, the scans remained inconclusive—hurtling through space toward them. There. She could feel it, distorting gravity along its path. She considered, thinking about where the object had been, where it was, where it would be.

More specifically, where it would be when the full power of the weapons systems on the Vectors and the Longbeam hit it all at once.

This shot could not be calculated using computers. It had to be done by feel, with the Force, by all the Jedi at once in a single moment.

"I have the target," she said. "Are we good?"

No answer from the other Jedi, but she didn't need one. She could feel their assent through the link Master Kriss maintained back on the surface of Hetzal Prime. It was faster than speaking, more effective.

"Let us become spears," she said, speaking a ritual phrase from her own people, the Duros.

Not wanting to take her hands off her control sticks at such a crucial moment, Te'Ami spared a tendril of the Force and used it to lift her lightsaber from its holster on her belt. Its hilt was dark cerakote with a heavily tarnished copper crosspiece. The blade, when lit, shone blue. The thing was scratched and gouged with use, and had an unsightly blob of solder up near the business end where she'd welded one of the components back on when it fell off. If there was an uglier lightsaber in the Order, she hadn't seen it.

But it turned on when she wanted it to, and the kyber crystal that powered it remained as pure and resonant as the day she found it on Ilum so long ago.

Could Te'Ami have refreshed the blade, if she wanted to? Absolutely. Many Jedi changed their hilts regularly, whether due to adjustments to fighting techniques, technological innovations, or even, on occasion, just . . . style. Aesthetics. Fashion, you could call it.

Te'Ami had no interest in any of that. Her lightsaber, ugly as it was, served as a perfect reflection of the great truth of the Force: no matter what a person was on the outside . . .

. . . inside, everyone was made of light.

The lightsaber moved through the cramped cockpit. It placed itself against a metal plate on the Vector's control panel with a soft, very satisfying click, staying in place via a tiny, localized force field. A low hum vibrated through the ship's hull as its weapons systems activated. A new set of displays and dials went live, glowing with the bright blue of her saber blade. Weapons on a Vector could only be operated with a lightsaber key, a way to ensure they were not used by non-Jedi, and that every time they were used, it was a well-considered action.

An additional advantage—the ship's laser could be scaled up or down via a toggle on the control sticks. Not every shot had to kill. They could disable, warn . . . every option was available to them. In this case, though, the settings would be at maximum. They needed to disintegrate the hyperspace anomaly, turn it into vapor, and that would require all three Vectors at full power plus everything the Longbeam had. One huge blast.

It would work. It had to work. Four billion defenseless beings on the Fruited Moon hung in the balance.

Te'Ami reached out again, checking her colleagues' readiness. There was something . . . from the thread leading to Nib Assek's ship. Fear . . . almost . . . panic.

"Nib, I'm sensing—" she began, and the reply came before she could finish.

"I know, Te'Ami," came Nib's voice. Calm, but perhaps a bit embarrassed. "It's Burryaga. He's having a hard time locking down his emotions. I think it's the stress of what we're doing. All the lives at stake."

"It's all right, little one," came Mikkel's gravelly tones, translated across the comm. "You are but a Padawan, and we are asking a great deal of you. Te'Ami, can we free him from the burden of helping us calculate the shot?"

"Yes," Te'Ami said. "There is no shame in this, Burry. Only an opportunity to learn."

Te'Ami reached out with the Force, gently curving the connection away from Nib Assek's Padawan. The Wookiee was silent. She could still feel the roil of emotions from him. Well, no shame, as she had said. Every Jedi found their own path, and some took longer than others.

"Let's go," Nib said, perhaps trying to make up for the delay caused by her student. "We're running out of time."

"Agreed," Te'Ami said.

She moved her thumbs up on her control sticks, first rolling them along the toggle wheel to tell the weapons system to fire at full power. Then she settled her hands on the triggers.

The object, speeding toward the moon. Where it had been. Where it was. Where it would be.

The other Jedi were ready. They would fire the moment she did, as would the linked systems in Joss and Pikka's Longbeam, every blast heading to precisely the same location in space.

Four billion people. It was time. Te'Ami tightened her grip on the triggers.

A squeal from the comm system, loud and insistent. A scream, or a yell—forceful, almost panicked. It startled Te'Ami, and if she were not a Jedi Knight, she might have inadvertently fired her weapons. But she was indeed a Jedi Knight, and did not fire.

It took Te'Ami a moment to understand what she was hearing—not a scream, but words. In Shyriiwook. Burryaga, saying something she could not understand. Loud, insistent, desperate. His emotions strong again through the Force, that same mixture of fear edging on panic.

"Burryaga, I'm sorry, I don't understand Shyriiwook. Are you all right? We're running out of time. We have to fire."

"No," Nib Assek said, her voice sharp, insistent. In the background, the whines and growls of Burryaga's voice, coming over her comm. "We can't attack."

"What are you talking about?" Mikkel said. "We don't have a choice."

"Burryaga is explaining it to me. The emotions we were getting from him—they weren't his. He was sensing them. He had to tune in a bit, overcome his own fear before he could understand."

"Please, Nib, just tell us what he means," Te'Ami said.

A long, whistling, mournful bit of Shyriiwook, and then a pause.

"The object," Nib said. "The one we have to destroy, to save the moon. It's not just an object. It's debris, part of a *ship.*"

Te'Ami let her hands fall from the control sticks.

"It's full of people," Nib finished. "And they're alive."

CHAPTER EIGHT

AGUIRRE CITY, HETZAL PRIME.
65 minutes to impact.

The Force sang to Jedi Master Avar Kriss, a choir that was the entirety of the Hetzal system, life and death in constant, contrapuntal motion. It was a song she knew well—she heard it all the time, everywhere she went. Here, the melody of the Force was off, a discordant jangle of death and fear and confusion. People were dying, or felt the dread of their imminent demise.

Threaded through that song—the Jedi, and the brave personnel of the Republic, and the heroic citizens of Hetzal itself, using the resources they had to try to save the people of these worlds.

The *Third Horizon* had landed not far from the Ministerial Residence in Aguirre City, the capital of Hetzal Prime. The Republic was coordinating its efforts with the Hetzalian government to try to stem the tide of the disaster—ensuring the evacuation proceeded in as orderly a fashion as possible, tracking the incoming projectiles, helping as they could.

Avar Kriss was still on the ship's bridge, still serving as the point of connection for the Jedi in the system, letting them sense one another's presence and location and emotional states. Sometimes words or images came through unbidden, but only rarely. It was all just a song, and Avar sang and was sung to.

Still, she was able to gather a great deal of information from what it told her. She knew that fifty-three Jedi Vectors were currently active in the Hetzal system. She knew which Jedi were working on the planet—for example, at that moment, Bell Zettifar, Loden Greatstorm's promising Padawan, was approaching the surface of Hetzal Prime at extraordinary speed.

Elzar Mann, her oldest, closest friend in the Order, was in a Vector of his own, flying a single-person version of the ship near one of the system's three suns. He was almost always alone. Avar was one of only two Jedi he worked with regularly—it was just her and Stellan Gios. This was mostly because Elzar was . . . unreliable wasn't exactly the right word. He was a tinkerer, if that term could apply to Jedi techniques. He never liked to use the Force the same way twice.

Elzar's instincts were good, and he didn't try anything too unusual when the stakes were high. Usually, his experiments in Force techniques did expand the Order's understanding, and occasionally he accomplished incredible things.

But sometimes he failed, and sometimes he failed spectacularly. Again, never when lives were on the line, but even that bit of uncertainty, coupled with Elzar Mann's general unwillingness to take the time to explain whatever he was trying to do . . . well, some in the Order found him frustrating to deal with. Avar believed that might explain his continued status as a Jedi Knight rather than a Master. She knew that bothered Elzar. He thought it was unfair. He didn't care about other Jedi's paths through the Force—why should they concern themselves with his? He just wanted to follow his road where it led.

Avar didn't understand Elzar's explorations any more than most of the Jedi, but the key to their relationship was that she never asked him to explain. Anything, ever. That arrangement had powered their friendship since their days as younglings together in the Jedi Temple on

Coruscant. That, and she just liked him. He was funny, and clever, and they had come up together through the Order, Stellan and Elzar and her, the three of them inseparable through all their years of training.

She pulled her mind away from Elzar Mann, listening to the Force. She sensed Jedi on the system's worlds, Jedi in Vectors, and still more on stations or satellites or ships, all around the system, helping wherever they could, usually in conjunction with the twenty-eight Republic Longbeams deployed by the *Third Horizon.*

The chain of connection through the Force even told her that others of her Order were on their way, doing their best to respond to Minister Ecka's original distress call despite being so far from Hetzal. Closest was Master Jora Malli, future commander of the Jedi quarter on the just completed Starlight Beacon, along with her second-in-command, the imposing Trandoshan Master Sskeer. Stellan Gios was powering in from his Temple outpost on Hynestia as if summoned by her thoughts of him a few moments before, whipping through hyperspace in a borrowed starship. And more besides.

Avar sent out a note of welcome, and called to every other Jedi she could reach, near Hetzal or not. Distance was nothing to the Force. Who knew how they might help?

So far, the death toll from the disaster was low, barely above the baseline churn of life and death constantly at work in any large group of beings. She was worried that could change at any moment—they didn't have a good understanding of what was happening here. Nothing about it felt natural. She had never heard of anything like this—a huge spread of projectiles appearing in a system, popping out of hyperspace with no notice.

She could not imagine what would have happened here if the *Third Horizon* was not in transit nearby after a refueling stop, or if their inspection tour of the Starlight Beacon wasn't interminably delayed by the project's overseer, an officious Bith named Shai Tennem. She had insisted on showing her Jedi and Republic visitors every last obscure element of Starlight Beacon's construction, pushing back their scheduled departure and irritating Admiral Kronara immensely. But if they had left on time, the *Third Horizon* would have been deep into hyperspace when Minister Ecka's evacuation order went out, too far to get to Hetzal in any reasonable amount of time.

If not for an overzealous Bith administrator, Hetzal would be dealing with this apocalypse on its own.

The song of the Force.

Between what it told Avar directly and the chatter she heard around her from the *Third Horizon*'s deck officers, she was able to maintain an up-to-date picture of the disaster, in all its moments large and small.

Above Hetzal Prime, a Republic technician completed repairs to an evacuation ship that had lost power on its way offplanet, so it could continue on its way to safety.

Near the second-largest gas giant, two Vectors fired their weapons, and a fragment was incinerated.

A Longbeam pushed past its limits as it raced to reach a damaged station at the system's outer edge. Its engines failed, catastrophically. Avar gasped a little at the cold, dark sensation.

And above the Fruited Moon, one very clear impression, as close to a message as could be sent through the Force under these circumstances—a sense from a Jedi Knight named Te'Ami that their understanding of what was happening here was utterly, tragically incomplete.

"No," Avar said, disturbed at the urgency of what Te'Ami was trying to pass along. Her emotions roiled, and the song of the Force shimmered in her mind, becoming quieter, less distinct.

Focus, she told herself. *You are needed.*

Avar Kriss calmed her emotions and listened. Now, thanks to Te'Ami, she knew what to look for. She called the other Jedi's face to her mind—green skin, high domed skull, large red eyes—and it took her almost no time to find what Te'Ami had tried to show her. In fact, now that she was looking, it was obvious. Avar spread her awareness through the system, pushing herself to the limit.

I can't miss one, she thought. *Not a single one.*

She opened her eyes and unfolded her legs, setting her feet once again upon the *Third Horizon*'s deck. Bridge officers looked at her, surprised—she had not spoken or moved in some time.

Admiral Kronara was speaking to Chancellor Lina Soh, who had called in via a high-priority relay from Coruscant. Her delicate, sweeping features were displayed on one of the bridge's commwalls. She looked fragile—which she absolutely was not. Kronara, in contrast, had a face that looked like a hammer would break against it. He looked hard—which he absolutely was. He wore the uniform of the Republic Defense Coalition, light gray with blue accents, the cap tucked under his arm in respect for the chancellor's office.

The resolution on the display was low, with sharp lines of static crossing Lina Soh's face every few seconds—but that was to be expected. Coruscant was very far away.

"Thank the light your ship was close enough to Hetzal to respond, Admiral," Chancellor Soh was saying. "We sent out aid ships as soon as we could, but even receiving the distress signal from Hetzal took time. You know how choppy the comm relays are from the Outer Rim."

"I do, Chancellor," Kronara responded. "We appreciate anything you can do. We're making progress here, but there will definitely be a large number of wounded, and I am sure a variety of essential systems will need repair. I'll relay word to Minister Ecka that you're sending assistance. I'm sure he'll appreciate it."

"Of course, Admiral. We are all the Republic."

Avar walked across the deck, passing Kronara as he ended the transmission to Coruscant. He glanced over at her, curious, as she stopped before the display screen showing the status of the disaster mitigation effort—all the ships, people, Jedi, Republic, locals. Red, green, blue, worlds, lives, hope, despair.

She tapped certain of the red anomalies on the screen with her fingertip. As she did, they were highlighted, each surrounded with a white circle. When she was done, about ten of the projectiles were indicated.

Avar moved back from the display, then turned to look at the bridge crew. They were confused, but polite, waiting for her to explain what she had done.

"I hate to say this, my friends," she said, "but this just got a lot harder. We have a new objective."

Admiral Kronara's weathered features twisted into a scowl. Avar did not take it personally.

"Does it replace the existing mission parameters?" he said.

"That would be nice," she said. "But no. We still have to do everything we came here to do—keep the fragments from destroying Hetzal—but now there's something else."

She gestured at the display, with its highlighted red dots, racing sunward.

"The anomalies I have indicated here contain living beings. This is no longer just about saving the worlds of this system."

Realization dawned on Kronara's face. His scowl deepened.

"So it's a rescue mission, on top of everything else."

"That's right, Admiral," Avar said.

A chorus of dismayed voices rose up as the officers realized that all their progress thus far was just the preamble to a much greater effort.

"How is that possible?"

"How many people? Who are they?"

"Are they ships? Is this an invasion?"

Admiral Kronara held up a hand, and the voices stopped.

"Master Kriss, if you say some of these things have people aboard, then they do. But how do you propose we mount a rescue? These objects are moving at incredible velocities. Our targeting systems can barely hit them as it is, and now we have to . . . dock with them?"

Avar nodded.

"I don't know how we'll do this. Not yet. I'm hoping one of you might have an idea. But I will say that every one of those lives is as important as any life on this world or any other. We must begin by believing it is possible to save everyone. If the will of the Force is otherwise, so be it, but I will not accept the idea of abandoning them without trying."

She moved her hand in a broad circle, encompassing the entire display board.

"This is all you have to work with—what we brought with us. Every Hetzalian ship is occupied with the evacuation effort, so all we've got are the Vectors and the Jedi flying them, plus the Longbeams and their crews. Find a way. I know you can. I'll send word to the Jedi. The Force might have an answer for us."

The bridge officers looked at one another, then scrambled into motion with a new surge of activity, as they began to plan ten utterly impossible rescue missions.

Avar Kriss closed her eyes. She stepped up into the air. The Force sang to her, telling her of peril and bravery and sacrifice, of Jedi fulfilling their vows, acting as guardians of peace and justice in the galaxy.

The song of the Force.

CHAPTER NINE

HETZAL PRIME.

60 minutes to impact.

Bell was falling. He had hoped he might be gliding, but no. Definitely falling. He had followed his master over the side of the *Nova,* leaping out of the Vector's cockpit to drop to the ground below. He had practiced maneuvers like this many times in the Temple, but there was generally some sort of padding involved in that situation, a safety measure if the Jedi-in-training couldn't quite muster the necessary concentration to use the Force to break his fall.

Now, gravity was gravity, and even the Force couldn't turn it off (though Bell thought perhaps Master Yoda could make it happen, if he focused hard enough). But you could convince the Force to slow you down, reduce the impact when you landed. Perfectly executed, you would alight on the ground like a leaf, or a snowflake.

What Bell was doing was . . . not perfectly executed. The Force seemed to be busy elsewhere, unwilling to listen to his requests for assistance. As the ground approached with alarming speed, Bell's focus left him entirely. He threw his arms up, opened his mouth to scream. As a Jedi, he knew he should be meeting his death with dignity, but this was about as undignified as you could get. Bell Zettifar was about to end his Padawan career by smashing into the ground like a rotten piece of fruit and probably splattering all over everything and—

—he didn't.

Bell slowed, and he rotated in the air until his feet were pointed at the ground, and he lit upon it . . . like a leaf, or a snowflake.

"You need more training," his master said, from not far away. With a smile in his voice.

Bell opened his eyes, and there was Jedi Master Loden Greatstorm, one hand raised, a smile on his face, too.

"Probably," Bell said.

"Definitely," Loden said, lowering his arm. "We'll work on it."

He looked up at the *Nova,* moving a hundred or so meters above them in gentle, autopiloted circles, biding its time until the Jedi required it again.

"That wasn't much of a fall, really," Loden said. "You barely had time to think before the ground came calling. I get it, Bell. This is my fault. But don't worry, I can fix it. When we're back on Coruscant, I'll throw you off the tallest supertowers we can find. Maybe you just need more time to commune with the Force. Some of those towers are thousands of stories tall. You could be falling for minutes. Plenty of time."

"Sounds like a wonderful idea, Master," Bell said.

"I agree," Loden said.

Bell turned to look at the reason Loden hadn't just brought their ship in for a landing in the first place. Hundreds of angry Hetzal Prime natives crowded around the compound the two Jedi had seen from their Vector, the home of this wealthy merchant or entertainer or businessperson. Above the high, spiked walls, the sleek curve of the starship waiting inside the compound was clearly visible.

Every person in that crowd had heard Minister Ecka's evacuation order and knew that a path offplanet waited inside the gates. Guards atop the walls seemed ill inclined to allow anyone to get inside—each held a powerful-looking rifle, and if their weapons weren't aimed directly at the milling crowd, they certainly weren't aimed away. If things got ugly, people would die. Many people.

Bell and Loden had drawn the attention of the evacuees—unsurprising. Two Jedi falling from the sky got noticed, even in the desperate circumstances these people found themselves dealing with. Loden walked to the nearest group, two men and a woman, one of the men holding a swaddled infant. They were afraid, unhappy, at the edge of hope—and Bell didn't need the Force to sense it.

"Hello," Loden said. "My name is Loden Greatstorm. I am a member of the Jedi Order. My apprentice here is Bell Zettifar. We're here to help. What's happening? Why aren't you being allowed to board that ship?"

One of the men looked up at the guards on the compound wall, then back at Loden.

"Because the ship belongs to the family that lives in the fancy house on the other side of that gate with all the spikes on it. They're called the Ranorakis. They pay those guards to make sure no one's gonna fly out of here but them. They're getting ready to leave—packing their fancy socks or some garbage like that. Taking their time while the rest of us wait out here."

The woman spoke up, her voice cracking.

"There aren't any ships left. They've all gone, and they aren't coming back. This is the only way offworld, and Minister Ecka's order made it sound like . . . made it sound like . . ."

Loden reached out a hand, touching the side of the woman's face, and she calmed, an ease returning to her manner.

"You will not worry," he said, in a low, resonant tone Bell recognized. Loden was using the Force to add weight to his words, to cut through the surrounding chaos and anxiety. "Focus on your family, your child. Keep them safe. I will take care of the rest."

The woman nodded, and even smiled.

"Come, Padawan," Loden said, and he began walking toward the gates, his stride determined. He didn't look back to see if Bell was following—but he didn't really need to. Where Loden went, Bell followed. If nothing else, just to see what his master was going to do.

The two Jedi walked through the crowd, which parted for them easily as soon as the people realized who they were. They were still dressed in the ceremonial garments they wore for the Starlight Beacon inspection—soft fabrics of white and gold, with colored accents here or there, held together by a golden clasp shaped into the insignia of the Jedi Order. For operations in the field they would ordinarily wear their leathers, sometimes even armor, depending on the task at hand, but there had been no time to change. The *Third Horizon* had dropped into the system, and off they went.

Bell thought that was good, perhaps. No one would mistake them for anything other than what they were. Sometimes just being a Jedi could solve problems. He knew he and Loden were an imposing pair, too—a human and a Twi'lek, both tall and dark-skinned, with lightsabers at their hips . . . their footsteps echoed with the full authority of the Jedi council.

Murmurs spread out from their passage like ripples on water, and the angry shouts and cries died down, until they walked through a silent crowd, all eyes on them. It seemed that Bell was not the only one who wanted to know what his master was planning.

Loden stepped up to the gates. He looked up, where two of the guards were stationed in battlements atop the wall on either side. This no longer looked like a home—it was more like a small fortress. Bell wondered what this family did, these Ranorakis, that would require them to hire such an extensive security staff. At least two dozen men and women stood guard up on the walls, and presumably more waited inside.

"Ho there, Master Jedi," one of the guards said, his tone companionable enough. "Can't let you in, either, sorry. Besides, looks like you have your own ship. Why don't you two hop back in it and fly on back to the Core Worlds. This is private property."

"I'm still outside the gate," Loden said. "Surely whatever authority you have doesn't extend beyond the walls?"

The guard lifted his weapon and let it rest on his shoulder. He spat, the bit of phlegm landing on the ground—outside the walls—with a wet splat.

"So you say," he said.

"I was told you won't let any of these people access that ship, despite the evacuation order issued by the planet's leader?"

"That's right."

"But the vessel could hold most of them. Maybe all of them, if you got creative."

"It's not my job to let them board, Jedi. It's my job to make sure they don't."

"Perhaps you should consider an early retirement," Loden said.

As always, there was a smile in his voice, but Bell recognized the meaning of this particular flavor of smile, just as he'd known when his master was using the Jedi mind touch to calm the refugee woman. Bell moved part of his tunic to one side, exposing his holstered lightsaber hilt.

Without looking at him, Loden raised a hand toward Bell and tapped two fingers together, the first and second on his left hand—a prearranged signal. It meant one very simple thing: *No. Don't.*

Bell forced himself to relax.

The guard captain seemed utterly unconcerned. Even a little amused.

"What do you think you're going to do, Jedi? Cut right through the walls with your lightsaber? Fight off every one of us?"

His master leaned forward, a smile now on his lips as well as in his voice.

"Sure," he said. "Why not?"

The guard's face changed. No longer amused. Now . . . confused. Concerned.

"Open the gates," Loden Greatstorm said. "I promise you. It's the best way forward. For all these people out here, but also for you. And all your friends up there, too."

The guard looked at Loden, and Loden looked at the guard. Bell knew how this was going to go, and he couldn't help but relish it, even though he knew relishing moments like this was very un-Jedi-like.

Loden hadn't even had to draw his weapon. Hadn't used the mind touch. Loden Greatstorm had just spoken a few well-chosen words, and now . . .

"Open the gates," the guard captain said, his tone weary, defeated.

"Thank you," Loden said.

He turned away, looking at Bell.

"We'll stay for a bit," he said. "Make sure this all goes smoothly. Then we'll head out and see if there's another place we might make ourselves useful. Yeah?"

"Yeah," Bell said.

Sounds, from behind them, and both Jedi spun. They were not good sounds. Blasters firing, and screams. They could not see what was happening, not through the crowd.

"Up," Loden said, and he leapt to the top of the wall, landing next to the very surprised captain of the Ranoraki family's personal guard.

Bell followed, and from the higher vantage point, they could see speeders, two of them, bulky, heavy things, each with deck-mounted blaster cannons, firing directly into the crowd.

Marauders, Bell thought, come to take the ship inside the compound, as desperate as anyone else left on Hetzal Prime, but significantly better armed.

They were attacking the defenseless crowd, clearing them out of the way so they could smash their way into the compound and steal the starship.

"Sabers," Loden Greatstorm said, giving the command.

The smile in his voice was gone.

CHAPTER TEN

HETZAL SYSTEM. ABOVE THE FRUITED MOON.
50 minutes to impact.

"We can't do this. It's impossible," said Joss Adren, current commanding officer of the Republic Longbeam designation *Aurora III*. "Just shooting the blasted thing would have been hard enough."

He stared at his cockpit display, depicting his own ship, the three Jedi Vectors flying escort, the massive hyperspace anomaly whipping through space that somehow contained living beings, and, of course, the densely inhabited moon that said anomaly was going to impact and probably eradicate in, oh, call it twelve minutes. In other words, the problem they were somehow expected to solve.

When they'd volunteered to take out a Longbeam and help where they could, Joss's primary motivation had just been that he wanted to try out one of the fancy new Republic ships. He'd never flown this model before, and it had supposedly had some nice little tweaks on the last design.

Not that he wasn't happy to help out, sure—but now he had people's lives in his hands. Like . . . a *lot* of lives, and while people might celebrate him if he succeeded, they would sure as hell blame him if he failed.

Joss cursed. Then he cursed again, then four more times.

"Is that really helpful?" said his copilot, Pikka Adren, second-in-command of the *Aurora III* and first-in-command of his heart.

"Don't tell me you can't relate," he said.

She looked a little bemused, a little irritated, and very focused. Also very beautiful, with light eyes and dark, curly hair and a pile of dark freckles across slightly lighter skin he loved to see and touch. His wife liked to tell him he was handsome, but he knew the truth: He looked like an engine block with a head stuck on top, with hair he kept cropped tight to his skull so he never had to think about it. Joss Adren assumed he must have some good qualities, otherwise he'd never have landed someone like Pikka . . . but he knew his looks were not on the list.

"I can relate to your frustration, dear," his wife said. "I still want to try saving these people."

"Well, of course I want to try, Pikka," Joss said. "I just don't see how."

The mission had begun as a seek-and-destroy. The target was one of the mysterious projectiles that had appeared in the Hetzal system. It was moving fast, but it was unarmed, and didn't appear to be able to alter its trajectory. They just had to blow it up before it hit the moon. Difficult, but not impossible.

But now, thanks to Te'Ami and their other three Jedi colleagues on this mission, they knew that the object was, somehow, inhabited. There were people aboard it. Living people.

So, while the *seek* part of the mission was done and dusted, the *destroy* part was off the table—at least until they'd managed to rescue the people inside. Once that was done—however they might do it, and that was still very unclear—they would still have to blow the thing up, because it was on a collision course with the Fruit Moon, or whatever the people in this system called it.

One tricky mission had become an impossible one, with the original tricky mission still nested inside it.

Joss sighed, then began running through his operational assets.

A Longbeam, with all its capabilities and weapons and tools—a pretty magnificent ship, honestly. You could do a lot with a Longbeam. Beyond that, they had three Vectors containing four space wizards, and he'd always been a little fuzzy on what they were actually capable of. Jedi could do amazing things, sure, but *which* amazing things?

He considered that, extremely conscious that every moment he spent trying and failing to find a solution meant this fragment, this ship, whatever it was, got closer to smashing into the moon, obliterating everyone aboard as well as the planetoid itself.

So, what could Jedi do?

They could use those laser swords of theirs pretty well. Always fun to see in action, but he didn't figure they would do much good just then. Jedi could jump high and run fast—but not as high as space, and not as fast as a ship moving at a pretty good percentage of lightspeed.

They could stand around and look cool. He'd seen them do that plenty of times.

They could . . . move things around with their minds.

Huh, Joss thought.

He turned to Pikka. "Magclamps?" he said, knowing he didn't need to explain further. She'd get it right away—one of the reasons they worked well together, on and off duty.

"Maybe," Pikka said, thinking. "What kind of cabling are they rigged with?"

"Egarian silk," Joss answered. "They just did a refit on all these Longbeams, swapped it in instead of the duralloy line."

"That's good. Egarian's got a higher tensile strength, and it's got the variable elasticity. More electricity you run through it, the more rigid it gets. If we could latch on to the object, and start pretty stretchy and ratchet up the tension slowly . . ."

"Exactly. Do it gradual, so the cables don't snap."

Pikka nodded, tapping her finger on the control panel, thinking hard.

"But we'll never hit it. Those clamps aren't like blasters. They're big, clunky. Bad for precision work. They're designed to tow stationary wrecks back to dock for repairs. The anomaly's moving too fast."

"Yeah, well," Joss said, "I had an idea about that, too."

He activated his comm system.

"Master Te'Ami," he said. He wasn't sure if the Duros Jedi actually was a Jedi Master, or a Jedi Knight, or some other rank in the Order, but he called them all Master. Better safe than sorry. Joss didn't know if the Jedi could even *get* offended, but why take a chance?

"Yes, Captain Adren?" came the Jedi's voice, cool and utterly without tension, even though she was facing the same impossible problems he was.

"I might have an idea. But I have a question. You know how you guys can move things around by thinking about it?"

A bit of a pause.

"We use our connection to the Force, but yes, I know what you mean."

"Can you stop things from moving around?"

Another, longer pause.

"I see where you're going with this, Captain, but we're not gods. We can't just stop that thing cold."

"Not asking you to," Joss said, rolling his eyes at Pikka, who grinned at him. "We have something aboard that might be able to slow it down, but it's not easy to use. We'll have to try to match velocity with the fragment, and we all know how fast it's going. It'll take every bit of engine power we have, and a lot of our fuel, just to accelerate to where we need to be.

"If you can slow it down even a little, even five percent, even one percent, it could make a big difference. At these speeds, even a minor downward shift in velocity would still mean a significant reduction in the resources we'd have to expend."

"One moment," Te'Ami said. The line went cold, and Joss figured she was probably talking to the other Jedi, seeing if they thought this would work.

The comm hissed back to life.

"We'll do what we can," the Jedi said.

"Excellent," Joss said. Then a thought, and he leaned forward and spoke into the comm again.

"And, uh, if you could maybe try to hold the fragment together, too, when you slow it down?"

"Why?"

"Because we're going to hit it with these big metal clamp things, and we don't know how fragile it is. We don't even know *what* it is. Might cause it to just shatter. So if there's anything you could do to, you know . . . prevent that . . . might be good."

A very long pause.

"This is the best idea you have?"

"Only idea I have, Master Jedi. If we can connect to the thing, we can reverse engines, full power, but gradual, slow it down. We're not seeing any drive signatures from it—it's like a projectile from a slugthrower. Like someone whipped a rock real fast. If we could get some opposing force on it, should drain down the velocity pretty quick. If, uh, it doesn't break apart. But that's where you guys come in."

The longest pause yet.

"As I said, Captain . . . we will do what we can."

"Great," Joss said.

He snapped off the comm and turned to Pikka.

"The space wizards don't seem very excited about this," she said.

"Eh," he answered. "They'll be excited when it works."

"Is it going to work?" she asked. "Or will the thing break apart, or will the cables snap and whiplash us off into space, or will we just not be able to latch on no matter what we try?"

"Eh," Joss said again.

He pushed the throttle all the way forward, and the Longbeam leapt into space, the engines roaring, every surface vibrating with power.

"Let's find out."

CHAPTER ELEVEN

HETZAL SYSTEM. INTERPLANETARY SPACE.
40 minutes to impact.

A line of four vessels, carrying approximately thirty-five hundred people, moved at a steady pace away from Hetzal Prime. They sought safety from the barrage of deadly projectiles that had infiltrated the system and continued to wreak havoc. From the farthest reaches all the way to the gas harvesting stations near the three suns that powered Hetzal's endless growing seasons, destruction reigned.

Two of the ships were passenger liners, and two were cargo freighters temporarily repurposed as transports for the duration of the emergency. While the passenger liners were capable of greater speed than the freighters, all four captains had opted to remain together as they traversed space on their way out of the system, so as to render aid to one another if needed.

Minister Ecka's evacuation order had asked all ships to reach "minimum safe distance" but was vague on what that might actually mean. To find their path to safety, the captains were relying on the Republic vessel that had transited into the system at the start of all this. It was coordinating efforts from the surface of Hetzal Prime, sending out a tracking feed. From that, the captains could see the path of the deadly rain of projectiles falling on the system. It gave them a sense of where safety might lie.

Based on what they could see, they should be out of the danger zone soon. After that . . . who knew? Apparently, the Republic and their Jedi colleagues were executing some sort of plan, but no one on the ships knew what it was, or when it would be possible to return to their homeworld. Assuming they ever could. For all they knew, the situation was permanent, and they would never set foot on Hetzal Prime again.

This turned out to be true.

In less than the blink of an eye, the ships vanished, replaced with four slowly expanding balloons of fire and vapor and shredded metal and molecular remnants of the thousands of people aboard. One of the projectiles had exited hyperspace directly in their path, and because the vessels had grouped together for safety, it pierced them all, one after the other, like a skewer through bits of meat. The ships were gone.

On the *Third Horizon,* Jedi Master Avar Kriss heard the new silence of all those souls, lost to the Force forever. Her mouth tightened.

She continued to listen. Something was off, a bad note in the melody. She tried to understand what she was hearing, sensing, knowing that she was stretching her abilities to their limits. There was too much happening in the Hetzal system all at once, and her mind was not truly capable of processing it. She was pushing, trying to make the Force reveal the answer to her—that was not the way. She needed to pull back, not shove forward. Let the Force give her what it willed, in its own time.

Avar slowed her breathing, slowed her heart, felt calm return to her mind and spirit. She listened again for the bad note—as she did, a projectile finally hit the surface of Hetzal Prime, a sea impact, destroying thousands of square kilometers of algae farms, sending water vapor high into the atmosphere and tsunamis outward in a rapidly expanding circle. People died—but hundreds, not thousands or millions, as the farms were mostly automated and droid-managed. Perhaps more would be lost when the waves hit the coasts, but it all could be worse, much worse. The hyperspace fragment was small, and greatly slowed by the water. It did not penetrate the planet's crust.

A bad note, certainly . . . but no worse than the other bits of ugliness and pain she was hearing. The system remained out of balance, despite the ongoing efforts of the Jedi and Republic to save it. No, what she was seeking was not a bad note.

It was a *missing* note. There was a hole, right in the middle of her awareness. Something she was not hearing, something the Force was trying to point out to her. But with everything else she was tracking—the anomalies, the fear of the people trapped aboard some of them, her own teams trying to help, and just the web of life within the system—it was all too complex, too distracting.

She was missing something. And if she could not find a way to hear it, she believed everything they were doing here might, in the end, mean nothing.

Avar Kriss opened her spirit as much as she could.

She listened.

CHAPTER TWELVE

SOLAR ARRAY 22-X. REPUBLIC LONGBEAM
AURORA IX.
35 minutes to impact.

"Now, Petty Officer," ordered Captain Bright, and Innamin activated the fire suppressor systems. A line of green foam arced out from nozzles mounted below the Longbeam's cockpit, impacting the flames rippling across the damaged sunfarm's docking ring.

The moment the fire was out, Bright maneuvered the ship forward, trying to get a good seal with the docking mechanism. It wasn't easy. The array had been badly damaged when the hyperspace projectile smashed through its outer arms, and the whole station was in a loose, fast spin. The giant mess of solar panels, bracing struts, and the large central crew compartment were all equipped with external thrusters, which were trying to compensate for the spin. But whatever droid brain was in charge of the anti-spin system didn't seem to understand that the mass of the array had changed drastically when it lost so many arms in the collision.

All the little attitude adjustments, vapor buzzing out into space from the maneuvering jets . . . they just made things worse. The central sphere, where the operations crew lived and worked, was vibrating, buzzing like a hive full of irritated insects. Connecting the *Aurora IX* to the station's docking system without destroying ship, station, or both required the most skillful possible flying.

Fortunately, Captain Bright was a very skillful flier.

"Let's get in there," he said, watching his control panel light up green as the diagnostics told him the docking seal was good. He looked up and saw his team—Petty Officer Innamin and Ensign Peeples, both of whom had suited up in emergency rescue gear pulled from the Longbeam's lockers.

"This station had a crew complement of seven," Bright said. "It's not that big, but there are still plenty of places to hide. They aren't responding to our comms, which means either they're injured or the array's systems were damaged when the projectile hit. We'll have to do a sweep. We'll split up, each of us taking a third of the decks. If you find someone, bring them back to the air lock. If you need help, call for the droid."

He nodded toward the floating silver cylinder hovering just outside the cockpit, vertically oriented and rounded on top and bottom. A pill droid. Very simple design, with one large, round crystal eye and a speaker grille below. It didn't seem particularly functional, but that was deceptive. Bright had seen these things work. The droid had a variety of extender arms hidden behind sleek panels on its body, and could use them for everything from moving wreckage off trapped victims to performing basic on-site surgery. Handy machine to have around.

"Let's go," Bright said, and pressed the release that opened the *Aurora IX*'s air lock.

A wash of furnacelike air flooded out from the damaged station, bringing with it odors of chemically tinged smoke, melted plastoid, and overheated metal.

"It's burning," Ensign Peeples said, his proboscis vibrating almost as intensely as the station itself. "It stinks. Maybe the solar array had too much pharphar for lunch."

"Yeah, well, I'm getting it, too—my tentacles are almost as sensitive as your nose, Peeples. Just put on your mask and take shallow breaths. We have a job to do."

The three operatives spread out through the station. The smoke thickened, and despite the tech-enhanced goggles they all wore, it rapidly became obvious that a visual search would be ineffective. The searchers called out as they moved along the decks, paused to listen for responses, then kept going.

Bright was becoming increasingly sure that everyone on the station was dead when he heard a weak voice call out from behind a collapsed control console.

"Please, I'm here . . . please . . ."

He moved toward the sound and saw a dark-skinned human sitting with her back against a bulkhead. Blood ran down the side of her face from a wound on her scalp. Another crewmember lay beside her, unconscious. She had taken his head in her lap but didn't seem to be able to offer anything else by way of assistance to the man.

"I'm from the Republic," Bright said to the woman. "My name is Captain Bright. Don't worry, ma'am, we'll get you both out of here. What's your name?"

"Sheree," she said, her voice weak. "This is Venn. I'm . . . not sure if he's . . . He might be dead. He hasn't moved in a while."

"Don't worry about that now, Sheree. Are the other members of your crew still alive?"

"I don't know," she said. "We lost contact with one another when . . . everything caught fire. The station's comms are down."

As I expected, Bright thought.

He pulled a comlink from his belt and lifted it to his mouth.

"Innamin. Peeples. I have two survivors. One is too injured to move. I'm going to call the pill droid and get them back to the Longbeam. Have either of you had any luck?"

As he spoke, he tapped a remote clipped to his belt that would summon the rescue droid to his location. Hopefully the machine would be able to do something for the unconscious man—Venn. And if not, the medical bay on the *Aurora IX* was equipped to handle a number of different emergencies.

Bright's comlink crackled to life.

"No other survivors yet, Captain," Innamin said, his voice clouded by static—evidently the damage to the station was causing interference. "But we have another problem."

"Talk to me," Bright said, watching the rescue droid glide silently into the room.

He signaled to Sheree that he was going to keep moving, continue his search. She nodded, her expression pained but grateful.

"I started on the lowest level," Innamin continued. "It's where they stuck the operational stuff for the station—power, life support, all that. I had a hunch and wanted to check the main reactor. I'm glad I did. It took some serious damage. It's unstable. If it's not repaired, it'll blow for sure."

Blast it, Bright thought. Not that he'd expected this to be easy, but this was an entirely different level of challenge.

"How long do we have?" he said.

"Honestly, sir, if it were up to me, I'd pull us out right now. It could go at any second."

"Can you do anything? Stabilize it, even just long enough for us to continue our search? I found two survivors—there are bound to be more."

Innamin was an engineer by training. Of the three crewmembers of the *Aurora IX*, he was the only one with the skill set to even consider fixing a damaged reactor. That also meant he was the only one who would be able to accurately assess whether he could do anything about it. Innamin could easily just say, *Sorry, nope, can't do anything, we need to leave now, we did our best,* and who would know the difference? The kid was young, had a lot to live for. Bright almost wouldn't have blamed him if he'd said it was time to go.

"I can try," Innamin said. "Might be able to buy us a few minutes."

Bright felt a surge of pride wash over him.

"We're all the Republic," he said.

"We're all the Republic," Innamin replied.

"We're all *dead* if we don't finish searching the station," Ensign Peeples chimed in from another deck. "I have another survivor. Badly injured. Send me the pill."

A tremor struck the station at just that moment, a quick tight snap, as if someone outside had whacked it with a durasteel rod a hundred meters long. It knocked Bright off his feet, and he barely caught himself before what could have been a nasty fall. He was sure this was it. They would all be blasted to vapor, three would-be heroes gone in an instant along with the people they were trying to save. But the shaking eased, and he still had a deck beneath his feet and walls to either side. The station was still intact. Bright decided to consider the incident a valuable reminder that they had to get the hell out of there.

"Buy us time, Petty Officer," he said, pulling himself to his feet. "And Ensign Peeples, I'll send the droid to you as soon as it's done handling my two survivors. I'll keep looking."

Bright began to run, sweeping his eyes from side to side, scanning the haze for person-shaped outlines.

"But by the light . . . both of you . . . *hurry.*"

CHAPTER THIRTEEN

HETZAL PRIME.

30 minutes to impact.

The two Jedi, Bell Zettifar and Loden Greatstorm, apprentice and master, sprinted toward the marauders' speeders. The blades of their lightsabers buzzed and snapped through the air as they ran. The weapons sounded like nothing else in the galaxy. To Bell, it was the sound of skill, and training, and focus, and the choice of last resort, and the art of the Jedi.

Lightsabers were designed to end conflicts. They were designed to injure no more than necessary, and in the horrible circumstance where death was the only possible outcome, they would kill quickly. No more damage would be done by a lightsaber than its wielder chose. There was no collateral damage with the lightsaber.

The hum of his blade made Bell think of all these things at once. He suspected the marauders they were rapidly nearing assigned an entirely different meaning to the sound. He thought it probably sounded like . . . consequences.

The marauders saw them coming—how could they not? Bell thought that was part of the point of a lightsaber, too. It was bright, it glowed, it was impossible to ignore. Between the sound and the light, an enemy was given warning, every possible chance to simply *not* fight, and wasn't that always the best outcome?

These evil people did not seem to think so. Evil . . . that was the right word. Anyone who would fire into a crowd of helpless people in an effort to blast their way into a compound and steal a starship . . . that was evil in its purest definition.

About twenty of the marauders waited, spread evenly between their two speeders. Both vehicles had large cannons mounted on the rear deck, and they swung to point at the Jedi, a loud hum splitting the air as the huge weapons powered up.

"Why has the Force called us to fight today?" Loden said.

"For life and the light," Bell replied.

The speeder's cannons fired, sending out a dense stream of blaster bolts, an overwhelming, ratcheting, spearing chaos, the sound of death.

Bell was not expert yet at many of the Jedi arts. Loden was right to push him, to take every opportunity to train him, to solidify his skills. He was a Padawan, and probably would be for some time to come. But the lightsaber . . . that had come naturally to him from the very start.

Loden and Bell deflected the blaster bolts, every last one. The shots were deadly, thick cores of high-powered energy racing at incredible speed—and all of that meant nothing to the Jedi's lightsabers. Nothing to the Force. The majority of the bolts were deflected skyward, away from the crowd, but both Jedi sent a few carefully aimed bolts back toward the speeders. They didn't need to coordinate—Bell took the speeder on the left, Loden on the right, each Jedi's choice obvious to the other through the Force. The bolts twanged off their blades with a sizzle of power.

The deck cannons exploded, becoming twisted, smoking, melted wreckage. The marauders operating those guns died—Bell sensed it happen, even shrouded as he was in the focus he brought to protecting himself and those around him, and through the connection he felt to the other Jedi in the system through Master Kriss's efforts on the *Third Horizon.*

The cannons were gone, but they were not the only weapons the marauders possessed. Small-arms fire shot out from the smoking speeders—rifles and scatterguns and blaster pistols. It didn't matter. Loden and Bell moved forward, inexorable, their blades flashing.

A splinter grenade shot out from a tube held by one of the marauders, directly at a knot of fleeing refugees. Loden Greatstorm reached out without breaking stride and the grenade took a right-angle turn, moving from the horizontal to the vertical, shooting straight up into the air, finally exploding harmlessly hundreds of meters above them. Shards of sharp metal that would have turned dozens into bloody meat fell instead on the cropland bordering the Ranoraki compound.

Bell sensed his Master's great displeasure at the attackers' choice, and almost, almost felt bad for them.

The two Jedi leapt into the air, somersaulting, swatting away more blaster bolts as they arced up. Say this for the marauders, these dark, selfish people—they were decent shots. Not that it would matter.

Bell landed on the speeder on the left, Loden on the speeder on the right, as if they'd discussed it. The marauders finally got smart, diving off their vehicles, scattering into the crowd—but not before the Jedi disarmed a few, with either well-placed lightsaber thrusts or by using the Force to yank their weapons away.

"Blast it," Loden said as the remaining villains, about eight, vanished into the crowd. "Some of them are still armed. They might take hostages. We need to get after them, now."

"I know, Master, but how do we—"

A snap, and suddenly Bell saw nothing but golden light—bright, blinding—filling his vision. His nostrils filled with the scent of overheated, ionized air. Heat and light and color—a lightsaber blade. A blaster bolt caromed harmlessly into the sky, a streak of light that until just a moment before was destined to drill a hole into Bell's forehead.

Bell understood. His master had just saved his life.

He looked past Loden's blade to see that the Ranoraki guards, still at their posts atop their still-sealed gates, had lifted their weapons and were firing directly at them.

"Fools," Loden said.

"What are they doing?" Bell said, lifting his own blade and deflecting a blaster bolt. "I thought you had an understanding with them?"

"They must have misunderstood the understanding," Loden growled. "They're taking their chance. They think between them and the marauders, they can take us down."

"This is insane," Bell said. "With everything else going on, they want to fight?"

"They're afraid. They're trying to carve out a little control from an uncontrollable situation."

From the crowd, more blasterfire as the remaining marauders saw their chance and fought their way toward the gates. It was turning into chaos, a full-on battle, as families of refugees fought back—clearly some had their own weapons, carried in case of emergency.

And still, every moment, the larger disaster loomed. The longer these people remained on the planet, the greater the chance they all died when a projectile impacted the surface. In fact, it seemed like something already had.

Far to the west, a huge, dark cloud was swelling up into the sky on a gigantic column, spreading out into a thick disk as it reached the upper atmosphere. Moans of terror rippled through the crowd of refugees. Massive clouds of darkness on the horizon were rarely a good sign.

"This has to stop," Loden said.

"I agree . . ." Bell said. ". . . but how?"

His master looked out at the fighting. Then he glanced at the sky, where the *Nova* still circled slowly high overhead. Or maybe he was looking for fiery trails spearing in from space, signifying doom falling on the planet, nothing a lightsaber could knock back no matter how good its wielder might be.

It turned out he was evaluating, deciding. Making a plan.

"Apprentice," Loden said. "Protect me."

Without waiting to see how his Padawan would interpret this order, Loden deactivated his lightsaber. Just in time, Bell deflected a bolt that would have blasted a hole right through his teacher's chest.

Favor repaid, Master, he thought.

Loden closed his eyes, holding his hand up in front of him, palm out. He snapped his fingers out, spreading them like a star.

That was all Bell could see—he stepped in front of his master, his lightsaber in a guard position, snapping blaster bolts back toward the guards on the wall.

Nothing will get through, he thought. *I will protect my master.*

He felt a surge in the Force behind him, and eight figures shot up from the crowd, rising into the air. The remaining marauders. Most dropped their weapons, but some sent a few shots wildly into the air, hitting nothing, yelling in fury, their limbs flailing, before their blasters were yanked from their hands.

Bell was in awe. This was the power of the Jedi. This, someday, could be him. Would be him.

Even the Ranoraki guards stopped firing as all eyes watched the attackers rise into the air. Higher, higher, three meters, five, ten . . . and then they dropped. They fell, like rocks thrown off a cliff, screaming, for perhaps a second and a half. Then they hit, and the screams changed to moans of pain.

They weren't dead. Bell would have sensed it. But these people would kill no one else. Not today, or perhaps ever.

Cheers erupted from the crowd, which both Jedi ignored. They did their work because it was right, and for no other reason.

"Thank you, Bell," Loden said.

"You're welcome, Master."

Loden lifted his lightsaber hilt. He pointed it at the gates to the compound, still locked, still sealed. He locked eyes with the guard captain.

He ignited the saber, and as the core of fire and light flashed into existence, the gates blew inward with a mighty crack, the lock obliterated by the Force and Loden's mastery. The heavy metal doors smashed against the inner walls of the compound so hard it seemed as if they might rip from their hinges.

"*Now* do you understand?" he shouted at the guards as refugees streamed into the compound, headed for the starship.

The guard captain watched the refugees for a long moment, then looked up at Loden. He dropped his rifle, as did the rest of the guards.

Loden lowered his lightsaber. He looked at Bell.

He smiled.

Then a moment of uncertainty, for both master and apprentice.

"Do you sense that?" Bell said. "From Master Kriss, on the *Third Horizon.*"

"Yes," Loden replied. "Something is wrong."

CHAPTER FOURTEEN

THE *THIRD HORIZON*.
25 minutes to impact.

Avar Kriss stood before the projection wall on the bridge of the *Third Horizon*, still displaying the Hetzal system. The crisis had evolved from a stage of reaction to one of management. No new fragments had appeared from hyperspace in some time, and many of the existing projectiles had been dealt with in one way or another.

She was still listening to the song of the Force, and she knew additional Jedi were beginning to arrive in the system, to use their skills to help.

As she watched the screen, she saw Jora Malli and Sskeer execute a complex maneuver alongside two Republic Longbeams, destroying a fragment moments before it could impact a transport carrying several thousand evacuees.

"That's done," Jora said over the bridge comm, entirely matter-of-fact.

"Thank you, Master Malli," Admiral Kronara said, standing to Avar's left. "I . . . wasn't sure you'd get there in time."

"Thank the Force, Admiral," Jora said, "and your teams. It was a joint effort. Now, if you'll excuse me, I'm going to see what else Sskeer and I can do out here."

Something is wrong, Avar thought. She knew this was true, down to her bones, but she couldn't figure out what felt so off.

"Call coming in from Coruscant, Admiral," called one of the bridge officers. "It's Chancellor Soh, asking for a status update."

"Put her through, Lieutenant. I think she'll be happy with the good news."

Kronara turned to her, smiling. He wasn't celebrating, exactly—people had died in this system, and they still didn't know what had caused the disaster in the first place—but he clearly felt like he had done his job well, on little notice and with no planning. Skill and training and inspired improvisation had saved the day here: the perfect outcome for a military man.

"I should know better than to say this," Admiral Kronara said, "but I believe the worst might be over."

You should know better than to say that, Avar thought. The Force was still singing in her mind, and right in the middle of it, still, a huge, blank spot. A silence. Something she was missing.

The admiral stepped to a comm station to take the call from the chancellor. Avar did not take her eyes off the screen.

What am I missing? she asked herself. *What?*

Something caught her attention—one of the hyperspace anomalies, deep in the system, not far from the largest of Hetzal's three suns.

Avar beckoned to the closest bridge officer, then pointed at the display.

"This," she said, pointing at the anomaly near the sun. "What is this, Lieutenant?"

The officer looked where she indicated.

"One of the fragments, Master Kriss," he replied. "It doesn't have any living beings aboard, and fortunately we can more or less ignore it."

"Ignore it? Why?"

He tapped a control on a datapad. A dotted line appeared on the display, showing the projectile's path. It would follow a short arc through the inner system before vanishing deep into the sun.

"As you can see," the lieutenant said, gesturing at the display, "it will just fall into the star and be vaporized. Fortunate, really—we don't have any ships near it. It exited hyperspace deep in the system, and most of our resources are deployed elsewhere."

Avar frowned.

"There's something else. Something about it. The Force drew my attention to it, and we need to understand why. Do you know what it is? Specifically, I mean?"

The officer hesitated, squinting at the screen as if that might tell him something new.

"It's too far away for our onboard sensors to get any additional information, ma'am," the officer said. "I can check with the Hetzalian administrators, though. They might have some satellites closer that could provide more information."

"Please," Avar said. "And hurry."

The officer nodded and moved away, headed for a communications console.

Admiral Kronara, back from his conversation with the chancellor, stepped up beside her. "What is it, Master Jedi?" he said.

"I don't know yet, Admiral," Avar replied. "Trust in the Force."

"Well, obviously," Kronara said.

"How is the chancellor?"

"Relieved, I would say. This wasn't a good day, but she knows it could have been much worse. Chancellor Soh asked me a lot of questions I couldn't answer yet—about the source of the anomalies, whether it would happen again, things like that. She's thinking long-term."

"That's her job," Avar said. "What do you think she'll do?"

"If I had to guess, she's worried this was some kind of attack. I know it's unlikely, but it's not impossible. Enemies don't usually announce their intentions to hit you ahead of time."

"They also don't usually send engineless passenger compartments filled with people, Admiral. What are those supposed to be? Some sort of invasion force?"

"I'm not going to pretend I know, Master Kriss. It could be some bizarre tactic we don't yet understand. The important thing is that we were here to help stop it, and—"

"Sir, ma'am," the lieutenant said, and both admiral and Jedi turned to look at him. The officer was pale, and Avar could sense the man was on the verge of despair. Like he had just stepped off a cliff.

"You know we've been collating our own sensor data with the in-system resources being coordinated through the minister's office in Aguirre City," he said. "Their primary tech is a man named Keven Tarr—he's been able to do some truly remarkable things, keeping their satellite networks running despite all the damage from the hyperspace incursions. It's all very impressive, actually, and—"

"Lieutenant, please," Admiral Kronara said. "What is it?"

The officer nodded and spoke again.

"Tarr diverted everything he has left to getting a scan of the anomaly Master Kriss indicated—the one the, ah, Force pointed out to her. Turns out it's a container module of some kind, huge, and it must have been damaged somehow. It's leaking. Just a little, but enough that Tarr's network could run a spectrographic analysis. It's . . ."

The lieutenant took a breath.

". . . it's liquid Tibanna. The whole thing. And the star it's headed for is an R-class."

Admiral Kronara swore, which came as a mild shock to Avar.

"Bad, I take it?" she asked.

The admiral stared at the display for a long moment, his jaw clenched.

"Honestly?" he said.

He turned to look at her.

"Couldn't be much worse."

CHAPTER FIFTEEN

HETZAL SYSTEM. ABOVE THE FRUITED MOON.
20 minutes to impact.

Three Jedi Vectors flew in formation above and to either side of the Republic Longbeam piloted by Joss and Pikka Adren. Te'Ami to the larger ship's right, Mikkel Sutmani to its left, and Nib Assek and Burryaga above. They had accelerated to the limits of their ship's capabilities, chasing the speeding projectile due to impact the Fruited Moon in a matter of minutes, killing billions—those on the moon as well as the people aboard the anomaly.

They had closed a great deal of distance, burning almost all of their fuel in the process, but were now within striking range of the object. Their sensors had finally identified it as a modular passenger compartment, the sort of thing snapped into cargo ship frameworks to temporarily allow them to transport travelers. Largely self-sufficient, with dedicated life-support systems and onboard batteries, even individual hyperspace field emitters linked to the mothership's navigation and propulsion. At the moment, it was functioning almost like a large escape pod, though without engines, unable to direct or slow itself. While that explained how it could have people aboard, it did not clarify how it had suddenly appeared in the Hetzal system from hyperspace with no warning.

Te'Ami had her suspicions. She visualized a ship traveling through hyperspace, a cargo vessel, with compartments dedicated to all sorts of cargo—raw materials, fuel . . . and passengers, probably settlers bound for new lives on the barely inhabited Outer Rim worlds. Something happens to that ship in the hyperlane, and it cracks apart. All of those bits and pieces reappear from hyperspace at once, and that event has the bad luck to occur at the transit point just outside Hetzal.

Most of the wreckage would be inert, just chunks of metal. But some, if properly shielded, could be those passenger compartments, the people inside still alive, but with no way to stop their tumbling flight through space, filled with the fear and panic Burryaga had sensed, waiting to die. Waiting for help that would not come.

But help had arrived, despite everything. The Jedi and the Republic were here, and they would save the lives of every last one of those people, and everyone on the Fruited Moon, too.

"Now," Te'Ami said, the command transmitted simultaneously to Nib, Mikkel, and Burryaga, as well as Joss and his copilot Pikka. It was time for everyone to do their part.

The Jedi had discussed their approach, but only briefly. Their task was, on the face of it, simple. They reached out with the Force, touched the passenger compartment on all sides, embraced it in all the power and energy they could command, and understood its nature as best they could. Every surface, every beam, strut, and cable, and most important—the lives inside it, the beings they were trying to save.

They looped the Force around the speeding fragment. Te'Ami had once seen a rodeo, on a world called Chandar's Folly. The point was to subdue enraged animals using only long lengths of rope or cable. The brave fools who participated looped the lassos around each creature's neck, leaping on its back and riding it until either they were thrown free or the beast eventually calmed.

Mostly, the would-be riders were tossed four or five meters into the air before crashing to the dirt. Sometimes the landing was hard, sometimes soft.

This was like that—they were lassoing the passenger compartment with the Force—but the chances of a soft landing seemed unlikely. The Jedi closed their loops around the racing chunk of wreckage and pulled back. Te'Ami's breath left her with a *whoosh,* her lungs emptying. Nothing had changed about her physical location—she was still seated in the cockpit of her Vector, speeding at the same velocity she had a moment before—but it didn't feel that way. It felt like she had been yanked out into open space and was being dragged along, utterly out of control.

It seemed impossible that anything the four Jedi could do would influence the speed of this thing in any way, but they had to try. Joss Adren had been clear—even a one percent change could be significant.

"Slow . . . it down . . ." she managed, speaking through gritted teeth. She could feel oil gathering in the sacs along her ribs, her body's involuntary response to great strain. The acrid stink of the stuff filled her cockpit, an evolutionary throwback and defense mechanism from the days when the Duros were liable to be eaten by any number of things prowling their world.

"Trying . . ." Mikkel spat back, strain in his natural voice slipping past the translator's efforts to subdue it. Te'Ami wondered how Ithorians responded to stress. Probably not by producing large amounts of horrible-tasting oil.

"Captain Adren," Te'Ami said, "we've done what we can. If you're going to do something, now is the moment."

"Acknowledged, Master Jedi," Joss replied. He sounded tense, too. "Remember, if you can try to hold the module together once we lock on, it'd be appreciated. This might get a little bumpy."

"We'll do our best."

"All right. Firing magclamps in three . . . two . . ."

Four metal disks shot out into space ahead of their formation, angling toward the passenger compartment. The thing was venting vapor from either a coolant or a life-support system, creating a thick fog into which the disks vanished. Thick, silvery lines unspooled—the cabling attached to the Longbeam's winches, with which they would attempt to slow the wreckage down. Three of the lines went taut, the other looping and coiling in space.

"We hit it with three out of four. As good as we can hope. We're gonna apply reverse thrusters. Get ready."

Through the Force, Te'Ami could feel new strains and stressors on the system, all its complex linkages and connections. Longbeam to wreckage, Force to Jedi, wreckage to Force, and now a new note of confusion from the poor survivors inside the compartment, who must have heard the thumps as the clamps engaged, probably sounding like kicks from a giant, with no idea what was about to happen to them.

Honestly, Te'Ami didn't know, either. The Longbeam activated its thrusters and dropped out of formation, the long, thick cabling stretching, growing thin, then impossibly thin, then vanishing to the naked eye. Captain Adren had told her this would happen, the silk that composed the cables was able to stretch almost to the molecular level and retain its strength. The cables were holding. The compartment to which they were attached . . . perhaps not so much.

"It's going to break apart," Nib Assek said. Burryaga whined mournfully in the background.

"No, it won't," Mikkel grunted. "We won't let it. Just . . . *hold it together.*"

"Stop talking and do it," Te'Ami said.

The overstressed box of metal, plastoid, and wiring did not want to continue to exist in its current form. It had been through too much, and knew it. It wanted to disintegrate, escape from the weight and heat and become a swarm of much tinier bits, all free to head off on their own trajectories.

If not for the Jedi, it would have done exactly that. They used the Force to keep the container in one piece, the loops of resistance they had used to slow it now used to maintain its integrity.

It didn't seem like it would work. It was too much all at once—on top of everything else, the exhausted Jedi had to keep their Vectors flying at top speed, close enough to the passenger compartment that they could maintain their links.

And in the back of their minds, distraction, as some new crisis burgeoned elsewhere in the system. An increasing sense of alarm swelling along Avar Kriss's network—but they had no time for that. They had their own crisis right here.

The wreckage ahead of them shifted, like a pile of stones about to tumble after one is removed, and Te'Ami opened her mouth and groaned, a sound of intense strain, as physical as internal. She could still feel the compartment pulling on her, and now she knew that if she let go, if she released her hold even a little, her Vector could be torn apart around her. Now it wasn't just the lives of the people aboard the compartment, or even on the moon, now so close she could see its disk looming in space, growing larger every second.

Te'Ami stopped thinking about any of those things. She closed her eyes and let the Force guide her. For long seconds, nothing but chaos, strain, stress. And then . . . a lessening. The slightest release in tension—but it made everything simpler. As Captain Adren had said, even a one percent reduction was meaningful.

Then one became two, and more, and the objects working against one another became a single system.

The compartment slowed. More, and more, until it came to a slow stop, the Longbeam reeling it in on its cables.

"Whoa," came Captain Adren's voice over the comm. "I really didn't think that would work."

"You certainly waited long enough to tell us," came Mikkel's reply. Even through his translator, he sounded utterly exhausted.

"Almost out of fuel," said Joss, ignoring the remark, "couple more seconds and we'd have had to shut off our thrusters. We couldn't have done that alone. Thank you, Jedi."

"We couldn't have done it by ourselves, either," Te'Ami said. "And the idea was yours. Whether you thought it would work or not, it did."

Pikka Adren spoke. "We can suit up and go over there, see if there's some way to extract the passengers. If not, we can tow it to a station, dock it there. At the very least, we can get them some medical attention. I'm sure they're banged up."

"All right," Te'Ami replied. "Thank you. We'll pass along how we achieved this—I'm sure other rescue teams will find the information useful."

She maneuvered her Vector up and alongside the passenger compartment, moving close. The module had portholes along its length, and in them, she could see faces. Beings of all types, all ages, all alive. She sensed their fear beginning to lessen, replaced with—

A huge flash of alarm shot through the system-wide net of awareness being maintained by Avar Kriss. Again, no words, but if the sensation could be translated, it would be just these words: "Jedi. You are needed. Now."

Something was very, very wrong.

CHAPTER SIXTEEN

SOLAR ARRAY 22-X.
10 minutes to impact.

The station heaved, throwing Captain Bright off his feet and into a wall. He hit hard, barely catching himself on a stanchion before an impact that would surely have cracked his skull.

The pill droid floating just a few meters ahead of him in the burning corridor didn't seem to notice the jolt at all—but then it wasn't in contact with the deck. It was floating, serene as ever, its stretcher attachment unfolded from its carapace, currently occupied by an unconscious, tiny Anzellan, purple drops of blood leaving a trail behind the droid.

They weren't far from the *Aurora IX*, and the Anzellan made seven rescued crewmembers from the solar array—the full complement. The job was done, and so far, they'd all survived, miracle of miracles. It was just a matter of whether they could get far enough away from the station before it blew. Which was imminent, as the series of increasingly urgent messages he'd received from the engineering deck suggested.

Bright lifted his comlink.

"Petty Officer Innamin," he growled. "What in blazes was that? I thought you told me you could keep this station stabilized?"

"What I told you, Captain, is that I explicitly could not do that," Innamin replied, his voice wavering between annoyance and utter panic. "The reactor will blow. There is nothing I can do about it. We just need to be gone when it does."

"All right," Bright said. "I have the last crewmember. We'll be at the Longbeam in about thirty seconds. Get up here, and we'll decouple and get gone."

The pill droid had reached the air lock, where Ensign Peeples was waiting; he had been tasked with stabilizing the other injured crewmembers of the solar array in the *Aurora IX*'s medical bay. His needlelike snout buzzed as he saw the Anzellan.

"Aww," he cooed. "Who's the cute little baby?"

Peeples picked up the injured crewmember and cuddled him against his chest. The pill droid's stretcher attachment snapped together and refolded itself in some ingenious way before disappearing back inside its carapace.

"Blast it, Peeples, that's not a baby. Get him to the medical bay, and make sure everyone's strapped in and ready to go. We need to fly, and it might get rough."

Peeples blinked his eyes, all nineteen of them, and Bright's tentacles told him the ensign was frustrated, presumably at his fun being ruined. But he turned, taking the Anzellan with him.

Then he turned back.

"By the by, an order came through, from the *Third Horizon*," Peeples said. "Full system evac. All rescue efforts are supposed to end, and all vessels are to head to hyperspace access zones and leave Hetzal immediately."

"They say why? Lotta people gonna get left behind."

Peeples shrugged, or performed the odd spasm that passed for a shrug with him, and walked away, crooning to the unconscious little being in his arms.

Another rumble from the station, and a blast of flame rushed down the corridor. Bright barely registered what was happening before the pill droid moved with a speed belying its usual languid grace. It inserted itself between the inferno and Bright. One of its side panels opened, and a nozzle emerged. Suppressor foam shot from it, intersecting with the flames, knocking them down, and only the merest wash of heat reached Bright.

He released the breath he'd been holding, then drew in another, realizing how close he'd just come to being cooked alive. He patted the top of the pill droid's cylinder.

"Thanks, pal," he said.

The pill droid emitted two short beeps. Bright couldn't understand Binary without a translator, but he took the sound to convey a sort of "just doing my job, sir" type of stoicism, which he liked.

He lifted his comlink again. "Innamin! Where the hell are you? If you don't get up here I'll leave you behind!"

"About that," came the reply. No longer annoyed, no longer panicked. Just . . . resigned.

That, Bright did not like. "What's the problem, Petty Officer?"

"I can't leave. I have to run a sequence on the reactor's control console, injecting coolant every few seconds, and if I stop, it'll blow right away. I was trying to set up some sort of automation, but the processors are damaged. I . . ." His voice cracked.

"No, we'll get you out," Bright said. "I'll bring the pill droid. We can show it the sequence. It'll run it for us while we get out and away."

"Captain . . . you should go. Coming down to save me will take time, and—"

"Shut up, Innamin," Bright said.

He gestured at the pill droid's ocular sensor, giving it the command to follow, and then he started sprinting toward the nearest set of deck ladders.

He made his way down the decks as quickly as he could, finally arriving at the reactor level. Innamin looked up, his face covered with sweat, so relieved he looked like he was going to faint.

"Hold it together," Bright said to the junior officer.

The station shook again, and didn't stop.

"We have *no time,*" Innamin said.

"Clearly," Bright said. "Show the droid the sequence."

"It has to happen when this gauge goes into the red," Innamin said, a scenario conveniently happening at exactly that moment. He tapped a quick run of five button-presses on the console, and the gauge slipped back a few notches. Not to green, but to orange, and that would have to do.

The sequence was not complicated. Bright got the order just from seeing it once. Evidently the droid had it memorized, too. It moved forward, taking Innamin's place at the console, waiting for the next opportunity to enter the commands.

"Go, right now," Bright told his subordinate. "Get to the Longbeam."

"Aren't you coming?"

"I want to make sure the droid can do this," he said. "Just go. Help Peeples. The light only knows what he's doing up there."

"Thank you, Captain, it . . . it means a lot."

"We're all the Republic," Bright said.

Innamin nodded and ran off, out of the reactor chamber, toward the nearest deck ladder.

"All right, you beautiful machine," Bright said, turning back to the pill droid. "Show me you understood."

The gauge slipped into the red, and the pill droid moved fast and sure, tapping the five buttons. The gauge fell back—less than it had the previous time, Bright noticed—and the station seemed just a bit less likely to shake itself apart.

"Okay, it's all yours," Bright said. "I gotta run. It's been wonderful working with you."

This time the droid did not respond, which Bright decided to take as a sort of resigned agreement. He turned and raced out of the room, following the path Innamin had taken. He reached the ladder and put his boot on the first rung.

This will work, he thought, more wish than belief.

And then he sensed it—or rather, his tentacles did, with their ability to pull out pheromones from even the most polluted environment. There was another being here, someone alive. Alive and hurt, if his receptors didn't steer him wrong.

Bright followed the scent trail, and there, behind a panel, was a Twi'lek, male, heavy, bruised, bleeding, and unconscious. He was dressed in the uniform of the station, and Bright didn't know if Innamin hadn't thoroughly searched this deck because he was distracted by the damaged reactor, or because the injured man was mostly hidden, or . . . well, it didn't matter, did it?

Just to see, Bright crouched down and attempted to lift the Twi'lek. His muscles strained, but the unconscious man was deadweight. He barely moved.

No, he thought. *No way.*

Bright gave himself a moment, just one, to think about his life, the things he'd done and the things he thought he might do. He thought about the Republic, and what it meant, and his own oaths to serve it and all its people.

And then he ran back to the reactor.

"I've got this," he said, pushing the pill droid out of the way and taking its position at the control console. He pointed his thumb back over his shoulder.

"You've got a patient, about nine meters past the deck ladder. Get him back to the ship. Now."

The droid rotated, swooshing quickly away.

Bright tapped in the command sequence, and the gauge slipped back a little—but less than it had the last time.

He spoke into his comlink.

"Innamin," he said. "You make it?"

"Yes, Captain," came the reply. "But where are you? You were supposed to be right behind me."

"Change in plans," Bright said. "I'm sending the pill droid up with one more evacuee."

"But we already got all seven crewmembers."

"Guess there were eight," Bright said.

"But the reactor," Innamin said, trailing off. Bright could almost hear the kid's mind working, coming to understand the reality of what was about to happen.

"Take off the minute you have the droid aboard. Don't wait. Get out of the system's gravity wells and jump away. Rendezvous with the *Third Horizon,* if you can. If not, get back to Coruscant. It seems like things are falling apart all over the system, not just here."

"But Captain, maybe—"

"No. Look. I've been easy on you as long as we've flown together, Innamin. The insubordination, the joking around . . . life's too short, and the ship's too small, I always figured. But all that ends now. Life *is* short, Petty Officer, pretty damn short indeed. I gave you an order, and if you do not follow it, I will see you court-martialed."

A long silence from the comm. They both knew how empty that threat was. Not the point. At last, Innamin spoke, his voice subdued.

"I can see the droid. It has the crewman. A Twi'lek?"

"That's right."

Bright entered the sequence again. The gauge slipped back. A little less.

The tremors on the station had risen to the level of a seismic event. The array was tearing itself apart.

"Go, Innamin!"

"We've . . . already undocked, Captain. Reversing thrusters now. Getting to minimum safe distance. Shouldn't be long."

"Good," Bright said.

The gauge was in the red again. Bright entered the sequence. This time, the needle didn't move. It just stayed in the red.

Bright sighed.

"Captain, we are away," Innamin said. "We are all the Republic."

"Damn right," Bright said. "We are all the—"

Heat and light and nothing more.

CHAPTER SEVENTEEN

HETZAL PRIME. THE *THIRD HORIZON*.
4 minutes to impact.

"Master Jedi, are you certain this is the correct choice?" Admiral Kronara asked.

Avar Kriss could sense his concern. He was a good commander, and although she was not technically part of his crew, she knew he felt responsible for her safety. Especially considering that if he did what she was asking him to do, he was probably condemning her to death.

"I am certain, Admiral," she said. "We've loaded as many refugees as we can hold, and more besides."

She glanced around the hangar. It was true. This room alone held hundreds of beings, with nothing other than the clothes on their backs. No one had been allowed to bring anything else. Every bit of available space on the huge cruiser had been allocated toward saving lives. And even then, people were still trapped on the planet's surface. Admiral Kronara and his crew had done their best, but the *Third Horizon* was just a machine, and there was a point where taking on additional mass would mean the ship could not take off, and no one would be saved at all.

"These people are afraid," Avar said. "I can sense it. You need to get them to safety."

"But if you fail, you will die," Kronara said, making one last attempt.

"I know that, Admiral, but there are billions of people down there who couldn't find a way off Hetzal Prime." Here she pointed, at the open sky visible outside the hangar's exit ramp.

The ship was a hundred meters up, stationary above the cropland outside Aguirre City, having left the starport after taking on as many refugees as it could.

"If I don't try this," Avar continued, "they will definitely die. Every last one."

"But can you actually save them? I've never heard of anything like this being possible—even with the Jedi."

Avar smiled at him.

"All things are possible through the Force," she said. "Now take the *Third Horizon* and go. I have work to do, and it's important that you deliver a direct report to Chancellor Soh about what you witnessed here. It's not enough to tell her over the comm. None of this should have happened. There's something wrong. I can sense it. Hyperspace is . . . sick, for lack of a better word."

"Of course, Master Jedi," the admiral said. "But you should deliver that report yourself. I still don't understand why you can't perform your task from open space? I don't know much about the Force, but I do know it works across great distances, and if you're safe on the ship, at least you'll have a way to escape if—"

Avar Kriss believed that the best way to win arguments was simply not to have them. She sprinted down the exit ramp and leapt, out into open air. The ship was hovering above a field of some blue grain she was not familiar with—all she knew was that it was absolutely gorgeous. She used the Force to slow herself, somersaulted, then landed lightly on plowed soil between two neat rows of the stuff.

The *Third Horizon* was already just a dwindling speck in the sky by the time she looked back up. Admiral Kronara had accepted defeat and was wasting no time leaving the system. That was good. They had very little.

Focus, she told herself. Time truly was short, and the task to be accomplished here was all but impossible.

A tank of supercooled liquid Tibanna, as large as a decent-sized starship by itself, was headed directly toward one of the Hetzal system's three suns, an R-class star. When it hit, the volatile nature of the substance, combined with the intense heat of the star and its unique nitrogen-heavy composition, would cause a rapid chain reaction that would result in the sun surging outward, flaring up to nearly double its size, putting out radiation that would cook the entire system in a matter of moments. The Hetzal system, in not much time at all, would cease to exist.

Unless the Force willed it otherwise, and used its instruments—the Jedi—to prevent it.

Kronara wouldn't ever understand why it was so important for her to stay on the planet. He couldn't touch the Force.

Avar needed to be on the surface of Hetzal Prime because the world was a planet of life. Now, the Force was everywhere, of course—even in the deepest, coldest reaches of space. She could always hear its song—but here, standing in this field, surrounded by growing things that had been tended with love and care by the farmers of this world, the song was *loud.* Loud and sweet.

Here, she did not have to spend any extra time or energy seeking a deep connection to the Force. It was all around her.

Avar Kriss lifted her comlink. She set it to broadcast-only, knowing that what she was about to say would bring questions from many of the other Jedi in the system, some of whom outranked her. Jora Malli was a member of the Jedi Council, and even if she was planning to step down in order to take up her post on the Starlight Beacon, she hadn't left the Council yet. Technically, she could order Avar to stop what she was doing.

Not that she would do that—probably—but why take a chance?

She thought about Elzar Mann, who did things like this all the time. *Better to ask for forgiveness than permission* was basically his entire credo.

He'll love this, she thought, and spoke.

"My Jedi friends, this is Avar Kriss. I am on the surface of Hetzal Prime. You know I've been watching you all work so hard to save this system and its people. You've done incredibly well. But something else is about to happen, something terrible, and we all need to act together to stop it.

"One of the hyperspace anomalies is headed directly for the system's largest sun—and it is a container of liquid Tibanna. I am told that when it hits, a rare chain reaction will result that will destroy everything in this system.

"It is up to us to move the container to a new path. We will ask the Force to come to our aid. It might not be possible, and anyone who stays runs the risk of dying if we fail. The *Third Horizon* is about to transit the system. Anyone who wants to leave can dock with it. My good wishes will go with you."

Avar waited. Though she had silenced her comlink to replies, the song of the system told her that no Vectors had altered course toward the rapidly accelerating *Third Horizon.* They had all decided to stay. The Jedi were with her.

"Let's begin," she said.

She lowered the comlink. This would not be done with words.

Avar sent the concepts through the link with her fellow Jedi. Each would receive it in their own way, a series of impressions that she hoped would resonate properly with each of them. A very simple plan, really:

There is a thing, moving very fast. It is very large, and very heavy. It needs to change direction. We will all find it together, and we will all apply the Force to it together in just the same spot in just the same way at just the same time, and we will move it so it does not hit the sun.

Simple . . . but enormously difficult. Space was large, and there were many Jedi, and coordinating their efforts so they did not fight against one another or cancel one another out or touch the Force at slightly different moments . . . well. That was the task. No use complaining about it.

Avar's lightsaber lifted from its holster, gliding up into the air through the Force. It floated up until the hilt was before her face, the crosspieces level with her eyes. The lightsaber ignited with a snap and a hiss, a bright-green beam spearing straight up at the blue sky and illuminating the field of blue grain around her.

The weapon began to rotate, slowly, like the blade of a windmill. It made a sound as it moved through the air, a low, droning hum. Avar breathed—in, out—and the blade slowly sped up. The tone of its passage through the air changed, no longer a low drone but a higher pitch, a lovely round note. The lightsaber moved faster, its blade now too fast to see; a green circle of light with a shining metallic center.

It was beautiful, but Avar closed her eyes. She did not need to see. She needed to hear. Her lightsaber was not just a weapon. Here, now . . . it was an instrument.

The note of the blade rose, becoming a clear ringing, the normal crackling hum and whine of a lightsaber in combat replaced by a pure, glassine tone.

Her awareness was the song of the saber, and she tuned the speed of its rotation until the note it produced was precisely in sync with—

Yes, Avar Kriss thought. *I hear it.*

Her mind snapped outward, the sabersong chiming in harmony with the larger chorus of the Force, in a single instant becoming the entire system and everything within it, and more particularly every single Jedi, each connected to the Force in their own way.

What she heard as a song, Elzar Mann saw as a deep, endless, storm-tossed sea. The Wookiee Burryaga was a single leaf on a gigantic tree with deep-dug roots and sky-high limbs. Douglas Sunvale saw the Force as a huge, interlocked set of gears, made of an endless variety of materials from crystal to bone. Bell Zettifar danced with fire. Loden Greatstorm danced with wind.

This was not the simple network she had built earlier. This was deeper. All of the Jedi were the Force, and the Force was all of them. And she, Avar Kriss, could touch them all, no matter how they saw the Force.

Now, though, she had to find their target. The module of Tibanna racing toward the sun. It was difficult now, with so many Jedi singing in her mind, a chorus to the Force symphony blasting at full volume. So many people, so many beings, so much life. Every grain in the dimly sensed field around her piping like flutes.

Somewhere in all of that was the module of liquid Tibanna racing toward the sun to destroy them all. It did not sing a song of its own, but that was itself something to be sensed. A silence, a caesura, a fermata of precisely the correct duration and size.

There, she thought.

She had it, without a doubt. It was—gone. She'd lost it.

"Blast it!" she said out loud, and everything wavered and almost faded away.

She'd lost the anomaly, and now couldn't find it again, not within the chaos of everything else moving within the system. It was like looking at a particular flower in a wind-tossed meadow, looking away, then looking back and trying to find the precise blossom again.

Time was fracturing away, shards of moments flying off into nothingness, never to return. She had to find it. She had to—she could not fail. It was her responsibility. No one else could . . .

No. What had she said?

We will find it together.

She had a system full of Jedi working alongside her. They each had their own connection to the Force—perhaps different from hers, but no less powerful.

Avar Kriss asked for help, and help came.

Estala Maru found it first. Avar could see the Force through his eyes—to Maru, the Tibanna bomb was a single light in a single window in a single small building of an endlessly spiraling nighttime city. But once Estala had it, it was only a matter of pointing the other Jedi to look in that direction as well, and then they all did.

But now the task did fall to Avar.

She drew her awareness back, gauging how close the bomb was to hitting the star—it would not be long. The heat of the sun was already causing steam to rise from the forward edge of the tank's outer shell. They had to act.

There is a thing, moving very fast. It is very large, and very heavy.

It needs to change direction.

We will apply the Force to it together in just the same spot in just the same way at just the same time.

Avar Kriss showed the Jedi what to do, and as one, the Jedi reached out to the Force. They did not hold themselves back. They acted with disciplined desperation, leaving nothing in reserve.

We will move it.

Not far from the Fruited Moon, Te'Ami lost consciousness, yellow ichor streaming from her mouth.

We will move it.

A group of five Vectors flying in tight formation lost control of their Drift, too much of their focus devoted to the effort to shift the Tibanna bomb. Two of the craft collided before control could be reestablished, and the three Jedi aboard those ships were lost.

We will move it.

Now, Avar thought.

Across the system, Jedi reached out to the Force. Some closed their eyes, some lifted their arms, some stood, some sat meditating on the ground while others hovered above it. Some were in starships, others on the surface. Many were alone, but others were with members of their Order, or were surrounded by small groups of people who could sense, somehow, the import of what was happening, even if they could not themselves touch the Force.

Dozens of Jedi, acting as one.

The galaxy *thrummed.* An invisible hand grasped the Tibanna bomb in a firm grip and threw it to one side. Gentle, but precise, like tossing an egg to someone you hoped would catch it without the thing shattering all over their hands.

Avar listened.

They had succeeded. They had moved the Tibanna.

But they had also failed.

The tank had not moved far enough. It would still hit the sun, and even now, she could sense the liquid heating inside the container, pressure building, preparing for an explosion that would presage the larger blast to come.

Again, she told the Jedi, those of whom could still hear and respond. Many had fallen unconscious at the strain of the first attempt, which meant the burden on those who remained was that much greater.

We have to try again.

Avar could sense the weariness in the song, of all her companions in her great Order, these heroes who had all stayed to save people they had never met and probably never would, people who would never know the choice or the sacrifice being made on their behalf. None of that mattered.

She felt her fellows toss aside their exhaustion, lift themselves up, renew their focus.

Not only that, but she sensed that other Jedi had brought their focus to bear as well—from Coruscant, from across the galaxy. Even Yoda, wherever he was with his little crew of younglings—his great, wise mind sang its own part of the chorus, heartbreakingly beautiful, a voice of pure light belying his physical appearance. Not this crude matter indeed.

Avar would not have believed such a thing was possible—but as she had told the admiral, through the Force, there wasn't a blasted thing that couldn't be done. Her great Order was with her, as she was with them, and the Force was with them all.

We will move it.

Another moment chosen, another great effort.

We will move it.

She felt the Jedi saying the words with her, each in their own way, through their own particular lens on the Force. No, not saying. Chanting. Singing.

We will move it.

More Jedi falling—mostly just collapsing where they stood, or spiraling off in their Vectors. Some managed to regain control, but others were lost forever. Rohmar Montgo. Lio Josse.

Jedi Knight Rah Barocci tottered and fell off the tower farm on the Rooted Moon where he had been helping a family whose daughter had suffered a seizure in the stress of the evacuation order. The daughter was calm, her crisis over, but Rah fell twenty stories and did not recover in time to save himself.

With every Jedi lost, the work became harder.

Elzar Mann, standing alone on a rocky promontory overlooking a pharm where the new miracle drug bacta was produced in extremely limited quantities, felt the strain, the inertia of the Tibanna bomb that did not want to be moved.

To Mann, the Force was a bottomless sea, never ending, in which all things swam. Brightly lit in its upper reaches, fading to darkness below, but all one great ocean. He reached out to it, letting himself race along its currents, going deeper than ever before, seeing and sensing things he had never before known. The sea never ended, and there was so much of it he hadn't seen. Strength flooded through him, his exhaustion vanishing. He added that power to that of his fellows, giving them everything he could.

We will move it.

. . .

. . .

. . .

. . .

And it will not hit the sun.

The Tibanna entered the outer photosphere of the Hetzal system's largest star. For a moment, a long moment, the song stopped. Avar Kriss heard nothing but silence.

The fragment burst out of the sun, only having touched its outermost layers, heated but intact, on a path that would take it harmlessly out of the system.

The song burst back into life.

Jedi Master Avar Kriss fell to her knees there in the field on Hetzal Prime. Her lightsaber hilt, now deactivated, hit the ground a moment later, embedding itself in the soft soil.

Avar let herself breathe. Two long breaths, then three. Then she raised her comlink.

"Thank you," she said.

Neither Avar Kriss nor any of the other Jedi in Hetzal knew that the events of those moments had been broadcast across the Outer Rim. The signal even found its way to the inner worlds of the Republic, though slightly delayed due to the limitations of the galactic communications network. The signal was sent by Keven Tarr, working from Minister Ecka's office in Aguirre City, still doing his job despite having had the opportunity to leave on the *Third Horizon.*

The broadcast was originally just a feed sent to the chancellor's office on Coruscant at its request, tight-band and secure, to allow Lina Soh and her aides to have the most up-to-date information on the disaster as it progressed to this final phase.

But Keven Tarr made a decision. If these were to be the last moments of Hetzal—his home and the home of billions of others—he did not want such a good place to die unacknowledged. He changed the settings on the feed, stripping out the security codes and sending it to every channel, every relay, every ear and eye it could find.

This, in its way, was a feat of technology just as impossible as what the Jedi were attempting.

In any case, the people of the Republic watched as the fate of Hetzal was decided. They stopped breathing as the Jedi came together to save these worlds, full of people they did not know. This small group of brave people risked their own lives to save others, and used their unique gifts to preserve, to help.

A gasp of dismay rose on a thousand worlds as the first attempt failed, and it was clear that the Jedi had not succeeded. Perhaps could not succeed. Some looked away, not wanting to see the flare of light as the star exploded, followed closely by the death of billions of sentient beings.

Others could not look away, and these people saw what happened next. The star did not explode. The people did not die.

Across the galaxy, cheers of relief and joy. Yes, scowls from those who lived in darkness, hoping for the Jedi to fail, to be crushed, to die—but they were few.

This was a Republic that valued and celebrated life and those who preserved it.

This was a victory.

For this day, at least, the light had prevailed.

It was over.

CHAPTER EIGHTEEN

It was not over.

In the Ab Dalis system, farther along the same hyperlane the *Legacy Run* had been traveling when it met its end, seven fragments of that ship emerged from hyperspace, just past the transfer point.

Not the largest nor the smallest was a chunk of the huge cargo vessel's superstructure, a durasteel support beam still attached to a large portion of the ship's hull.

The fragments were moving at just below lightspeed, but all were unpowered, electronically inert, and well inside the normal transfer point from hyperspace where vessels could arrive in the system. The sensor arrays and early warning systems did not pick up the anomalies until it was far too late, and even if they had, there was no Republic Cruiser full of Jedi nearby to save the day.

All seven fragments were traveling along the system's ecliptic, but Ab Dalis was not as densely populated as Hetzal. Space was immense, and the fragments were, in comparison, tiny.

Six of them hit nothing, passing through the system and out the other side without incident.

The seventh hit a glancing blow on the most densely populated world of the system, a swampy wasteland interrupted only by city-sized factories, slums inhabited by the workers who operated those factories, and, here and there, the towers inhabited by those who profited from both. The fragment was vaporized in the impact, but the concussion flattened one of those cities, and the slums, and the towers.

Approximately twenty million people were killed.

This was the first Emergence.

Interlude

The Nihil.

Ab Dalis. Never a lovely world, always shrouded in swirling, brown-tinted clouds as if the swamps on the surface were trying to escape the planet's gravity. Now, though, it looked even worse than usual. The orbital impact had forced an enormous cloud of vaporized water and mud into the air, and much of that had ionized, causing gigantic lightning storms to flicker across the planet's atmosphere.

It looked like some form of hell.

A convoy of six freighters made its way through the system, away from the ravaged planet. They held the entire workforce, along with their families, of Garello Technologies, a midlevel materials research and manufacturing concern based in the Keftia district. Beyond the people, the freighters' holds also contained much of the company's most important research, databases, machinery, and financial resources. All of it had been loaded aboard the six starships to bring it offworld for safety while the disaster unfolded on Ab Dalis, a massive effort that consumed all of the day and night that had passed since the impact.

The company's chief executive, Larence Garello, had made the company's other starships available to the Ab Dalisian government for relief efforts, but he had chosen to take care of his people and his business first. Many people relied on Garello Technologies, and he wanted to ensure that when the crisis abated, every person who put his trust in him would be safe and sound, and would still be working for a company that could continue producing the ideas and products that supported so many.

Many Ab Dalisian business owners at Larence's level scoffed at him for going to such great expense to temporarily pack up his operation and move it offplanet, but he didn't care. The oligarchs and trillionaires cared more for a single durasteel beam in their factories than the people who worked in them. Larence was wealthy, yes, but that was because good people in his employ gave him their all. He was damn well going to take care of every last one.

The convoy was headed to the system's outer edge, where it would stop to wait to see how the situation developed.

But before the ships could reach their destination, they encountered something strange.

It looked like a storm, or a storm cloud, perhaps. A massive, blue-gray swirl of vapor out in space, dense and threatening, and directly in the convoy's path. Faint lights flickered from deep within it, like spark-flies at dusk above the Ab Dalisian swamps.

The lead ship in the convoy was the *Arbitrage*, captained by a dark-furred Shistavanen named Odabba, a good, steady hand who had worked for Garello Technologies for over a decade. He scanned the cloud, but the sensors could not provide any information. He gave the order for all ships to divert course, to go around the thing, whatever it was. Better safe than sorry.

But there was no safety—not anymore.

The storm cloud lit up. A massive, jagged spike of energy shot out from the middle of the cloud, lashing out past the *Arbitrage* to impact one of the other ships in the convoy, the *Maree's Diligence*, named after Larence Garello's mother.

The other ship glowed brightly for a moment, surrounded by phosphorescent fire, then went dark, its running lights deactivating along the length of its hull and engines fading out. The *Maree's Diligence* began to drift away from the rest of the convoy, all its systems clearly offline.

Captain Odabba ordered the convoy to raise shields and prepare for battle—but all six ships were freighters, not warships, and in the rush to evacuate the planet, no guard fighters had been arranged. The cargo vessels were all but unarmed, with only a few light laser cannons each.

Another flash from the cloud, then another, and now it was impossible to think of them as anything but lightning strikes—huge blasts of energy at a scale difficult to process. Each of these two last strikes found a target in Garello's convoy, but by now the shields were up, and while they didn't cripple the vessels the way the first against the *Maree's Diligence* had, both ships' defenses took a significant hit.

But each flash of light had illuminated the cloud from the inside, and for just a moment, the beings aboard the convoy had seen what was waiting for them. Ships. Many ships.

As if the third and final strike was a signal, the vessels hiding in the strange cloud shot out, a buzzing, whipping swarm. They were ugly, blocky things, with spikes protruding from them in no discernable pattern. They looked like tools designed for beating someone to death. Most were sized for one or two pilots, but some were larger, and in the center of the cloud a much bigger vessel waited. It was at least equal in size to one of the convoy's freighters, but this was no cargo ship. This was a cruel thing, built for war, for destruction.

All of the ships had two things in common, no matter their size or design—three bright slashes down their sides, like war paint, and a strange attachment to their engines, a metal lattice like a half-moon filled with rippling green fire, of unknown purpose.

Laser bolts began to lance out from the convoy's freighters, anemic and thin in comparison with the threat they faced. There were . . . so many.

Word began to spread among the people of Garello Technologies and the convoy's crews. Hope died, replaced with panic and terror. They had seen the lightning strikes, and the insignia on the ships. They believed they knew who was attacking them.

The Nihil.

Captain Odabba gave the order to run, to turn and race back to Ab Dalis. He knew it was futile, but less so than fighting, and perhaps some of the ships might somehow reach safety.

The Nihil. A year ago, neither Larence Garello nor anyone in his employ had even heard the name. But in the past months, the word had taken on an almost talismanic quality across the Outer Rim, like a plague, or a hunting beast that could not be escaped or fought.

The Nihil were raiders, thieves, murderers, kidnappers. They could be anywhere, at any time, appearing from nothing. They worked in space, on planets, in cities, in the wilderness. They moved like spirits and killed like devils. Whether they were actually monsters or just acted with monstrous savagery was unclear. What was known about them was dwarfed by what was not.

The most important things known about the Nihil were these: They took what they wanted and destroyed what they didn't, and while occasionally you heard a story about someone surviving an encounter with the Nihil, you never heard a story about someone fighting them off.

A large segment of the enemy ships surrounded the disabled *Maree's Diligence*, swirling around it in a manner chaotic but somehow aware, like winged insects swarming a corpse but never colliding with one another.

Projectiles fired from each of the Nihil attack ships. Not laser blasts or missiles. These were something like harpoons, and each dug deep into the hull of the unshielded, defenseless freighter.

As one, the Nihil vessels rotated 180 degrees, so their engines faced the *Maree's Diligence*, and then those engines fired. Long tendrils of flame shot out from each ship, and the Nihil vessels strained at the cables attaching them to the freighter.

From the bridge of the *Arbitrage*, Larence Garello watched in horror, thinking of the people on that ship, the thousands of people on that ship.

Their families. He had told them to bring their families, that he would keep them safe.

The *Maree's Diligence* ripped apart.

It did not explode, other than a few flickers of flame here and there. Presumably this was due to the fact that the ship's systems were largely inert after the Nihil's first strike. Whatever the cause, it shattered and tore, its inner passageways and compartments venting to space. Smaller objects and bits of debris came spiraling out into the void, and Larence Garello, chief executive of Garello Technologies, knew that some of those objects were his people.

"Keep firing!" Captain Odabba shouted to his bridge crew. "I've called for assistance from Ab Dalis, and they'll send what they can. We just need to hold on."

Larence was not a military man, but even he knew these words rang hollow. Ab Dalis was consumed with a planetwide catastrophe. Their government was corrupt and ineffective after generations of catering to all those oligarchs and trillionaires, and might not send anyone to help even if they could.

Another blast fired from the lightninglike weapon, emanating from the largest vessel in the Nihil force, the warship at its center. It hit one of the other freighters, which went cold and dead, as had the *Maree's Diligence.* Everyone left in the convoy assumed that this ship, too, would shortly be ripped apart and plundered by the Nihil corpse-flies.

Indeed, enemy ships surrounded the disabled freighter, and the cables shot out again . . . but this time something different happened. Perhaps the freighter's reactor was not completely inert, or some other error was made, but the cargo ship exploded. A ball of white light enveloped the Garello Technologies vessel as well as many of the swarm of Nihil surrounding it, and while Larence Garello's heart ached at more of his people lost, he felt a beat of savage triumph at the thought that at least they had taken some of the bastards with them.

"We're being boarded," Captain Odabba said, his voice grim, staring at the alerts and threat indicators rippling across his screens. "I'll open the weapons locker. We don't have enough blasters for everyone. Anyone with military experience gets priority. Everyone else . . . find something to fight with."

He moved away from the command console toward the bridge annex, where the freighter's limited complement of weaponry was stored.

But before he could take two steps, the bridge hatch smashed open, as if kicked inward by a giant. It skidded across the deck, smashing into and presumably killing a member of Captain Odabba's crew. The Klatooinian woman died without making a sound.

Three white canisters shot into the room from the exterior corridor. Before they hit the deck, they exploded, and the bridge was filled with thick, dense, blue-gray gas. It was instantaneous. One moment the air was breathable, the next it was like being lost in a fog . . . or a storm cloud, perhaps.

Larence Garello tried to hold his breath, but the shock of the events had left his heart racing, and he was not as young as he once was. He took in a gasp of air—but it was not air, and his system reacted near instantaneously to the poison.

He looked up to the hatchway, where the Nihil were entering the bridge. He saw them through swimming, fading vision, saw the masks they wore, and knew that whatever they were beneath, they wanted the galaxy to see them as monsters.

Larence Garello sucked in one final, burning breath, and knew he would not be one of those rare few to survive an encounter with the Nihil.

PART TWO
The Paths

CHAPTER NINETEEN

CORUSCANT. MONUMENT PLAZA.

Lina Soh rested the palm of her hand on the rough surface of Umate, the tallest peak of the Manarai range. The mountain's summit was some twenty meters above her head, and its base was somewhere 5,216 levels below, at the very bottom of the city-world that was Coruscant. This was the one spot left on the planet where its original topography could be seen. Farther below, the mountain's structure had been incorporated into the city, becoming a sort of hive of tunnels and passageways and chambers surfaced by durasteel and permacrete, barely distinguishable from other parts of the planet. But here, a bit of wildness remained.

People from all over the Republic came to Monument Plaza to see Umate, and many did as Lina Soh had—felt its surface and took a moment for reflection. A darkened ring around the peak's base served as evidence of the countless hands that had touched it over the generations. All those minds, all that sentience, all those many perspectives. Umate meant different things to different beings—endurance, the imperturbability of nature despite the efforts of sentient beings to remake the galaxy, even just the novelty of a natural thing in an artificial world.

To Lina Soh, chancellor of the great Republic that was bringing light to the galaxy's many worlds, stitching them together into an enlightened union in which anything was possible, Umate meant . . . choice.

The city-world's planners could have removed the mountain at any point in its millennia of history, but generation after generation had not. They had repeatedly made the decision—the choice—to preserve this one place, this one thing. Many political systems had claimed Coruscant in its day, from brutal empires to the purest democracies, but all had chosen to keep Umate as it was, Monument Plaza climbing upward century by century as new levels were added to the city's surface.

Progress was inevitable and crucial, but was not the only goal. Mindfulness was also important. Choice.

Chancellor Soh stepped back from the mountain. She turned away. Matari and Voru lifted their great heads and stepped toward her, the huge, beautiful beasts sensing her mood and knowing she was ready to move on. The two targons—twins, a red male and a yellow female, both taller than she was with thick fur and tufted ears—took their accustomed stations at her side, keeping pace as she moved away from Umate. The giant cats accompanied her everywhere, acting as guards, companions, even sounding boards. She often spoke aloud to them as she worked through ideas or plans. The creatures did not understand her words, but targons had low-level empathic abilities, as unusual as that was in a predator species. Matari and Voru might not comprehend . . . but they understood. More than anything else, the creatures were utterly loyal. Lina worked in politics. Loyalty was the quality she valued above all else.

The surface of Level 5,216 surrounding Umate's peak had been turned into a greenspace, with effort being made to replicate the original plants and trees that would have been visible at the mountain's base untold millennia earlier when the planet's surface was still accessible. No one really knew if the park designer's choices were accurate, but it was certainly lovely enough.

Ordinarily, Monument Plaza was full of tourists, all waiting their turn to touch Umate, a long line stretching most of the way through the park to Senate Hill. Now, though, the area was empty, cleared by the Coruscant Security Force. Lina could have held this meeting in her offices, or indeed, almost anywhere on the planet, but she liked being here. More than any other spot, it was here that she felt connected to the rest of the Republic. It drove her security teams crazy, because she was theoretically vulnerable to aerial attack while out in the open (though she thought Matari and Voru might find a way to bring down a speeder, if push came to shove). Lina was not worried about an attack, aerial or otherwise. This was the heart of the Core, and the Republic was at peace, barring the occasional regional squabble. She was as safe in Monument Plaza as she was in her own bed.

Let's hope that's still true, she considered, thinking about what had happened with the *Legacy Run* and all it could mean.

Norel Quo, her primary aide, an unpigmented Koorivar, unusual among his people, was waiting a respectful distance away.

"Are you ready, Chancellor?" he said.

"I am, Norel," Lina answered. "I hope no one's annoyed that I took a moment. I don't come here enough, and considering the conversation we're about to have, I thought it might be worth centering myself."

"You're the chancellor of the Republic," Norel said, turning to keep pace with her as they walked away from the mountain and deeper into the park, Lina's blue-clad Republic Guards falling into formation around them. "They'll wait."

The path curved around a grove of billian trees, their flutestems whistling in the evening breeze, leading to a small clearing beyond. There, Soh's appointment waited—a group of some of the most powerful people on the planet, and therefore the entire Republic. Four Jedi: the Quermian Yarael Poof and Togruta Jora Malli, both members of their Council; Malli's second, the imposing Trandoshan Jedi Sskeer; and Master Avar Kriss, who had been directly involved with the resolution of the *Legacy Run* disaster in the Hetzal system. Senator Izzet Noor, of Serenno, the spokesperson for the majority of the Outer Rim Territories. Jeffo Lorillia, her transportation secretary. And finally, Admiral Pevel Kronara, of the Republic Defense Coalition, the organization created from the pooled resources of many worlds to handle the rare regional flare-ups that could not be managed via the forces of any one planet alone. Kronara did not command the RDC, but he was a high-ranking member with direct knowledge of the matters to be discussed.

A few Coruscant Security Force guards were discreetly positioned around the edge of the clearing, and a polished copper-colored servitor droid stood nearby, ready to provide any required aid.

The seven people were chatting among themselves, but fell silent as Lina approached. She walked straight to Avar Kriss, smiling. She extended her arms and took the Jedi's hand in both of hers, clasping it and looking the other woman in the eyes. Avar seemed tired, but that was no wonder, considering the ordeal she had been through.

"Master Kriss, on behalf of the entire Republic, please accept my gratitude for everything you did out there in Hetzal. You and the other Jedi saved billions of lives, not to mention helping to secure food production for the Outer Rim."

"We are all the Republic, Madame Chancellor," Kriss replied, giving a little smile of her own. "We did what we could."

"It's inspiring, and symbolic of everything I want this Republic to be. We all help each other, and we all grow and thrive together."

Lina released the Jedi's hand, giving her another smile as she did. She looked at the rest of the group.

"I have decided to expand the hyperspace closure another five hundred parsecs around Hetzal until further notice."

Senator Noor let out a low whistle. He was a thin, tall man, aged but vigorous, bald but for a lush fringe of white hair that he wore long, letting it drape over the collar of his bright-green robes.

"That will strangle that part of the Outer Rim, Chancellor. Do you have any idea how much traffic moves along those routes? Trade, transportation, shipping . . ."

"I'm not talking forever, Senator. But these Emergences keep happening—how many do we have so far?"

Admiral Kronara gestured at the servitor droid, and it projected a flat map of the Outer Rim into the air, centered on Hetzal, displayed in red. A number of other systems were also marked with the color, creating a very rough circle around the site of the original disaster. A red ring surrounded it all—the current boundary of the hyperspace lane closures.

"Fifteen at current count, Chancellor," Admiral Kronara answered. "We might be missing some because, obviously, not every fragment of the *Legacy Run* impacts a planet. We're assuming other pieces are emerging from hyperspace undetected."

"And we still have no idea what caused this?"

"Not yet," Secretary Lorillia replied in his thickly accented Basic. "My analysts have never seen anything like it—but we are working on the problem."

"So, in theory," Lina said, "it's possible that any ship traveling through hyperspace could be destroyed in a similar way?"

The transportation secretary nodded, uncomfortable. He was a no-nonsense Muun, and disliked uncertainty of any kind. His goal—the point of the entire galaxy-wide bureau he ran—was to keep the spaceports humming and cargo running and passenger transports arriving and departing precisely on time. The idea that there could be a problem with hyperspace, the barely understood system that allowed the entire Republic to exist . . . well, Lina thought this might be poor Jeffo's worst nightmare.

"The risk of another similar disaster is why I've closed the lanes, and why they will remain closed until we know more," Lina said.

Lorillia's thin lips twitched, and he lifted his hands, tapping his long, thin fingers together once, slowly, then again. Lina gave him a reassuring pat on the shoulder.

"It's all right, Jeffo. I realize this makes your job a thousand times more challenging, but I'll give you all the support I can. You understand why this is necessary, I hope. The Emergences are bad enough. We simply cannot have another ship fall apart like the *Legacy Run.*"

She gestured at Kronara and Avar Kriss.

"Next time we might not have Jedi and Republic heroes nearby to save the day."

Secretary Lorillia gave a tight nod, pulling himself together.

"Of course, Chancellor. You can rely on me. I will make it work."

Lina took a moment to consider the reports she had received, then turned to the members of the Jedi Council standing nearby, listening intently but volunteering nothing.

"Anything from your side of things?" Lina asked.

"We can say that these events do not seem to be the result of direct action by Force users," Yarael Poof said, the Quermian's head weaving back and forth on his elongated neck like a flower in a breeze. "We are not all-knowing, but as of now we have no evidence along those lines."

"I was at Hetzal," Jora Malli added, a petite woman in the white-and-gold tunic of the Jedi Temple. She seemed a little frustrated; she kept tapping a finger against one of the beautifully striped head-tails that draped down across her chest. Togrutas had a certain regality as a species, with their montrals arcing out from their heads like crowns and the head-tails like natural robes across their bodies. Even their coloration contributed to the effect; in this case the bright orange skin and striking white facial markings suggesting a masked ball. Lina knew these characteristics were no more than the result of evolution, camouflage coloration, but they combined to give Togrutas a certain natural authority when interacting with most of the galaxy's sentient beings. Jora Malli used that to full effect, whether consciously or not.

Lina had only dealt with the woman a few times in the past, but she had gotten the sense that Jora had a tinge of un-Jedi-like impatience. She liked to push problems until answers revealed themselves, trying many things until something worked rather than considering all angles and taking one decisive action. She preferred, in a word, to be busy.

That was why, Lina presumed, the Jedi Council had given Jora Malli the job of running the Order's section of the new Starlight Beacon station in the Outer Rim. The station would be the first responder for virtually every Republic- or Jedi-related issue in that massive expanse of space. She would hold equal command with an RDC admiral and a Republic territorial administrator, with all significant decisions made by a majority vote. One problem to solve after another, endless negotiations and tinkering, and a thousand things to do at once. It was the perfect assignment for her.

"While Sskeer and I arrived after the *Legacy Run* tragedy had already begun," Jora Malli went on, "if the Force has been used to cause it, I think either I or one of the other Jedi in the system would have sensed that. Master Kriss in particular was closely connected to the Force from almost the very start of the events."

Sskeer hissed his agreement.

Senator Noor stepped toward Lina, inserting himself into her line of sight, a mildly aggressive act that caused Matari and Voru to flatten their ears. The senator seemed not to notice—the idea that mere beasts would dare to violate his person not even crossing his mind.

"Chancellor, I must ask again," Noor said, "how long are you planning to keep the hyperspace lanes closed? Not every Outer Rim world is self-sufficient. Billions of people depend on those lanes for food and other essentials."

"Obviously I won't let people starve, Senator," Lina said, a little exasperated. "I've already got one crisis—I won't start a second one trying to solve it. I just want to decrease the odds of another disaster at least until we understand what we're dealing with. If need be, I'll authorize limited shipping of essential goods through the lanes."

She turned to Kronara.

"I'll ask you to enforce the ban, Admiral. Can you coordinate with the other RDC commanders to station cruisers at the applicable hyperspace beacons? I don't want anyone reactivating portions of the navigation network. No navigational updates will keep these lanes from being used."

"It'll be a larger mobilization than anything we've done for some time, Madame Chancellor, but certainly."

"Thank you," Lina said.

She took two steps forward, until she was directly before the map of the Outer Rim Territories hovering in midair.

"We all want this over as soon as possible. Besides the immediate goal of preventing further death and destruction, you know I have plans for this part of the galaxy. The Starlight Beacon station will make the Republic more than just a distant ideal making brief appearances in the Outer Rim when our starships fly through, or we attempt to collect taxes. We will be there, with them, helping, from Bunduki to Bastion."

Chancellor Soh tapped her index finger on the map, and a single glowing starlike dot appeared, more or less in the center of the region interdicted by the ongoing hyperspace disaster.

The Starlight Beacon. Finally finished after a lengthy, challenging construction process, the huge waystation was built to serve many purposes: a Republic embassy that could also serve as a fortress if necessary; a projection of security presence to discourage raider and marauder activity. A Jedi outpost containing the largest single contingent outside the Coruscant Temple itself, where they would research and teach and listen for the guidance of the Force. Cultural spaces showcasing the beauty of the many worlds making up the sector. A communications relay that would boost transmission times in the region by a factor of ten. The most state-of-the-art medical facilities in the Outer Rim—even now, survivors of the disasters in the Hetzal and Ab Dalis systems were being treated on Starlight despite the station not being formally open just yet.

Chancellor Soh had plans for many Great Works, extending from infrastructure to culture—the Republic Fair, the ongoing construction of comm relays throughout the galaxy, cracking the code on bacta cultivation, negotiation of a new treaty between the Quarren and Mon Calamari, all sorts of innovations technological and otherwise—but the Starlight Beacon, and the other planned stations of the Beacon network . . . they were how she would be remembered. The greatest of the Great Works, bringing the Republic out from the Core and making it truly a galactic entity.

It was all hugely expensive, though, in both credits and political capital. Even in an era of enlightenment and peace, when trade flourished and the coffers were relatively full, there were those who preferred the status quo. Their view: Certainly, things were good now, but they could always turn bad, and why spend credits now you might need then? The Republic was huge, and creating complete consensus was impossible. A group of three people might all face the same problem and find three utterly different solutions—multiply that by trillions and it gave some sense of what it was like to run a galactic government. But Lina had done it, not by making promises she had no intention of keeping, or making threats, or abusing the power of her office. She had simply done her best to show the worlds of the Republic what they might be if they all came together. How much better things could be. How unique this moment was in history, and how they needed to seize it and move forward and, ideally, extend it so the many generations to come could know the peace and prosperity they all now enjoyed.

The Starlight Beacon symbolized everything she wanted for the Republic, and every member of the Senate knew it. If it succeeded, the rest became that much easier. If it failed . . .

"I will not jeopardize lives," the chancellor said, "but you all know how important it is, for many reasons, that the Starlight Beacon dedication ceremony takes place as currently scheduled."

Jora Malli spoke, her tone milder than before—this was a question to which she had an answer.

"I was just at Starlight. It's finished, but for perhaps a bit of polishing and cleanup," she said. "A short delay shouldn't have much impact on the schedule."

She gestured at Avar.

"Master Kriss was there recently as well, just before the *Legacy Run* disaster, for the inspection tour, reviewing the Jedi quarter. How did it seem to you?"

"As you say, Master Malli," she answered, "I'm not an expert, but Administrator Tennem explicitly said Starlight Beacon could hold its dedication ceremony as scheduled. If not for the blockade, the last little touches would be complete in a few weeks from now. She does not seem the type to exaggerate."

"All right, then," Lina said. "Let's figure this out. I have questions."

She lifted her hand and started to tick them off on her fingers, one by one.

"How many fragments remain of the *Legacy Run*? Do any of them contain survivors, and if so, is there a chance those people could be rescued? They're all Republic citizens, and if we can save them, we must.

"Is there a way to predict where any remaining Emergences might happen? And most important . . ."

She closed her hand into a fist.

". . . what actually happened, and why? Is hyperspace safe, or is this all just getting started?"

No one responded. They all knew better than to speculate.

"I am asking all of you to find out. You represent administrators, politicians, the security forces, and of course the Jedi. Some of you were present at the *Legacy Run* disaster. Between you, there should be more than enough skill and connections to determine what happened and prevent it from happening again. The resources of the Republic and all the authority of my office are available to you. Create any teams you like, draft anyone you think might be useful. The Starlight Beacon is due to open in thirty days. I would like to use the occasion to celebrate a Republic triumph over adversity. I do *not* wish to open that station while a huge swath of the galaxy is locked down, underscoring the Republic's inability to keep its citizens safe. Use the Starlight Beacon dedication as your deadline. *Figure this out,* my friends. I believe you can."

Chancellor Lina Soh reached out to either side, burying her hands in the fur of Matari and Voru, taking comfort in their warmth and presence. She looked up above the tree line, to the very peak of Umate just twenty meters above. Once, the mountain must have dominated this part of the planet, the queen of the entire Manarai range. Now it was just a small chunk of stone poking up from the surface of a world that had utterly swallowed it up, dwarfed by everything around it.

Umate remained, though, the benefit of a choice made generation after generation to preserve the mountain even in this attenuated form. Lina Soh appreciated that—the way societies could choose heritage over progress, represented here in living stone.

But to the chancellor, Umate had a second meaning. A symbolism she would never voice, never speak aloud, as it went against the general spirit of optimism and hope and possibility that was a cornerstone of her government and indeed, the Republic itself.

That meaning was this: There was nothing so big it could not be swallowed up. Nothing so strong it could not be humbled. Nothing so tall it could not be made small. Not a mountain, and not the Republic.

"I am not prone to dire pronouncements," the chancellor said, still looking at Umate's peak, "but if this continues to get worse, and we somehow lose the ability to travel through hyperspace, all of this ends. There will be no more Republic."

Her gaze shifted from the mountain to the night sky beyond. Coruscant was a city-world, radiating light at all hours, making it impossible to see many stars even in the depths of night. Just a few points of light were visible, shining faintly, separated by great swaths of emptiness.

"Just worlds, alone in the dark."

CHAPTER TWENTY

HETZAL SYSTEM. THE *THIRD HORIZON*.

The assembly droid moved the bit of wreckage into place, its manipulator arms making minute adjustments to the small metal fragment. How the droid knew where to place the piece in the overall puzzle being assembled, or the original purpose of any given chunk of wreckage—that was a task for an advanced computational motivator circuit, and beyond what Elzar Mann could easily understand. To him, one ragged piece of durasteel looked very much like the next.

The process seemed to be working, though. Inside a large rectangular area of space, illuminated by huge floodlights, the outline of the ship that was once the *Legacy Run* was clearly visible. About a dozen of the assembly droids were working to pull pieces of wreckage from the open bay doors of a huge cargo freighter parked just outside the range of the lights. One by one, the droids pushed bits of metal and plastoid into place in the reconstruction zone, some as large as full compartments, and some as small as a single wire. It was as if they were trying to rebuild the starship out of pieces of junk they had found here and there.

That was more or less the task, actually. Wreckage from the initial disaster in Hetzal had been collected after it dropped out of hyperspace, tracked by a huge network of satellites and monitoring stations and telescopes. The system had been bashed together during the disaster by an apparently brilliant local named Keven Tarr—a pale, quiet young man who was at this very moment standing a meter or so to Elzar's left. He wasn't alone, either. A whole group had gathered to bear witness to the destroyed starship, staring silently at the wreckage through a viewing panel on the *Third Horizon*'s observation deck.

Not much was left. The assembly droids were doing their best, but many pieces of the *Legacy Run* were destroyed on their impact with objects in the Hetzal system, or had simply whipped through the system and vanished before they could be collected. Some had appeared in other systems via the Emergences, of which there had been eighteen to date. Those pieces had been brought here as well, when possible. But still more might be in hyperspace, waiting to Emerge in their own right and wreak devastation in some other part of the Outer Rim. That was the point of trying to pull the wreckage together: to estimate how much still remained to be found.

To see how bad it could really get.

Elzar noticed that one of the smaller pieces of wreckage was drifting out of true, possibly disturbed by one of the assembly droids jetting away, or just moved by a gust of stellar wind. He lifted his hand and made a subtle gesture. The piece moved back into place, as if guided by an invisible touch.

He felt eyes on him and glanced to his right, where Jedi Master Avar Kriss was looking at him. Of course she had sensed him using the Force—that was Avar's gift, one among many. She called it the song, and she heard it always.

Elzar winked at her. Avar rolled her eyes, but the side of her mouth lifted up in a little smile. She couldn't help it.

He knew Avar thought he used the Force for frivolous purposes from time to time, but he couldn't understand the viewpoint. If you could use the Force, then you should use the Force. What, you were supposed to save it for special occasions? It wasn't as if the Force would run out. Avar heard a song, and Elzar saw a sea, of endless depth and breadth. The Force never began or ended, and it was impossible to use it up.

So if Jedi Knight Elzar Mann could help out a struggling assembly droid with a little push from the Force, why not? What was the harm?

He knew Avar agreed, even if she'd never admit it. The little smile told him everything he needed to know.

"How much of the *Legacy Run* do we have here?" asked Jeffo Lorillia, the Republic's Secretary of Transportation. The poor man seemed tense. A muscle in his endlessly long forehead seemed to have developed an involuntary twitch. That was understandable. The man's entire job was to ensure safe, reliable travel throughout the Republic, and yet the chancellor had just extended her hyperspace blockade for the Outer Rim another fifty parsecs after the eighteenth Emergence near Dantooine.

Keven Tarr consulted a datapad he was holding.

"I've got schematics here for the ship's superstructure," he said, "and the manifest from the shipping company that lists everything it was carrying. I'd say we've got about a third. Your brain takes the outline we've built here and fills it in, tells you you're seeing a full ship . . . but we really don't have that much."

Elzar thought it looked like the ghost of a ship, but decided not to make that observation in a system where so many people had died. Ab Dalis had gotten it worse, of course—twenty million dead on its primary world was an unspeakable tragedy—but Hetzal had suffered plenty of damage. And more to come across the Rim, it sounded like.

"So this won't be over for ages," Senator Noor all but moaned. The

Outer Rim representative understood the consequences of the hyperspace closures just as much as Secretary Lorillia. These worlds were already considered by some to be backwaters, and if you couldn't even travel to them . . . well. The galaxy contained many worlds. Easy to forget a whole sector, if need be.

"We don't know that, Senator," Avar said. "The investigation has barely begun."

Senator Noor shot a glare at Avar. "And meanwhile, Madam Jedi," he spat, "the poor, beleaguered people of the Outer Rim, who depend on the shipping lanes for their very existence, creep closer to chaos with every moment. I am already hearing reports of hoarding on a number of worlds, and the economic impact mounts with every passing day."

Noor pointed out the viewport at the remains of the *Legacy Run,* spotlit and floating in space.

"Why are we even here? It's a wrecked cargo ship. What does it matter? You need to get out there, find out what happened. Find out who did this!"

"You believe the disaster was deliberate, Senator?" Elzar asked. "An attack?"

Noor threw up his hands.

"What other conclusion should I draw? Hetzal is the agricultural heart of the Outer Rim. Perhaps some planet farther Coreward became jealous of the credits flowing here and wanted to wreck our food supply. Maybe it was the Selkath, angry about the prospect of bacta putting them out of business. All I know is neither the Republic nor the Jedi are doing anything to find the culprit. You're just staring out into space! What are you even doing here? You're not part of the chancellor's committee!"

"I assure you, Senator, this man is never just staring at anything," Avar said. "Let me introduce you to Elzar Mann, a Jedi Knight of my long acquaintance. He was present here in the system during the disaster. He was instrumental in helping the Jedi prevent the Tibanna fragment from impacting the sun. Without his strength, Hetzal would no longer exist."

"We all did our part," Elzar murmured. Somewhere inside, though, he was pleased Avar had noticed. Dozens of Jedi working together in that final moment—no, thousands, really, if what Avar had told him was accurate—and despite all that, she knew what he, specifically, had done.

"Of course," Senator Noor said. "We appreciate your efforts. But my point remains. We're running out of time. After all, the chancellor's precious Starlight Beacon languishes out in space, waiting to be brought online. What if an Emergence hits *that,* eh? I bet *then* you people would finally get moving."

Elzar Mann reached out and placed his hand over the senator's mouth. Above his fingers, he could see the man's eyes go wide with shock.

"Shh," Elzar said. "We're moving, I promise. Just not in ways you can see. The Force doesn't feel the need to announce its actions. It just acts."

He removed his hand. The senator was stunned into silence, which was the idea all along. In fact, everyone present seemed pretty surprised as well.

Sometimes, Elzar believed, it was important to remind people that, no matter how important they thought they were, they were, in fact, just people.

He could probably have accomplished the same goal via the mind trick—Noor's mind seemed weak, like most politicians'—but Avar absolutely would not approve, and Elzar knew it. Normally, that wouldn't matter so much. Avar Kriss was an old, close friend, which meant they could disagree, even squabble like nesting screerats, and come out the other side just fine. But now, here . . . things were different.

The Council had put Avar in charge of the Jedi's response to the Emergences, due to her actions during the *Legacy Run* disaster. It was a huge assignment, and who had she chosen as her partner for the investigation? Oh, none other than Jedi Knight Elzar Mann.

Now, why had she done that? Elzar thought he knew. He and Avar had a history, sure, and worked well together, and he was good with many Force techniques, including some pretty obscure ones—but he didn't believe any of those were the reason. Plenty of other Jedi were just as qualified as he was. Elzar figured Avar picked him because doing well on this mission could help him attain the only real achievement he cared about within the Jedi—making Master. When you were a Master, you could pursue your own studies, move forward through the Force on your own terms. In fact, the Council expected Masters to do exactly that. It sounded like paradise, but a paradise that had thus far remained elusive. Doing well with the *Legacy Run* investigation, showing the Council that he could help the Order with its goals just as much as his own: It could make a huge difference.

In other words, Avar Kriss had chosen him as her partner because she was trying to help him . . . and Elzar didn't want to give her any reason to regret the choice.

So, no mind trick. Well, not unless there was no other way.

"I'm good at anticipating problems, Senator," said Avar. "My colleague here, Elzar Mann, is good at solutions. He tends to find a unique way through most issues, paths others can't see. I promise we'll figure this out. As you said, we're running out of time."

She turned to look out once again at what remained of the *Legacy Run.*

"I see two problems here to be solved. They encompass everything else. First, the Emergences. We need to ensure nothing like what happened in Hetzal and Ab Dalis happens again.

"Second, we need to figure out whatever is causing the Emergences—which may be what also caused the original disaster. I believe this wreckage could help us with that, but that's just a hunch. I'm not a forensic scientist. Still, I know amazing things can be learned from even tiny bits of material, if the right kind of analysis is applied. Are we doing that?"

"Yes. I have technicians from my department going over the data, and we learn more with every new piece we find," Secretary Lorillia replied. "So far, nothing conclusive, but there may be an easy way to get a much clearer picture."

He gestured to a vidscreen in the chamber, displaying a detailed schematic of the *Legacy Run* in its original, pre-destruction form.

"This class of cargo carrier has a dedicated flight recorder system. Extremely durable, specifically hardened to survive catastrophic disasters. It could tell us more about what transpired in the final moments before the *Legacy Run* disintegrated."

"I thought of that, too, Secretary, but the assembly droids haven't found it yet," said Keven Tarr, reviewing his notes. "It could already have Emerged somewhere else, or it might still be in hyperspace."

"Impossible to tell," said Lorillia. "We'll just have to wait and hope it gets found."

"Well," Keven said, "I had an idea about that. The surveillance network I engineered during the disaster was designed to monitor the entire solar system in real time, and track the debris as closely as possible. Pick up new fragments as they emerged from hyperspace and follow their paths. This is what it looked like while it was happening."

He held up his datapad, triggering its projection function to display a larger image of the system. Long, thin lines wove through Hetzal, all headed on gently curving arcs toward the three suns at its center.

"There's a lot of data here," Keven said. "And when I link it with the other eighteen Emergences . . ."

He tapped his datapad a few times, and the image changed, now expanding out to encompass a good section of the Outer Rim. More thin lines appeared here and there—eighteen sets beyond the original deadly bloom in Hetzal.

". . . it sort of makes a picture. I don't really have it yet. I don't have the processing power. But if I could get enough droids, probably navidroids because they're good at calculating hyperspace routes, I might be able to figure out where Emergences would happen. And if I could do that, then we could get ahead of them, and maybe find the flight recorder, if it's still out there."

Everyone was silent.

"That's . . . very impressive," Elzar said. "You should do that."

Keven shrugged.

"I'd like to—but I can't."

"Why not?"

"I just said. I need droids."

"There are droids everywhere. Take those," Senator Noor said, gesturing out the viewing panel at the assembly droids.

"I need a lot."

"How many?"

"If it's navidroids, the very newest models, then . . . twenty or thirty thousand, maybe. Like I said, they're good at this kind of thing. If it's regular droids, or older navvys, a lot more. Like a hundred thousand. And whichever kind we use, they'd all have to be linked together to make it work. Pretty big problem to solve."

More silence.

"The chancellor said we could use every resource, didn't she?" Avar said.

"Yes, but tens of thousands of navidroids . . . that's . . . hmm," Secretary Lorillia said, pursing his lips, thinking through the problem. "Many of those models are built directly into the ships they work with. Those could get here fairly quickly, but some would have to be . . . hmm. The Republic doesn't have that many, but perhaps we could acquire them from manufacturers . . . hmm."

"You should get started," Elzar said. "The sooner we begin, the sooner we might be able to get ahead of these Emergences. We can save lives and, ideally, find the flight recorder."

Avar spoke.

"I've been thinking about something the chancellor said, too.

There's at least some chance this isn't a onetime problem—that there's something wrong with hyperspace on a larger scale. Do we have any idea how we might approach that? I'm not sure I even know where to begin."

"If you want to know about hyperspace, I have the people you should talk to," Senator Noor said. "They don't live out here anymore—they moved to the Mid Rim when the family struck it rich—but I can make the introduction."

"Who?" Elzar said.

"The San Tekka clan."

"I know that name . . . the prospectors?"

"They prefer the term explorers. They're an odd bunch, but no one knows more about hyperspace than they do. If there's something wrong, they'll probably be able to help."

"All right," Avar said. "Secretary Lorillia, will you work on the navi-droid issue with Keven Tarr? Elzar and I will meet with the San Tekkas to see if we can learn anything. Let's all stay in touch. As the senator pointed out . . ."

She looked again at what was once the *Legacy Run.*

". . . we're running out of time."

CHAPTER TWENTY-ONE

NO-SPACE.

"Who are we?" Pan Eyta roared, his already deep voice bellowing out of his huge chest, amplified and distorted by the mask he wore, which was itself a distorted version of his native Dowutin face, with massive, heavy brows and horns sprouting from its chin. His words crashed out across the sea of faces staring up at him and the others at his table. Most in the crowd wore masks of their own, of many designs but one purpose. A few thousand people, from many worlds across the galaxy, unified by a desire to *take* and *kill* and *eat.*

"THE NIHIL!" came the response, a thunderclap rolling back at him.

"What do we ride?" Lourna Dee cried, lifting a clenched fist on a thin, bare arm cabled with muscle. She was Twi'lek, of about forty years, whip-thin with green skin the color of swamp water, emaciated lekku with bone-white stripes dangling from the back of her head. She wore armored leather made from the hide of a kell dragon and a mask to match, with just the one arm bare and a single long-bladed knife sheathed on her thigh.

Lourna stood next to Pan Eyta on a raised platform at one end of the Great Hall of the Nihil, at a banquet table covered with rich food and potent liquor. Dozens more of these tables were placed throughout the hall, amid towers of flame pushing back the endless night. They were laden with indulgences for all to consume from as they chose. Food, drink, drugs. As much as they liked.

"THE STORM!" the Nihil shouted back.

The third and final of the Tempest Runners shouted out his own question. This was Kassav, an aged Weequay with skin like sun-dried meat, wearing only a fur cape, stained leather trousers, and his own mask—a thin plate of hammered metal with slits cut into it for eyes, nose, and mouth. A horrible parody of a face.

"Who guides us?" he bellowed.

"THE EYE!" came the answer, and at these words, the Nihil turned toward another platform, set lower than that of the Tempest Runners, where one person sat alone, at an empty table.

Marchion Ro.

He wore a mask, too, but not like the others. His was unique, even in the Great Hall of the Nihil. Smoked transparisteel with a single symbol slashed into it, a primitive, brutalist etching, swirls and lines that evoked a stylized planet-killing superstorm as seen from space, with its central eye centered roughly over his face. His clothes were simple—black pants and jacket over a sleeveless white tunic, and tight leather gloves with padding at each knuckle. His limbs were long, and what parts of his skin were visible were slate-gray. He wore no obvious weapons.

Marchion tilted his head back, gazing out into the void that surrounded them all. Strange lights flickered in the far distance, at the edge of vision, through the full spectrum. The Nihil called this place No-Space, and only they knew how to get there, via secret roads through tortuous hyperlanes unmapped in the galactic databases. Roads delivered by Marchion Ro, and his father before him.

The Great Hall of the Nihil had no walls or ceiling, just invisible vacuum shields creating a dome of breathable air above a broad durasteel platform hundreds of meters long. It looked and felt as if it were adrift in the great nothing.

The symbolism was obvious, and intentionally so. With the Nihil . . . all was light and life. Outside . . . cold, empty death.

"What do I see?" Marchion Ro said, his voice quiet, a breath, not a scream. The crowd hushed to hear it. "What does your eye see for the Nihil?"

"WHATEVER WE WANT!" came the answering roar, immediate, every voice lifted—hungry and certain and joyful.

Marchion looked at Pan Eyta and nodded. This was the Dowutin's show. The gigantic being adjusted the lapels of his leather suit, stylishly cut, its pale turquoise color chosen to set off his yellow skin.

"That's right," Pan said. "*Whatever we want.* Just like in Ab Dalis. We killed that convoy *dead.* We ripped those ships down to the *bones* and took everything they had, and now everyone who fought alongside me there gets a share, through the Rule of Three. With the Nihil, everyone eats."

Pan Eyta pointed out off the platform, into the strange wilderness of No-Space, where the emptiness was interrupted only by the fleet of ships that had carried the Nihil to this place. Marchion Ro cast his eyes across the vessels. No two exactly alike, and all reflecting the taste and cultures of their owners to some degree. They did all share a certain brutalist aesthetic, and the glowing, green half-spheres that were the Path engines, the navigational miracle provided to the organization by Marchion and his father.

The Nihil's ships, large or small, looked like armored, spiked fists, coming to pound you into nothing and harvest your corpse. No curves where a straight line would do. Sharp edges, a lack of overall symmetry. The smaller, fighterlike Strikeships, larger Cloudships and Stormships, all the way up to the three corvette-sized vessels of the Tempest Runners. Kassav had the *New Elite,* Pan Eyta flew his *Elegencia,* and Lourna Dee . . . she called her ship the *Lourna Dee.*

Much larger, imposing, looming behind the rest of the Nihil fleet with a silhouette like a marine predator, was Marchion Ro's flying palace and fortress, its empty, echoing corridors the only home he had—the *Gaze Electric.*

"That's why we all came here today," Pan Eyta said. "That's why we're celebrating. We fly together and we die together, and when we come back . . . we reap the rewards."

Pan gestured toward Lourna Dee and Kassav.

"I also gotta give my gratitude to my fellow bosses here. Ab Dalis was a job that came through my Tempest, but both Lourna Dee and Kassav gave support with their crews. They'll all get their piece, too."

He reached to the table and lifted a massive goblet of spiced wine, showing it to the crowd, then turning to Marchion Ro.

"And here's to the Eye of the Nihil, who gave us the Paths to make it all happen. Couldn't have done it without him."

Pan Eyta tilted his head back, lifted his mask, and drained the goblet, wine splashing to the floor. The crowd roared its approval, and Marchion Ro held up an acknowledging hand to the cheering Nihil.

"But you know . . ." Pan said, setting down his goblet, "we could have done better. There were six freighters in that convoy, and we only took five."

He affected a dissatisfied air, shaking his huge head.

"We lost one in the attack. One of them blew up just as we were ripping it open, and whatever it had for us . . . now it's just hot dust."

He arced out his arm, sweeping it across the Great Hall.

"Where's the Storm who was in charge of the crew assigned to that freighter?"

A ripple across the assembly as heads turned, looking to see who would own up to the mistake. A few long moments passed, but eventually the pressure grew too great, and a man stood. Part of Lourna Dee's Tempest, by the minimalist clothing he wore. His species was hard to identify, but his mask had big, curling horns running down over the ears, little white slits for eyes, and the ever-present filter assembly over his nose and mouth, the better to survive the various chemical weapons the Nihil often used in their raids. He had three jagged white stripes on his tunic, signifying his rank within the organization.

"Huh," Pan Eyta said, turning to Lourna Dee. "Looks like he's one of yours, Lourna. You mind if I . . ."

"Be my guest," Lourna said, her voice without affect—she never revealed much of what was going on behind her eyes, ice-blue and ice-cold. "His name is Zagyar."

"Zagyar!" Pan Eyta cried, pointing at the man. "Bring the rest of your crew up here. The Clouds and Strikes."

Zagyar nodded at the group sitting at his table, and they stood as well. Seven men and women, all masked, all different except that they shared the white, slitted eyes of their leader. The Clouds had two of the jagged stripes somewhere on their clothing, and the Strikes, just one. They walked forward as a group, the other Nihil parting to let them through, to stand before Pan Eyta and the others.

"What happened, Zagyar?" he said. "Why did we lose a sixth of what we went out there to get?"

The Storm, to his credit, didn't try to dissemble. He just answered, plain and clean. No embellishing or hiding the truth. Marchion Ro respected that.

"One of my Strikes, kid named Blit, miscalculated her harpoon shot. Hit one of the freighter's fuel tanks. That's all it took. Boom."

"I thought it was something like that. Is she here, that Strike?"

"No. Blit died in the explosion. Most of my crew did. I've only got these seven left. Couple Clouds and five Strikes."

Zagyar gestured at his people.

"I see," Pan said. "But someone has to pay for that mistake. Everyone lost when that happened. *I* lost."

He pointed down at Marchion Ro, still seated at his own table, a meter or two below the Tempest Runners.

"The *Eye* lost. It needs to be made right. For the Nihil."

Zagyar, again, showed no fear or anger—just responded, clear and honest. Marchion Ro could see how the man had become a Storm, and that was not an easy thing to do. You rose in rank in the Nihil by succeeding, and by doing whatever it took to make sure other people didn't.

"The Strike who screwed up paid with her life. Seems like that's something."

"It's something . . . but that Strike isn't here. You and your crew are all responsible. One of you could've given Blit better guidance, could've helped her. You didn't, and there has to be a price, and someone has to pay it. I'll let you decide."

Zagyar hesitated, looking at his crew, one after the other, the masks making it impossible to know what they were thinking.

A chant began, at the back of the hall and rapidly moving forward, until every one of the Nihil was saying the same three words.

"Pay the price!"

"Pay the price!"

"Pay the price!"

Zagyar's crew tensed. Looked at each other, quick little furtive glances, not knowing who would be the first to move. Blasters were forbidden in the Great Hall, but they all had their blades, and hands were reaching toward hilts.

"PAY THE PRICE!"

Marchion Ro turned his head, looking toward the edge of the platform, where a line of glowing blue-white lights marked the border between light and life, and freezing void. He hated the little pageants Pan and Lourna and Kassav put on, pitting Clouds and Strikes and Storms against one another.

The Nihil all worked under the same banner, and all used the Paths Marchion gave them, but that was as far as it went. They were chaos. Everyone out for himself, each Tempest ready to undercut the others. Any Nihil would slit another's throat at the slightest provocation or opportunity for profit.

The Paths could take the Nihil anywhere in the galaxy, but they refused to see it. The only one who could see the potential of the organization was, inevitably, the Eye. But the Eye was not in control. Each Tempest had its own boss, its Runner, and Marchion Ro had no real influence over what any of them did. He got his share of the payouts of any jobs that used his Paths, by the Rule of Three . . . but that was all.

The Eye could see . . . but the Eye couldn't act.

Sounds of struggle came to Marchion Ro's ears, but he didn't turn to look. Someone was paying the price.

He watched—all the Nihil watched—as one of Zagyar's crew was dragged to the edge of the platform, screaming and pleading about how unfair it all was, how loyal they were. Marchion Ro didn't know who had been chosen. Maybe Zagyar himself. It didn't matter. The lesson was clear.

Every Nihil was expected to contribute. Either you made the organization richer, or you made it stronger. And one way to make something stronger . . . was by removing what was weak.

A body drifted away into the void of No-Space, still moving. Not for long.

Pan Eyta turned back to the Nihil. He spread his arms, taking them all in, while gesturing simultaneously at the feast tables and fountains filled with various intoxicants, and death sticks and piles of uppowder and downfire.

"Now enjoy yourselves, my friends," he said. "You've earned this."

He stepped down from the table as the Nihil resumed their celebrations. If any of them harbored misgivings about what had just occurred, they kept it hidden, behind masks and fistfuls of food and sniffs of powder. Music kicked up—loud, with a sound like sheets of metal being hammered in complex polyrhythms.

"We need to talk," Marchion Ro said, looking at the three Tempest Runners.

Kassav frowned. "It's a party, Marchion. Didn't you hear Pan? Lots to celebrate. Why don't you just relax?"

Marchion Ro stared at the man for a full three seconds.

"There's business to discuss," he said. "It's important, and I want to talk about it while we're all in the same place, and before you three get too drunk to think."

The Tempest Runners looked at one another, none of them happy.

Lourna Dee shrugged. "Fine, Marchion, fine. Let's go on back."

Marchion Ro stepped down off the raised platform and walked toward the far end of the platform, the Tempest Runners falling in at his side. Nihil at all levels reached out to them, offering hands in greeting, desperate to make some connection with the organization's leadership.

The group reached a small structure built at the far end of the Great Hall; it housed the air lock and docking mechanisms, as well as a small complex of rooms that offered privacy, when required. Two droid sentries guarded its entrance, and bowed their heads as Marchion and the Tempest Runners passed. The droids were well over two meters tall, matte-black, and in lieu of even rudimentary features, the three lightning bolts of the Nihil glowed on their faceplates in sharp blue-white. They carried no weapons, and needed none. Their limbs and bodies were studded with sharp spikes, their hands set in fists made of heavy alloys that could smash bone and tissue into pulp.

Inside, once the entry portal had sealed, Marchion turned to face Kassav, Lourna Dee, and Pan Eyta, each solely responsible for and with complete authority over a Tempest, one of the three great divisions of the Nihil.

"Good party," Kassav said.

Kassav was always the first to talk. Predictable as the sunrise. Either he hated silence, or he was pathologically focused on ensuring no one ever forgot he was there.

Marchion Ro pulled off his mask, reaching up and running a hand through his long, dark hair, untangling it. The energy in the room changed, even though the Tempest Runners had seen Marchion unmasked many times. His appearance tended to have a particular effect on those around him—slate-gray skin, wholly black eyes, a certain angular leanness to his physique . . . for many of the galaxy's species, the features of Marchion's people meant *predator,* on some deep instinctive level.

"Is it a good party, Kassav?" Marchion said. "All I saw was a big party. Numbers. Lots of new faces out there. From all three of your Tempests."

"We always need new blood," Pan Eyta said. His voice was so low, some of his syllables dropped into subsonic ranges, giving him a wavery, resonant tone. "Strikes find other people to join, and when they get enough of a group under them, they move up to become a Cloud. If they make their name, they get to be a Storm. That's the way it works, since always. You know this. Been like that since back when your father was the Eye."

Marchion Ro was more than a little certain that one of the three people standing before him had murdered his father—Asgar Ro. Custodian of the Paths and Eye of the Nihil until Marchion inherited the position and all that went with it on Asgar's death. But he didn't know which of the Tempest Runners had done the killing, and he was just the Eye. They were the bosses and had a thousand soldiers each. He only had one real ally, and she wouldn't be much good in a fight.

"I know the way it works, Pan," Marchion said. "But the Paths aren't a limitless resource. Too many people means we can get spread too thin. We need to slow things down."

"No one's gonna like that," Lourna Dee said. "We don't slow down. We're the Nihil."

Marchion placed his index finger on his helmet.

"The Paths come from me. So now I'm saying we need to be a little careful about the next stage. That's all."

"Is this about the Republic again?" Pan Eyta said. "We've been over that. We know they're opening that station, that Starlight Beacon thing, but that doesn't mean they'll be coming after us. They think we're small time. They've never bothered us before, and they don't even have a military. How would they get us, anyway? We've got your Paths, right?"

The Dowutin adjusted his suit again—that polished turquoise leather. Pan was particular in his tastes. Everything was well chosen, from his clothes to the food he ate to the music he listened to. The Nihil in his Tempest tended to be the same way. From the beginning, Pan had chosen his first Strikes, and they had chosen theirs, and like called to like.

Each of the Tempests reflected its Runner—Pan's people were precise . . . planners. Kassav's group was chaotic and impulsive, all of his Strikes and Clouds and Storms chasing the next score, the next insane story they could brag about while so high on smash they could barely talk. Lourna Dee's group was subtle, introverted, keeping their intentions close until the result was achieved. Also, in general, her people were the cruelest among all the Nihil.

"It's not just the Starlight Beacon, it's that *Legacy Run* thing in Hetzal," Marchion said. "These Emergences are causing disasters all over the Rim. My people in the Republic tell me they're digging in hard. They've set up an investigation—even pulled in the Jedi."

"Jedi," Kassav said, baring his sharp little teeth. "I've always wanted to kill one. That'd be a story to tell."

Marchion knew Kassav had never faced a Jedi. Neither had Marchion Ro, but his family had a history with them, and he had grown up hearing stories. Even a few could destabilize or destroy the grandest aspiration. They could . . . tap into something. It wasn't just the Force. It was their Order itself. It gave them a confidence, a structure, a willingness to make choices to serve the larger purpose of spreading light in the galaxy. It made them bold, and made them strong. He was not afraid of the Jedi—but only a fool wouldn't consider them a serious threat.

"You're welcome to try to kill as many Jedi as you want, Kassav," Marchion said. "Just give us the name of the Storm you think should take your place as Tempest Runner after you're dead."

He waited before speaking again, letting his gaze shift to each of them in turn, letting his cold, dark eyes do most of the work. The silence turned to tension, and Marchion just kept watching, daring any of them to challenge him again. They didn't. They wouldn't. Not openly, anyway. He knew any one of these three would cut off his head in an instant if they knew how to access the Paths directly, but he kept that secret close.

"Here's what I'm worried about," Marchion said. "All three of you run your operations pretty independently, and you have crews doing raids all over the Outer Rim. Chancellor Soh put a hyperspace blockade in place, and it gets bigger with every Emergence. The Nihil are just about the only ships that can travel these days, because we have the Paths. What if the Republic comes across a Nihil crew and figures out we can do what we do? Or the Jedi? We don't want the Order on us, or the Republic Defense Coalition."

He shook his head.

"I know the Republic doesn't have a standing military. Doesn't matter. We aren't big enough to take them on, even if it's just an RDC task force. They'd wipe us out. I say we need to lie low. No new operations for the time being. No more Paths. If your people give you grief, tell them the Eye sees something special in the future, something big. A new initiative."

"Does the Eye, in fact, see that?" Lourna Dee asked. "A new initiative, I mean."

"I'm always thinking of the next thing, Lourna," he said. "You know that."

Kassav and Pan Eyta exchanged a glance.

"Just doesn't sound like us," Kassav said.

"I call the vote," Marchion said.

"Then I vote this is a big pile of bantha droppings," Kassav said. "The Nihil don't stop. We need to keep *riding that storm.*"

"You know," Pan Eyta said. "I think I agree with Marchion. I say we take a little break. Just for a while. Maybe we should take a little time to plan, strategize—figure out how we operate if the Republic's gonna be poking around in our territory."

"Pff," said Kassav. "Of course. You and your people just got fat off that job in Ab Dalis, so you don't need to eat for a while. What about the rest of us?"

"Maybe you should've given me more of your people to help, Kassav," Pan said. "One little Cloud worth of crew was all you could spare? Please. Anyway, I don't mind a little break. Maybe I'll take a vacation. Get tickets to the opera on Cato Neimoidia."

Kassav made a disgusted noise, deep in his throat.

The rest of the vote was moot. In any decision related to the Paths, ties went to the Eye, a long-standing rule. With Pan's vote, it was at least a two-against-two decision for putting a hold on new Nihil activity, at least until the heat from the *Legacy Run* died down. Lourna Dee hadn't spoken, but her decision was irrelevant—and it wasn't surprising she had waited to make her views known. She seemed to prefer that people knew as little as possible about what she was thinking. Whether that was pathological or tactical, Marchion didn't know. Probably some of both.

"I guess that's that," Lourna Dee said. "But I still want to pitch you on a job."

"Oh?" Marchion said, his voice thin.

Pan Eyta and Kassav didn't seem particularly thrilled, either. Tempest Runners could authorize raids within their own crews without asking any of the others, but anything that would require Paths needed a full-on vote. Usually, that meant Marchion was the deciding factor, because most of the time the two Tempest Runners who didn't have a stake in a given job voted against it. Not a bad system, really. As Eye, Marchion was the custodian of the Paths, and so he should have the loudest voice in deciding how they were used.

"I have a new group in my Tempest," Lourna continued. "Seven Strikes under a Cloud. Came to me with a really interesting plan, actually—they found this settler family on a mining world, very connected. My guys want to kidnap them, hold them for ransom from their rich relatives. It's smart."

"No, Lourna. I told you. We all just agreed. No raids until the heat dies down from Hetzal."

She stepped toward him, her thin face focused, her eyes intense.

"I'm telling you, Marchion, it'll be easy. The planet is Elphrona, which doesn't have much of a security force, and apparently the family decided to go all rustic, live way out on their own in the middle of nowhere. Easy pickings. We'll be in and out."

Marchion went still, which Lourna took as an invitation to keep talking.

"The Cloud asked for some Paths. You know . . . just in case. I know we're under pressure, but this is a new group, lots of potential. I want to bring them into the fold, give them a chance to prove their worth. I'm telling you, too—this operation will have a huge payoff."

"Elphrona . . ." Marchion said. "There's a Jedi outpost on that planet."

"Is there?" asked Lourna Dee, in a way that made it clear she had already known.

Marchion went silent. The Nihil were not just another group of raiders, like the thousands that operated in the Rim. They were special, powerful . . . and the reason for that was the Paths. In all the ways that counted, they made the Nihil what they were. They allowed crews to use hyperspace in ways denied to every other ship in the galaxy. Microjumps, leaps to locations inside gravity wells, entering hyperspace from almost anywhere as opposed to having to run elaborate calculations or travel to a non-occluded access zone . . . they allowed the Nihil's ships to appear and disappear at will, like spirits. They could be anywhere, at any time, and no defenses could stop them.

The Paths made the Nihil what they were, but they came from a single, unique, not inexhaustible source, and Marchion had placed significant demands upon that source recently, both to fuel the Nihil's growth and to support plans of his own. The *Legacy Run* disaster was not the only reason he wanted things to cool off for a little while.

Lourna Dee's idea, though . . . it had possibilities.

There was no need to hold a formal vote. Lourna Dee was obviously for it, and the Eye's two votes would ensure it went ahead, if Marchion Ro agreed.

"Fine," he said. "Send me the plan, what you think you'll need, and I'll get you some Paths. But do not do anything to get the attention of those Jedi. Get in, grab the family, get out."

"Thank you," Lourna Dee said, and left. As ever, the woman never said a word more than she needed to.

Kassav and Pan Eyta glanced at each other, then back at Marchion Ro.

Pan shrugged. He left, following Lourna Dee back to the celebration outside.

Kassav did not.

Marchion lifted his mask and replaced it on his head.

"Dunno how that was fair, Ro," the Weequay said. "You giving Lourna Dee a job, giving her Paths, but saying Pan and me gotta stop. I got people to feed, too. I got like a thousand people in my Tempest, and ain't one of 'em gonna be happy with this. How about I send you some ideas, maybe you choose one and I can get something going? You'd get a share, too—a full third to the Eye, just like always. Don't you want that payday?"

They returned to the Great Hall, walking past the spiked guard droids, who once again inclined their heads as the Eye and the Tempest Runner passed.

Marchion walked to the edge of the platform, Kassav close on his heels, right up against the blue lights that marked the border of the vacuum shields.

"Your father never would have done something like this," Kassav said. "Shutting down the Paths? Forget it. Not Asgar Ro. He wasn't any kind of coward, no way."

Marchion Ro went very still.

"My father's dead, Kassav," he said. "I'm the Eye now. You can do whatever you want with your Tempest, but the Paths come from me. You don't like it? You want to make a play for me, try to take what I've got? Go for it. Just be aware . . ."

He gestured out at the void.

". . . there's a price."

CHAPTER TWENTY-TWO

THE OUTER RIM. ELPHRONA OUTPOST.

"What are you waiting for?" Loden said.

Bell crept closer to the edge of the cliff and peered over. The ground didn't look any closer than it had the last four times he checked. He looked back at his master, who had his arms folded. He was smiling, but it was one of those smiles that felt much more like a deep, disapproving frown.

Get on with it, that smile said. *Unless you'd prefer to be a Padawan for the rest of your life.*

The Jedi Order had established outposts across the less-settled sectors of the Republic, both as an opportunity to explore new regions and to offer assistance to any who might need it in those wilder zones. Not as large as full temples, they were staffed by crews of three to seven Jedi, often with a wide range of experience. Getting "outposted" was a common part of the Padawan training regime, and this was what Bell was doing on Elphrona. He and Loden had been there for a while, though they did get the occasional offworld assignment like the Starlight Beacon tour that had ended up with them in the middle of the

Legacy Run disaster. They were originally due to be rotated back to Coruscant after that via the *Third Horizon*—but Chancellor Soh's hyperspace blockade had gotten them sent back to the outpost for the duration.

The Council thought Jedi might be needed in the Outer Rim more than usual during the crisis. So far, though, the blockade didn't feel much different from the usual sort of outpost life. For Jedi Padawan Bell Zettifar, that meant constant orders from his master to do utterly impossible things under the guise of "training."

The wind kicked up, pushing Bell back from the cliff's edge. He inhaled the unique scent of Elphrona—hot metal and dust.

The Order often built its outposts to fit in with the natural surroundings and culture of the planet where they were based. The outpost on Kashyyyk was a huge tree house. On Mon Cala, it was a gigantic raft grown from coralite, kelp dangling from its underside, providing a reeflike habitat for local sea creatures as it drifted with the currents.

Elphrona was a dry world of slate and clay, topographically diverse. Almost its entire surface was covered by long mountain ranges, composed primarily of iron and other ferrous minerals, which curled along its surface in arcs that followed the pattern of the planet's magnetic fields. From orbit, it looked beautiful—like a calligrapher had inscribed the entire world with some unimaginably enormous pen. From the ground, it looked exactly like you would think a huge ball of dusty metal might—a world whose bones were close to the skin.

In this hard place, the Jedi had built their outpost out of a mountainside, or rather into it. A face of the iron mountain had been sheared away, carved with laser chisels into a columned templelike entrance. The entrance was flanked by two massive statues of Jedi Knights, their lightsabers out and held in the ready position. The Jedi wore hooded robes of a style that felt like a nod to an earlier era. Above the doors, a gigantic symbol of the Order, the upswept wings embracing a spear of starlight shining up and out into the galaxy.

Bell didn't love Elphrona—he would have been happier with that Mon Cala posting, for instance, where breezes smelled of sea and life, not rust—but he did love the outpost. It was simple and majestic at the same time. Everything the Jedi should be.

It was dawn, and the rising sunlight caught the electrum of the Jedi symbol, setting it alight with reflected fire. The view from the clifftop where he stood could not be improved. It was perfection.

Bell Zettifar, Jedi Padawan, soaked it in. Then he began to turn around, intending to tell his master, Jedi Knight Loden Greatstorm, that he was not ready for this particular exercise today, and wanted to read up on the techniques a bit more before he just *jumped off a perfectly good cliff.*

"I believe in you," he heard Loden say from a few meters behind him.

Bell felt his master reach out to the Force, and then something like a hand in the center of his back. And then he was shoved hard, right off the cliff.

Some thirty kilometers away was the settlement of Ogden's Hope, a fairly large town built and maintained on the dreams of those who thought they might be able to transform the planet's mineral wealth into a fortune of their own. The mining industry on Elphrona was over a century old, but the planet's governments over the decades had successfully resisted the efforts of the huge galactic concerns to buy up and consolidate its resources. The entire planet was divided into a grid, and no one family, corporation, enterprise, or association was allowed to own more than four claims at a time.

That meant much of the planet remained unclaimed, and who knew what treasures might be waiting under the surface, ready to be discovered? Earlier strikes had turned up rare minerals, aurodium and platinum, even stranger substances—a vein of resonance crystals, once.

Elphrona was a planet-sized treasure vault, and somehow, it belonged to everyone who lived there. Ogden's Hope, as a place, was well named. It was a place of possibility, where everyone had an equal chance at success and freedom. Chancellor Lina Soh cited Elphrona often in her speeches as emblematic of the spirit of the Republic. It was a hard place but, generally, a good one.

To this good place, a family had come, from a populous, wealthy world in the Core. A mother, a father, a son, and a daughter. They acquired two claims next to each other, an hour's speeder ride from Ogden's Hope—longer if you ran into a rust storm. They built themselves a place to live, with the help of their droids. The first version was just a rough, ugly structure of permacrete, nothing more than a shelter from the sun and wind, but in time it had become theirs. More rooms, more windows, a greenhouse, a second story, decoration, all the little touches that transformed housing into home. They dug into the soil, looking for whatever treasures might be beneath their feet.

The family could have used their droids to do most of the work—but that was not why they had come to Elphrona, and so they all did their part. The children studied with their droid tutors and grew taller every day. The parents worked, and planned, and believed they had made the right decision for themselves and their family.

Until one early morning, the mother, whose name was Erika, looked up from a delving droid she was repairing to see a strange cloud not far from their home. It was odd, unlike anything she had ever seen. For one thing, it hugged the ground like a fogbank. But Elphrona was a dry world. There was water, but it circulated deep below the surface in underground rivers and channels. Rain was a once-per-decade event. So, fog . . . no. It couldn't be.

Even beyond that, this cloud looked odd . . . it had a sheen to it, like a metallic blue. Like a storm cloud, really, though she hadn't seen one of those since she left her homeworld some years back. And it seemed to be moving with direction, or purpose. Toward them.

"Ottoh," she called to her husband, who was not far away, spreading feed for their small herd of steelees. The long-legged beasts were clustering around the trough, their excitement at getting their morning meal obvious. "What do you suppose that is?"

Ottoh turned to look. He froze. Unlike his wife, he kept up with galactic affairs—he had not entirely cut himself off from the news of the Republic. And so he had heard stories, and he knew what it meant when a storm came creeping toward your home, or business, or family.

"Get Bee," he said, dropping the sack of feed he was holding. "I'll find Ronn. We need to get in the house and seal it up. Now."

Erika didn't ask questions. She didn't hesitate. They were many kilometers from help, and even a good world in the Outer Rim Territories was full of danger. She called for her daughter and ran to the house.

"Ronn!" Ottoh shouted, not taking his eyes off the cloud. "Get in the house *right now*!"

Within the approaching fog, figures were beginning to become visible, ten or so. He couldn't make out details yet, but he knew who they were. He had heard the stories—of impossibly vicious marauders who appeared from nowhere and left the same way, leaving nothing in their wake but terror that they would return.

The Nihil.

Bell reached out to the Force. He knew that, as a Jedi, he could survive this fall. He had seen Loden do similar things many times in the past—most recently on Hetzal Prime, but in training, too. Loden could drop like a rock and then slow himself at the last moment for a perfect landing. It wasn't flying—no Jedi born without wings could fly as far as Bell knew—but it also was not exactly falling.

Bell knew it could be done, and he knew Loden Greatstorm believed he could do it. His master—probably—would not have used the Force to shove him off that obscenely high cliff otherwise. Bell thought the Jedi Council would frown on inadvertent Padawan murder—but he also thought Loden could talk his way out of it, probably by arguing that the Order had no use for a Padawan who couldn't master something as simple as a controlled descent.

All of this flashed through Bell's head in the merest second after his plummet began. With a massive effort, he forced himself to focus, to find the flame of the Force within and fan it into greater life, and through it connect with the air currents rushing past his face and whipping through his dreadlocks. Loden had given him instruction on how to execute this maneuver safely, though he was frustratingly vague in his description of how it was supposed to work.

In general, the idea was to guide yourself to the updrafts, and use them as a foundation to slow your fall. Once you figured that out, you were somehow also supposed to use the Force to push against the ground as it drew closer. The two elements could slow you down enough to land safely. Bell had achieved it easily enough in Temple training when falling from lesser heights, or if dropping onto a repulsor pad that would prevent any real injury.

But now, when plummeting from a cliff, facing a horrendous maiming *if he was lucky,* he could barely even remember what Loden had told him to do. He knew the real challenge here was not mastery of the Force, but mastery of fear—always the Jedi's greatest test.

A test he was about to fail. And from this height, he knew even Loden Greatstorm could not catch him. This was it. The end. Bell closed his eyes. The fear rushed in, and he didn't even fight it. He asked for serenity, and hoped he would just die quickly and not be left in broken agony on the jagged iron rocks at the base of the cliff.

The wind stopped rushing past him.

Bell opened his eyes and saw the ground, a meter or so below him. Then he dropped, hitting hard, though not as hard as he would have if his fall had not been stopped.

He rolled over, groaning, and a shadow fell across him.

"You need to figure this out," Indeera Stokes said. "Loden really is going to kill you one of these times."

She extended a hand, and Bell took it and let the other Jedi pull him up. Indeera was Tholothian, with dark skin only a few shades lighter than Bell's own, elegant white tendrils in lieu of hair, and eyes so blue they almost seemed to glow, just like every member of her species Bell had ever met. Her leathers were scratched and worn, with the Jedi insignia in white on one shoulder. She wore her lightsaber holster on a strap of yellow webbing slung diagonally across her chest, and kept a dark-gray nanofoil scarf wrapped around her neck—useful as a mask in dust storms, and moldable into almost any shape she might need.

Standing at Indeera's side was a small, four-legged creature, mostly mottled black, white, and gray, but with spots of red and orange here and there, and bright-yellow eyes. A charhound, native to Elphrona. She took a few steps forward and nuzzled at Bell's hand; he scratched behind her ears, and the little beast purred with pleasure.

"Hi, Ember," Bell said. "Nice to see you, too."

He gave the charhound one last scratch and looked back at Indeera.

"Did Loden ask you to catch me?" he said, brushing dust off his own leathers, originally bright white but now well worn in, stained and mottled, evidence of hard use.

"Yep," Indeera said. "No shame in it. No Jedi is perfect at everything from the start."

She held out his lightsaber hilt. He hadn't even felt it fall from his side. Bell took it and slipped it into his own holster, worn at his hip.

"No shame . . ." he said.

Loden knew he'd fail from the beginning.

"I just don't get why he won't let it go," he said. "I clearly can't do this."

"Because one day you'll fall off a cliff for real, and he wouldn't be doing his job if he didn't try to keep you from dying when you do. Jedi fall off things a lot. You need to be ready."

Indeera turned toward the path that led back up toward the outpost.

"Come on," she said. "Porter is making breakfast. Nine-Egg Stew, and he told me he found some stone peppers, too."

"You think Loden will let me eat before he throws me off the cliff again?" Bell said.

"I'll insist," she said. "No one should die on an empty stomach."

"Wow," Bell said, "so kind of you."

He followed her up the path, Ember keeping pace at his side.

Ottoh lifted the single-lens ocular and set it against his eye. The device had a setting that allowed him to see through the walls to pick up heat signatures from outside—good, because the Nihil had already killed their homestead's security cams. The monitors in the safe room were just throwing out static.

Now, not all the parts of the fancy security system they'd had installed when they moved out to the claim had failed. The automated reinforced durasteel shutters had worked as promised—slamming down over doors and windows as soon as the family was safely inside—but without the cams, they were almost blind.

All Ottoh had was the ocular, and the rough outlines it provided on its infrared setting. The Nihil showed up as purple-and-red outlines, with strange, misshapen heads. Ottoh had seen hundreds of different alien species in his day, but he'd never seen anything like the Nihil. It made him think they were probably wearing masks, which aligned with both the stories he'd heard and the fact that they used gas to hide their movements and incapacitate their prey. But knowing that didn't make them any less threatening. They were monsters, looming up from nowhere.

The gas was definitely still out there, too, even if the ocular couldn't pick it up. The family's herd of steelees were all lying on their sides in their pen, unconscious or dead, and as far as he knew nothing had touched them.

"Will the seals keep out the gas?" Erika said, evidently thinking along the same lines.

"That's what the company promised. The safe room's supposed to be impervious to all but the highest levels of blasterfire, and impermeable to chemical and radiological weapons."

"You didn't say explosives," his wife said. "What if they brought explosives?"

Ottoh didn't answer.

"Well, whatever they brought, I'm ready to fight," she said, and he set down the ocular and looked over at her.

Erika tapped her datapad one final time, then held it up for Ottoh to see, displaying the elements of the plan she had come up with.

"I think the speeder, right?"

"Yeah," Ottoh said. "At the very least it'll buy us time. Maybe someone will see the explosion, or maybe the Nihil will just leave."

Now it was his wife's turn to stay silent.

"Any luck, Ronn?" he called to his son, thirteen years old, with everything that came with that age. But now, no angst, no pushback, just doing exactly what he was asked to do in an effort to keep his family alive.

Ronn was using the family's comlink, trying to reach someone in Ogden's Hope who might be able to help. Their daughter, Bee, nine, was curled up against him for comfort, holding a stuffed varactyl toy she hadn't touched for years, as far as Ottoh knew.

"I can't get a signal through, Dad. I checked the weather, and there's a big rust storm between us and Ogden's Hope. It's messing with the transmissions, I think."

"Keep trying, son," Ottoh said. "Your mother is going to buy us some time."

A huge *boom* from below—not an explosion, but the sound of metal on metal. Ottoh looked through the ocular again, to see that a cluster of four Nihil had gathered around the front door to the house. They were positioned as if they were holding something, all four gripping it together, but the ocular's heat setting couldn't pick out the object. A battering ram made of cold durasteel, he guessed.

"They're trying to break down the door," Ottoh said.

Another *boom*.

"Now, Erika!" Ottoh said.

His wife pressed a control on her datapad.

Outside, Ottoh could see their four delving droids coming up out of sleep mode in the droid pen not far from the main house. Their outlines through the ocular were green and yellow—they put out a different kind of heat than the Nihil—but all were clearly visible.

The machines left the pen and moved quickly, accelerating through the yard. The delving droids were industrial machines, loud and powerful, designed to punch holes into hard ground and remove the resulting rubble. There was no way for them to move stealthily, even though the gas presumably still circulating outside probably gave them a little cover. The quartet of droids split—two heading for the group at the front door, and the rest toward the speeder.

Ottoh took a moment to appreciate the skill in what his wife was doing—simultaneously overriding the autonomous functions of four droids, taking control and making them operate in ways they were not designed to work, running them fast, guiding them via feeds from their monitor circuits on a tiny datapad display. All that complexity to manage, and each droid was moving in a straight line, unerring, right toward their targets.

"Good, Erika . . . you're doing it!"

"Don't . . . talk to me . . . right now . . ." she said, her voice tight with concentration.

Blaster bolts, hot white through the ocular, began zipping out from both sets of Nihil—the four at the front door and another six clustered around their speeder. The raiders had noticed the approaching droids . . . no surprise there.

The machines were tough, built to withstand high impacts and temperatures, but they weren't impervious. One of the droids stopped moving, then another.

"Faster, Erika! They're knocking them down!"

His wife didn't answer, just flicked him a momentary glance. Ottoh understood. She was running the droids from her datapad. She knew when they became inoperative right away—she didn't need his updates. He knew that—he'd known it when he spoke. He just wanted to . . . *do* something.

From behind him, he heard his son's voice, talking quickly, and Ottoh realized he'd actually gotten someone on the comlink. Ogden's Hope maintained a small communal security force; all the claims paid into its budget every year. Their station wasn't so far away. If the family could just hold on a bit longer . . .

A third droid stopped in its tracks, hot green sparks shooting from where its head had once been attached to its neck.

Just one droid left, and Ottoh watched as the machine barreled forward. He saw it dodge a Nihil shot, and again marveled at his wife's skill. What operator could make a delving droid *dodge*? The one he was married to, apparently.

The last droid took a hit, dead center, and its speed slowed to a crawl.

"Blast it!" his wife said.

"Is that it?" Ottoh said.

"No," Erika answered, her voice cold and certain. "It's not."

Ottoh heard his wife's fingertips tapping furiously on the datapad, and whatever rerouting and adjustments she did seemed to work. The last droid lurched forward, careening ahead at a rapidly increasing rate of speed. The Nihil weren't done shooting, but the droid seemed all but impervious. It lost an arm, then another. Half its head disappeared, but it didn't stop.

It reached the Nihil's speeder, and Ottoh yanked his eye from the ocular just before the lens flared white. A huge sound from outside, not a *boom* but a *BOOM,* this time definitely an explosion.

The delving droids were mining machines. Sometimes they dug, sometimes they sorted, sometimes they lugged debris . . . and sometimes they blasted holes in dense, metallic rock with small pellets of high-powered explosive. From the sound, Erika had just set off every bit of the droid's load at once.

"Hnh," his wife said, her tone satisfied. "How many did I get, dear?"

Ottoh raised the ocular to his eyes and looked outside. The scene was radically altered—the Nihil's speeder was gone, as was the delving droid, both replaced by hot, twisted metal and leaping flames. He turned down the brightness, looking for . . . there. He counted outlines . . . four, close to the fire, and none of them moving. But two others were still alive, one slowly dragging himself away from the wreckage, and another being pulled free by the team that had been using the battering ram at the front door. That group, unfortunately, had been mostly sheltered from the blast by the house.

"Not enough," Ottoh said. "But it helps."

He lowered the ocular and turned to his son, who was speaking to Bee in a low, kind voice.

"Did you get someone, Ronn?" Ottoh said. "I heard you on the comlink. Is help coming?"

Ronn looked up. His face was bleak.

"I got through to Ogden's Hope security, Dad," he said. "I told them what was happening. The man on the other end was asking a lot of questions, but he stopped when I told him the Nihil were here. He . . . he just . . . he said they're too far away to get here in time. The man said he was sorry . . . but he just sounded like he was afraid. I've tried calling back, but they won't answer."

"Cowards," Erika spat.

From below, a sound: a *thud,* of something heavy hitting their front door, and then a voice.

"You shouldn't have done that," it called, floating up from outside, low and strange. "We were just going to take you."

thud

"Now we're going to hurt you, too."

"You want more stew?" Porter Engle said, looking down into Bell's empty bowl. "Falling's hungry work, I guess."

Across the table, Loden chuckled. Bell didn't care. He was over it. He'd figure out the Force falling eventually, and even if he didn't, that was no reason to turn down a second bowl of Porter's Nine-Egg Stew.

Porter Engle was a legend. He'd been in the Jedi Order for over three hundred years, a burly Ikkrukki who, at this point, was more beard than being. He had explored full careers in most of the primary Jedi roles in his time—teacher, explorer, diplomat, warrior—and the stories told about him in any one of those occupations would be enough to ensure his status in the chronicles. He had just one eye, for example, the other lost long ago, a long scar down his face a story of its own. But now he was nearing the end of his span, and his latest and final calling seemed to be cook. The stew really did have nine different kinds of egg in it, but Porter would only reveal five of them. The remaining sources were either too rare or too revolting for him to divulge. Whatever was in it, the stuff was *good.*

Below the table, Bell felt Ember stir. She was lying across his boots, her internal heat warm and prominent even through the thick leather. The hound was no fool—of all the Jedi of Elphrona, Bell Zettifar was by far the most likely to slip her a bite or two during meals.

The creature had appeared one day at the building's entrance, skinny, trembling, and with an infected wound on her rear haunch.

Indeera treated her injury, Porter fed her, Bell named her, and Loden had allowed her to stay, declaring that the Force had brought them a new member of the team. That was a neat workaround to the Order's rule against forming attachments, because of course you were supposed to take care of your fellow team members, and make sure they were safe and happy and well fed and their coat was brushed and . . . well. The Jedi of the Elphrona Outpost had all become extremely fond of Ember the charhound, rule or no rule.

"Yes please," Bell said, holding up his bowl. "It's fantastic today."

"It's the stone peppers," Porter said, pleased, ladling up another serving of the thick yellow stew. "Found some nice hard ones at the market."

Veteran Jedi could live wherever they liked once the passage of time naturally reduced their ability and desire to participate in the more active work of the Order. Most remained at the Coruscant Temple, which maintained lodgings for all its older members, to live out their days as they pleased. Porter Engle had taken the opposite approach, actually requesting an assignment to the Elphrona Outpost. He seemed intent on remaining as useful as possible despite his age, and an outpost was the best way he knew to ensure his three centuries of Jedi experience could directly help the galaxy.

In an average day, an Outpost Jedi might be called upon to settle a dispute, defend a town from marauders, bring criminals to justice, teach children, offer medical assistance, or just wield the Force in any of the ten thousand ways it could be used to help people. Not every problem required a Jedi to solve it, but when a problem did rise to that level, people tended to be glad they lived on an outpost world.

"Starlight Beacon's almost ready for the dedication," Loden said as Bell dug into his second bowl of stew.

"Just a few weeks," Indeera said. "But the chancellor's hyperspace closures might push that back."

"Mm . . . I hope not," Porter Engle said, taking a seat at the head of the table. "It wouldn't be the end of the world if it didn't open on time, but I know it's important to the chancellor's future plans that everything runs smoothly. I'd like to see it, too. It sounds beautiful."

"It is," Loden agreed. "Wouldn't you say, Bell?"

"Gorgeous," Bell said. "There's a biosphere zone, where visitors can check out actual re-creations of various worlds in the Outer Rim Territories. Dantooine jungle, an ice flat from Mygeeto . . . I liked it."

Loden dropped his spoon into his empty bowl.

"The idea is to showcase the diversity of the worlds out here," he said. "They'll rotate the biospheres from time to time, bring in different creatures . . . it's very ambitious."

Indeera spoke, not looking up from the datapad she was perusing.

"The whole station is ambitious. And it's just the first of many, right? The chancellor's got a whole network of Beacons planned, I think. I read about it."

"That's what they told us at the conclave," Bell answered.

"Lina Soh and her Great Works," Porter Engle said. "I think she's fantastic. If there was ever a time for Beacons and relay networks and outreach, it's now. I remember when the galaxy was just pulling itself together, a few centuries back . . . we couldn't think about anything but survival, really. We should use this time of prosperity to build something meaningful for the future."

"Do you think the Order's outpost network will close down once the Beacons all come online?" Bell asked.

"I hope not," Porter said, leaning back and putting his hands behind his head. "This sort of life suits me just fine. Every day's a little different, seeing what comes, helping people however they need it . . . not so bad."

He signaled a servitor droid, which trundled over and began clearing the breakfast dishes. They were sitting in the outpost's dining chamber, a comfortable, low-ceilinged room, one of eight set just off the main chamber, a tall, circular area designed around a huge Jedi Order symbol inlaid on the floor. Sleeping chambers, the kitchen, storage, the hangar, a sparring room for lightsaber training . . . all of it was accessible from the central zone, just as the Force touched all things equally.

"Speaking of which," Porter went on, "what do you all have on deck for the day?"

"I'm going to take one of the Vectors to a spot down in the southern hemisphere," Indeera said. "Some miners think they found a vein of essurtanium. I've never actually seen it before—supposed to have really rare properties, maybe even a little Force-reactive. I was hoping to buy a sample, bring it back here so I could study it."

"Take Bell with you," Loden said.

"What, so she can throw me out of the cockpit?" Bell said.

"You are very wise, my Padawan," Loden said.

"Well, I'm going to wash the dishes," Porter said. "What about you, Loden?"

"A claim to the north is having trouble with a nest of chromants. I thought I'd go give them a hand."

"Can't they just bring in an extermination unit?" Indeera asked.

"Probably," Loden said, "But maybe I *want* to fight a hundred chromants."

Bell shook his head. He also wanted to fight a hundred chromants, but he knew better than to ask. He was jumping out of another Vector, and that was that.

A low whistle from the central chamber, and all four Jedi turned their heads toward the sound—the signal for an incoming transmission on the outpost's emergency comm system. Loden reached out and tapped a control set into the tabletop, bringing the transmission into the room. A voice sounded, quiet, filled with tension.

"Uh, Jedi . . . this is . . . no. Don't wanna get involved. But there's a homesteader family, about thirty kilometers to the southwest of town. Two parents, two kids. The Blythes. I caught a transmission to the Ogden's Hope security station, I monitor that channel on my comlink, like a hobby. Anyway, they were calling for help. The family's being attacked . . . by the Nihil. Ogden's Hope security won't go. Afraid, I think. I'd be afraid, too—the stories we hear about the Nihil . . . But the person who called in . . . it was a *kid.* He sounded . . . it sounded really bad. Maybe you could go out there? Help somehow? I'm sending the coordinates. I can't get involved, not with the Nihil. But I just . . . thought you should know."

The message ended.

Ember sensed the tension in the room. From below the table, she coughed out one small sound, like a boot stepping on a piece of charcoal.

"The Nihil," Indeera said.

"The family," Porter Engle said.

His voice had gone very cold. Perhaps for the first time, Bell looked at the man and no longer saw the joking, bearded Ikkrukki chef he knew so well, inventor of the Nine-Egg Stew. Instead, he saw the Jedi they once called the Blade of Bardotta.

"Let's go," Loden said.

CHAPTER TWENTY-THREE

THE MID RIM. NABOO.

Avar Kriss leaned on the ornate, carved-stone railing and looked out across the lake to a small, forested island rising to a low peak in its center. A small settlement of low, orange-shingled buildings crouched together by the lakeshore, but otherwise the island looked like pristine wilderness.

"Varykino," Elzar Mann said, stepping up beside her.

She glanced at him. He looked good. Happy, his dark eyes shining, a grin lighting up his face, though that could be due to the drink in his hand, some green stuff in a stemless glass bowl. She didn't know what it was, but she knew Elzar, and so odds were it was the finest intoxicant their hosts had available. And considering their hosts, that meant it was probably very fine indeed.

"Very what?" she asked.

"Varykino," he said, gesturing with his drink toward the island. "That's the name of the island. It's an artists' retreat, a place for creative outcasts to live together and think deep thoughts. There's a poet there, a man named Omar Berenko. Supposed to be brilliant."

Elzar glanced at her. He ran a hand through his dark hair, cut short, with a natural wave to it.

"Sounds nice, actually," he said. "We should remember it, once we're too old for the Order to make use of us anymore. I wouldn't mind spending my days in quiet contemplation. Maybe figure out how to catch fish with the Force."

He took a sip of his drink, and his face took on an impressed expression.

"As long as we lay in a steady supply of this stuff. By the light, that's good."

"Let me try," Avar said, and he handed her the bowl.

She sipped the liquor, a spicy, soft taste that left her tongue tingling.

"No arguments here," she said. "That's delicious. But go easy. We're here to do a job."

Elzar had one last swallow, then set the bowl down on the railing; a shining golden servitor droid promptly scooped it up and quietly withdrew, hovering not far away in case the two Jedi required anything further.

"Are your owners on the way?" Avar asked the droid. "We've been waiting for some time."

"Of course, Master Jedi," the droid replied, in a lovely chime of a voice. "Masters Marlowe and Vellis are completing some urgent business, but have notified me that they will be here momentarily. If you wish, you may take a seat while you wait."

The droid gestured with one long, languid limb toward a seating area deeper in the lanai—plush couches and seats with various refreshments laid out on a low quartz table. She assumed this was where Elzar had gotten his drink. So much wealth on display here—just owning an estate in the Naboo lake country was out of reach for any but the richest families in the galaxy. Nonetheless, the feeling created by the décor was not one of ostentation, but of care and taste. The owners of this home were not trying to overawe—every choice was made with an eye toward simplicity and integration with the natural environment. Which, of course, was impressive in its own right.

As if to underscore the point, a gentle breeze blew across the patio, rippling through the millaflowers dangling from vines hanging from the arbors overhead. Their fragrance saturated Avar's senses, and the song of the Force swelled with the beauty of it all.

It was easy to forget they were there to continue the investigation into the ongoing galactic emergency. She forced herself to focus. Quiet contemplation could wait for retirement—and for a moment, just one, she let herself consider the idea of spending that time with Elzar Mann—something she would never tell him; he would never let her hear the end of it.

Another Emergence, another tragedy, had happened in the Ringlite system, and several thousand people had died. Only the valiant efforts of the system's security squads had prevented something worse. Chancellor Soh had widened the hyperspace cordon once again. Senator Noor hadn't protested this action—the necessity was obvious—but the pressure was mounting to solve the mystery once and for all.

This meeting today could be the key.

As if they had read her mind, two men appeared at the edge of the patio and walked toward her and Elzar. Marlowe and Vellis, the scion of the San Tekka empire and his husband.

Both were pale, with blond hair and blue eyes. The similarities stopped there; Vellis's face looked chopped from granite while Marlowe's features were softer. They did seem a pair, though, and like their home, everything about them radiated wealth and comfort and ease.

She wondered what Marlowe's ancestors would think of what the family had become—the San Tekka family made its fortune a century or so ago as hyperspace prospectors, rough-edged people finding routes through the wild spaces of the galaxy, like planetary explorers searching for passes through deadly mountain ranges. Hyperspace prospecting was just as dangerous; many who tried it ended up lost forever, adrift in nothingness with no way to get home. The San Tekkas seemed to have a knack for it, though, and consistently found the shortest, fastest ways to get from here to there in the galaxy. They sold those routes to traders, governments, and entrepreneurs, and in some cases set up hyperspace toll lanes, where navigational data could be downloaded for a fee. All that revenue added up. These days, the San Tekkas were among the wealthiest families in the galaxy, and their teams of prospectors—now called hypersurveyors to give the trade a sheen of respectability—continued to sniff out lucrative new paths between the stars.

The galaxy was endless, and people would always want to traverse it more quickly and safely.

"Welcome to our home," Marlowe said, extending a hand to Avar. "It is an honor to have Jedi guests."

She took the hand and shook it briefly. Elzar did the same with Vellis.

"Please, let's sit," Vellis said, gesturing to the couch. "The servitor droid tells me you've already sampled the attar of spinsilk—one of my favorites as well. But there's much more you can try. Anything you like."

"Thank you," Avar said.

The group sat, and Avar gently reached out with the Force to sense the emotional state of their hosts. They were utterly relaxed. Not that she expected anything else. A gorgeous lakeside patio with the love of your life at your side and enough credits for a thousand lifetimes? Of course the San Tekkas were relaxed.

"Senator Noor told us you're investigating the dreadful disasters in the Outer Rim," Marlowe said, pouring a glass of something red and handing it to Vellis. "I'm not sure what we can do to help, but of course we're more than happy. Izzet is an old friend, and we know he has responsibility for the Outer Rim. Anything he needs, really."

"Not to mention all the people in the firing line," Elzar said, a slight edge to his voice.

"Of course," Vellis said. "We are all the Republic."

"The Emergences are bad enough, and we're working on a system to predict where they're going to happen next," Avar said.

"Oh really? That's interesting," Marlowe said. "How is that possible?"

"Hetzal Prime happened to have a genius systems analyst in their Technology Ministry. He's trying to build a network of navidroids . . . linking their processors together to use the data we have so far about the original disaster and all the Emergences. It's not a sure thing. The problem seems to be getting enough droids to run the calculations."

Marlowe and Vellis exchanged a quick glance—information passed between them, some unseen communication even Avar couldn't detect.

"We can probably help with that," Vellis said. "We have a proprietary set of algorithms we use to model likely hyperspace routes. If your analyst on Hetzal is interested, we can send a few of our navulators—hyperlane specialists—to help him refine his system."

"Generally, we like to keep our trade secrets confidential," Marlowe added, "but there are lives on the line."

"Thank you very much," Avar said. "That's generous. We'll put you in touch with the analyst—his name is Keven Tarr. I'm sure he'll take any help he can get."

"That's not really why we're here, though," Elzar said.

"Oh?" Marlowe said, raising a thin eyebrow.

"It's not just about stopping the Emergences. We want to make sure nothing like the *Legacy Run* ever happens again, and in order to do that, we need to know what caused it. Your family knows more about hyperspace than anyone, or so Senator Noor tells us. Do you have any theories?"

"Well, we've read the HoloNet reports, but they're a little light on details. Do you have any additional information?"

Elzar reached into his tunic and produced a datachip, which he handed to Vellis.

"That's everything we have so far. The Republic Transport Bureau's personnel have analyzed the wreckage, and based on the wear patterns, it looks very much like the *Legacy Run* disintegrated in transit."

"A collision?" Marlowe said.

"No," Avar said. "It seems that the ship attempted to execute a maneuver that stressed its superstructure beyond its capabilities. I'm oversimplifying, but it seems to have ripped itself apart."

Vellis and Marlowe were silent for a moment. Vellis set his glass down. Avar didn't think he'd even tasted his drink.

"I'm sure you both know this, but the nature of hyperspace means that there is never any reason to maneuver at all. It's empty. There's nothing to hit. Routes are precisely calculated to ensure collisions like this are impossible."

"We know that," Elzar said. "Everyone knows that. But . . . something happened out there, and people continue to die and suffer across the Outer Rim. Pretending it's impossible just wastes time."

He pointed at the datachip Vellis was still holding.

"We're examining a few possibilities. It's all on the chip. Our first thought was pilot error, but we looked into that. The captain of the *Legacy Run* was a woman named Hedda Casset. Ex-military, a decorated veteran. It's hard to imagine she would make a mistake that would result in the destruction of her ship. By all accounts, she was steady and focused."

"A mutiny?" Marlowe asked.

"Why?" Avar replied. "It was a ship full of settlers. A routine run from the Core to the Outer Rim Territories. Nothing unusual or extremely valuable aboard."

"Strange things can happen psychologically when you're out in deep space," Marlowe said. "We have stories from our family's history you wouldn't believe. Madness creeps in before you know it."

"Fair," Elzar said, "But this was a straightforward run on a well-traveled route. RTB officials interviewed some of the survivors we rescued, and they didn't suggest anything along those lines. Mutiny's low on the list."

"Maybe the ship malfunctioned?" Vellis ventured.

"Not impossible, but unlikely," Avar continued. "The *Legacy Run* was an old vessel, but we know from its maintenance records that Captain Casset kept it in top condition, and it had a full overhaul two runs before the trip that killed it."

"Our working theory is that it encountered something in the hyperspace lane, and it tried to avoid running into it," Elzar broke in.

"Impossible," Marlowe said. "I just told you. Hyperspace doesn't work that way."

Avar caught a flicker of an impulse from Elzar. Not a word, not a message, but something she understood all the same. She had known Elzar Mann for a very long time—they were younglings together, and Padawans, and that created a connection, a bond through the Force that meant sometimes they didn't have to use words to understand each other.

But if Elzar *had* used words, she knew what she was sensing from him would mean: *He's lying.*

Elzar was better at sensing deception than she was. Now, when it came to her particular gift, a native understanding of the way the Force touched all life in the galaxy, she thought there might not be a more skilled Jedi in the Order than herself. Well, perhaps Master Yoda. But as far as understanding people . . . Elzar Mann was an expert. She didn't think he even needed to use the Force to do it.

Avar suspected he was considering a use of the Force right then, however—what most Jedi called the mind touch, and he called the mind trick. He found it a more honest way to describe what was actually being done. Elzar would lift two fingers in a subtle gesture and touch Marlowe San Tekka's mind with the Force, and then Marlowe would do whatever Elzar said next.

The mind touch was a tool of the light, Avar knew, but she preferred indirect approaches to such a focused intervention in another person's path. Elzar had his reservations as well, but viewed the technique as a way to open people to the truth, to provide clarity, to allow them to feel the will of the Force. To put it another way—he was a problem solver, and the mind touch certainly solved problems.

Avar sent an impulse of her own across their link, one he would recognize immediately, simple and straightforward.

No.

Elzar turned and looked at her, his face expressionless but easy for her to read. His mouth quirked up into a quick little smile—*okay, you got me*—and then he looked back at the San Tekkas.

"Are you absolutely certain a collision is impossible, Vellis?" Avar asked. "Perhaps a derelict ship, or an asteroid . . . ? Surely there must be a way for an object to be left adrift in the hyperspace lanes."

Vellis shook his head. "Hyperspace is not like realspace. Once a ship—or anything else—enters it, there's no way to encounter anything. You're in a bubble of space-time that nothing else can interact with, because each lane is, as far as we can tell, its own distinct plane of existence."

Avar knew she would remember those words every time she traveled in hyperspace for the rest of her life. A jump to lightspeed had become such a routine event, but each time it happened was a step away from everything familiar, a journey into a new universe, some new realm. The song of the Force was beautiful, but sometimes its indescribable vastness left her feeling insignificant, despite all her focus, all her training. It could leave her reeling.

Another impulse from Elzar: *Lying,* and again, from her: *No.*

"Be that as it may," Avar said, "the *Legacy Run* died, along with many people aboard it, and millions have died since in the Emergences. Your family has spent more time studying hyperspace than anyone in the galaxy. Have you ever encountered anything like this?"

"No," Marlowe said flatly, and this time there was no signal of falsehood from Elzar.

"So you don't think it's a problem with hyperspace?" Elzar said.

"We'll look at your data," Vellis said, holding up the datachip, "but as of now, it's hard to imagine something like that. I don't think you have to worry about another *Legacy Run.* Our guess, based on more than a century of experience out there in the lanes . . ."

". . . this was a onetime event," Marlowe finished.

Avar stood up, and Elzar, masking his surprise, did the same.

"Thank you," she said. "We can't tell you how much we appreciate your sending your people to help Keven Tarr in Hetzal. We're going to move on to our next appointment—but if we think of additional questions, can we reach out?"

"Of course," Marlowe said, standing as well. "As we said, it is an honor and a privilege to assist the Jedi and the Republic with anything you might need."

Final pleasantries were exchanged, and Avar and Elzar left the San Tekka compound, heading for the Longbeam that had brought them to Naboo, waiting on a landing pad just outside the gates.

"They were hiding something," Elzar said. His tone was light, but she knew he was frustrated. A familiar emotion from him. He was always reaching . . . pushing.

"I'm sure they were, Elzar. They're businesspeople. We don't know that what they held back is even relevant. The San Tekkas didn't seem malicious. The opposite, really—they're offering to share some of their most closely held secrets to help save lives."

Elzar was silent, but she felt a grudging acceptance from him.

"Let's continue our investigation, see if there's more we can learn. If need be, we can return and question them again. We made progress here. Be pleased."

"The drink was good, at least," Elzar said, and walked ahead, toward the waiting Longbeam.

The breeze blew across the lanai, and Marlowe and Vellis San Tekka sat in silence, looking out across the lake at the isle of Varykino, where strange geniuses toiled in isolation, creating art that, more likely than not, would never be seen by anyone beyond the shores of the little island.

"You know who this sounds like, don't you?" Vellis said.

He lifted his wineglass, tapped his fingernail against its rim a few times, then set it back down on the quartz table.

"It's not possible," Marlowe answered. "She can't still be alive. She'd be beyond ancient."

"I hope so," Vellis said. "For her sake, by all the gods . . ."

The sun sparkled off wavelets on the lake, and both men thought about the history of their clan, and where their great wealth had truly come from, and the great tragedy at its heart.

". . . I hope so."

CHAPTER TWENTY-FOUR

HYPERSPACE. THE *GAZE ELECTRIC*.

Marchion Ro's flagship traveled through hyperspace—but in a way no other ship in the galaxy could. Its course was not set, moving from one access zone to another, through a well-defined hyperlane. No . . . the *Gaze Electric* didn't move, it maneuvered. The massive ship plunged and rose, making impossibly tight turns, diving into tiny offshoots of the main road and finding itself in an entirely new urspace. It followed routes that could not be seen and could not be repeated.

Its path was charted by Mari San Tekka, and Marchion Ro let her have her head—she had complete control over the ship's navigation systems, and if the ride got a little bumpy sometimes, even terrifying, so what? These rides made Mari feel happy and good—they let her test her theories, work out new ideas.

Piloting the *Gaze Electric* calmed her down, made her feel like she was in a good place, so that when Marchion asked her for specific Paths, she was able to provide them without exhausting herself or getting frustrated.

He looked through a viewport at the strange, unreal landscapes through which she was taking the ship. Like flying through a snowstorm made of flowers built of bright-green light. Beautiful and horrifying all at once.

Traveling through hyperspace under ordinary circumstances was an entirely different experience. You entered the lane, you flew through the unchanging, swirling nothing for some set period, and then you exited back to realspace.

But Mari's flight was like that of a fast-winged insect, zipping from blossom to blossom, changing direction without bowing to considerations of inertia, acceleration, or deceleration.

These abilities came at a cost, both in wear and tear and fuel, though the *Gaze Electric* was specially equipped to handle them via a Path engine of unique design. The very first, in fact, similar in appearance to those on all the other Nihil ships but greatly enhanced in capabilities. The engines allowed the Nihil to translate the Paths into actual navigational data that would be rejected by any conventional system as being *impossible*—they were the key to everything, now and in the future.

Marchion had owned the huge vessel for a very long time, and his father before him, both of them haunting its empty spaces designed for thousands, now through time and treachery inhabited by only a few. The Ros, father and son, had no homeworld; they left it behind long ago. The ship was as close as Marchion got, just as Mari San Tekka was the nearest thing to family he had left.

Marchion Ro peered in at Mari, who lay in a sealed oblong pod with a clear front panel. Wires ran from it to power sources in the deck, and large tanks of various medical chemicals bubbled nearby, their contents dripping into tubes running into the pod. The machine was essentially one large medical capsule designed to keep Mari as healthy and comfortable as could be managed for a human who had been alive for well over a century.

Mari had dialed in to the particular focus she found while doing these runs, her eyes flickering, charting routes through the swirl of hyperspace that her mind was uniquely capable of seeing. No other being seemed able to do it, and no navidroid came close. Droid brains could chart routes along already established paths, but what Mari did was nothing like that. Mari found the roads between the roads, via some mix of instinct and unconscious mathematical analysis that operated on a level she couldn't explain.

Marchion had asked her, of course—many times—as had his father, and his grandmother. If Mari San Tekka's gift could be replicated, then there truly was no limit to what could be accomplished. Mari had tried, but it was like explaining why there were always more stars the farther you traveled, the deeper you looked. Some things just were, and could not be explained.

Or duplicated.

When Mari San Tekka died—and that day could not be far off, despite the best medical technology in the galaxy being applied to extending her life span—the Paths would die with her. And at that point, the thing that made the Nihil more than just another marauder gang carving out territory in the Outer Rim would vanish.

Marchion pressed a control on the exterior of Mari's medical pod, and spoke.

"Can you bring us back, Mari?" Marchion Ro said.

The old woman ignored him, and the *Gaze* leapt again. Marchion braced himself against the shock without thinking. Some people could barely keep their feet when Mari San Tekka took the ship on one of her little voyages, but he had been experiencing it since he was a child.

"Mari?" he said again.

No response. Hyperspace swirled outside the viewports, and Mari's eyes tracked it, seeing paths visible only to her.

Marchion Ro frowned. He pressed another control on the medical pod's console, and Mari's entire body tensed as a mild electric shock coursed through it.

He wished she weren't making him do it. The woman was not

robust, and he didn't know how many jolts she could take. Her doctor, a rotund Chadra-Fan named Uttersond, had once described Mari San Tekka's heart as a paper lantern.

But he didn't have time for her to be lost in her mind. He had plans, and questions, and the Nihil needed Paths, and the Paths came from Marchion Ro, but truly from this old woman to whom he had tied his entire future, this woman he *kept alive* and *pampered* and she just wanted to fly his ship halfway across the galaxy instead of just—

He pressed the button again, and Mari's body went rigid.

—giving him—

Again.

—what he—

Again.

—*needed.*

Mari San Tekka collapsed back against the cradle in her medical pod, and then her body trembled and shook. Her mouth gaped open, spittle shining at its corners, and her eyes rolled back in her head.

An alarm began to sound, a low, insistent beep, which he knew would summon Dr. Uttersond. Marchion Ro tapped another control and the alarm ceased.

He leaned over the medical pod, watching Mari San Tekka endure her seizure. The pod went through its emergency procedures; needles extended on actuator arms from its sides and slipped into the protruding veins on the woman's stick-thin arms, as flat metal paddles slid beneath her robes to stimulate her heart.

Maybe this is the end, he thought. *Everything I've done, all those years of planning . . . it could be over, right here, today.*

The idea had a perverse appeal. Fascinated, he watched Mari San Tekka's trembling, tiny body, wondering if his life was about to embark on . . . well, an entirely new path.

His finger hovered over the alarm for Uttersond, and he didn't know what the idiot doctor could do, but perhaps something, and was pressing it even as Mari San Tekka coughed, a sharp barking sound, and her seizures ended.

Her eyes opened, and she looked around her in wonderment. They locked on Marchion, and she smiled, broad and kind and open as a child.

"Why, Marchion, hello," she said. "Did I lose myself again? I'm sorry. You know how I get when I take us traveling. There's just so much to see, you know."

Her index finger twitched on the control panel beneath her hand, and Marchion felt the *Gaze* drop from hyperspace.

"It's all right, Mari, everything's just fine."

Mari swiveled the medical pod, taking it vertical, so instead of looking up at him she could stare him right in the eye. Her mind was clouded by age, but her gaze was not—her eyes were clear and focused, and she never seemed perturbed in the least by his own black orbs.

"Well, that was a good one, in any case. Found a new path between Pasaana and Urber. Should reduce travel time by a third, maybe more. It'll make you a bundle!"

Mari San Tekka had been a hyperspace prospector since she was six years old. Something had happened to her as she traveled out in the interstellar wilderness with her family, and it had changed her. Changed her mind. Opened her up so she could see things no one else could—the Paths. For some years, she had used that ability on behalf of her people, and brought them wealth and renown . . . but that fame brought with it a price.

Marchion Ro's own family had taken Mari San Tekka . . . stolen her, no reason to call it anything other than what it was. They had used her skill to find things they believed they needed back then, and then they had just . . . kept her. Told her whatever stories were required to keep her happy and working. Handed her down from generation to generation, until eventually she took up residence on the *Gaze Electric.*

Mari San Tekka seemed to believe she was still working as a prospector. Sometimes she thought Marchion Ro was her father (or his, or his grandmother), sometimes her son, sometimes her jailer, sometimes her business partner. Her sense of time had gotten muddled over the decades—though her skill at finding new hyperlanes had not diminished, and not just the Paths Marchion requested for Nihil raids. Mari had charted new, secret routes all over the galaxy, from the Deep Core to Wild Space. She seemed to think Marchion Ro was selling them to the Republic, or whatever form of government she thought was currently running the galaxy. That belief was consistent no matter what identity she assigned to him.

In fact, Marchion didn't use Mari's new routes at all. He stored them on the *Gaze Electric*'s central database. There could be a time when they would be valuable to him . . . but many things had to fall into place before that day could come.

Still, it kept Mari San Tekka happy to believe she was making herself useful, and when she was happy, it was easier to get her to do what he actually needed.

"Thank you so much, Mari," Marchion said. "You can input them to the computer, and we'll reach out to buyers right away. You're fantastic."

Mari smiled, suddenly shy. She was so *good,* so *ignorant.* Marchion hated how much he needed her.

"How are things going with your work, Marchion?" she asked. "That big fancy plan of yours. Are you making progress?"

Marchion had told this woman things . . . things he had told no other living being. He told himself it was because he needed her expertise, and not because he had no one else to tell.

He considered her question. The Paths, and Mari herself, were his legacy, passed down to him from his father. Asgar Ro hadn't created the Nihil, nor had he ever ruled them. Neither did Marchion. Both served as the Eye, which sounded impressive, but in truth the Eye just provided a unique service—the Paths—for which the Nihil's true bosses, the Tempest Runners, paid extremely well.

Asgar Ro did not bring the Paths to the Nihil just for the credits it would give him, though. He had a goal in mind—redemption and revenge, for his family and many others. He had not lived to see it come to fruition, and had passed the task to his son.

Completing that work would require transformation—the Nihil would need to become something entirely different than the selfish, ravaging, disorganized band of criminals they currently were. Until very recently, Marchion Ro had not been able to see any way to get it done . . . but now he had no choice. For centuries, the Republic had largely left the Outer Rim to govern itself, but now things were changing. They were building a huge station, the Starlight Beacon, and what they called galactic outreach he called force projection.

The Nihil had to evolve now, before it was too late and the Republic brought their law and order and control to the Outer Rim. And of course, the Jedi. Couldn't forget about them.

"My plan is . . . ongoing," he said, answering Mari's question. "Some stumbling blocks along the way, and the next steps will require some serious subtlety. It's a dangerous time for me, in some ways. Actually, I was hoping you might help me with something."

Mari lifted a frail hand, and her smile faded.

"Oh, you want some Paths. Do I have to? I just did so much work finding that new route . . . it wore me out, it surely did. Can I do it later? After a nap?"

Shock her, Marchion thought. *Shock her again and again until she burns inside that blasted pod.*

"No," Marchion said. "It's just a question. I just wanted you to think about something. The chef made your favorite for dinner—we can have it brought in, if that helps."

Mari sighed.

"All right, Marchion," she said. "If you really need it. You know, your father never worked me as hard as you do. I miss him."

Marchion Ro's finger twitched toward the button that would trigger another shock to the medical pod. His father was dead. Marchion did not and would not walk that man's path. Mari San Tekka and the Tempest Runners could make as many little jabs as they wanted, suggest he could never measure up. It didn't matter. His father was dead.

He took a deep breath and clenched his gloved hand into a fist.

"Thank you, Mari," Marchion said. "Here's what I'd like you to do."

He pulled a datachip from his belt and plugged it into a reader on Mari's medical pod. Information displayed on the inside of the canopy in bright blue—rapidly scrolling lines of data that described the last moments of what was once the doomed *Legacy Run* as it scattered through the Hetzal system. Mari San Tekka's eyes sharpened, scanning the information, missing nothing.

"Oh dear," she said. "That poor ship. What a tragedy."

"Mm," said Marchion Ro. "It didn't stop here, either. Pieces of that ship have been popping up out of hyperspace all over the Outer Rim. They're calling them Emergences. There's one part in particular—a section of the bridge that contains the ship's flight recorder. The Republic is looking for it, because they think it will tell them things they want to know about what happened to the *Legacy Run*."

"Yes, I see," Mari said, still tracking the data as it rolled along her medical pod's canopy.

"They're trying to build a huge sort of machine—lots of navigational droids linked together—and they hope they can use it to predict where the missing pieces of the *Legacy Run* will show up. I just want to know if that's possible. Can something like that actually be done?"

Mari did not hesitate. She laughed, a surprisingly rich sound. Marchion had no idea where it came from. Her chest looked like you could collapse the whole apparatus with the flick of a finger.

"Of course, you silly. I could do it for you right now. I can tell you where every last piece of this ship will show up. Won't take long at all. Just . . . I'm very tired."

Marchion froze. Everything was clear—in that single moment, every step he would need to take was revealed to him. There were options, branching routes, he would have to make choices, improvise . . .

but it was all one path, and it led to what he'd been looking for all his life.

His comlink chimed, and he lifted it from his belt.

"Yes?" Marchion said.

"She had another seizure," came Dr. Uttersond's squeaky voice through the comlink. "I saw it on my monitors."

The Chadra-Fan's voice was exceedingly irritating even when he wasn't affecting the scolding tone he was currently using.

"She's fine," Marchion said.

"No, sir, respectfully, she's not. She needs to rest. No more prospecting, no more Paths, nothing for at least a week. She is frail, and needs to rebuild her strength."

"Thank you, Doctor. Understood."

"Do you, sir? Because sometimes I wonder. I think—"

Marchion ended the transmission. He watched Mari San Tekka, the innocent smile on her face as she watched pieces of the *Legacy Run* kill and destroy throughout Hetzal.

"I would appreciate your help very much, Mari," he said. "I need to go do a few things, but I'll be back later. Can you get started right away? I'll have the chef bring you your dinner. You can work while you eat."

The old woman didn't answer. She waved a hand vaguely, her medical pod slowly rotating back to a horizontal position. She was going deep again, her mind flickering along swirling roads only she understood, as she began to work the problem.

Marchion Ro left Mari's chamber, heading for the ship's bridge. The *Gaze* was almost entirely crewed by droids and hired personnel from outside the Nihil. He couldn't trust the Clouds and Storms, and certainly not the Strikes. Not any one of them. Not even the Tempest Runners were allowed aboard his ship. None knew where the Paths came from, but if they ever found out, well . . . anyone could keep a medical pod running.

When he arrived on the bridge, a beautiful chamber carved entirely from the trunk of a single huge wroshyr tree, imported from Kashyyyk and shaped by artisans at breathtaking expense, Marchion moved to his captain's chair without a word to his deck crew. He tapped the button that raised privacy screens around the seat, all of which doubled as comm displays.

Another button, and Kassav, Pan Eyta, and Lourna Dee appeared on the displays.

"Let me guess, you're scared of the big bad Jedi and don't want to give us any Paths," Kassav said, as ever the first to speak and the last to shut up.

Pan Eyta and Lourna Dee remained silent.

"I am not afraid of the Jedi, Kassav. However, because I am not an idiot, I take them seriously as a threat. They could destroy everything we've built."

Kassav looked like he was about to say something else, so Marchion just kept talking, not giving him the chance.

"I know you've all been frustrated that we've been lying low," he said. "No raids. Well. You know that new initiative I mentioned? It's on. We're going to change things up. I'm going to get the three of you a list of the Emergences—the ones that haven't happened yet. Go over them, see what opportunities you can find for us. Only catch is no Paths. You'll have to plan your operations without them. Just standard tactics and techniques."

Lourna and Pan said nothing, but he could see them calculating, thinking, trying to decide how much this would help or hurt them, what sort of game he was playing, how they could benefit or change his mind, or whether it was finally the time to actively embark upon the plans he was sure both had to murder him, steal everything he had, and take the Paths for their own.

For once, Kassav didn't speak right away. He probably was thinking the same things as the other two.

"I'm actually impressed," Kassav finally said. "This is pretty good. But since we'll be doing the jobs ourselves, and you aren't actually giving us any Paths, the split should be different. I say the Eye doesn't get a third for these. How about . . . ten percent? That seems fair."

Marchion gave him a smile that was not a smile at all.

"Here's what I can do, Kassav—if you don't want the Emergences, I can give them to Pan Eyta and Lourna Dee. Or none of you. Your choice. But if you take the Eye's information, you pay for it like you usually do, or no more Paths, ever. Returns get divided up like usual. The Rule of Three applies."

Kassav didn't like this. Marchion didn't care.

"The Republic is trying to figure out where the Emergences will happen, too, and they'll be there right away after they happen, so use your best people," he said. "You'll want to get in and get out. Maybe you find a disaster site and loot it. Maybe you ransom off the information about where an Emergence will happen . . . but do it anonymously, with the funds going to our dark accounts. My point is, be subtle. If the Republic figures out that someone knows where the Emergences are happening, it could lead them right back to us. We don't need that kind of heat."

He leaned forward.

"That all make sense?"

The Tempest Runners nodded, and Marchion Ro cut the connection. He thought for a moment. It was all so clear now. So clear. He pressed a control on the armrest of his captain's chair.

"Get the old lady her dinner," he said.

CHAPTER TWENTY-FIVE

ELPHRONA.

A clang, and the vehicle shuddered. Bell heard Indeera curse under her breath, but they didn't slow down. If anything, they moved faster, the engine's roar increasing in pitch.

Ember stirred at Bell's side, anxious, and he stroked the hound's pelt, feeling the temperature variations across the creature's coloration.

"It's all right, girl," Bell said. "Indeera just bumped into something. We're fine."

They were riding in another vehicle custom-designed by Valkeri Enterprises for the Jedi—a Vanguard, the land-based equivalent to the Vector. It was also sometimes called a V-Wheel, even though the thing didn't always use its wheels to get around. Every Jedi outpost had at least one as part of its standard kit, and the machine was engineered to operate in all of the many planetary environments in which those stations were situated. It could operate as a wheeled or tracked ground transport, or a repulsorlift speeder for ground too rugged for even tank treads. A Vanguard even had limited utility as an amphibious or even submersible vehicle, being able to seal itself off entirely as needed. It could do everything but fly, and that came in handy on Elphrona, where the planet's strong magnetic fields made certain regions utterly inhospitable to flying craft.

The overall aesthetic was analogous to the Vectors—smooth, sleek lines, with curves and straight edges integrated into an appealingly geometric whole. Behind the seats in the driver's cabin—currently occupied by Indeera Stokes and Loden Greatstorm—was a large, multipurpose passenger area, with space to store any gear that a mission might require. Vanguards were more rugged than Vectors, but were built with many of the same Jedi-related features as their flying cousins. The weapons systems required a lightsaber key, and many of the controls were mechanical in nature, so as to be operated—in an emergency—via an application of the Force rather than through electronics.

No Jedi would use the Force to accomplish something as easily done with their hand—but lives had been saved by the ability to unlock a Vanguard's hatch from a distance, or fire its weapons, or even make it move. Bell didn't think he could do it, and he wasn't sure Loden could, either. Indeera . . . maybe. She was by far the most technologically minded of their crew. She usually drove whenever they took the machine out—today was no exception.

Indeera had chosen the most direct course to their destination, a straight shot through the landscape across a low-slung set of hills. A road did exist, running from the outpost to Ogden's Hope and looping back out to the claim zones, but it was an indirect route. Using it would take time they did not seem to have, based on the emergency message they'd received. So the ride was bumpy, uneven . . . but it was fast, especially with Indeera at the controls.

The Vanguard crested the rise.

"Smoke," Loden said.

Bell turned to look through the Vanguard's windscreen and saw what his master was referring to—a wide column of dark smoke, far ahead and in their path, revealed now that they were over the hills.

"If that's not the Blythe homestead, it's right next door. Do you think . . ." Indeera said.

"I do," Loden replied. "The Nihil, from what I've heard, are destroyers. They take what they want and wreck what's left. They use gas attacks, too—that could be what we're seeing."

"Looks like a fire to me," Indeera said. "Take the wheel, Loden. I'm going to run out a Veil, see if I can get a look at what we're heading into."

"And it gives us a chance at a multifront response if the Nihil are still there, or if they left any surprises," Loden said.

Indeera nodded. She got up from her seat as Loden grasped the control wheel. The Vanguard slowed.

Indeera made her way back to the passenger compartment, moving past Porter Engle, who sat in silence, his single eye blank, staring at nothing.

Outwardly, the Ikkrukki was calm, but Bell sensed roiling energy in the man. Porter Engle, the kindly cook, inventor of ingenious dishes and dispenser of useful aphorisms, was being set aside. What was appearing in his place felt like a dormant volcano beginning to wake—simmering and ready, filled with unimaginable power. The ancient Jedi was summoning up a ghost: one of his former lives. A version of himself the Padawans told stories about. Someone the sort of people who attacked defenseless settler families should pray they never met.

"Are you all right, Porter?" Bell said.

"Yes," the old Jedi answered without shifting his gaze.

Bell decided to leave it alone. He wasn't afraid of Porter—they were both Jedi, after all. But . . . he wasn't sure how he felt about meeting a ghost.

Indeera slipped past them to the rear of the vehicle, where its two Veil speeders were stored on racks, one above the other. Like all the Valkeri Enterprises gear built for the Order, they were designed for Force-users, and as such were delicate, highly responsive machines. Little more than a seat strapped to a hollow duralium frame, with a single repulsor and four winglike attachments that sprang out from its sides, a Veil was basically a flying stick. But if you knew how to ride them, they were incredibly fast and maneuverable. A group of skilled riders, with lightsabers out and ready, could take down entire platoons of armored vehicles while sending blasterfire back at their attackers.

Veils were also incredibly fun, and Bell took one out to ride through the hills and valleys around the Elphrona Outpost whenever Loden gave him a rare hour off.

Indeera lifted one of the Veils off its rack, then kicked out at the switch that opened the Vanguard's rear hatch. It flipped up, metal-scented air roaring into the compartment.

"Be careful," she said to Bell, and then Indeera leapt out, the Veil's wings flipping open as she did. He saw her catch the wind and flit away, gone in a blink.

Bell pulled the hatch closed. He got up and moved toward the front of the Vanguard, passing Porter, who said nothing. He sat in the driver's seat recently vacated by Indeera. Ember lay between them, and Loden reached down to pat the creature's head without taking his eyes from what lay ahead.

Through the windshield, the source of the smoke column was revealed as a burning, two-story home, the centerpiece of what had once been a small, neat homestead—what looked like a mining operation.

Loden slowed the Vanguard to a stop a few hundred meters from the fire. He looked at Bell. "Do you sense any survivors?"

Bell reached out with the Force. Nothing. Cold emptiness. "No," he said.

"Neither do I," his master said. "But we need to check anyway. See if we're missing someone—or if there are clues to what happened. We will find justice here, one way or the other."

Loden opened the door on his side of the driver's cabin and stepped to the ground. Bell followed suit, Ember slipping down after him. Porter appeared a moment later, his hand resting lightly on the hilt of his holstered lightsaber.

Bell realized he'd never seen the old man draw it. Not once.

Loden lifted a comlink and spoke. "We've arrived at the Blythes' claim, Indeera. Looks like the Nihil burned the place. We're going to look around. Do you see anything?"

"Nothing," Indeera's voice replied. "I'm on a rise about half a kilometer away. I can be there quickly if anything happens. I'll let you know if I see anyone coming."

"Good," Loden said, and slipped the comlink back onto his belt. "Let's go, but slowly."

He took a few steps ahead, toward the burning house. They passed a corral, where several terrified steelees rushed and stamped, their eyes huge, nostrils flaring. Porter lifted a hand.

"Easy, friends," he said, and the beasts calmed immediately, sinking to their haunches, huddling together in their pen.

"Wrecked speeder," Loden said, pointing at a smoldering pile of wreckage not far from the house. "Bodies, too. And a bunch of mining droids—taken out by blasterfire. My guess is the family tried to use the droids to defend themselves. Didn't work, or not well enough."

Porter called out from over at the steelee corral, where he was squatting, peering closely at a patch of disturbed ground by its gate.

"The Nihil took some of the family's steelees when they lost their speeder. I can see the whole story right here in the dirt. Six people, four captives."

He stood, and his face seemed cold enough to extinguish the fire. "Two of them are kids."

Bell looked more closely at the house—there was something on the door. It looked odd, like writing, or . . .

He stepped closer. The door to the Blythes' home had been marked by three jagged lines zigzagging from top to bottom. The edges were ragged, savage, as if carved by a vibroblade running low on charge.

"There's something here," he said, and took another step.

The lines looked like . . . lightning. Three jagged lightning strikes.

The heat from the fire was intense, but the symbol was fascinating, in some primal way. He moved closer, needing to see it as clearly as he could.

Ember barked, a sound of sharp, unmistakable alarm.

Bell stopped and turned to look at the charhound.

"What is it, girl?" he said, and then he noticed why Ember was trying to warn him—four trails of raised dirt, moving toward him at incredible speed.

Mole mines, Bell had time to think, and then he did two things.

First, he pushed Ember with the Force. He tried to be gentle, but the point was to shove her back out of harm's way. Whatever damage he did to her, it couldn't be as bad as getting caught in an explosion. Then Bell leapt, straight up, unholstering his lightsaber as he did.

The mole mines were designed to race toward their target just below the surface of the ground, and then shoot up into the air, exploding at roughly a meter high, sending out a ring of horizontal shrapnel along with a crown of intense heat and flame. They were deadly, and cruel—most people never even had a chance to recognize they were being attacked before they were killed.

Two of the mole mines popped out of the ground—dark-gray cylinders with grinding, gear-filled mouths at one end, the means by which they yanked themselves through the soil. As Bell reached the top of his leap, he seized both with the Force and flung them as far as he could into the air, a reflexive move he hoped would do the job.

The remaining two mines had not left the dirt, their primitive brains unsure where their target had gone now that he was no longer standing.

A huge sound, a *whoomph,* then a second a moment later, as both airborne mines exploded.

Bell felt a wash of heat—intense, but survivable.

He fell, seeing the endpoint of one of the mole mine trails just below him, and aiming himself toward it as best as he could.

Bell landed, stabbing his lightsaber into the ground, impaling one of the two remaining mines. The final explosive shot up into the air, and he reacted without thought, the Force as his guide, slicing it in half before it reached the apex of its leap.

The two halves of the mole mine, neatly bisected, fell to the ground, and Bell looked up.

He saw that Loden and Porter were dealing with their own attacks—each in their own way. Loden was using the Force to yank the mines out of the ground before they got anywhere near him, sending them flying high into the air to explode harmlessly over the rust flats. Porter was in a low crouch, his lightsaber out and lit, a bright-blue blade he held in a reverse grip.

He was simply slicing the mines in half as they popped out of the ground. One after another—the maneuver Bell had performed just once and didn't even truly understand how he'd managed, Porter was doing again and again. The expression on his face never changed. His blade flashed, and the metal fell, and he remained untouched.

Both Bell and Loden were transfixed. They were both good swordsmen, and Loden had some claim to being great. But this was like nothing they had ever seen. Not at the Jedi Temple, not from Master Yoda or Zaviel Tepp, or even old Arkoff. Bell couldn't imagine what it would be like to face Porter Engle in combat.

The display of skill was beautiful, and they could not stop watching, and so they did not see the mole mine that burrowed its way beneath the Vanguard, then shot up and destroyed itself in a paroxysm of joyful self-immolation. The explosion ripped the transport in half and shoved Bell and Loden to the ground in an impact they were barely able to cushion with the Force.

"You all right?" came Indeera's urgent voice. "Loden! Porter! Answer me! What the hell is going on down there? Everything just started blowing up!"

Loden groaned and rolled over onto his back. He pulled his comlink from his belt.

"We're okay, Indeera," he said. "Just a few surprises the Nihil left for us. Mole mines. Seems to be over now. But we lost the Vanguard."

"If they left mines, it means they thought they might be followed," Indeera said. "Means they got away."

"I think so, too," Porter said, walking up, his lightsaber back in its holster. "My guess is they have a ship parked somewhere in one of the transit zones. The magnetic fields are rough around here, so they couldn't just land by the house and take the family. They had to land, then speeder in. Then the family killed their speeder, so they stole the steelees and set out to ride back to their ship."

"How are we supposed to catch them now?" Bell asked, pushing himself up off the ground. "The V-Wheel's done."

"Still got three steelees left," Porter said. "I can saddle them up, and I can use the Force to convince them to work with us, to give us everything they've got to save their people. If we hurry, we can catch these monsters before they take the family offworld."

"Do it," Loden said, then lifted his comlink again.

"Indeera, we're going after the Nihil—there are beasts here we can ride. You head back to the outpost and get a Vector. We might need it to follow them off the planet."

"Got it," Indeera said. "May the Force be with you."

Loden replaced his comlink in his belt and walked toward the burning remains of their Vanguard. The vehicle's two halves were now separated by several meters, shards of debris scattered amid the open space between them. He stopped near what was once the driver's compartment.

"What are you doing?" Bell asked.

"The internal systems on the Vanguard are hardened against attack. In theory, you can blast a thousand holes in one and the wheels will keep turning. Now, this poor V-Wheel isn't going anywhere ever again, but maybe it can still make itself useful . . ."

He lifted his hand, and a long metal panel on the front of the wrecked Vanguard began to vibrate, lifting away slightly from the rest of the machine.

"Help me, Padawan," he said. "This thing's on tight."

Bell lifted his own hand, and the blackened metal panel tore free, flying backward and skittering across the ground. Loden bent and peered into the Vanguard's inner workings.

"Mm," he said. "Looks intact."

He gestured with his hand, closing it into a fist, and Bell heard the sound of metal bending and snapping from inside the engine compartment—little spangs as of thin clasps being stressed beyond endurance.

Loden reached into the machine and withdrew a metal tube about a meter and a half in length, with a sort of wire basket on one end containing a compact power module. Wires stretched and pulled as he lifted the assembly out, electronics connected to a flat metal panel dangling below the tube as he freed it from the Vanguard.

Bell watched as his master quickly wove the wires into a sort of strap and slung the whole thing over a shoulder. The tube's ends protruded beyond his back at shoulder and hip.

"Oof," Loden said. "Heavy."

He looked at Bell, and noticed his Padawan's questioning look.

"Just in case," Loden said, and grinned.

Porter returned from the corral, holding the reins of the three silver-sided steelees, now saddled and ready.

"Connect with your mount as best as you can. These are good beasts, but we'll be pushing them hard. You'll need to explain to them how important all of this is."

Bell wasn't sure what that meant, exactly, but he assumed he'd either figure it out or be thrown from the steelee and left behind.

He put his foot in a stirrup and pulled himself atop his mount—not as smoothly as he might have liked, but the important thing was that he was aboard. The steelee whickered, sidestepping and shaking its head. It stamped a hoof, marking its irritation at having an obviously inexperienced rider, and sparks flew from where the metal hit stone.

"Which direction, Bell?" Loden said, already in his own saddle.

Bell reached out, looking for fear, pain, anger . . . and found it. Not as far away as he might have thought, either. They had a chance.

"That way," he said, pointing.

They went.

CHAPTER TWENTY-SIX

SALVATION-CLASS REPUBLIC MEDICAL FRIGATE *PANACEA*.

"I'm uncomfortable with this, Master," Burryaga said. "We were just doing our job."

He spoke in Shyriiwook, and as far as he knew, the only person within a parsec who could understand him was his master, the Jedi Knight Nib Assek, standing at his side. But he didn't want anyone to think he was complaining, or didn't want to be there; this was a solemn occasion. They were both in their Temple attire to mark the moment. For him, that was just a sleeveless, layered tabard with an azure sash, but Nib was in the full white and gold, her long, gray hair tucked up in a bun, her boots and her lightsaber hilt both polished to a highly reflective shine.

"This isn't for us, Padawan," Nib said. "We're here to give these people some closure, some peace. They wanted to meet us. Come on. It won't be so bad."

The two Jedi were standing near the entrance to a high-ceilinged, cathedral-like chamber. The huge room took up most of the middle portion of the *Panacea,* a gigantic medical aid ship, one of Chancellor

Soh's earliest Great Works. In the years since its completion, the vessel had been sent to various conflict zones, disaster sites, and areas affected by outbreaks of contagion, tangible evidence of the Republic's commitment to its citizens, especially the weakest. Most recently, Soh had dispatched the vessel to the Hetzal system to collect and treat survivors of the *Legacy Run* disaster.

The *Panacea*'s huge central chamber, called the viewdeck, was a transparisteel dome. Under ordinary circumstances, the dome revealed whatever happened to be outside the ship, but in deference to most of the room's occupants, a different choice had been made. Instead of the dark void of space, circuitry within the dome had rendered its surface opaque, with subtle green and blue tones moving through it, and warm yellow light shining down from above. Calm sounds played softly in the distance—burbling water, wind through leaves. The ship's medical psychologists had subtly re-created the colors, sounds, and feel of a planet very like the one the settlers aboard the *Legacy Run* had hoped to make their new home. That was, if their transport ship hadn't been destroyed in an instant of terror and flame, throwing them out of hyperspace and into a disaster that was not yet over.

Burryaga was tracking the Emergences closely. Because he had been present at the start of the disaster and played a fairly central role in its resolution, he felt connected to the whole terrible situation on a deep level. He wanted to stay involved, and help however he could, until the whole slow tragedy finally came to an end. Among other efforts, he read the daily report issued by the chancellor's office on the status of the crisis. Recently, it was focused on burgeoning unrest as the effects of the ever-growing hyperspace blockade were felt. But it discussed the Emergences, too. Current count: twenty-one, and one of those last had caused the destruction of an orbital shipping facility over Dantooine that was coordinating a massive aid shipment to the increasingly beleaguered systems of the Outer Rim Territories.

Nib Assek walked out toward the center of the viewdeck, where thirty or so people were gathered, chatting among themselves in low voices. The *Panacea*'s staff had set out refreshments, and most of the people had drinks in their hands. It was like a party . . . but it wasn't.

These were the first survivors of the *Legacy Run* to be rescued, the very ones whose fear Burryaga had detected just before he, Nib, Te'Ami, and Mikkel Sutmani nearly destroyed their passenger module. The survivors had gathered here to meet their Jedi and Republic saviors—it was both an attempt at closure and a chance for them to express their gratitude in person. It all made Burryaga uncomfortable—you didn't thank Jedi for being Jedi.

Joss and Pikka Adren, the married Longbeam pilots, didn't seem to have any such qualms. They looked completely at ease, already talking to some of the *Legacy Run* passengers. Burryaga didn't have an issue with that, of course—they'd been an integral part of the rescue, and he was glad they were here, if for nothing else than to take some of the social load away from him.

Burryaga surveyed the *Legacy Run* survivors. Through the Force, he could sense the strange tension in these people—an odd mix of regret, shame, exultation, and relief. Survivor's guilt, he supposed.

Nib greeted a young couple warmly, embracing them one after the other. As she released the second woman, she flickered her fingers toward Burryaga, in a signal that he knew meant "advance into battle"—one of their private Master-apprentice signals.

Burryaga sighed and stepped forward, adjusting his sash, the polished weight of his lightsaber hilt a comfort in its holster at his side. It shone just as brightly as Nib's, though his was fashioned from the amber of a white wroshyr tree from the Wookiee homeworld of Kashyyyk, with a broad crosspiece in electrum. Not that he expected to use his weapon in this place, but "advance into battle" felt pretty accurate. His master knew how much he hated gatherings like this. None of these people would be able to understand him. Sometimes that was good, because often people assumed people who didn't speak weren't listening. Useful when he was trying to gather intelligence—but this wasn't actually a battle, and he wasn't in enemy territory. It was just a strange sort of social event, and he couldn't imagine he'd learn much no matter how many conversations he overheard.

That said, he knew Avar Kriss had asked Nib to gently inquire as to the experiences of the *Legacy Run* survivors, to see if any details about the disaster might manifest. Master Kriss and her partner, Elzar Mann, were looking for clues about what had happened. She thought some of the survivors could have repressed memories that might emerge with a bit of time and distance from the original event. But seeking that information was his master's job, not his—he couldn't see how he could ask people to tell him their stories under the circumstances. None of them could understand a word he said.

Maybe if the *Panacea* had a translator droid aboard—but no, just a few therapy droids, with their wide-eyed faces and serene way of moving, and some pill droids floating around. It was a medical ship, after all.

Burryaga walked up to three people chatting quietly among themselves—a Mimbanese couple and a human female. They seemed washed out, reduced. Even the scarlet skin and huge, blue, pupil-less eyes of the Mimbanese seemed pale. He understood that. They had all spent what must have seemed like an eternity tumbling through space in that cargo compartment, certain they were going to die at any moment. Burryaga held up a hand in greeting.

"Hello," he said in Shyriiwook, expecting and receiving a very familiar set of blank looks in response.

"Master Jedi," the Mimbanese male replied, in Basic. "It's an honor to meet you. We're all so grateful for everything you did."

"Of course, sir," Burryaga replied. "No need to thank us. All life is precious, and we are all the Republic."

More blank looks. He suppressed a sigh.

"Hey, Burry," he heard a voice say, and looked over.

It was Joss Adren with his wife, Pikka. Both had drinks in their hands and seemed utterly relaxed. He didn't know how they did it. Maybe it was the drinks. The two pilots walked up to the little group.

"You guys might not know this," Joss said, "but this is Burryaga. He's the reason you're all alive."

"Uh, dear, perhaps there's a better way to phrase that?" Pikka said. She wasn't tiny, for a human, but next to her husband, she appeared so. Joss Adren looked like a tree trunk with a head on top.

"But it's true," Joss said. "We were getting ready to blast you guys into vapor—I mean, we didn't know you were aboard. We thought you were just another fragment, and wanted to make sure you didn't smash into anything. But then Burryaga here got on the comm and started yelling up a storm—he sensed you in there, and stopped us from firing just in time."

He grinned.

"But it was close. I mean *close.* One more second, and—"

Pikka hit him in the arm, hard.

"Ouch," Joss said.

"Come on, darling," she said, leading him away.

The three survivors were staring at Burryaga. He felt hot and wanted to start panting, but knew some people saw that as a threatening move, but he was a Wookiee, and of course his teeth were sharp, and—

"Is that true, what he said?" the Mimbanese woman said. "Was it really that close a thing?"

He nodded, and their faces went very thoughtful, and Burryaga felt very embarrassed. They were treating him like he was some sort of . . .

He decided to take the opportunity to escape, and headed for the refreshment tables. He was starving—which wasn't unusual. His fur was light in color, mostly golden, with streaks here and there of the darker mahogany. He was in his prime growing years. He ate every chance he got.

The refreshment tables were full—the *Panacea*'s droids had made sure of that—but a glance told him it was all cheeses, breads, fruit, fresh-cut vegetables, spreads and dips and sweets . . . not a bit of meat. Wookiees could eat almost anything, but at that moment, Burryaga felt he needed fortification beyond what mere carrotins and pipfruit could provide.

Still, food was food. He took what was offered, filling a plate and beginning to graze. If nothing else, a full mouth might mean no one would engage him in conversation.

Munching away on a bright-green fruit he'd never had before, actually quite good, Burryaga cast his eyes across the room, this strange reception held amid a sort of illusory meadow floating in the middle of deep space. Little knots of people—Nib Assek in animated conversation with a family, Joss in the middle of a story to another group, who were smiling. Pikka holding a woman's hand, listening earnestly to whatever she said.

Burryaga spared a thought for the two *other* Jedi who had been involved with rescuing these people—Masters Te'Ami and Sutmani. How had they managed to escape this assignment? His mood souring, he ate the core of the fruit, seeds and all, crunching it into nothing and swallowing.

He turned back to the plates of food, thinking he might try one of the cheeses next, when someone caught his eye. There, off to the side, standing at the very edge of the white floor, staring out at the swirls of blue and green on the viewdeck's dome, a human boy, red-haired, speaking to no one. One of the therapy droids stood not far away, its broad, cheerful face slowly cycling through a range of warm, pleasant pastels as it spoke to the child. Burryaga wasn't always expert at estimating ages of other species, but he thought the boy was ten years along, maybe a little older.

He wasn't answering the therapy droid, despite the best efforts of the helpful little machine. Just staring, thinking whatever thoughts occupied his mind.

Burryaga set his plate down and walked in that direction, reaching out with the Force as he did. He sensed an immense sadness coming from the boy, mixed with . . . guilt. Guilt for something monstrous and immense, nothing someone of his age should ever have any reason to feel.

He walked up to the boy. The child's eyes were hollow, just pits in his face.

"I'm Burryaga," he said, touching his chest, even though he knew the boy couldn't understand. He pointed at the child. "What's your name?"

The gestures were universal enough, obvious, and the boy smiled sadly.

"Serj," he said. "Serj Ukkarian."

Burryaga gestured over toward the other survivors, a questioning expression on his face.

Serj looked over, a long, slow, sad look that did not seem to end, as if he was searching for something among the survivors he knew was not there. Someone, more like.

He shook his head.

Burryaga reached out and folded the boy up in an embrace. He couldn't understand why anyone hadn't already done this. When someone was hurting, you did what you could to heal them.

When someone was lost, you found them.

With the Force, he did what he could to soothe poor Serj. He couldn't take away his bad feelings, but he could take some of the weight, make them a bit easier for the boy to bear.

Serj held himself rigid, but slowly began to relax, setting down some part of whatever he was carrying. Burryaga felt him begin to shudder in his arms, and realized the boy was crying.

"I did it," Serj said, his voice muffled against Burryaga's chest. "It's all my fault. I was slicing into the bridge systems because Captain Casset thought she was so smart. I wanted to show her she didn't know as much as she thought—I was going to put a holovid on the bridge screens, but right when I got in, I saw . . . I saw . . . and then the ship ripped apart, and I was in compartment eight, but my mom and dad were in compartment twelve, and they still haven't found it, and I think . . . I think . . ."

He collapsed into sobs. Burryaga held him for what seemed like a long time.

The boy wasn't quite done talking, though, and Burryaga listened to everything the child had to say. Eventually, when Serj seemed to be talked out, he released him and stepped back.

"You," he said, tapping the boy gently on the forehead, "did nothing wrong."

He touched his fingertips together, then pulled them apart gently, miming an explosion.

Burryaga shook his head gently, and gave Serj a smile.

"You did nothing wrong," he said again.

The boy surely could not speak Shyriiwook –but he could understand, and he did.

Burryaga steered Serj over to Nib Assek, who was chatting with another group of survivors.

"You need to hear this, Master," he said.

She looked at him, curious.

"This is Serj Ukkarian," Burryaga said, patting the boy on the shoulder, who suddenly seemed very nervous indeed, which made sense—being the focus of Jedi attention could be intimidating. "He fears he lost his family in the disaster, and we should do everything we can for him."

Nib Assek nodded.

"Of course," she said. "Everything we can."

Her tone was respectful, but also a little curious. His master didn't understand why he had brought this child to her—after all, nearly everyone on the viewdeck had a sad story to tell.

"Serj accessed the bridge systems on the *Legacy Run* just before the accident," Burryaga said. "He was playing a prank, nothing serious, but as part of that he sliced into its screens, and when he did, he got a glimpse of whatever it was they ran into out there that caused the ship to disintegrate."

"That's fascinating," Nib said, purposely avoiding looking at Serj so as not to spook him. She could sense his state as well as Burryaga could—well, perhaps not as easily as he could, emotions were his particular strength in the Force—but the boy's tension and confusion blazed out like a burning tree at night. A youngling on his first day at the Temple would be able to sense Serj's turmoil.

After a moment's thought, she turned to the boy, going down on one knee, putting herself at his level.

"Burryaga tells me you're very brave," she said.

Serj didn't answer.

"He also tells me you saw something when you sliced into the *Legacy Run*'s systems, just before the disaster began. We're trying to do everything we can to stop the Emergences, and prevent something like this from ever happening again. I know it has to be a painful memory, but can you tell me what you saw, Serj? Can you explain it to me?"

Serj looked at the Jedi, his eyes gone hollow and distant again.

"Lightning," he said. "It looked like three strikes of lightning."

CHAPTER TWENTY-SEVEN

ELPHRONA.

"We're going to be all right," Erika said, looking her children in the eye as she said it—first little Bee, then Ronn.

Ronn was older, just a few years from being ready to go off on his own, but at that moment they both just looked like babies, terrified and desperate for reassurance from their parents.

The Nihil with them in the cart snorted.

"Yeah," she said, "just fine."

She wore a mask, like the others, but Erika knew she was Trandoshan from the look of her arms—long in comparison to the torso, gray pebbled skin gleaming in the sun, ending in hooked white claws. A single line of jagged blue paint bisected her mask from forehead to chin. She held a rifle, and had a holstered blaster and the galaxy only knew what other weapons.

Erika and her family weren't going to overpower this woman, even if all four of them managed to free themselves from the plasticuffs pinning their arms behind their backs. They were two miners and their kids, and Ottoh was barely conscious; he'd taken a nasty punch to the head when the Nihil finally pulled them out of their house.

No, they weren't going to be all right.

But you didn't say that to your kids.

"Just stay brave," Erika said.

They were racing along a dirt track that curved between two sets of hills. Iron on the left, magnetite on the right, the field generated by the two part of the reason ships couldn't fly through this part of Elphrona, and the reason they weren't already in the Nihil's starship headed off-world. With their speeder gone, the Nihil had decided to add livestock rustling to their list of crimes and stolen five of the Blythes' herd of steelees to make their getaway.

The kidnappers had harnessed two of the creatures to pull the repulsorcart in which the family was currently riding. Another three kept pace alongside, one Nihil per mount. They were inexpert riders, Erika noted with contempt, slumping in the saddles, holding their weight all wrong. They kept digging in their heels and slapping the creatures' haunches in an effort to coax out more speed, not realizing that if they would just sit on them properly, the steelees would move twice as fast.

Not that Erika intended to tell them that. The slower their party moved, the better. Because someone was coming after them, and the longer it took the Nihil to reach their ship, the better the odds the people behind them could catch up.

Ronn had noticed it first. He was sitting in the cart facing away from the direction they were moving, which meant he had a view of everything behind them.

Her son had gently nudged her leg with his boot. Three short taps—obviously a signal. She looked at him, mouthed a word: *What?*

He didn't move, just cast his eyes to one side, looking past her, then back to her. Then back to looking past her, toward the path they had traveled, then back to her.

Ronn nuzzled up to Bee and said, loudly, "Don't cry, Bee, this dumb lizard's not going to hurt you," which had earned him a kick from their Trandoshan guard that he bore in silence, her brave, brave son. It had also earned Erika a moment to turn her head and look behind them, where she saw what Ronn had seen—sparks, in the distance.

Not close, but not so far, either. She had looked several times since, taking any opportunity for a quick glance, and their pursuers were getting closer, moment by moment.

The sparks were identical to those kicked up by their own mounts every time a steelee's hoof struck against a metallic rock—wild steelee herds running at night were one of the natural wonders of Elphrona. They made a loud noise, too—a sharp, quick *tchk*—which helped to disguise what had to be similar sounds emanating from the riders coming up behind them.

Three, she thought. She couldn't quite make out any details, but it seemed like three, riding side by side.

No one seemed to have noticed besides the two of them. Their Trandoshan guard was keeping her eyes on her captives. And of course, the Nihil weren't looking anywhere but dead ahead. They were hanging on for dear life, trying to stay in their saddles.

She gave Ronn a questioning look, and he responded with as much of a shrug as he could using just his eyes. He didn't know who was on their trail, either—and Erika knew he hadn't been able to raise help from Ogden's Hope.

Maybe the settlement's security squad had found their spines and sent a team out to help—but they'd be in a speeder, not as mounted riders.

It didn't make any sense—but it was a little bit of hope, and hope was in short supply at the moment.

She risked another glance back, just to see if they were getting closer, and this time her luck ran out. The guard saw her doing it and looked, too. She saw their pursuers immediately—impossible to miss, now. The sparks were shooting up to either side like the people chasing them were riding along a road of flame.

The Nihil stood in the cart and yelled out to the rest of her crew.

"Trouble! We got people comin' up behind, fast! Looks like three of—"

And then Ottoh, who as it turned out was not unconscious but merely pretending to be, waiting for a moment like this, holding his own hope in reserve, clicked his tongue sharply against the roof of his mouth three times. It was a loud sound, and all five of the steelees, well trained and well loved by her husband, knew the command and obeyed immediately.

They stopped, their duralloy hooves locking into the ground with the organomagnetic field that allowed them to climb even the steepest of Elphrona's mountains—here, the maneuver simply removed all velocity cold, in one quick, snapping movement.

Velocity, but not momentum, not inertia. Three of the Nihil were thrown from their saddles, whipping forward at enormous speed. Their guard, too, who was in the worst possible position when the steelees stopped—standing, unbalanced, in a fast-moving repulsorcart. She shot up and out, as if fired from her own rifle.

A moment later, a thick, hard sound, between a snap and a thud, the sound of something very hard breaking when it hit something even harder.

Erika didn't see it happen, because she, along with the rest of her family, was pressed together against the front edge of the repulsorcart, a tangle of limbs and pressure and future bruises. Despite that, she was fairly sure she now knew what it sounded like when a Trandoshan's skull split open against hard ironstone.

And good bloody riddance.

"Is everyone all right?" Erika said.

"I'm okay," Bee said. Tough little kid.

"Hurt my hand, but it's nothing too bad," Ronn said.

"I'm sorry I couldn't warn you," Ottoh said, pulling himself out of the tangle. "It wouldn't have worked if it didn't surprise them. "Now try to do what I do."

He rolled himself onto his back, then pulled his legs up close to his chest and extended his arms as far as they would go, trying to get his cuffed wrist out and over his feet, so at least he'd be able to use his hands again.

Erika got ready to repeat the maneuver herself. If they could use their hands, maybe they could find a way to get free, or at least to run.

The butt of a rifle slammed down on Ottoh's head, and he slumped. His eyes went blank and dazed. He was alive, but Erika didn't know how much of him was left just then. Her husband wouldn't be cooking up any more surprises, of that much she was sure.

The Nihil weren't gone. They had fallen, some had fallen hard, but they were still there, and they still had guns, and now they were very angry. The one who hit her husband lifted his rifle for another crack, and she knew this one would most likely crack his skull for good if the first blow hadn't.

Erika lunged forward, covering his body with hers, trying to intercept the blow.

"No!" she cried.

The rifle hit her in the side, and she curled up against the pain, which was immediate and immense. But better her than Ottoh.

"Move or you die, too," the Nihil growled, its voice low and strange.

Someone else outside the cart grabbed the attacker and pulled him back. Erika was struggling to breathe, but she could still hear.

"Don't kill any of them."

"Asaria's dead. She's *dead*."

Asaria, Erika thought, *what a lovely name.*

"These stupid *miners* killed *half* of us already, Dent."

"Damn right," she heard Ronn whisper.

"It's time for some *payback*."

"I said *no.* Every one we kill, that's twenty-five percent of our take. I'm not worried about the people we lost—it doubles our share. But we lost a *speeder,* too, and that means we're in the red on this. We need every credit we can get. Don't kill *any* of them. You're just a Strike. I'm the Cloud. You do what I say."

A long moment of silence, and Erika knew that the lives of her husband and maybe the rest of her family were dependent on how much respect this Strike had for his Cloud, whatever that meant.

"Fine," the first Nihil spat, and she heard him walking away.

Erika exhaled slowly.

"Ottoh," she said.

No answer. She decided she would just believe he was still alive. Hope was a choice—and not unwarranted, either. In the distance, she could hear a sound. Hoofbeats. Their pursuers were catching up.

"We need to kill whoever's coming after us," the Nihil's leader said to the rest of her crew—a Cloud, she had called herself. "Egga, Rel, get up in the hills, on either side. Find spots where you have a good view of the canyon. Mack, Buggo, and I will keep going for the ship. We'll take the family with us, so they'll have to come this way. Take them out."

Erika listened as these arrangements were put into play, and with a jerk, the cart began moving again, rapidly picking up speed.

But now there was no guard, and she was able to complete the maneuver her husband had shown her, getting her hands in front of her as opposed to stuck behind her back. First, she felt Ottoh's pulse—steady and strong. He was unconscious, but maybe that was all. Her husband attended to, Erika turned to her children. She touched Bee's face and kissed her, and then took Ronn's hands in hers.

"You're both being so strong, so brave. We're so proud of you."

"Is Dada all right?" Bee asked.

"He will be. Don't worry about your father. Just stay calm, and be ready to do whatever I ask you to do, when the time comes. For now, try to get your hands out in front of you, like I did. You're a little wriggly worm. You can do it, I know you can. You, too, Ronn."

She watched as both her children contorted themselves as she had requested.

Now what? she thought.

Erika had an unconscious husband and two children to save somehow, and—

She remembered their pursuers. Help, maybe, and on its way.

She reached up to grasp the edge of the cart and pulled herself up, looking back. Surely they had to be close—and they were. The delay from Ottoh's trick with the steelees had done its job. They couldn't be more than five hundred meters back.

She could see them now—three figures, riding well, riding fast—these were experienced wranglers, nothing like their captors.

Erika wanted to yell out, to tell them they were riding into a trap, but she didn't think they could hear her, and didn't want to do anything that would cause the Nihil to decide a seventy-five percent profit margin would be fine after all.

Then something happened.

Three lines of light blossomed from the riders coming up fast behind them: one gold, one blue, one green, and Erika realized what was happening, who these people were.

"By the light," she breathed. "They're Jedi."

CHAPTER TWENTY-EIGHT

HYPERSPACE. THE *NEW ELITE.*

"You guys ready to ride the storm?" Kassav shouted.

He held up a bulb of smash, bright blue and soft, with a slim nozzle at one end, designed to make the drug accessible to just about every type of gas exchange anatomy in the galaxy. Whether you had a nose, a trunk, stomata, a proboscis, or just some weird hole in your face, you could use a smashbulb. Which was good, because his team had all those options and more.

The crew of the *New Elite* lifted their own bulbs, anticipatory grins on every face. Music vibrated every surface; big, booming wreckpunk, where every instrument the bands used was made from the re-forged wreckage of crashed starships.

Kassav took a good, long puff, and *boom,* his mind lit up. Everything was sharper, brighter. He could do this. He could. He could *do this.* He could do it all.

He watched as his crew did the same—a few ran the smash straight into the gas filters of their masks, a neat trick that intensified the effects. Saw the energy ripple through them, that charge, that rush, that sugar candy hit that made everything glow and buzz and hiss. He dropped his empty bulb on the deck and grinned.

"Feels *good,* don't it?" he shouted, spitting the words. "Feels like the *Nihil,* right?"

His people roared. Some were twitching in time to the music. Some were just twitching.

"Okay—you all enjoy—give it a minute, but then take the rounder. We need to be sharp for this. Let's ride the storm, not let the storm ride us, yeah?"

By way of example—you needed to provide an example from time to time as a leader—he reached into his tunic and pulled out a small orange-and-yellow pill. He held it up, showing it to his crew, then popped it into his mouth and bit down. Almost immediately, the smash high took on a new, swirling quality, like waves in a storm-tossed sea. Huge, powerful, you needed to watch yourself—but these waves . . . you could surf.

It reminded him of hyperspace, a little. Not the normal kind, but the weird roads of Marchion Ro's Paths. Kassav turned to look out the bridge's viewport, watching as the hyperlane rolled on past. Tunnels built from endless ribbons of light, many colors, washing and tossing and weaving into one another. There was some meaning there, but he wasn't smart enough to figure it out.

He had no idea where the Paths came from. Marchion Ro was cagey about it, never giving too many details, and his father had been the same way. Kassav sometimes wanted to find out the secret at blasterpoint or, even better, at the edge of a blade, but the Ros were not stupid people. Or at least, Asgar hadn't been. He knew what he had with the Paths, and knew people would want it. And while Marchion Ro wasn't his father, not even close, he'd inherited all the safeguards Asgar set up. The *Gaze Electric,* those gnarly guard droids he used . . . it was hard to get close to Marchion. He'd made it clear that the Paths themselves had their own safeguards, too. If he died, so would they. That hadn't happened when Asgar died, but then again,

Marchion didn't have a son to whom he could pass the family business.

But it wasn't just starships and murder droids protecting Marchion Ro. It was also the structure his father had insisted the Nihil adopt when he'd brought them the Paths so many years ago. Before that, the group was much smaller, barely a gang, really. It kept its operations to a tiny corner of the Rim, close to Thull's Shroud by Belsavis, pulling off whatever little jobs it could. Asgar Ro had shown up one day and offered them the Paths, in exchange for a third of the take of any operations that used them. But that wasn't all—he wanted a vote, too.

Any jobs that used the Paths required a full vote of the three Tempest Runners, plus the Eye, and any tie vote went the Eye's way. It didn't seem like such a big deal at the time, but it meant that he, Pan Eyta, and Lourna Dee were always against one another in a way, always courting the Eye's favor to get Paths. In theory, they could all team up to try to go after Marchion, but there was too much bad blood. Most of the time, Kassav could barely be in the same room with Lourna Dee and Pan Eyta, much less contemplate sharing the throne with them.

Marchion was all alone, and should be completely vulnerable . . . but somehow, he wasn't. He was protected, by the system his much smarter father had set up. It was annoying . . . but it worked.

Hell, Kassav had copied a lot of Asgar's ideas for his own Tempest.

Kassav had three Storms up at the top of his Tempest's hierarchy: Gravhan, Dellex, and Wet Bub. They all wanted to be him, but they would never work together to get rid of him, because then none of them would be the Tempest Runner—they'd still just be three Storms sharing power. Yep. It was a good little system.

All three of those Storms were on the bridge of the *New Elite,* and they'd all blown smash right when he did. He didn't know if they'd all taken the rounder, or if the Clouds and Strikes in their crews had, either . . . but that was all right. A little edge wasn't such a bad thing. The Nihil were all about edge. It wouldn't be a problem, as long as everyone did what they were told.

And everyone would. That was the other thing that made the Nihil such a great system, even if this particular truth was hidden down deep, making it hard to see unless you were near the top of the organization. On the surface, the Nihil were all about freedom, about breaking away from the galaxy's systems of control. Forget the Republic, forget the Hutts, forget anything but doing what you wanted when you wanted. That was the sales pitch, how they got people to join up. Ride the storm, baby, ride that storm.

But once you were a Nihil, you still had a boot on your chest, even if you didn't always feel it because of all of the burn parties and smash and the thrill of taking what you wanted, when you wanted. You still had to do exactly what your bosses above you said, and the bosses above them. If you didn't, at best you didn't get your share of the Rule of Three. At worst, you got a vibroblade in your neck, or you got thrown out of the Great Hall the hard way. Everyone had to stay in line, everyone paid their price. Well, everyone but Marchion Ro and the Tempest Runners—him, Lourna Dee, and that flashy brute Pan Eyta, did he even realize how stupid he looked, a Dowutin trying to be fashionable? Anyway.

The Nihil was just another form of control, an engine designed to roll credits up to the people at the top of the organization.

Yeah, good little system.

Kassav surveyed his crew, the upper echelons of his Tempest. Gravhan, Wet Bub, and there was Dellex right up front, her one organic eye gleaming from the smash—oh yeah, she definitely hadn't taken that rounder—and their crews arranged behind them.

"Here's what we're gonna do," Kassav said. "We're gonna string these jerks along, make them pay us so much money there won't be more than two credits left in the whole blasted system. We're gonna take 'em for everything they've got, and they'll be *happy we did.*"

Everyone liked that—lots of savage grins and appreciative words from the crew.

"We're about to drop out of lightspeed in this system called Eriadu.

They're hurting pretty bad from the Republic's hyperspace blockade—not enough food to go around down there. Word is the people are ready to overthrow the governors. So those guys are already in trouble, and they ain't gonna want any more. Perfect for us.

"Everything will start to happen fast once we show up—we gotta cut this close because of the way the Emergences are lined up. Storms, you all got your crews briefed? Everyone knows their job?"

"Dunno about these other two jokers, Kassav, but my line knows their business good," Gravhan said, fingering a tusk. He was a Chevin, mostly just one huge head to look at him, with wrinkled gray skin and wisps of long blond hair on his scalp. He looked slow and ponderous, and maybe he was, but Kassav had once seen him rip a security guard in half with his bare hands. They were robbing a bank in a tiny settlement on some backwater ice planet. Gravhan had just grabbed the guy, and . . . well, if Kassav's Tempest had a motto, it would be something like *Strength Wins,* and Gravhan was the perfect example of that. Just ask that security guard.

"My people are ready, too, boss," Dellex said. "I've been drilling them ever since you laid out the plan."

"I bet," Gravhan said, and a few of his Strikes chuckled, people too dumb to know that you didn't want Dellex on your bad side.

Kassav had known the woman for a long time, even had a little thing with her a while back. He knew she thought she was ugly as sin, and that's why she kept spending all her money on fancy mechanical upgrades. She was making herself beautiful, one shiny new body part at a time. But all that metal didn't do her personality any favors. She was getting prettier, sure, but colder, too. Kassav had a feeling those chuckle-happy Strikes in Gravhan's crew might find themselves with their skulls crushed some night soon.

Oh well. Not his problem. There were always more Strikes.

"Affirmative," said Wet Bub, giving a thumbs-up from where he sat at the ship's primary computer console.

Sometimes people figured Wet Bub was called that because he was a

Gungan . . . but that wasn't the only reason. Used to be, when he'd go on raids, he'd end up covered in blood, head-to-toe. Like, soaked. Happened enough times that people got to calling him that, and he never killed anyone who said it, so he must have liked it. Hard to tell what Wet Bub did or didn't like, sometimes.

Bub was also a slicer, though. A damn good one—he'd been breaking into computer systems ever since he was a kid, and now he used that skill to do all sorts of ugly things in his personal time. Intrusive, cruel things.

Also not Kassav's problem.

"Let's do this," he said.

The *New Elite* fell out of hyperspace into the Eriadu system. Not much starship traffic on the scopes—not surprising. The planet hadn't gotten much in the way of fuel shipments recently, not with the blockade on. The lack of traffic also meant the system's monitoring satellites had probably already spotted them. That was fine—they weren't here to hide, and if the Eriaduans wanted to send out a few patrol ships to take a poke at them . . . well, that was where Dellex and Gravhan came in. Their gun crews were *tight.*

"Wet Bub . . . go," Kassav said, pointing at his lieutenant.

Bub set to work, accessing the system's communications network, pushing on through whatever access codes and security measures were in place, going higher and higher, until he found what he was looking for.

He tapped a few last buttons, then gave another thumbs-up.

"You're in, bossman," he said.

A voice came over the bridge's speaker system, raspy and sibilant and cold. The voice of someone powerful, who wasn't used to things happening that she hadn't ordered.

"Who is this? This is a restricted comm network," said Mural Veen, current planetary governor of Eriadu. "And what the hell is that . . . music?"

Oops, Kassav thought.

He tapped a control, and the wreckpunk volume dropped to a whisper.

"Hi there, Governor," Kassav said. "I'm your new best friend."

Silence from the other end of the line. She was waiting to see what he wanted.

"You might have seen a ship drop out of hyperspace out near the edge of the system. That's me, and all you need to know about us is that I can get through Chancellor Soh's hyperspace blockade when no other ship can do it. So, that's the first thing you should keep in mind as this little chat moves along. I can do things no one else can."

"Let me guess," the governor said. "You sneaked through the blockade, and now you're going to offer to sell us food at some ridiculous rate? I don't respond well to extortion."

"That remains to be seen, ma'am," Kassav said, putting an emphasis on the last word, getting a little chuckle out of the Nihil on the bridge, all listening like this was the best holoplay they'd ever seen.

"But I'll tell you one thing," he went on, "I am offended that you think we're just ordinary smugglers. We're much more than that."

"Then who the hell are you?" she said.

"I told you. I'm your new best friend. Your savior, in fact."

A silence.

"I might not know who you are, but I know where," Mural said. "My teams just pinpointed your location. I'm ending this call and sending out security cruisers to bring you into custody. I don't know your game, but you can explain it from inside a cell on Eriadu. If you resist, we'll blow you into atoms."

"You sure you want to do that?" Kassav said, teasing it out.

"Absolutely. Goodbye. I don't have time for this."

"Actually," he said, "I agree. Three Emergences are headed for your system. They'll be here soon. We know where they'll happen, and when. We can stop them for you, if you pay up."

"What are you talking about? No one can predict the Emergences."

"And no one can fly in hyperspace in the Outer Rim, either."

"I've heard enough. We're sending the cruisers. You can tell my interrogators what you know."

"If we see your ships heading our way, we'll leave, and you'll be the reason billions of your people die."

Kassav grinned. The rounded-off smash high was getting better by the second. He felt like he was flying, pushed along by the crest of the drug's wave, arms extended, unstoppable. He knew all along this was a good plan. He'd gone over the list of Emergences that Marchion Ro had given the Tempest Runners and seen this opportunity right away. It was an opportunity so good, in fact, that he had forgotten to mention to Marchion or the other Runners that he was intending to take advantage of it. Oops. What a shame. No Rule of Three was gonna carve up this score, no way.

Kassav realized he hadn't yet told this stuffy governor woman what he was asking for. He shook his head. He really needed to stay focused.

"Governor, it's easy. If you give me fifty million credits, no one has to die. I can stop the Emergences, and you'll save your people's lives. I can make it real simple for you, too . . ."

He lifted a finger, and Wet Bub sent over the encrypted banking information that would allow Governor Veen to untraceably deposit the cash directly into a darknet account controlled by Kassav. Not a Nihil account—this was one of Kassav's own.

"You're insane," the governor said.

"You're skeptical. I get that. Here. Let me help you out."

Kassav lifted a second finger, and Wet Bub sent over another short string of information.

"You just received the coordinates for the first Emergence. Not too far from my ship, as a matter of fact. We picked this spot for a reason. Check it out."

Kassav held up a third finger, and chopped his arm downward toward Gravhan, who nodded and turned to his gun crew at their weapons stations.

"Any moment now . . . any moment . . ." Kassav said.

A piece of the doomed *Legacy Run* dropped out of hyperspace about thirty light-seconds from the *New Elite,* exactly where Kassav had predicted it would. Thank you, Marchion Ro and the Paths and whatever mastery of hyperspace allowed him to know the routes all the fragments would take—it was about to earn Kassav millions of credits.

He glanced at the targeting holos projected on the vidwall on the bridge, which had already locked onto the fragment. It looked like a compartment, intact. He'd heard that some of these things had people on board, settlers who had been aboard the ship before it disintegrated.

Oh well. Not his problem, either.

"Fire," Kassav said.

Gravhan's team was very good. A spread of laserfire and torpedoes shot out from the *New Elite*'s weapons array, headed straight for the fragment. They all impacted at once, hard, and the compartment vaporized, vanishing from the battle array on the vidwall. Perfect shot. Of course, they'd known what they were aiming at ahead of time, and had planned this all out . . . but still, it had to look impressive.

"There," Kassav said, turning back to look out the front viewport where, somewhere sunward, Governor Mural Veen was probably feeling a bit less sure of herself. "Now you see that I'm on the up-and-up. Two more Emergences coming. Next one's in ninety seconds. You have the account information. Pay up, or face the consequences."

"You bastard," Governor Veen said.

"Could be," Kassav said. "Never knew my mom *or* my dad, though. Don't think it matters. What matters are the choices you make in your life, not where you come from. Like the choice you need to make right now, Governor."

The seconds ticked by. Kassav glanced over at Wet Bub, who shook his head. No transfer yet. A bit disgusted, Kassav gave him a go-ahead gesture.

Another set of coordinates was sent, with twenty seconds to spare before the Emergence. The *New Elite* wasn't close enough to this one to get there in time. This time, the Emergence was going to happen, and nothing was going to stop it. But still . . . it could serve a purpose.

"You just got the coordinates for the second Emergence," Kassav said. "You could have stopped what happens next, Governor. Remember that."

Another piece of the *Legacy Run* flashed back into realspace, moving too fast for anyone to react.

Eriadu had one primary export—lommite, a mineral used in creating transparisteel, the alloy that formed the main component for starship viewscreens and portholes. When Chancellor Soh put her blockade in place, the cargo transports heading offsystem with full loads of lommite were stuck with nowhere to go. Those transports had clustered together in an open space not far from the nearest spot where it was safe to enter hyperspace, waiting for the moment the lanes reopened.

The fragment ripped through one of them, causing it to detonate immediately—and the shock waves took out four other vessels before they got their shields up.

"Ouch," Kassav said. "That was a few hundred crewmembers, easy . . . not to mention all that lommite. What'll that cost your system, Governor? Big money, I bet. Now you're in a worse spot than you were before. And remember, one more Emergence on the way. You've got about four minutes. And this time it won't be hundreds dying. It'll be billions. Even you, probably. You've got the account information. Don't wait too long."

"This is evil," the governor said. "You realize that, don't you?"

Kassav turned to face his Tempest and rolled his eyes—more laughter.

"You're laughing?" came the incredulous words over the comm. "You're *laughing*?"

"Yeah, Governor. It's funny, that's all. It's not evil. It's *business.*"

"You're sending these Emergences somehow, aren't you? You're doing this. It's the only way it's possible."

"Does it matter? Time's wasting, Governor. Two minutes."

Kassav was getting a little nervous, truth be told. They needed to move, fast, to get in the path of the third Emergence, otherwise they wouldn't be able to stop it—and he figured it was important that they *did* stop it, otherwise, well, this scam might not work so well next time, would it? He wasn't even sure he'd go back to the Nihil at all after this, not with fifty million credits in his account and an entire Tempest loyal to him, and a list of all the other Emergences he could exploit.

Yep, Marchion Ro was absolutely not his father, just handing out valuable information like that. The man had this weird sense of loyalty to the Nihil. He thought they were something more than they were. The Nihil were a gang of criminals, and if there was one thing Kassav knew about criminals, it was this: You couldn't trust them.

He was a perfect example.

Ninety seconds.

"Governor, you're running out of time."

"You're monsters."

"So are you, if you don't save your people."

"Fine," Governor Veen spat. "The funds are being transferred now."

He looked at Wet Bub, who gave him another thumbs-up. Kassav pointed at Dellex, who fired up the engines for the burn that would put them in the path of the third Emergence just as it appeared.

Gravhan's gun crew got to work again, preparing the salvo that would destroy the final fragment and earn them their pay.

"You should know," Governor Veen's voice came over the speaker, "I've been transmitting our conversation to Senator Noor, who will spread it along the entire Outer Rim. We've also sent along a scan of your ship, even matched its silhouette in the databases—the *New Elite,* owned by Kassav Milliko—that's you, I presume. You got your payday, Mr. Milliko . . . but I think your troubles are just beginning."

"Troubles? What troubles? We're saving lives. We're the *heroes,* Governor."

Kassav spoke for the benefit of the Nihil around him listening to every word, but his stomach felt a little . . . Maybe he hadn't thought this through all the way. Oh well. Nothing to be done about it now.

"Go," he said, pointing at Dellex.

She nodded, and the ship jumped, but the timing was tight. So tight that Gravhan's crew would have to fire the very second the burn ended. That was okay, though. They had time.

But they didn't. The third Emergence occurred just as expected, and yes, the *Legacy Run* fragment was headed straight for Eriadu's inhabited moon, estimated population one point two billion. Gravhan's team fired their weapons exactly as scheduled, right on time.

Except the target wasn't there. The *New Elite* had miscalculated its microburn, and had hugely overshot the spot they were aiming for. They were nowhere near the Emergence, and the laser blasts and torpedoes flashed out, hitting nothing.

Kassav realized immediately. He shot a glance at Dellex. She knew it, too. She was looking right at him.

"Boss, I must have . . . I must have screwed up the nav calculation. I don't know how it happened."

Kassav had his suspicions. Her one organic eye was still glinting, awash in the smash, and he knew for sure she hadn't taken that rounder. It didn't take much to mess up a nav calculation, and Dellex was normally a champion at it because of her mechanical components, but this time . . . this time . . .

The *Legacy Run* fragment smashed into the moon. Everyone on the bridge saw it happen. It was projected up on the vidwall, clear as day. Big debris cloud mushrooming out from the surface, shock waves starting to roll across the little world, lots of fire and those dark clouds you got with the really huge explosions. Like a storm, kind of.

A voice came over the comm, echoing out across the now utterly silent Nihil. No chuckles from them now. Just silence.

"You will pay for this," said Governor Mural Veen, her voice maybe the coldest thing Kassav had ever heard. "This I vow: *vengeance.* The people of Eriadu are hunters. You and all the monsters with you have now become our pr—"

Kassav tapped a console, and the voice went silent.

He looked at his Tempest and knew what they were thinking.

One point two billion people.

Oh well.

Not his problem.

"Get us out of here," he said.

"Where?" said Dellex, her voice uncharacteristically subdued.

Kassav thought. These people on Eriadu knew his name. Knew his ship. He had their money, but he didn't like the sound of what that governor was saying. She didn't seem like the type to let things go. He'd need protection. Needed to be part of something bigger. Needed . . .

"Back," he said, resigned. "Back to the Nihil."

CHAPTER TWENTY-NINE

HETZAL SYSTEM. THE ROOTED MOON.

Keven Tarr looked out across the plateau. The sight was breathtaking.

Fifty-seven thousand, eight hundred and seventeen navidroids, linked together into one massive array. All different models, all different sizes—from the latest compact, self-powered units equipped with legs or other mobility attachments allowing them to move from ship to ship, to processor units ripped from the vessels in which they had been originally installed. The computing power varied greatly from droid to droid, but all in all, it was an impressive arrangement.

If just getting the droids had been a challenge (aided by the heroic efforts of Secretary Lorillia, it had to be said—he had requisitioned navidroids from all over the galaxy), then assembling them into the array was nearly as hard. The idea was to set up a number of processors running in parallel, so various sections could address different parts of the problem at the same time. Keven had designed the system from top to bottom, but linking it all up by himself would have taken months, time they didn't have. Beyond conceptualizing the thing in the first place and getting the droid components, he'd also needed to assemble a team of engineers trained in positronic architecture and network structuring, a lot of them.

Hetzal had a few people with the necessary skills, but nowhere near enough. The San Tekkas had sent a dozen of their navulators, people who wore strange implants that wrapped around their shaven heads, allowing them to run calculations with droidlike precision that also retained the conceptual leaps organic minds could achieve. Incredibly useful, but still not enough to get the array built in any reasonable amount of time. Once again, pulling together the required resources had been about using connections available through Senator Noor, Secretary Lorillia, and their own various allies, and they had come through and then some. Keven had systems engineers on-site from as far away as Byss and Kuat. *We are all the Republic* had never seemed more true.

Keven had no idea how much it cost in influence and actual capital to get this thing built, and he didn't really care, either.

He just wanted to turn it on.

The system had three primary nodes, each with its own subnodes. All three main elements were assigned a different part of the overall calculation. The first was designed to create a computer simulation of the original disaster using all available data. The second modeled all the known Emergences thus far, and the third, by far the biggest and most complex, ran a particular algorithm designed to figure out where the next Emergences would happen.

That third node was the tricky one. The other two were just describing things that had already happened. The third one had to predict the future.

And if I can do that, Keven thought, *I'm basically a Jedi.*

But of course he wasn't. A few actual Jedi were standing just a little distance away—the pair he'd met a few times before, who had helped with the San Tekkas. Avar Kriss and Elzar Mann. They seemed like nice people, but honestly, he was nothing like them. Avar was all quiet confidence and utter competence, and Elzar looked like someone out of a holodrama, with his olive skin and dark, wavy hair—just a beautiful man.

Keven Tarr was probably closer to a droid, or one of the navulators (though he didn't have to wear those weird implants, thankfully). He liked systems, and rules, and the systems and rules behind those rules and systems. That's what everything was, really. Systems and rules.

That statement was true of people, and it was true of droids, and it was true of the entire galaxy and everything in it. The deeper the systems you learned to access, or the rules you understood, the greater the change you could create. That was what had helped him rise so quickly on Hetzal, all the way to a prime posting in the Ministry of Technology before he was twenty-five. When he was still a kid, he figured out that four different crops were interacting in a complex sort of relationship, and that a routinely exterminated pest wasn't a pest at all but in fact a symbiotic partner to the crops. If the plants were just allowed to occupy the same fields at the same time rather than being kept separate, and the so-called vermin were allowed to live, not only would overall yields be higher but the seeds and grain the crops produced would be of better quality. Beyond even that, a sort of hybrid fruit would emerge twice a year that couldn't happen without the contributions of all four plants.

That little project had gotten him all he really wanted: access to bigger and better systems he could spend his time trying to understand. The Hetzalian authorities gave him increasingly important assignments, from developing crop rotation algorithms to modeling weather, all of which he found deeply engaging and rewarding. The only thing he found frustrating was how slow it could seem. He couldn't just dig into anything he wanted, even with his high-level role in the system's Ministry of Technology—there were still many things he could not access without permission.

That was his choice, though. Keven knew he could be one hell of a slicer, breaking into computer cores of all types, but he didn't hold with that. He believed in law, and he believed in the Republic. He had decided long ago that the only way he would ever work with the really significant systems was if he could earn those privileges through his skill and dedication.

Well, now that moment seemed to have arrived. It didn't get much bigger than what he was about to try to do.

He, Keven Tarr, was going to slice hyperspace.

A soft, cool breeze touched his face, drifting across the plateau overlooking the array. A good sign.

Keven glanced at the other observers standing not far away, chatting quietly among themselves. If he'd had his preference, the first test of his machine would have happened in private in case something went wrong, but it was all too important, time was too short, and too much had been invested in creating the array. Many people, powerful people, had chosen to back Keven's idea, and they all wanted to be present to see whether that idea was worth a damn.

Senator Noor and his aide, Jeni Wataro. Secretary Lorillia. Minister Ecka. The two Jedi, of course, who were chatting with Marlowe and Vellis San Tekka, who had, honestly, been incredibly helpful. Beyond supplying the twelve navulators, they had also provided hyperspace modeling tools far beyond anything Keven would have been able to access on his own. He'd signed all sorts of agreements with their company's legal department saying that he'd never use the tech for anything else, but that was no problem. Actually, he thought he might see if the San Tekkas wanted to work with him after this was all over. Hetzal was his homeworld, but he was ready to move on. The planet was a system, too, and he'd sliced it about as well as he could. Onward, to bigger and deeper.

Of course, if he couldn't make the array work, none of those exciting possibilities would happen. If you said you would *try* to do something, people heard that as you *would* do something, and if you didn't achieve the goal then they thought you had failed. And blamed you for trying at all. It wasn't exactly fair, especially because predicting the future with a massive computer array made from wired-up droid brains was basically impossible. But that was how the system called society worked, and Keven Tarr would never be powerful enough to change that set of rules.

His situation was binary. Succeed or fail. He'd done everything he could to make sure it was the former, and that was all.

He lifted a comlink and spoke. "You guys got that last batch of droids linked up?"

A crackle—this many droids in one spot was causing interference. You could taste it in the air, like touching your tongue to new metal.

"One more left," came the response from Chief Innamin of the Republic Defense Coalition—Petty Officer Innamin until recently, promoted based on his heroic efforts during the *Legacy Run* disaster. He and his shipmate, Peeples, then an ensign now a lieutenant, had decided to stay in-system after the disaster to help however they could, as a way of honoring the sacrifice of their captain, Bright, who had died during a rescue attempt on a solar array.

Keven liked that the two officers were contributing their skills—thought it was noble and good. More important, Innamin had the necessary engineering training to be particularly useful here on the Rooted Moon, and to supervise Peeples, even though the lieutenant was technically his superior officer. Peeples didn't seem to mind, and had even offered to swap ranks with Innamin. The chief declined, after letting out a heavy sigh. In any case, the duo was currently completing the wiring for the subnode tasked to model the fifth Emergence.

Privately, in a way he would never, ever voice, Keven wished there had been a few more Emergences. Every single one was a data point, and so far there had been thirty-three. Not bad—a pretty good set—but the more information his machine had to draw on, the better. He wouldn't get a second chance at this, for many reasons.

Mostly for one reason, in fact, something he had purposely decided not to tell the kind people who had helped him gather all these rare and valuable machines for his array.

Keven sent a furtive glance at Jeffo Lorillia, the Republic's transportation secretary, not far away on the plateau and deep in conversation with Senator Izzet Noor, his long face uncharacteristically animated. Lorillia had pulled in incredible favors to bring so many navidroids together, and on such short notice. The Outer Rim was still in its hyperspace quarantine, much to Senator Noor's intense frustration, but Secretary Lorillia's requisition had taken so many navidroids out of circulation that it wasn't just the Outer Rim experiencing shortages. Shipping all over the Republic was beginning to be affected.

Yes, if Keven's algorithm performed correctly, they would know where the Emergences would happen next, and could end the blockade—but that was a big if. He only had fifty-seven thousand droids, when the number he actually needed was more like twice that. The calculations he had to run would now take at least double the time, even pushing his system to the limit. That much stress on the machine for that long would generate . . . well. He had his doubts about how many of these hugely precious electronic brains would make it through the process. That was the essential fact he had chosen not to share with Secretary Lorillia. The array, once powered on, would be hungry, and what it ate . . . was navidroids.

But this was the solution he had. He had to try—even though he knew what would happen to him if he failed. That's what good people did.

"Peeples! Get your toe out of there! What do you think you're—oh, that's actually a pretty good idea, I guess," Chief Innamin said over the comlink, his voice a little distant, as if he had turned to yell at someone on his side of the transmission. Then he came back, strong and loud. "We're good here, Mr. Tarr. Linkage complete."

"Thank you, Chief—and you can call me Keven. Clear the area, and pull out any other teams you see out there. Get off the plateau, back up here on the observation platform."

"Huh? Why?"

"Just pull everyone back, all right?"

Keven lifted a datapad, the central control unit for the entire array. He shot off a quick prayer to the Vine Matron, patron saint of the area on Hetzal Prime where he had been raised, then tapped the single button that turned the whole blasted thing on.

Farther along the plateau, Senator Izzet Noor fanned his face as the huge networked array of navidroids hummed into life. It sounded like a hive of insects—not even a sound, really, more like a sensation, just below the level of true perception. He was also praying, but not to the Vine Matron, more of an unfocused "please, please, please" muttered under his breath.

All over the Outer Rim, worlds were on the verge of revolt. While the chancellor had authorized aid shipments to worlds suffering from lack of hyperspace transit, it was still far from life as usual, and the occasional shipment of emergency rations wasn't the way to quell unrest.

If this Keven Tarr's insane droid scheme didn't work, he'd have to go to Chancellor Soh and beg her to reopen the hyperlanes, regardless of the danger. At a certain point, she would have to see that the damage being done to the people of the Rim outweighed the risk of another *Legacy Run*–style crisis.

"Can you believe all this?" Noor said to Jeni Wataro, his closest aide going on ten years. She was Chagrian, with blue skin and thick, horn-tipped tentacles curling out from the sides of her head and draping down across her chest. Wataro was essential to his work in endless ways. Every politician could use a Chagrian aide, Noor believed.

"What do you mean, Senator?" Wataro said.

Noor gestured vaguely out at the gigantic droid array spread out on the plateau before them.

"All *this,* Wataro. Use your eyes. We're going to such massive expense, and there's no guarantee that this will even work. I don't see any reason why we can't just reopen the hyperlanes.

"And you know what?" he continued, turning to her. "Someone else out there clearly already has the ability to predict Emergences, based on what happened at Eriadu."

Wataro nodded.

"Why are we doing this stupid droid thing when Admiral Kronara and the RDC should just be hunting down whoever tried to extort the Eriaduans?" Noor went on. "That Kissav person—I think that was the name Governor Veen said. We find them, we ask them where the next Emergences will be! Done. Easy."

Noor frowned out at the array again. The initial hum had deepened into an unpleasant buzz—not a sound, but a feeling, deep in his bones.

"I respect the chancellor's choices, but I wish she would consider a different approach," he said.

"Perhaps you should run, Senator," Jeni said.

She always said this, and he knew it was a sort of passive-aggressive thing, like she was pointing out his hypocrisy in criticizing the chancellor when he never *actually* ran for the office.

"Maybe I will, Wataro—maybe I just will," he said. "Wait and see."

A large screen was set up on the observation deck above the array, currently displaying a rough approximation of the *Legacy Run* disaster, accelerated to ten times the actual speed at which it had occurred. Keven Tarr, the Jedi, the senator, and the other Republic and local officials watched solemnly as the events played out. Many of them had been there while it happened—people had died. Not as many as could have, but still—this was a tragedy, and no one spoke as they watched.

Keven looked down at his datapad, which provided him with another essential information set—the status of the navidroid array. All 57,817 processors, running incredibly high-level calculations at the very limit of their capability. Keven could, with a few taps, expand any of the three main nodes to look at subnodes, smaller groupings, even individual droids. The array was designed to work like a massive brain, with neurons, nerve cells, all of it.

The readouts gave him the speed at which each node, unit, and individual droid was running—useful, but not the primary data points upon which Keven was focused. No, he was concerned with another figure, also displayed at the far end of each long chain of data . . . the heat.

This many processors running together at full capacity was basically one enormous oven. Keven had planned for it as best he could—that was why the array was outside, in the wind and the relatively cool temperatures of the Rooted Moon. He could have built it in space, but heat didn't dissipate through vacuum—it would have been even worse out there.

Many of the droids had internal cooling units—that was the source of the hum rising off the plateau, now getting louder, more insistent. Keven didn't need to check his datapad to know the temperatures were rising, and fast.

Fortunately, the observers all seemed to be riveted by the events unfolding on the large display screen: every brave rescue of *Legacy Run* survivors, every tragic death, every hairbreadth escape. Keven, despite the burgeoning issues with the array, took a moment to appreciate the enormity of what the Jedi and the Republic teams had accomplished here.

The Hetzal system should be gone. It was astonishing that he was still standing here, on the surface of the Rooted Moon. He shook his head, watching the simulation as the final fragment sped toward Hetzal's sun, the tank of liquid Tibanna that had almost destroyed the entire system. He remembered these moments clearly—he had been certain he would be dead in moments, knew it down to his bones . . . and that hadn't happened.

The Jedi had come together to move a gigantic piece of metal that did not want to be moved, in precisely the right way, in perfect coordination though millions of kilometers from one another.

It was impossible. Yet somehow, they had done it.

Keven watched it happen again, the fragment skipping away, just missing one of the system's suns. It seemed so simple, so easy on the screen. He knew it had taken everything the Jedi had. Some of them had even died in the attempt.

They had succeeded. He could not fail now.

The simulation of the *Legacy Run* disaster was complete, and a second node kicked into life, this one modeling the first Emergence. The display showed the seven fragments appear in the Ab Dalis system, and the impact of the last on the planet. The watchers stood in silence—another tragedy, but this one not prevented by a miraculous Jedi intervention.

Keven, however, had stopped looking at the screen. He could not take his eyes from his datapad. The temperatures were rising faster than he had anticipated. For his algorithm to work, the systems had to continuously model everything that had happened, every detail, every fragment, every trajectory, all at once. As each new Emergence was added to the simulation, the load grew greater.

It felt like heat was already rising off the plateau. Surely that was his imagination. Keven wiped his sleeve across his forearm—damp.

No. Not his imagination. The array was running hot, and they still had almost thirty Emergences to model.

Senator Noor shifted uncomfortably. He turned to his aide, gesturing out at the air above the droid array, which was shimmering, heat haze rising into the early-morning sky.

"Wataro," he said. "Is that . . . how this is supposed to work?"

"I . . . I'm not sure," she replied, taking a cloth from her tunic and blotting little green dots of sweat that had appeared on her forehead.

Keven was worried about Node Five. Secretary Lorillia had done his best, but obviously not everyone was willing to give up their best, state-of-the-art navidroids, no matter how noble the cause. A good number of the droids in the array were older models, or even retired from active service. They could still do the job, but not as well or as fast as the others.

He had distributed the older droids throughout the array in an attempt at load balancing, but inevitably, some sections ended up with a few more of the less-capable machines. Node Five was one of those. The heat was rising quickly, and it was just a matter of time until—

A shower of sparks shot up from the array, and Keven didn't have to look at it to know it was coming from Node Five. One of the older navidroids had blown its circuits, the heat essentially frying its computational matrix to sludge.

"Blast it," he said.

"What's happening, Tarr?" he heard Senator Noor call over.

Keven didn't answer. He didn't have time. If Node Five went down, then the whole simulation would have to start over, and he knew they probably wouldn't let him do that. This was most likely his only shot. Fortunately, he had anticipated the problem—at least to some degree.

A phalanx of pill droids floated off to one side of the array, all equipped with cooling units able to send out blasts of wintry air wherever they might be needed. Keven had kept them in reserve until now, but it was clear that the time had come.

He tapped his datapad, and several of the pill droids zoomed over to Node Five, shooting out cold air from their vent attachments that immediately brought the temperature down. Fine. It was fine.

As long as the pill droids' coolant held out, and as long as he didn't lose too many more navidroids. Fifty-seven thousand, seven hundred and twelve, now—and he really shouldn't have even tried this with less than seventy-five thousand.

Node Seven was starting to run hot, and Keven had learned his lesson. He sent another few pill droids in that direction to cool it down before anything went wrong.

This can work, he thought. *I can do this.*

Node Fourteen came online, modeling the nineteenth Emergence, and it overloaded immediately, hard, fifty droids at once shooting the same set of sparks Node Five had just produced. Maybe an error in the linkage, maybe that was just a particularly complex part of the simulation.

"No!" Keven shouted.

He was dimly aware of voices in his vicinity, asking questions, offering advice, concern . . . he couldn't spare time for them, not even a moment. The array was on the verge of a cascading failure.

Twenty pill droids whipped over to Node Fourteen—half of what he had left, and they were barely two-thirds of the way through the simulation.

They're going to blame me, he thought. *They're going to say it was my fault. I was just trying to help. I did my best. I did my—*

A hand touched his arm, and Keven jumped. He looked—it was the Jedi, Avar Kriss. A few steps behind her, the other one, Elzar Mann—they always seemed to be together.

"Be calm," she said, and he was. He felt better, just having her there.

"What's happening?" Avar asked.

"The array's producing too much heat, but I can't stop the simulation now. Either it runs to the end, or there was no point to any of this. We haven't learned anything new yet, either. If we stop now, it's all a waste."

Another rain of sparks—Node Eleven. Three hundred and eighty-two droids gone, all at once. Fifty-seven thousand, eight hundred and sixteen left.

Keven sent the rest of his pill droids to cool down that section, which would work for a bit, but a glance at the datapad showed him at least four more nodes in serious trouble.

Nodes Three and Eight blew. Fifty-seven thousand, three hundred and eighty-four. If they got below fifty thousand, it was over. No amount of reshuffling and load balancing would create processing power where it didn't exist.

The breeze died, and that little bit of additional cooling it provided vanished. There was nothing more he could do. It was over.

Avar Kriss continued to use the Force to help the young man hold back his panic. It wasn't easy. Keven Tarr wanted to spiral out of control. He felt guilt, shame, frustration . . . none of which were fair or earned, probably, but emotions were rarely logical.

She looked at Elzar. "Any ideas?"

"He needs to cool everything down?"

"That's what he said."

"Okay," Elzar said, his tone thoughtful. "I might have an idea. I've never tried it, but the theory is sound. You'll be able to sense what I'm doing. Anything you can do to help would be appreciated. I can't imagine I'll be able to do this alone."

Elzar seated himself on the ground, folding his legs together, then lifted his arms and closed his eyes. Avar reached out, trying to follow what he was doing. He was calling on the Force . . . but to do what?

She suspected this was one of his . . . refinements. Ideas were constantly popping into his head, ways the Force might be used to do new things, new ways the light side might answer his call. He failed, all the time, but she found his commitment to bringing new ideas to the Jedi inspiring. To Elzar Mann, what the Jedi were was nowhere near as interesting as what they could be.

Avar listened to the song of the Force . . . and suddenly she understood what Elzar was trying to do.

Impossible, she sent to him, a concept basic enough to be conveyed through the very loose emotional linkage the Force could give them.

He smiled, not opening his eyes.

Help me, he sent back.

Elzar Mann was talking to the air. It was hot here at the surface, above the furiously working droids, but much cooler high above. The hot air was rising, as it liked to do, but slowly. Not fast enough.

He asked the Force to help with that, and it responded, though sluggishly. Air was heavier than it looked.

Then, an easing, and he knew Avar was with him. That was good. Everything was easier when she was at his side. Literally, in fact—he opened his eyes briefly to see that she had knelt next to him, her forearms resting loosely on her thighs, her palms facing upward and her eyes closed, her face tilted up toward the sky.

The small patch of heated air rose higher, both Jedi creating currents to waft it into the sky above the plateau. This did very little to cool the navidroid array, though that was not really the idea here.

As the hot air rose, it reached cooler zones higher in the atmosphere. The heated air carried moisture with it, evaporated from the surface. Those tiny molecules of water found one another, touched, connected.

Elzar and Avar did it together, nudging the air, helping it do what it wanted to do anyway, helping the individual bits of water become one. Elzar felt something like exultation. Not pride—that was not the Jedi way—but joy in a difficult job being done well, by two people connecting on a deep level, without any need to explain to each other what they were doing.

They had always been this way, ever since their Padawan days. Their connection made many things better—but if he was being honest with himself . . . it also made some things worse.

The two Jedi worked. Elzar felt exhaustion creeping over him. He and Avar were only working with a small region of the atmosphere, a relatively tiny volume of air. Shaping it, molding it, trying to bring it to a critical mass that would let the moon's weather systems do the rest of the work—essentially creating a seed—but it was still grueling. Sweat poured from his body, and he knew that was only partially due to the heat rising off the array. Every breath became an effort, and his chest felt like it was being pressed in a vise, as if the air moving above was being sucked directly from his lungs.

But Elzar Mann did not stop, nor did Avar Kriss, and slowly, something began to appear in the sky above the plateau. Huge, gradually darkening as the moments passed.

A cloud.

Fifty-one thousand and eighteen navidroids remained, and while Keven had managed to keep the simulation intact—the vidscreen was now playing out the thirty-first Emergence, which meant they were just minutes away from being able to move past modeling things that had happened to projecting things that *would* happen—but there was no way the array would last that long. Every single remaining droid was in the red, even the most advanced models. Keven was maneuvering the pill droids above the entire array in big, sweeping arcs, trying to chill the whole thing at once. It was working, to some extent, buying them additional seconds—but his datapad also displayed their coolant reserves, and most were down to single digits.

At this point, all he could hope for was that they might be able to predict an Emergence or two . . . even a few might help prevent a future tragedy. They almost certainly wouldn't be able to find the *Legacy Run*'s flight recorder system, which was obviously the secondary goal of all this—it would help them understand what had happened here and, hopefully, prevent it from ever occurring again.

But you took the good where you found it, and so Keven kept using the systems he had left, pushing them as far as he could, even as another few hundred navidroids burned out and died.

Something hit the back of his neck, startling him. It was soft, maybe an insect, or—

Another impact, this time on the back of his hand as it moved rapidly across his datapad's surface, and he realized what was happening.

"It's . . . it's raining," he heard Senator Noor say.

And suddenly, with a rumble of thunder, it was. Rain, pouring down over the array. Steam hissed up from the overstressed navidroids, and Keven had to swipe the side of his hand across his datapad to clear the water so he could read it. Temperatures were dropping rapidly, across every node. The navidroids were hardened for operation in vacuum—a bit of water wouldn't hurt them.

Clouds of steam drifted up from the array, and Keven turned to look—first at the Jedi, Avar Kriss and Elzar Mann, who knelt side by side, arms lifted, eyes closed, trembling with sustained effort as the rain soaked their tunics. The Jedi looked as if they were trying to lift a starship with their bare hands. The sun was still bright off the plateau, and the light shone through the rain, causing a glinting spectrum to surround them both.

Beyond the straining Jedi, the vidscreen finally displayed something new: a zone of uninhabited space where the thirty-fourth Emergence would occur.

There had only been thirty-three Emergences to date.

The system worked. It was predicting the location of future Emergences, and as long as the rain held up, it would remain stable.

Keven realized that he hadn't failed after all. He, Keven Tarr, a farmer's son from Hetzal Prime, had sliced hyperspace.

What a strange galaxy this was.

CHAPTER THIRTY

ELPHRONA.

Porter Engle bent low over the neck of his steelee, whispering to it, even as he calmed its shaking muscles with the Force.

"You are a luminous being," he said. "There is no pain, there is no fatigue, there is no fear. You are light and speed and there is nothing in this world more beautiful. I am here with you. We are together. We will do great things. We will save this family."

The blade of his lightsaber hummed as he rode, chasing the bastards who had kidnapped four innocent people from their very home. What had Loden called them? The Nihil.

Porter Engle was not angry. He had been a Jedi for almost three centuries. He knew all too well where anger could lead. He had found a better way to express his emotions when faced with situations like this. He was not angry.

He was certain.

Certain that a great injustice had been done.

Certain that he could set it right.

And, most of all . . .

. . . he was utterly certain these . . . *Nihil* . . . would never do anything like it again.

One way or another.

He had taken the point position, riding a little ahead of Loden Greatstorm and Bell Zettifar. He liked them both. Loden had a sense of humor about things that was very welcome among the Jedi. Porter had met many in their Order who took things far too seriously. Life was long, and they had the gift of the Force. Why be stoic? The vows didn't mean they were dead.

And Bell . . . Bell was a wonderful young man. Still figuring himself out, but he was only eighteen years old. He shouldn't know very much about himself at that age anyway. But someday, he would be the kind of Jedi held up as an example to future generations.

Assuming Loden didn't kill him in training first.

Porter brought his focus back to the task at hand. Jagged ironstone slopes scraped up to either side, and the way ahead narrowed. The Jedi didn't slow, but they brought their steelees into line, moving through the canyon single-file.

The Nihil with their captives were still some distance ahead, but the Jedi were gaining. Wouldn't be long now. He recalled battles long past, pulled up strategies for hostage situations. The Nihil clearly thought the family was valuable, and wouldn't want to hurt them unnecessarily. That gave Porter and his team an advantage. Still, they would need to move fast. The best would be for one of them—Loden, probably—to use the Force to yank the family free of the Nihil, while he and Bell moved on the kidnappers.

Odds were these Nihil had never fought Jedi before—most people hadn't, and even if they'd heard stories, mere words couldn't do the experience justice. So they might not know how foolish it would be to try to fight using blasterfire. A blaster bolt fired at a Jedi was essentially the same as shooting at yoursel—

The tiniest whiff of danger, whether some signal from the Force or just long instincts honed from many other rides through many other narrow canyons with enemies on the horizon. The sound of a blaster rifle firing. Porter Engle whipped up his lightsaber, moving to deflect the attack—but it was not aimed at him.

His steelee reared up, pain filling its mind and heart and echoing through Porter. He pulled back his link to the animal and leapt free as it crumpled to the ground, digging up furrows in the hard dirt with its metallic hooves. He somersaulted in midair, using his lightsaber to knock back a few more shots. The Nihil had clearly hidden themselves up in the hills, waiting to ambush the Jedi.

Porter landed.

"Cowards," he spat.

More blasts rained down, from either side, but now he had the angles figured, and the angles and pace of blasterfire told him the story. Only two shooters.

"Keep going!" he called to Loden, who had slowed his mount slightly. "Don't let the other Nihil get that family to their ship! I'll take care of these monsters and join you as soon as I can."

Loden nodded without a word, and he and Bell raced ahead, deflecting a few errant shots as they went.

Porter Engle stood alone in the canyon, the body of his dead mount not far away, a noble animal who had only done her best.

"You think you're smart, eh?" he called up. "Shot my steelee right out from under me."

Silence from up in the hills. No shots, no movement. Perhaps they were, in fact, smarter than he gave them credit for. They were undoubtedly circling around, trying to get a bead on him from a new spot. Let them.

He shouted up toward the tumbled rocks above.

"Before you killed my steelee, I will admit I had not decided how to deal with you. All possibilities were on the table. But that creature lived in the light, and you stole it away. You had no right. Thank you for showing me exactly what you are. Makes things much simpler for me."

He rotated slowly, his lightsaber up, scanning the hills. He knew what was going to happen. Anyone who aimed for a man's mount rather than shooting at him fair and square, anyone who attacked from ambush, was also the sort of man who would—

Blasterfire, three shots, right at his back. Of course.

Porter spun, blocking the first, the second, and sending the third right back from where it had come. Movement from up in the rocks, and he leapt, higher than he was sure these Nihil cowards would have thought possible. Straight up, and he saw the man who had shot at him. Porter threw his lightsaber, and it sliced out, a spinning disk, inescapable.

The Nihil sniper ducked behind an ironstone outcropping, thinking it would shelter him. It did not. The blade sliced through the rock, and then it sliced through the man, and Porter regretted that a living, thinking being, a child of the Force, had made choices that brought him to such an end.

The second ambusher shot at Porter before he had landed from his great leap, and before he could retrieve his lightsaber. He was in midair, without his primary form of protection, making the situation a bit complex to handle—but Jedi lost their weapons from time to time, and any Jedi Knight worth the title put in the hours developing strategies for unarmed defense.

Porter Engle reached out with both the Force and his hand, palm out, and deflected the bolt back, sending it caroming back off toward the hills. Not strictly necessary. He could have pushed it away with his mind, or frozen it in place. But flicking a blaster bolt away like an insect . . . it made a certain statement.

"I saw you, friend," he shouted up, calling his lightsaber back to him. "Saw right where you're hiding."

The hilt smacked into his hand with a *whap* he always found utterly satisfying, his thick fingers slipping into grooves worn into the metal cylinder from tens of thousands of hours of practice and combat.

"And soon I'll see you again," he called.

Porter Engle sprinted toward the hill, moving faster than the Nihil could probably see, leaping up and over and from side to side. No more blaster bolts. He had a feeling the surviving Nihil had thought better of this whole ambush and was making a run for it.

When he made it to the top of the rise, he learned that he was right. The Nihil was sitting on another steelee, trying to get the beast to move, digging his heels into its sides. He wasn't shouting at the poor creature, its head down and hooves dug in hard—he knew better than to make that kind of noise—but Porter knew that under ordinary circumstances he'd be cursing at it, using every horrible oath he could dream up.

"I bet you're the one that shot my animal," Porter said.

The Nihil whipped around, his blaster firing, and the conflict ended the only way it could.

Porter was utterly certain.

The Nihil toppled off the steelee, a smoking hole through his mask.

Porter Engle wasted no more time on him. He deactivated his lightsaber and slapped it into his holster, then approached the traumatized steelee, his hand outstretched.

"Hey there, fella . . ." he said. "You are a luminous being. Whaddya say you and me go do some good?"

The steelee looked at him, its eyes wide. He touched its flank, and it calmed. He wrapped his hands in its bridle, preparing to heave himself up into its saddle.

And then the Nihil with the hole through his mask *sat up.* He lifted his blaster to fire—and Porter Engle realized the raider was probably of some species that kept its brain elsewhere in its body, meaning he could survive a headshot, meaning that Porter Engle, whose hands were occupied with the steelee, was about to die.

These thoughts ran through his head, along with an odd moment of sadness about a refinement to one of his pie recipes he would now never get to try, and he prepared his spirit to join the Force.

A black, gray, and red-orange blur leapt off the rocks, directly at the injured Nihil.

Ember, Porter Engle thought in astonishment. He'd forgotten all about her.

The charhound opened her jaws and a huge gout of yellow flame spat out, enveloping the Nihil before he could bring his blaster to bear. A strange, hollow scream emanated from the raider's mask, and he rolled on the ground, trying to put out the fire that had consumed his body. Ember did not stop, just continued torching the Nihil until at first he stopped screaming, and then he stopped moving.

Then she closed her mouth and padded up to Porter Engle, who gingerly bent down and scratched her behind one ear. She felt hot, like his oven back at the outpost. He supposed that made perfect sense. She must have followed them all the way from the wrecked homestead, he and his fellow Jedi so focused on pursuing the Nihil they hadn't thought to consider who might be pursuing them.

"Good girl," he said. "Very good girl."

Porter climbed aboard the steelee, and he was off, headed down the slope at a ready pace with Ember loping alongside, racing after Bell and Loden and the family they were trying to save.

Loden Greatstorm and Bell Zettifar had steadily gained ground on the Nihil they were chasing, but had not completely closed the distance. Now the kidnappers' ships were visible, parked on the rust-colored sand just outside the no-fly zone. Two, looking like welded-together piles of cubes and spikes, and both marked with the three lines they'd seen on the door of the Blythe homestead. The Nihil had almost reached the vessels, along with their prisoners, still being pulled along in the little cart.

"We'll never catch them in time," Bell said.

"I know," Loden said.

He removed his hands from the reins of his steelee, but the creature didn't slow its strong gallop, sparks shooting up with every step. Bell assumed his master was steering his mount via his knees and a judicious application of the Force. In a single smooth motion, Loden swung the metal tube he had salvaged from the wrecked Vanguard around his body, placing it atop one shoulder. He pulled his lightsaber from his holster, slapped it against the flat plate connected to the tube's electronic components, and the power unit on the far end lit up glowing gold, the same color as Loden's blade.

Bell realized what Loden had taken from their vehicle—the Vanguard's laser cannon, its kyber-keyed anti-ship weapon. He held his breath. He couldn't believe this was about to happen.

Loden *fired,* and a bolt of golden light shot from the end of the tube, like a lightsaber blade but somehow denser, more *there.* The edges of a saber blade faded out into an intense whiteness—but this blast thickened, darkened, into an amber like the first rays of an autumn sunrise. And the *sound*—Bell heard it with his bones, not his ears. In the moment of the weapon firing, all other sounds ceased.

Bell's steelee reared up, and he had to fight to get it under control—and so he missed the bolt's impact. He heard it, though, an utterly unique sound of metal being overheated in an instant and flashing into vapor, followed by two distinct *thunk*s.

When his mount was calm, moving forward again to catch up with Loden—whose steelee hadn't missed a step, of course—Bell saw what the weapon had done. One of the Nihil's two ships had been sliced in half, the middle section of the vessel just . . . gone. The two remaining edges had fallen to the ground, sparks and flame already shooting up from the superheated edges.

"Whoa," Bell said.

He nudged his steelee to greater speed and called ahead to Loden.

"Get the other ship!"

"I can't," his master answered, pointing ahead with the smoking weapon before tossing it to one side, where it clattered onto the hard, metallic soil and was left behind in an instant.

Bell looked where Loden had indicated. He understood immediately. The Nihil had realized the danger to the one ship they had left, their last remaining escape route, and had repositioned themselves, moving the cart containing the kidnapped family so it was directly in the line of fire. The Vanguard's cannon wasn't a precision weapon, at least not removed from its housings in the vehicle. He couldn't risk the shot—it would almost certainly hit the family.

"Maybe for the best," Loden said. "If I'd fired twice the whole thing might have blown up in my hands. I had to leave the cooling module back with the V-Wheel."

"What are we going to do, Master?" Bell asked.

"Whatever we can," he replied.

Not reassuring. If Loden Greatstorm was out of ideas, things were dire.

They were getting closer to the Nihil, and the complications of the situation were starting to overwhelm Bell's ability to plan. He would have to trust in the Force, let it guide his choices.

Something happened up ahead. Bell and Loden heard a blaster fire, and a moment later a person was thrown from the cart. The Nihil sped on, leaving the body lying motionless on the hard ground.

"That wasn't a Nihil," Bell said. "No mask. Did they kill one of the hostages?"

Loden remained silent.

The Jedi raced forward, details becoming clearer with every meter. The victim was the mother.

"She's alive," Bell said. "I can still sense her."

As if to validate Bell's words, the woman lifted an arm from where she lay—a weak, pain-filled gesture, even at a distance.

Beyond her, the Nihil had almost reached their ship.

The Jedi reached the woman. They pulled their steelees to a stop and leapt from the saddles. She had a smoking hole in her side—probably non-lethal, at least not right away.

"Please," she said, her voice small, thin, "my children, my husband. Please, you have to . . ."

"We will," Loden said, his voice confident—whether real or for the woman's benefit, Bell did not know. "What is your name?"

"Erika," she said. "Erika Blythe."

Loden reached a hand toward her blaster wound.

"Erika, I can help with your injury, using the Force. I can stabilize you long enough to get you back to our outpost—there's medical treatment there."

"But my family," she said, her voice getting stronger as Loden did what he could for her wound.

"We'll save them," he said again.

Across the hardpan, all three heard the same sound—the Nihil ship's engines activating.

"No!" Erika Blythe cried, trying to struggle to her feet. Bell didn't know what she thought she could do, but the despair in her voice was deeper than any pain she might still be feeling.

Loden stood, taking his lightsaber from its holster.

"What is it, Master?"

The Nihil ship took to the air, moving up and away quickly. Loden ignited his blade.

The ship curved in the air, turned, and headed back. Straight for them.

"Are they going to kill her?"

"No," Loden said. "She was bait. They knew we would stop to help her. They're going to try to kill *us.*"

The Nihil starship whipped toward them, ugly and brutish, the three lightning strikes painted on its hull in reflective paint gleaming in the harsh glare of Elphrona's sun.

"Get behind me, Padawan," Loden said. "Protect Erika."

How? Bell thought. *That's a starship.*

But he was dutiful. Lacking any other ideas, he placed himself between the Nihil ship and the injured woman, and reached for his lightsaber.

Loden changed his stance, putting himself side-on to the approaching starship. His front knee was bent, and he held his saber hilt in both hands. He looked like a durasteel wall. Unbeatable.

But that's a starship, Bell thought again.

The Nihil fired, a rain of blasts from their ship lasers. Most went wide—a person was a small target for a starship—but a few were dead-on.

Loden Greatstorm roared, a battle cry echoing out into the empty deadlands of Elphrona. His lightsaber flashed, too fast for Bell to understand what he did, and the laser bolts wicked away. Loden's feet skidded back, kicking up rust-colored dust, and he grunted, as if he had been hit hard in the stomach by a huge, heavy maul.

He fell to his knees, his saber blade flickering out, as the Nihil ship whipped past overhead.

"Master!" Bell cried.

"I'm . . . all right," Loden said. "But . . . I don't think I can do that . . . again."

Bell looked up. The Nihil ship was coming around for a second attack run.

He lit his lightsaber, the green blade flicking into humming, buzzing life.

He turned side-on to the starship. He bent his front knee. He made himself a wall through which no evil could pass.

There's no way, he thought. *If Loden could barely do it . . .*

There might be no way. There was also no choice.

Bell reached out to the Force.

Laserfire, high in the air. Five shots.

Bell braced himself, looking inward, not up.

A new sound—an explosion, like a cough, muffled.

That was . . .

He snapped his head up just as two Jedi Vectors overflew the Nihil starship, which was now leaking thick black smoke from one of its engines.

They circled around in an incredibly tight curve, a two-craft Drift, and as they banked Bell saw that only one of the ships actually had a pilot.

"Indeera," Loden said, pushing himself painfully to his feet. "By the light, look at her go."

In awe, Bell realized what he was seeing. Indeera was *flying both ships.* Some of the Vectors' functions could be operated remotely via the Force in cases of extreme emergency—but operating was one thing, and piloting was another. Indeera was mirroring her motions in her own Vector in the second ship, a feat of concentration Bell could barely comprehend.

It was spectacular.

The Nihil seemed more terrified than impressed. Their ship jerked up and headed for open sky, accelerating slowly, trailing smoke.

The two Vectors came in for a landing not far from Bell, Loden, and Erika— not as smooth as they might, skittering along the ground a bit before coming to a halt, but considering what Indeera was doing, Bell was not inclined to criticize.

Both cockpits opened, and Indeera stood.

"Come on!" she cried. "We can try to catch them before they make it to the hyperspace access zone and jump away."

Loden turned to Bell.

"I would bring you, apprentice, but you have to get Erika back to the outpost. You have two steelees. Once you're there, put her in the medbay and—"

"I know what to do, Master," Bell said. He wasn't disappointed, exactly, but he knew where he could help the most, and it wasn't slowly and carefully taking Erika Blythe back to their outpost.

"She won't make it," came a voice.

Bell and Loden turned, to see that Porter Engle had appeared, as if from nowhere, Ember at his side. A third steelee stood nearby, and the ancient Jedi was down on one knee next to Erika, with his hand hovering above her wound.

"This is serious. She needs treatment on the way. I'll have to take her back. I'm the best medic of the four of us, by far."

Loden wasted no time. The Nihil were getting farther away with every second.

"May the Force be with you, Porter," he said. "Bell, with me."

He ran toward the waiting Vector.

"It's time to fly."

CHAPTER THIRTY-ONE

DEEP SPACE. REPUBLIC LONGBEAM
AURORA III.

Pikka Adren stretched, feeling her muscles ease a little. She wanted to ask Joss to rub her shoulders, but the thirty-ninth Emergence was set to happen soon enough that she didn't want to risk him being out of the pilot's seat when it happened. They still had a few minutes, but there was no reason to take a chance.

Her husband could give her a massage later. Assuming "later" ever actually arrived. Somehow, they'd been swept up in the efforts to solve all the backscatter from the *Legacy Run* disaster, and that was all well and good—they were getting hazard pay and doing something noble besides. But they were supposed to be on *vacation.* She had booked them a trip to Amfar once their shift helping to build the Starlight Beacon was over, and those days had come and gone. She'd lost the deposit, and had no idea whether the Republic would let her expense it, and—

Ugh. She was annoyed at herself for focusing on something so petty. She and Joss were literally saving the galaxy here. Or at least a good chunk of it.

But still. She was supposed to be on a beach right now, wearing something tiny, sipping something delicious, lying next to her handsome husband who was also in something tiny, thinking about later, when they would both ditch even those tiny things and think of inventive ways to make each other feel good.

"You ready, my darling?" Joss said.

He sounded excited. Clearly he wasn't thinking he'd rather be on a beach. He lived for this stuff.

But really, she thought, *so do I.*

Couple of spanner-slinging contractors out saving the Outer Rim Territories, doing it together, doing it in style. Not so bad.

"Ready, my darling," she said, putting her hands back on her console.

"I just checked with the rest of the team," Joss said. "Everyone's good to go. Whatever pops out, we can handle it."

Pikka murmured in agreement, pulling her mind away from Amfar and back to the task at hand. Somehow the Republic had figured out how to predict where the Emergences were going to happen—she'd heard a story about some sort of mega-processor made out of tens of thousands of droids linked to the Force that could predict the future, but that surely had to be nonsense. In any case, they had identified three spots as the most likely candidates for where the *Legacy Run*'s flight recorder would emerge, and had set up a team to intercept them, one after the other.

Other teams were working to recover potential survivors from other Emergence sites—it was possible some could still be alive in passenger modules despite the length of time since the original disaster, and all efforts were being made to bring them home. Those missions were obviously hugely important, but the flight recorder was crucial—it would provide information about how the ship had been destroyed in the first place, and help prevent it from happening again.

The hyperspace blockade of the Outer Rim was still in effect, and Pikka knew that many worlds were hurting. She'd heard rumors of food riots in the sinkhole cities of Utapau, even though Chancellor Soh had authorized special aid shipments. And of course, Starlight Beacon's construction had finally been completed, but the dedication and official opening were on hold. As a matter of professional pride, that stung a bit. That place would be beautiful, and help so many people. She and Joss had worked hard on their little part of it, and she wanted to see it operational on time.

The retrieval team included four Longbeams and two Jedi Vectors—it was her old friends Te'Ami and Mikkel Sutmani, which made sense. After all, the four of them had devised the techniques used back in Hetzal that had saved the Fruited Moon during the original disaster. They'd refined those ideas, and now, whatever happened, they'd be ready for it.

Pikka thought this Emergence would probably just be a piece of wreckage, nothing interesting about it. If so, they could just let it go. They were in an uninhabited region of space, far from anything to which a chunk of former starship might pose a threat.

"Weapons hot," she said. "Everything else is good to go, too—magclamps, fuel looks good, the whole deal."

"Great," Joss said. "As soon as we're done here, we'll have to zip away to the next Emergence spot. We'll barely have enough time to get there."

"You really think we might get in a fight?" she asked.

"I doubt it, but you know what happened at Eriadu. Someone else out there predicted an Emergence, too. Three, actually. We're looking for a ship called the *New Elite,* a modified corvette. Admiral Kronara went over it at the mission briefing. We don't know how they're involved, but there's at least some chance they might show up here, too. We need to be prepared for anything. If we get into a fight, we get into a fight."

Privately, Pikka was planning to just let the Jedi handle it, if it came to that—she wasn't afraid of a firefight, but she was basically a mechanic. She was more than happy to leave combat to the highly trained space wizards.

"Here it comes," Joss said. "Thirty-ninth Emergence in five, four, three . . ."

"... two, one," Belial said, from his post at the monitoring station. "There it is."

"Scan it, and tell me if it looks like the flight recorder," Lourna Dee said.

She was standing with her arms crossed on the bridge of her flagship, the *Lourna Dee,* looking out at the little fleet the Republic had put together for their little mission. Bunch of heroes. Hooray.

Lourna Dee loved her ship, and that was why she had named it after herself. Anyone who had an issue with that was welcome to discuss it with her. So far, no one ever had.

Each of Marchion Ro's Tempest Runners had a personal warship, a testament to its owner's taste as well as the possibilities inherent in the Nihil as an organization. Work hard, hunt well, follow the Paths, and you, too, might someday own a customized battle cruiser. Kassav's *New Elite* felt like the interior of a trashy nightclub. Pan Eyta's ship, the *Elegencia,* was beautiful, with surfaces covered in soft leather, lighting designed to perfectly accent every lovely little tasteful design choice he made.

The *Lourna Dee* was unique in a completely different way.

The cruiser was outfitted with all sorts of devices and shielding that made it all but impossible to pick up on a scan. Heat baffling, ablative plating, double-sealed engines that recycled almost all of its exhaust signature into the ship's life-support and weapons systems, and more. It cost her a pile of credits, but it made her Tempest's flagship nearly invisible to even the most powerful sensors.

Usually, an attack by the *Lourna Dee* went like this: The enemy pilot thought, *Wait, where'd that ship come fr—* and then they were blasted into vapor.

Here . . . well, it remained to be seen. The *Lourna Dee* packed enough punch to take out four Longbeams and a few wispy little Vectors, if she could take them by surprise and kept moving. But that could mean revealing her ship, and that was *not* on the menu for this operation. The Tempest Runners were in rare agreement when they voted to approve this mission: The Nihil needed to avoid *any* suggestion they were connected to the Emergences or the *Legacy Run.*

There were two reasons for that. First, obviously, was Kassav's massive screwup at Eriadu. His stupid attempt at extorting that planet, the one that had gone so wrong *and* was so obviously a shot at taking the entire proceeds of that job for himself, shone an unwelcome spotlight on the Nihil. The Eriaduans had splashed Kassav's name and the specs of his ship all over the HoloNet. While there was no direct connection to the Nihil, that was still more heat than they wanted. And after that, Kassav had had the nerve to come crawling back to the Great Hall. He'd offered up the thirty million credits he said he'd made on the Eriadu job and asked for protection.

Pan Eyta and Lourna Dee had wanted to throw Kassav out of the hall right then and there—the hard way—but Marchion Ro had voted to keep him around, to give him a chance to fix his mess. Said something about how his experience might be useful, since he was an old-timer, and how his Tempest was so loyal to him . . . maybe it wasn't a good time for unrest in the crews. Mostly, though, since Kassav didn't get a vote it was her and Pan against Marchion's two votes, and since by Nihil tradition ties went to the Eye . . . Kassav was still around.

The *second* reason this mission was so important was because of something Marchion Ro had learned from one of his Republic spies—the primary aide to that blowhard Outer Rim senator you always heard blathering on the HoloNet, Noor. According to the spy, the Republic investigation had turned up some pretty strong clues that the reason the *Legacy Run* blew up in Hetzal was because it encountered a Nihil ship in the hyperlane, traveling along a Path. Marchion had run some data, and it all seemed plausible. Pretty unwelcome surprise, that.

And now the Republic had built some kind of super-droid that could run high-level hyperspace analyses. It gave them the time and location of all the upcoming Emergences, including some where the *Legacy Run*'s flight recorder might show up. If the Republic investigators found it, they could probably use it to get definitive proof that the Nihil were connected to *everything*—not just Kassav's botched job in Eriadu, which you could argue would have happened whether he was there or not, but also every death in Hetzal, the deaths in Ab Dalis, and the rest. Jedi had died in Hetzal. If they knew the Nihil were the reason . . . well, Marchion Ro seemed pretty wary of the Order, and Lourna Dee didn't much like the idea of them coming after her, either.

The whole Nihil operation could be at stake. The Republic could not be allowed to find that flight recorder. They had to destroy it, and there was really only one Tempest Runner for the job . . . Lourna Dee with her stealth-equipped battle corvette.

So here she was, lurking in the system Marchion Ro had sent her to via a Path, staying hidden, waiting to see if this Emergence would give her a target, or if she would need to move on to the next spot on the Eye's list.

"It's not the recorder," Belial said, looking at his screens.

The Devaronian was just a Cloud, not yet a Storm, but Lourna Dee thought he'd level up pretty soon. The guy was smart, capable. Cool in a crisis. Unemotional. People like that fit right into her organization.

"Looks like one of the passenger compartments."

"Huh," one of her other lieutenants said, a human named Attaman. "You think they're still alive in there? They must have been traveling through hyperspace for weeks."

Lourna Dee didn't answer. She watched the little flares of light in the distance as the Republic team went into action, doing their heroic thing, working on a no-doubt heroic rescue.

She almost gave the order to fire. She wanted to.

A spread of missiles could maybe take out all six ships and the

Legacy Run passenger compartment, too, so fast they wouldn't even have time to realize they were dead.

But as satisfying as that would be, it might go wrong, and they already had enough heat on them. Marchion had been extremely clear, on the verge of actually trying to give her an order. "Don't let them know you're there unless you have to. Unless the flight recorder shows up, you just move on," he'd said.

She'd need to put him in his place sometime soon. There was a hierarchy to be observed. Honestly, she wished she could just take him out of the picture entirely, and if there wasn't such a good chance she'd just end up fighting Kassav and Pan Eyta, too, she'd probably take her chance. Win or lose, she doubted Marchion would blame her for it. That was the Nihil way.

Maybe later, once all this heat from the *Legacy Run* situation died down.

"Set coordinates and get us out of here," Lourna Dee said.

Marchion Ro had provided Paths for the whole operation, routes through hyperspace that ensured they'd get to the next location well ahead of the Republic team. And if that Emergence happened to be the flight recorder, well.

Maybe she'd get to kill someone today after all.

"That's it," came Joss Adren's voice over the comm. "Scans confirm this fortieth Emergence is the bridge section that had the *Legacy Run*'s flight recorder built into it. I'll be damned—I don't know the Republic's megadroid figured it out, but they nailed it. Everyone, get into position. We're down a Longbeam, but we planned for this. We'll run retrieval plan four—based on the fragment's trajectory, that should work best. Just stay cool and do your part."

Mikkel Sutmani pushed his control sticks forward, and his Vector surged ahead. He sensed Te'Ami doing the same off his starboard wing, somewhere out of range. He could see the three remaining Longbeams up ahead, moving into position.

The fourth Longbeam in their original party had stayed behind at the last Emergence point to assist the *Legacy Run* survivors on the fragment. The traumatized settlers required medical and therapeutic assistance—a few of their number had died on their unimaginable journey, and the horror of that experience would not be easily resolved. They would be taken to the *Panacea,* relocated from Hetzal to a collection point near the Starlight Beacon site, where they could connect with other survivors and work with personnel now well trained in dealing with their particular issues. The situation was awful—but at least they were alive, and no longer hurtling through space toward a slow, excruciating death.

Mikkel put the survivors out of his mind, refocusing on the task at hand. Their role here was much the same as it had been in Hetzal during the original disaster—use the Force to slow the piece of the *Legacy Run*'s superstructure while the Longbeams latched on with magclamps and reeled it in. The fragment was still traveling at incredible velocity, but they'd all practiced the maneuvers many times. What was originally almost impossible was now . . . well, not exactly routine, but doable.

"Let's dig deep for this, eh, Te'Ami?" Mikkel said, switching to the Jedi-only comm channel, hearing his translator convert his native Ithorian speech into Basic so she could understand. "The Republic captain is confident, but we have one less Longbeam than we planned for. This might be more challenging than we expect."

"Agreed," Te'Ami said.

Their ships swooped down toward the speeding fragment, the same arc, the same velocity—as one.

"I was thinking, Te'Ami," Mikkel said. "After the episode at Eriadu, it seems clear that the Republic and the Jedi will be working to hunt down this Kassav person. I was considering volunteering for that mission. It seems a good use of my skills. I was wondering if you might do the same? We work well together—that's clear—and you're a remarkable Jedi. I'd be proud to have you as a partner."

"Why, Mikkel," Te'Ami said, amused. "I don't think I've ever heard you say so much at once. Have you forgotten your vows? We Jedi are not to form attachments."

"I'm not *attached,*" he rasped. "I just think we could do good work together. Bring a little light to the galaxy. Our skills are complementary."

"I think I'm going to report you to the Council," she said.

"Whatever you think is appropriate," he said, his voice stiff, both in reality and through the translator.

She laughed.

"I'm teasing you, Mikkel," Te'Ami said. "I'd be very pleased to partner with you on a mission. If the Council agrees, we'll get out there and scour every last corner of the galaxy looking for—"

The Vector's threat display lit up. Missiles, from nowhere, a wide spread of them, at least a dozen, headed straight for the flight recorder fragment.

"What is this?" Mikkel said.

"They're headed for the fragment," Te'Ami said. "They're trying to destroy the flight recorder."

"Hnh," Mikkel said. "Perhaps it's Kassav again. Looks like we'll get to work on that mission a little sooner than we expected, Master Te'Ami."

"Seems so, Master Sutmani."

Mikkel pulled his lightsaber from its holster and held it against the activation panel on his instrument console—his weapons display unlocked and went live, glowing green as it linked with the crystal in his lightsaber hilt.

On his screens, he saw that the Longbeams were also aware of the threat—the three ships were scattering, moving into a position to try to shoot down the missiles.

His systems tracked back to the projectiles' point of origin to . . . nothing. Empty space. This many missiles implied a good-sized war vessel, but nothing like that showed up on his scope.

He put the question aside. The identity of their attacker could wait. Protecting the fragment—that was the thing.

Mikkel began to fire, blasts whipping out from his Vector's lasers toward the missiles. By this point, the Longbeams had begun to shoot as well—a combination of offensive and defensive systems deployed to either destroy or distract the missiles. It didn't matter which, as long as none of the projectiles reached the flight recorder.

One of the missiles veered toward one of those defensive measures—a cloud of static-activated foil emitted by one of the Longbeams, designed to present an appealing false target to the weapon's tracking systems. The Longbeam that had sent out the chaff held position, already shifting toward another target, clearly assuming the missile would explode automatically once it hit the foil. Instead, the weapon entered the shifting, spinning cloud . . . but no explosion. Mikkel sensed what was about to happen, but he was too far away. There wasn't enough time. He reached for the Force, but there was *not enough time.* The missile emerged from the other side of the chaff cloud, impacting directly against the Longbeam's hull.

Now the explosion came.

"Blast it!" came Joss Adren's voice over the comm.

Nothing else was said. The Jedi and the two remaining Longbeams went to work, not knowing the source of the missiles, not knowing if they would die at any moment—just doing the job they could do.

Lourna Dee watched as a few more of her missiles were shot down, or exploded harmlessly against Longbeam-deployed defenses. She still had five left in play, though, and only one needed to hit its target. Victory was just a matter of time.

She had plenty more missiles in reserve, too, though she didn't want to deploy another salvo unless absolutely necessary. The *Lourna Dee* had changed position immediately after firing, but the Republic crews knew she was out there now. There was a good chance they would lock onto the *Lourna Dee*'s signature immediately if she fired again.

The goal was to destroy the flight recorder and leap away. That was all.

Though if it came to it, she would happily destroy every last one of these ships and the flight recorder, too.

Happily.

Mikkel fired, and the missile he had targeted exploded, just seconds before it would have reached the fragment.

He exhaled, breath escaping from each of his mouths.

Just two projectiles left, and neither was in range for him. It was up to the others now.

He watched as Joss and Pikka Adren's Longbeam fired out those magclamps they were always so proud of—a whole grand array, most likely every one their ship had, reeling out on their endlessly long, thin cables—and the missile changed course, pulled in by the attracting force of the clamps.

Ingenious.

The missile exploded, and while the magclamps had certainly been destroyed, there was still one more surviving Longbeam, and it could retrieve the flight recorder—the mission could still succeed.

One more enemy missile remained, and Te'Ami was headed toward it on an intercept course. Neither of the Longbeams was in position to reach it, or Mikkel himself—but Te'Ami could knock it down, no problem. She was a fantastic shot.

And indeed, a spread of laserfire shot out from the front of her Vector—off target but zeroing in . . . and then another missile appeared on Mikkel's scopes, headed directly for Te'Ami. His targeting computer tried to resolve the location of their attacker. A vague, flickering outline appeared on his screens—and disappeared. Whatever was shooting at them clearly had some sort of cloaking system—but that was not the primary issue.

"Te'Ami! There's another missile! I can't—"

"I see it, Mikkel. Quiet now. I have work to do."

Mikkel Sutmani watched, his helplessness at the destruction of the Longbeam a few moments ago amplified a thousandfold. Te'Ami increased her Vector's speed, trying to simultaneously outrun the missile racing toward her and catch the original projectile before it hit the flight recorder.

Her Vector bucked and wove, laser blasts shooting out, all misses, as she attempted to hit her target while evading what had targeted her.

Mikkel slammed his own Vector forward, knowing, once again, that he didn't have time. He reached out with the Force, knowing that through it anything was possible, knowing he *could* reach the missile chasing Te'Ami's ship and could cause it to veer off or detonate. He could sense its speed, its outline, the metal of its casing, the superheated exhaust gases shoving it forward toward his fellow Jedi.

"Got it," came Te'Ami's voice over the comm, satisfied, content.

Mikkel almost had the missile . . . he could feel it, almost as if it were gripped in his hand. He could destroy it. The Force was his ally, and a powerful ally it was. He squeezed the missile . . . and suddenly, in a blast of violent flame, it was gone. But not by any action of his.

It was gone.

And so was Te'Ami.

The loss hit him like a blast wave, no less intense than the one that had killed his colleague. Mikkel clenched his fists, searching his spirit for calm.

His Vector's targeting scopes lit up with data—the full outline and location of the ship that had murdered Te'Ami, as well as detailed specifications of its armaments and defenses.

"Whoa, you guys seeing this? Target acquired—battle corvette . . . ugly-looking thing," came Joss Adren's voice. "Not the *New Elite*, another ship. Master Sutmani, how about your Vector and my Longbeam go after it while Captain Meggal grabs the flight recorder?"

Mikkel did not answer. He did not ask where this information had come from, or any questions at all, really. He just pushed his control sticks forward, as far as they would go, and his Vector's engines roared in response.

I have work to do, he thought.

"Blast it!" Lourna Dee cried, more emotional than she generally preferred to be.

The cursed Jedi had shot down her last missile before it could reach the flight recorder. Yes, that particular Jedi had died, but Lourna still had not succeeded at the mission, and it seemed like she'd probably revealed her position, too. She had a Longbeam and a Vector headed straight for her.

"Do we fire more missiles?" Attaman asked.

"Yes," Lourna said. "Send out the rest—everything we've got. We'll kill these idiots, too, and then go after the fragment."

The *Lourna Dee* shuddered slightly as the rest of its complement of missiles fired—another half dozen, trailing exhaust as they raced out toward the two growing dots of light headed toward her cruiser.

The Jedi . . . the blasted Jedi in that blasted Vector . . . shot down *four* of them. The other two were headed for the Longbeam, and it killed one with a laser blast and distracted the last with a flare.

"Who . . . are these guys?" Belial said.

He was worried. Lourna Dee could hear it. So, for that matter, was she. The *Lourna Dee* wasn't designed for straight-up fights. It was built to strike from hiding, kill its target, and leap away. It was light on armor, light on shields, and didn't have much in the way of laser cannons, either.

Could a Longbeam and a Vector actually take out her flagship? Just those two little vessels?

She decided she didn't want to find out.

Kassav or even Pan Eyta might have tried, gotten into some sort of doomed last-stand situation, but she was smarter than either of them. When circumstances change, you run the odds, you run the options, and then you pick the best choice you've got. And here, there was only one.

"Plug in the Path to get us out of here," she said. "We lost."

CHAPTER THIRTY-TWO

ABOVE ELPHRONA.

Ultident Margrona—just Dent since she was a teenager, she hated the name Ultident, thought it sounded prissy—yanked off her mask and let it fall to the floor of the cockpit. She didn't care if the stupid miners saw her face. She needed to breathe, needed air.

"They're on us, Dent!" Buggo said. "Comin' up fast!"

Dent knew that. The Jedi had landed a glancing blaster shot on their engines, and about 80 percent of top speed was the best they could manage. They had a Path from Lourna Dee that would let them get out of the system, but her ship's Path engine needed to calculate the jump from a specific region within Elphrona's gravity well—and that area was too far away to reach before the Jedi caught up. She'd heard stories about what these Vectors could do. They might look spindly, but those ships could take them apart, shot by shot. It wouldn't even be a contest. They'd end up with their engines completely gone, floating in the void, and then it'd be a hostage scenario, and how would that work out?

You're a Cloud, she told herself. *You wouldn't be a Cloud if you weren't smart. You aren't some stupid Strike. Think this through. Ride the storm.*

If the Jedi disabled their ship, they could buy time by threatening to kill the two kids and the dad until . . . what? The Jedi wouldn't let a band of Nihil kidnappers go. They'd board the ship eventually, and would probably kill Dent and her crew with their lightsabers right then and there, frontier justice. *Maybe* they'd get taken to prison on Elphrona instead.

Bad either way. Utter failure. Not very Nihil. She could just imagine what everyone would say. "You remember that gal Dent? Screwed up the easiest job ever—a snatch-and-grab on some nowhere planet. Got herself and all her Strikes killed. What an idiot."

She spared half a thought for the two Strikes she'd left back down on the planet, the ones she'd already written off. She guessed it was possible Egga and Rel were still alive down on the planet somewhere, fighting the good fight, two loyal Strikes doing as their Cloud ordered.

They were both so stupid—just went along with what she told them to do even though *obviously* she was sending them off to get killed to buy time for her, Mack, and Buggo to get off the planet with the cargo. No, those two idiots were dead, for sure. They hadn't called in, and if they'd taken out the Jedi they would have asked for a pickup.

Ugh, she thought.

This *was* supposed to be the easiest job ever. She was so proud of herself for thinking it up. She'd heard that these four people had tried to go it alone in the Outer Rim, live "*authentically,*" cut themselves off from their rich family on Alderaan. It made her so *mad.* They had everything, these Blythes, and they threw it away to go dig in the dirt. But some people didn't have a choice like that. They were born in the dirt and they'd die there—people like her. Until the Nihil, anyway. Lourna Dee had recruited her with a promise . . . they were all in it together, they were a family, a new family . . . it all sounded so good. And it was *working,* too. She'd made Cloud, and found Strikes of her own to command—it was all coming together.

And then when she'd come up with this idea to take the Blythes and ransom them back to their rich grandparents on Alderaan, and her Storm had liked it and taken it to Lourna Dee herself, and then she'd taken it to Marchion Ro and he'd liked it, too, and she'd gotten the Paths she needed to pull it all off. It was *supposed to work out.*

But then, Jedi.

"Boss! What are we going to do? Boss!"

Buggo, bugging her, like he did. She should have sent *him* up into the hills to ambush the Jedi. But he was her second cousin's husband, which was family in a way, close as she had.

Laser blasts zipped past the cockpit—warning shots.

Mack was on the guns, returning fire, but she had no confidence in his ability to shoot down a Vector. They moved like ghosts, flipping and moving around and doing impossible things. Like the Jedi themselves, in fact.

Dent reached forward and tapped a few buttons on her control console. She wasn't supposed to make contact while on a mission—signals could be tracked—but what did she have to lose?

A voice came over the comlink—her Storm, a funny, charming Ugnaught named Zoovler Tom.

"Dent!" he said, happy to hear from her, apparently. "What's the good word? You got the packages we sent you to pick up?"

"Got 'em," she answered, trying to keep the panic out of her voice. "But we ran into trouble. Jedi, chasing us. Ship's damaged. We won't be able to make it to the transfer point before they get us. We need a new Path, right now. We're still in atmosphere, so it'll be a tricky one."

"Jedi, huh?" Zoovler said, no longer so happy. "Path at such a low altitude . . . that's gonna run into trouble with the planet's gravity well. That's a big ask, Ultident."

Dent frowned. She'd told Zoovler her real name once, in a moment of booze-filled closeness at one of the rallies. Now he was using it, just like a weapon. Blasted little nothing man, thought he was so special, so superior because he was a Storm. He was just an Ugnaught. If she made it out of this she'd poison his drink next time, and laugh at him as his ugly little face turned black.

"Send me your coordinates. I'll have to run it up the line," the Storm said. "Don't call again. Either you'll hear from me with a new Path . . . or you won't."

The connection went dead.

Think, she thought.

It would take time for Zoovler to talk to the other Storms, then they'd have to decide whether to talk to Lourna Dee, and she'd make the call on whether to ask the Eye for another Path or just cut her loose. She was just a Cloud . . . the odds weren't good. But she knew the Blythes were valuable, and if this whole thing could somehow be pulled out of the fire, everyone stood to gain—including Zoovler, including Lourna Dee, even including Marchion Ro.

That was the system. That's why the Nihil worked. Everyone did things their way, lived how they wanted, took what they wanted . . . and everyone got a piece, so it was in everyone's interest to keep the system going.

But if the Jedi caught them before all of that thinking and requesting happened, no one would get a damn thing. Especially Ultident Margrona.

"Mack," she said.

"Yeah," he answered, still firing at the Jedi chasing them, his shots hitting nothing but air.

"Take one of the kids," she said. "The little girl. Throw her out the air lock."

"Uh . . ." Mack said, doubt in his voice.

"What, now you got *qualms*?"

"No," he said. "I don't care, except that we already lost the adult human female. Now we lose another one, we're cutting our return in half."

You idiot, she wanted to scream. *Who cares about money, when if we don't get away there's no profits, no credits, no life. We'll be dead, you dumb Strike!*

"The Jedi will try to save the kid," she said, forcing a patient tone into her voice. "That's what they do. Might give us a chance to get away."

Mack grunted, and she heard him get up and head toward the back of the ship, where their three remaining Blythes were tied up in the cargo hold.

"Ride the storm, Dent," she whispered to herself. "Just ride the storm."

CHAPTER THIRTY-THREE

THE OUTER RIM. THE *THIRD HORIZON.*

"So that's what caused so much pain," said Chancellor Lina Soh, from her offices on Coruscant.

She was looking at a hi-res holo projected by one of her comms droids, while Avar Kriss and others from the Emergences task force were watching a vidscreen in the *Third Horizon*'s briefing chamber—but the images were the same: the last thing the *Legacy Run*'s scanners saw before the ship tore itself apart.

That thing was a ship, blocky and ugly, with three bright, jagged stripes across its hull—exactly as described by Serj Ukkarian on the *Panacea.* Three lightning bolts, which Senator Noor's people had confirmed as the insignia used by the Outer Rim marauders known as the Nihil. The vessel was moving through hyperspace, but not along the path of the swirling hyperspace tunnel, as had been the case with every ship Avar had ever seen. The Nihil ship was moving *across* hyperspace, at a right angle to the *Legacy Run*'s direction of travel, with strange red-and-gold turbulence rippling in its wake.

"I was given to understand something like this was impossible,"

Lina Soh said, her left hand idly stroking the head of one of her two giant pet cats—Avar knew their names, Matari and Voru, they were famous throughout the Republic, but she didn't know which was which.

The chancellor's words were slightly delayed, a factor of the distance between Coruscant and the Outer Rim Territories. Senate-level comms were given the highest priority over the relays, but parsecs were parsecs. That would change, hopefully—improving the galactic communications network was one of Lina Soh's planned Great Works—but not if they didn't solve the issue at hand.

"It should be impossible, Chancellor," Vellis San Tekka said, sitting at the table next to his partner, Marlowe, who nodded in agreement.

Avar sensed something there. Some unspoken communication between the San Tekkas. A careful choice of words.

Maybe Elzar was right, she thought. *Maybe we should have pushed them a little harder.*

Clearly he thought so. He was sitting across the table from her, and caught her eye. Nothing more than the tiniest glance, but she knew exactly what he was thinking, even without Force-related assistance.

She offered Elzar a tiny shrug. Whatever the San Tekkas knew, their help had been genuine and invaluable. Keven Tarr had told her there was no way he could have completed his navidroid array without their assistance. She didn't know whether that was true—the Hetzalian engineer was clearly a genius—but the San Tekkas had certainly helped Keven finish the array more quickly, and speed was of the essence here.

The genius in question was on another screen, a comms droid projecting his holo against one of the briefing chamber's other blank walls. Tarr had stayed on the Rooted Moon in Hetzal, and was using his array to process the data retrieved from the *Legacy Run*'s flight recorder. The massive, stitched-together computer brain had been completely repaired from the damage suffered when it first activated. In fact, not just repaired, but enhanced. Chancellor Soh had ordered Transportation Secretary Lorillia to provide Keven Tarr with as many navidroids as he needed. If he wanted a million, he was to get them, no matter the cost.

"Can someone summarize our conclusions thus far, please?" Lina Soh said.

Everyone looked at Avar. Somehow she had become the leader of the task force, despite sharing the room with an admiral, a senator, and various other high-level luminaries.

"We have learned that a group calling themselves the Nihil was directly connected to the catastrophe in Hetzal and the subsequent Emergences. They're a low-level marauder operation working in the Outer Rim—raiders, basically. They've done some terrible things, but they're a regional problem, handled by defense forces and security teams on a case-by-case basis. As bad as they are, they're small time.

"It seems—though this is informed speculation—that whatever happened in Hetzal gave them the ability to predict Emergences, much like Keven Tarr's navidroid array. They've used that ability twice that we're aware of. First, in Eriadu, as part of a botched extortion attempt. And second, at the fortieth Emergence, where they attempted to prevent our teams from retrieving the *Legacy Run*'s flight recorder, as they knew it would tie all of this directly back to them."

"That's where we lost one of your colleagues, the Jedi Knight Te'Ami, and two brave pilots in a Longbeam—Marcus Augur and Beth Petters, correct?"

Avar inclined her head slightly in silent agreement. The chancellor considered for a moment, scratching behind her targon's ear and getting an appreciative purr in response.

"Do we think these Nihil caused the *Legacy Run* disaster on purpose?"

"It doesn't seem like it," Elzar Mann said.

He gestured to the main vidscreen, which was still displaying the Nihil ship crossing through hyperspace, running on a loop.

"This is clearly a ship, and armed. If they wanted to destroy the *Legacy Run,* they could have fired their weapons. They didn't. The *Legacy*

Run just tore itself apart trying to evade this thing. Besides, as Master Kriss pointed out, this is a bunch of Outer Rim raiders. Opportunists, not planners. This all seems like a horrible accident."

"An accident that they promptly tried to profit from at Eriadu," Senator Noor said, pounding his fist on the table. "An accident that has cost the Outer Rim Territories dearly in lives, opportunity, and treasure. They must be held responsible."

Behind him, his aide nodded, a blue-skinned Chagrian, slim, tall, and precise in dress and manner. Jeni Wataro, Avar recalled.

"They will," Chancellor Soh said, holding up a hand. "First, we need to know whether it can happen again. San Tekkas . . . what is your view?"

Marlowe and Vellis glanced at each other briefly before speaking.

"We believe this was a tragic fluke, Chancellor," Marlowe said. "We do not think there is an overarching issue with hyperspace. However, this"—here he pointed at the vidscreen, still displaying the brutish ship looping across the *Legacy Run*'s path, over and over again, trailing its strange red-and-gold wake—"suggests the Nihil have an understanding of hyperspace that is at best unique and at worst hugely dangerous. That should be investigated, and quickly."

"Well, perfect, then," Senator Noor said. "You heard the man, Chancellor. Hyperspace is fine. The Outer Rim is suffering—and I know you want the Starlight Beacon to come online. It's time to reopen the lanes."

"Not yet, Senator," she said. "We know what happened, more or less—but just because it was an accident once doesn't mean it couldn't be done purposely in the future. It's not such a leap for marauders to become terrorists. This threat has to be eliminated."

Senator Noor began to sputter out a protest.

"Enough, Noor," Chancellor Soh said. "I've made my decision. I know you're concerned about the Rim. I am as well . . . but I'm responsible for the entire galaxy, and in case you've forgotten, hyperspace goes everywhere. If the Nihil can attack us in the lanes, nowhere is safe."

She turned to look at Admiral Kronara, standing at the far end of the briefing room.

"Admiral, I want you to activate the defense provisions in the RDC agreements. Gather a fleet from the treaty worlds and hunt down the Nihil. I've read the reports—even if there really is no further danger to hyperspace, these are still dangerous criminals who should not be able to operate with impunity. Even if they confine their raids to the Outer Rim, we are all the Republic."

"Very good, Chancellor," he said, sounding pleased.

Then again, he was an admiral.

"Do you have any idea where the Nihil are based?" Chancellor Soh continued. "Their headquarters?"

"If I may, Chancellor," Keven Tarr interjected, raising a hand. "I've already set my array to calculating the likely origin point of the Nihil vessel that caused the *Legacy Run* disaster. It originated in a spot near the Kur Nebula. I don't know if that's their base, but it's a place to start."

"Very good, Mr. Tarr," she replied, then looked out across the *Third Horizon*'s briefing chamber.

"You have all done very well so far," she said. "You discovered the cause of the *Legacy Run* tragedy. Now I give you a new assignment. You are to make sure it never, ever happens again. Whatever it takes."

Chancellor Lina Soh leaned forward, and both of her giant cats lifted their heads, their ears flattening in a threat display as they sensed their master's emotional intensity. Avar, despite herself, despite all her skill and training, found herself glad that half a galaxy separated her from this woman. She did not envy the Nihil, who now found themselves under the gaze of a person who had demonstrated the will to reshape an entire galaxy.

"I want these Nihil brought to justice," the chancellor said. "Every last one."

CHAPTER THIRTY-FOUR

NO-SPACE. THE GREAT HALL OF THE NIHIL.

This is the *moment,* Marchion Ro thought. *The new beginning.*

He stood in the center of the huge platform that was the Great Hall of the Nihil, open on all four sides to the nothingness of No-Space. Unsettling multicolored lights flickered in the far distance, nothing interrupting them but the silhouettes of the vessels that had brought Marchion and the three Tempest Runners to this forsaken, desolate place. The hall was empty—no feast tables interrupted its expanse, and the four of them were alone and unmasked.

Marchion looked at these people—Kassav, Pan Eyta, and Lourna Dee. They resented him and they resented one another, and all believed they could do better than the rest. There was no unity. There was no purpose to the Nihil, other than a desire for profit and a shared love for taking from others, flouting the system. That had to change.

This was the moment.

"I heard from my spy in Senator Noor's office," Marchion said. "The Jedi and the Republic have accessed the flight recorder they got when Lourna Dee failed her mission."

Lourna Dee blinked but didn't say anything.

"They know we were responsible for the *Legacy Run* disaster," Marchion continued. "One of Pan Eyta's Clouds was returning from a raid, using a Path, and ended up almost smashing into the *Run.*"

"That's not our fault!" Kassav said. "How were we supposed to know—"

"It doesn't matter if that wasn't our fault. Eriadu sure as hell was," Marchion said.

For once, Kassav shut his mouth.

"So, it's what happened in Hetzal, all the Emergences, Kassav's idiotic move at Eriadu, and then Lourna Dee basically proved we're involved when she tried and failed to get the flight recorder," Pan Eyta said, his voice like rubble falling off a cliff. "We're all over this. This is bad."

"What do you think's going to happen?" Lourna Dee said.

"They'll hunt us down," Pan said. "The Republic and the Jedi, too. We're not just some regional raider crew anymore. We're a threat to them. We caused the whole damn hyperspace blockade. They'll want to make an example of us."

"Look, we've had a good run," Kassav said. "Everyone's made money. It's not like we have to do this. We can just . . . go."

"And all those Storms and Clouds and Strikes in our Tempests? The ones who follow us, believe in us. What about them?" Lourna Dee said.

Kassav shrugged. "They can do whatever they want. They want to keep the Nihil going, keep riding the storm, that's their business. Nothing saying we can't ever retire. What, we gotta be Tempest Runners until the day we die? What about living off the spoils of a lifetime of hard work?"

Pan Eyta snorted. "You think they'll see it that way? They'll think we cut and run."

Kassav shrugged again. "The Nihil are about freedom, right? Do what you want, when you want. Well, maybe I want to get the hell out of here before a Jedi pulls out their lightsaber and cuts off my head."

"Didn't you once say you wanted to fight a Jedi?" Marchion Ro said, his tone mild. "Get yourself a good story to tell?"

Kassav said nothing.

This is the moment, Marchion thought.

He punched Kassav right in his stupid, cunning, savage face. Marchion's gloves were reinforced with armored plates and acceleration compensators; he could punch a hole in a durasteel wall and not feel a twinge of pain. He heard the sound as Kassav's stupid, cunning, savage nose crumpled under his fist, and by the Path it felt good.

Pan Eyta and Lourna Dee didn't move. They seemed stunned. This was not something the Eye did. The Eye didn't fight, especially not the Runners. He didn't have a Tempest to back him up. The Eye got a third of the take and was happy with it.

Change can be challenging, my friends, Marchion thought.

Kassav staggered back, his eyes gone wide, blood gushing from his nose—but only for a second. The man was no stranger to pain, and Marchion supposed he was no stranger to surprise punches in the face, either. Kassav's eyes narrowed and his hand ducked inside his fur cape, where he kept a secret blaster in violation of the Great Hall's rules. Marchion had known about it for years.

Marchion whipped up his arm, and one of the vibro-stars he kept in a sheath along his wrist whickered out. It sheared through half of Kassav's hand along with the butt of his blaster, and chunks of metal and flesh fell to the floor.

Kassav, to his credit, tried to keep fighting. Blood spurted from his nose and sprayed from what was left of his right hand, and yet he lunged forward, swinging a pretty credible punch with his left.

Marchion caught it, spun, and threw Kassav to the platform. He landed with a hollow, wet sound in a pool of his own blood.

"Nngh!" Kassav said, the first sound he'd made since the fight began—the man was tough, there was no doubt about it.

Marchion put his boot on the Tempest Runner's chest. Not lightly, either. He pressed hard, like he wanted to shove the man right through the blasted deck, into the empty space on the other side.

"I am the Eye of the Nihil, as was my father before me," he said. "We made this organization what it is, and I will not watch you destroy it with your selfishness, fear, and weakness. You made a mistake at Eriadu, Kassav, and it showed us your belly. You need to remember how this works, Chief. The Nihil need to stay strong. And one way that happens . . ."

He bent at the waist, his eyes narrowed, his teeth bared.

". . . is by cutting out the weak."

Marchion pressed harder with his boot.

"I have a plan to fix this," he said. "Fix all of it. Do you want to hear it?"

Marchion Ro put a little more weight on Kassav's chest, and the man groaned. He nodded. Marchion stepped back and watched as Kassav pulled himself to his feet.

"I understand why you're all worried. This isn't a good situation, and it's on the verge of getting worse. But listen to what I have to say," Marchion said.

The Tempest Runners looked at him, wary but interested.

"This will solve everything," Marchion said. "Get the Republic off our backs, maybe even kill some Jedi. It'll be back to business as usual. No more Emergences. Just the Paths, and the plunder. We can start bringing in new Strikes again. The good times will keep on rolling."

The wariness dialed back, and the interest dialed up, even from Kassav. Marchion knew it would. None of them wanted to go it alone, without the Paths. They'd all made piles of credits from the Nihil, but they spent it as fast as it came in, on fancy ships and fancy clothes and elaborate banquets. Their greed would make the decision for them.

"Look—we're smarter, and faster, and we've got the Paths," he went on. "We're ten steps ahead of the Republic. I'm telling you, we can fix this whole thing. The Nihil are my whole life. I'm not walking away without a fight."

"We're listening," Pan Eyta said.

"Okay," Marchion said. "We can get the flight recorder back, and without that, the Republic won't be able to find us. We can lie low for a bit, reorganize, even move to the Mid Rim . . . the Paths let us work anywhere in the galaxy."

He pointed at Kassav and Lourna Dee, one with each hand.

"You both made big mistakes, and your crews saw you do it. People are talking. You look weak. Your Storms have to be thinking maybe this is their chance for a hostile takeover. You can fix all that. Do it right, you'll be heroes to your Tempests."

He smiled at them, a big, encouraging smile. They didn't seem reassured.

"Kassav, I've gotten word from my Republic sources that the flight recorder was damaged when the *Legacy Run* blew up. They got some data from it, but not the full set, not enough to find us. It's being sent to a special facility to extract the rest. You can intercept the transport and destroy it.

"Lourna Dee, go to Elphrona and help your crew there finish that kidnapping job. We might need funds, and since that operation's already in progress, we might as well bring in some credits, show the crews we're still taking their needs into account. This is a time for unity. We have to come together.

"I'll give you both the Paths you need to get it done."

Lourna Dee nodded. Then, after a moment, so did Kassav.

"Do you . . . need me to do anything?" Pan Eyta said.

That was unusual. A Tempest Runner asking the Eye for orders was just . . . not the way it was done. The dynamic had shifted. They could all feel it. The moment for them to leave had come and gone. They had acknowledged that if they were going to stay with the Nihil and reap all its benefits, then they needed the Eye to save them from themselves.

"No, Pan," Marchion said. "You're fine for now."

"Should we vote?" Lourna Dee asked.

"Absolutely," Marchion Ro said.

They did. It was unanimous.

"Go," Marchion said. "We don't have a lot of time. Save the Nihil."

The Tempest Runners left, heading for the air lock.

Marchion let them get a few steps away, then spoke.

"Kassav," he said.

The man turned back.

Marchion pointed.

"Don't forget your hand."

CHAPTER THIRTY-FIVE

ELPHRONA SYSTEM.

Bell couldn't believe what he was seeing—a hatch along the hull of the Nihil ship had opened . . . and a small figure had been tossed out. Just . . . thrown, like nothing.

He gasped. Loden, ahead of him in the pilot's seat, put the Vector into a steep dive.

"Padawan," his master said. "You will save the child. I will continue on and save the others. Do not fear. I am so proud to have been your teacher.

"I believe in you."

The Vector's cockpit levered open, the wind rushing past, so loud that speech was impossible.

But what more was there to say?

Bell unclipped his safety harness and leapt out.

Immediately gravity took him, and he fell into a spin. That didn't matter. They were kilometers above the surface of Elphrona, which meant he had some time, but not much. If he was going to save the little girl—and he was sure it was the little girl, a *child,* tossed away by the Nihil like garbage—he needed to focus.

He pushed away his awareness of Loden's Vector shooting back up into the sky, continuing the chase alongside Indeera in her own ship. He forgot about the ground, the sky, everything but the Force, and searched for a tiny spot of light within it, the sense of a lost child who needed to be saved.

There.

Bell could barely open his eyes against the rushing wind. He wished he had a pair of goggles . . . but truthfully, he didn't need them, or his eyes, either. He had the Force.

He wrapped his arms and legs tight to himself and angled his body down, feeling himself shoot forward as he became more aerodynamic.

Bell reached out to the Force, asking it to push him even faster. The little girl was flailing, and that surely created some wind resistance, but they would both reach terminal velocity soon enough, and then he wouldn't be able to catch her. The second or so of fall before Bell had leapt from the Vector had undoubtedly given her a significant lead.

But the Force answered, and perhaps the sleekness of his Jedi leathers let him shoot forward more quickly than he otherwise might. All he knew was that he was getting closer. The Blythe child's terror was looming in his senses, rising, her fear overwhelming.

He put it aside.

As he approached, he reached out and used the Force to pull the little girl to him. He enfolded her in his arms. She struggled—of course she did—who wouldn't?

He pulled part of his tunic over their heads, enough to block some of the wind, then looked at the child. He didn't know that he'd ever seen someone so frightened.

Bell pointed to the Jedi insignia on his chest. Miraculously, she calmed. She knew what he was, and she thought she was saved.

Not yet, Bell thought.

He pulled her close, cupped his hand over her ear to block the wind, and spoke.

"Close your eyes," he said. "I'm with you now. You're not alone."

He had no idea if she had heard, but he'd done what he could to calm her. Now he had to focus.

Bell glanced down, squinting against the wind. He was looking for a soft spot—water, maybe, even a slow slope they might be able to roll down—anything to ease their landing.

There was nothing. Just the rough landscape of the planet—the swirls of the magnetic mountain ranges, and rust plains between. Elphrona was not a soft world.

They were falling, from a height a hundred times higher than anything he'd ever tried in training, and even then he'd never landed successfully. For a moment, he hoped against hope that perhaps Porter Engle could miraculously appear at the last minute—but the Ikkrukki was far away by then, and in any case, he had his own Blythe to save.

No one was coming to save him, or the girl. He had to do it all, and he had to do it alone.

Bell opened himself to the Force. He did not think about the ground. He thought about the child in his arms, and how unfair it was that these things had happened to her.

He knew he had the power to save her, to let her continue living in the light. Why would the cosmic Force have given him his abilities, if not for this very purpose?

The wind was not his enemy, nor gravity itself. They were both part of the Force, just as he was, just as the child was. If he fought them, he was fighting himself.

He should not try to fight. He should try to understand.

Bell Zettifar relaxed.

He came to know something profound—perhaps something about the Force. Perhaps something about himself, something he would try to understand more clearly later. He thought it was the reason that he had been so bad at saving himself from falls, despite his master's best efforts to teach him.

Being a Jedi was not about saving oneself.

It was about saving others.

The roar of the wind past Bell's ears lessened, becoming no stronger than a powerful breeze. He could hear the little Blythe. She was praying, or chanting. He couldn't understand the words, but it was the same short phrase, over and over.

The wind quieted further, to silence. Bell opened his eyes. They were barely ten meters from the ground, and they drifted downward, slow as a leaf, to land gently on the slate-colored ground. He could understand what the girl was saying now.

"I'm not alone."

He sat up. The girl clung to him.

"We're okay now," he said. "What's your name?"

She looked at him, eyes wide.

"I'm Bee," she said. "But that's just what people call me. My big name is Bailen."

"That's a little like mine," he said. "I'm Bell. We're safe now, Bailen. Everything's going to be all right."

The child gave him a dubious look, the look of a kid who knew she was being told something untrue by an adult, no matter how much she wanted to believe it. Her face cracked, and she burst into tears.

Bell just held her. He looked up at the sky, searching for the Vectors or the Nihil ship. Nothing. Not even an exhaust trail.

Everything's going to be all right, he thought.

He didn't believe it, either.

Interlude

The Council.

Jora Malli positioned herself before the comms droid that would transmit her image to Coruscant, to the Chamber at the very top of the Order's great Temple where the Jedi Council met to deliberate. At that moment, she was aboard the *Ataraxia*, the Jedi's beautiful, elegant starship, almost a temple in and of itself.

The ship had dropped out of hyperspace near Felucia, expressly so Jora could attend this particular meeting with maximal stability and clarity of signal. It was, in all likelihood, the last vote she would ever take as a member of the Jedi Council. The Starlight Beacon would be brought online very soon, at which point Jora would officially step down from the Council and take on her new role running the Jedi quarter on the massive space station.

Jora Malli had missed many votes in the past—while she took her role seriously, she generally believed she could serve the light more effectively out in the galaxy than sitting in the Jedi Temple. But this day's deliberations were significant, and the entire Council had assembled, those not physically present on Coruscant sending their image via high-priority holotransmissions, as Jora was doing.

The comms droid projected an image of the Council Chamber for Jora to see: the elegant circular room with huge windows in every wall providing uninterrupted views of the Coruscant cityscape. It was day at the Temple, and the sun shone in, illuminating the beautiful mosaic inlaid upon the floor. The windows were symbolically significant, as well—the High Council conducted its business in the open, with nothing to hide.

Twelve seats were set at equal intervals around the room, each sized and designed for its particular occupant. Yarael Poof, Rano Kant, Oppo Rancisis, Keaton Murag, and Ada-Li Carro were present in person. Six others, including herself, were appearing via hologram, with yet another droid in the Council Chamber projecting their images to the other attendees. Eleven Council members, all but Master Rosason, in the midst of a delicate diplomatic negotiation from which she could not step away.

Jora thought about her Padawan, Reath Silas.

She wished he were there with her. He could learn many things from observing a Council meeting. Truth be told, she just missed the young man.

Reath was seventeen, a good student, but perhaps not entirely thrilled that he would soon follow his master to the Starlight Beacon instead of remaining on Coruscant. The frontier held little interest for him. Well, of course. Reath was, in fact, seventeen. No space station, no matter how exotic, could compare to the greatest city in the galaxy.

She had left him behind to give him a bit more time on Coruscant before he joined her in the Outer Rim, a small kindness she had been happy to provide. But just as his time in the Core was done, Reath had been pulled into a mission alongside two more experienced Jedi, Cohmac Vitus and Orla Jareni, both Knights. She had questions about Orla, but Cohmac was steady. Reath would be fine, if perhaps a little frustrated at losing his last bit of time in the Core.

Ah, well. Such was the life of a Jedi. Better to get used to it early.

She glanced at Sskeer, sitting across the table from her, watching silently, his long, clawed arms folded across his chest. He looked imposing, as always, a slab of scaled muscle and sharp teeth in Jedi robes. Trandoshan Jedi were rare, because the planet's culture was built around predation and supremacy, ideals that did not always mesh well with the precepts of the Order. Even when Trandoshan children did have an affinity for the Force, it was unusual for them to be brought to the Jedi Temple for training. But Sskeer had not only made it to Coruscant, but had also excelled, becoming a full-fledged Jedi Master. All things were possible.

Jora didn't imagine she would have direct need of him during this Council meeting, and she thought he knew that, too—but Sskeer was never far, and it was often when she'd thought she'd have no need for him at all that he'd come in most handy. Sskeer had personally saved her life four times.

And counting, she assumed.

The meeting began—and the matter to be discussed truly was important. The chancellor of the Republic, Lina Soh, had asked the Jedi to participate directly in a mission she had authorized for the Republic Defense Coalition to hunt down and either imprison or eradicate a group of Outer Rim raiders who called themselves the Nihil.

These people had interfered with the galactic hyperspace lanes in what appeared to be an effort to extort systems out of enormous sums of money. Bad enough, but their actions had also caused the deaths of billions of people and paralyzed a wide swath of the galaxy.

The Nihil must be dealt with. The only question was the role of the Jedi in that action.

Jora listened as the various Council members presented their arguments. Great emphasis was placed on interpreting the will of the Force, listening for the voice of the Force, taking direction from the Force, and so on. Jora found that a little tiresome. A philosophical vortex.

For her, it was very simple. The Jedi were deeply connected to the light side of the Force. Whatever choice any Jedi made was, therefore, the will of the Force. Study and focus allowed the Jedi to become better instruments of that will, certainly, in much the way that a well-maintained lightsaber functioned better than one that had fallen into disrepair—but getting caught up in an endless debate about what the Force might want was paralyzing. A waste of time.

"This is a military action," Master Adampo said, stroking the long white whiskers dangling from his chin, his voice strong and direct. "The Jedi are not a military force. I believe it is that simple."

"But we have been a military force in the past," said Oppo Rancisis. "In fact, our predecessors waged and won the Great Sith War. There is endless precedent in the chronicles for this sort of thing."

"True, but we are not at war now. We are the farthest thing from it," said Rana Kant.

"Not the farthest," replied Yarael Poof. "There have been times in our history when the Order was reduced to but a handful of members."

"Why are we talking about history?" said Ephru Shinn, the newest member of the Council, a Mon Calamari, selected by Yoda to hold his seat while the great Master was on his sabbatical from Council business. "We should be concerned with now, not old empires or victories or defeats. What is our role in this Republic, at this precise moment?"

She lifted a hand.

"I believe that the Jedi should, at all times, present to the many peoples of the galaxy a way of life centered on peace. We must show them the way. The Republic is uniquely receptive to such an idea at this moment."

"Yes, but we are guardians of two ideals, are we not?" said Yarael Poof. "Sometimes, unfortunately, they come into conflict. We must always strive for peace, but also justice. Peace without justice is flawed, hollow at its core. It is the peace provided by tyranny."

"I do not believe there has been a single instance of the Jedi getting involved in the military matters of galactic government that has generated anything but endless complexity," Ephru replied.

"So we should strive only for simplicity? The galaxy is not a simple place, Master Shinn," said Grandmaster Lahru.

And on it went. Jora listened, but did not speak, letting the other Council members make their positions clear. Those positions settled with five in favor of agreeing to the chancellor's request to include Jedi in the mission against the Nihil, and five against.

The final choice was down to Jora, which seemed appropriate to her, since it would be her ship, the *Ataraxia*, that would accompany Republic forces on the mission.

The other members of the Council looked at her, waiting for her to speak. And so she did.

"You know I am not much for words. I prefer to act. In this case, I think the decision is simple enough. It's the same question I ask myself whenever I do anything at all."

She again wished Reath were with her, thinking of the lesson he might learn here. She would have to pass it along to him later.

"Does the action I'm about to take bring more light to the galaxy?"

She spread her hands.

"In this case, I believe the answer is clear. The Nihil have snuffed out countless people across the Outer Rim, and caused endless strife and suffering. We should act to reduce their ability to do anything like this again. I will take the *Ataraxia* and accompany Admiral Kronara's fleet."

"And then what?" asked Oppo Rancisis. "Do you have any sense of what you will do once the Nihil are found?"

"Yes, Master Rancisis," Jora said. "Whatever the Force wills."

PART THREE
The Storm

CHAPTER THIRTY-SIX

THE OUTER RIM. THE KUR NEBULA.

The *New Elite* dropped out of hyperspace near a bright-green nebula that cast the ship's bridge in a sickly, swamplike hue. Kassav hated the color. He was from Sriluur out in Hutt Space, a dry world where the only time you saw something green was when it was covered with mold. Green was unnatural, a bad shade, a bad omen.

Lot of those going around.

The ship's bridge was silent—no music. Kassav didn't feel like it. He stared down at what remained of his hand as the medical droid attended to it, sealing off the slashed-open flesh, patching it up as best it could. His options seemed to be to retain a claw with a few fingers still attached, or just lop off what was left and go for a prosthetic. Either way, his blaster hand was never going to be the same. He'd have to learn to shoot with his left.

Marchion Ro, Kassav thought. *Marchion blasted Ro.*

"Did the Eye tell you when those Republic ships would show up?" Wet Bub said. "We're bringing plenty of firepower—should be able to knock down anything they bring. Get rid of that flight recorder thing Marchion Ro told us about . . . and then it's back to business!"

The Gungan grinned, his huge, idiotic teeth glowing like cave mushrooms in the weird light from the nebula.

"I'm sick of all this waiting around," Bub went on. "We're the Nihil. We need to ride the storm!"

Kassav looked up from the wreckage of his favorite hand, scowling at his lieutenant. "Listen, you stupid cloaca. You're gonna wait as long as I tell you to. And then you'll *do* exactly what I tell you to."

Wet Bub held up his hands, his two perfectly fine hands, like he was rubbing it in, and backed away. "Right, boss," he said.

Bub looked like a corpse. A moldy, three-weeks-dead corpse. Kassav glanced around the bridge, at the rest of his crew. Everyone did. That blasted nebula.

Outside the bridge viewport, he saw the rest of his Tempest dropping in, as ordered. About a hundred ships, mostly small—Strikeships and Cloudships—with a scattering of larger vessels. Assault craft, modified freighters, that kind of thing.

His people, all loyal to him and him alone. They were all Nihil, sure, but these crews didn't take orders from Pan Eyta or Lourna Dee . . . and definitely not Marchion Ro.

Kassav considered his fleet, casting his eyes from one ship to the next. Basically his entire Tempest, barring a few of his people off on jobs. Might not be the prettiest in the galaxy, but it was powerful. It could cause some real damage. Pan Eyta chose stuck-up thinkers for his crews. Lourna Dee picked liars and sneaks. Kassav . . . now, he had always chosen warriors. He thought if it came to it, his Tempest could probably take Pan Eyta's and Lourna Dee's groups combined. Warriors, every one of them, and they all believed the same thing, a lesson Kassav had learned by the time he could walk: When you're in a battle, you never stop fighting. Win or die.

In fact, looking at his Tempest swarming around the *New Elite,* the idea occurred to him, and not for the first time: Did he really need the

Nihil at all? Why not just take his people and go? Head across the Rim, find somewhere else to work. The Paths were useful, but he didn't need them, and he sure as hell didn't need Marchion Ro. It was a big galaxy. He could start a new Nihil; he'd learned all the techniques—no reason he couldn't use them somewhere else.

But none of this blasted storm business. He was sick of it. Maybe something to do with . . . fire. That could work. Sparks on the bottom, then flames, blaze, inferno . . . yeah, that could work just fine. And him at the top, as the sun. Kassav, a big, powerful star around which all else revolved.

Perfect. It would work like a charm. There were always people looking for something to belong to, a way to get ahead—and the Republic was rich, fat—ready for plucking. The Jedi investigators Marchion was so scared of were looking for the *Nihil,* not him specifically. Yeah, maybe they knew his name, his ship, after Eriadu . . . but he could change both. If Marchion Ro and the other Tempest Runners loved the organization so much, let them take the heat and figure out how to deal with everyone who wanted the Nihil gone.

In fact, why the hell was he waiting around for those Republic ships with that stupid flight recorder? Better if they kept it, and used it to track down Marchion and the rest of the Nihil. It would solve two problems at once. He had his entire Tempest assembled right here. He could give the order to leave right now.

Kassav waved the medical droid back. He reached for the communications controls on his command chair, a little awkwardly with his bad hand, and began to key in the code for a fleet-wide transmission.

Goodbye storm, hello fire, he thought.

Dellex, over at the monitoring station, spoke.

"Ships dropping out of hyperspace, Kassav."

He looked at her, his eyes narrowed.

"The Republic transports?"

She leaned forward, as if she couldn't believe what the screens were telling her.

"It might be the Republic, but it's not just a few ships," she said, and looked back up at him, her organic eye gone wide.

"It's . . . a battle fleet."

Admiral Kronara stood on the bridge of the *Third Horizon,* analyzing the tactical display, focusing on the rapidly updating data about the enemy forces provided by his ship's sensors. It looked like his coalition was about to face the full Nihil fleet—and this didn't seem like a force of disorganized marauders, either. Dozens of ships of all sizes, from fighters all the way up to a central flagship, some kind of custom-built thing about the size of a standard corvette. Scans were already building a picture of its military capabilities, which seemed fairly significant. It was no pushover. None of the ships out there seemed to be, in fact. Every single one was armed, with everything from laser cannons to magnetic mines.

There was potential here for a battle the likes of which he, a ranking military commander in the Republic, hadn't seen in decades. That was the problem with how good Chancellor Soh was at her job. The Hutts were quiet, the Mandalorians hadn't kicked up any trouble since before he was born, and the largest engagement most of his people ever got to handle was on the level of a skirmish. There wasn't even a standing Republic fleet—just the odd *Emissary*-class cruiser like the *Third Horizon,* and various smaller support and tactical ships.

By and large, sectors and planets handled their own security. On the rare occurrence of a more serious threat, the Republic Defense Coalition treaties could be activated. Prosperous worlds like Chandrila and Alderaan were called upon to supply ships and personnel under the command of Republic military officers, which were returned to their homeworlds once the crisis was complete. That's what had happened here. On the chancellor's orders, Kronara put out the call, and he'd managed to assemble a good-sized task force. Most of the treaty worlds had been more than happy to contribute matériel—all wanted a chance to strike back against these Nihil, the criminals that had crippled the galaxy.

Under his direct command, Kronara had the *Third Horizon,* with its Longbeams and a fairly robust complement of Incom Z-28 Skywings—in fact, his hangars comprised most of the small division of attack craft under direct Republic control. Beyond that, RDC member worlds had contributed five *Pacifier*-class sector patrol cruisers, each with a crew of a hundred, as well as their own Longbeam and Skywing squadrons. And . . . another group was on the way. Not a signatory to the RDC treaty, and not necessarily the people he would have invited along, but also not the sort of people you could easily refuse. Especially considering the tragedy visited upon them by the Emergences.

Another ship was visible on his display, outside his command authority but certainly an ally: the *Ataraxia,* the one large starship under direct control of the Jedi Order. It was a beautiful ship, designed to subtly evoke the Order's symbol with its hull and sweeping, curved wings accented in white and gold. While the *Ataraxia* would be permanently stationed at the new Starlight Beacon station once it opened, today it had come to offer support to the RDC task force. The ship was lightly armed, but it could carry a large number of Vectors, and on this day its hangars were full. Before the ship arrived, Kronara hadn't been certain the Jedi would participate at all, despite Chancellor Soh's request. The Jedi were linked to the Republic in many ways, but they could and did go their own way whenever they thought it was appropriate. Whatever their reasoning, he was glad the Order was here. Jedi tended to come in handy.

Admiral Kronara would never wish for war, but he would take any opportunity he got to assemble a coalition task force and get real-time combat and coordination training. Even better, there was no moral ambiguity about the situation. These Nihil were clearly on the wrong side of history. A fully justified military action against a significant force? A chance to make the galaxy safer? Yes. He'd take it.

He refocused on the display, thinking through the tactics he was about to employ. His forces were in green, in disciplined, uniform rows. The Nihil were a swirling, chaotic blob of red. A lot of ships out there. Made it difficult to predict how things might go. Kronara had studied the few bits of intelligence available on the Nihil, gathered by security forces from various Outer Rim worlds. By reputation, they were a pretty savage bunch. More troubling—reports suggested they could almost appear and disappear at will. He didn't know what that meant, but it suggested they could have some very unique tactics to deploy.

Well, let them. He had some tactics of his own.

He looked again at his own small fleet on the display. Not exactly an armada, but plenty of force, all things considered.

If the Nihil wanted a fight, they'd get one.

Admiral Kronara keyed his comlink, calling over to the *Ataraxia* in order to coordinate his initial moves with its commander, Master Jora Malli. He knew her decently well—she had a strong military mind, as much as any Jedi could, and was slated to run Starlight Beacon's Jedi temple once the station became operational. But since that had not yet come to pass, she was here, in command of the Order's response to the Nihil.

"Master Malli," he said, "we're going to attempt to contact the Nihil command ship. Occlusion from the nebula means there aren't many spots to jump to hyperspace, and we've blocked most of them off. The majority of the Nihil ships don't look big enough to have onboard navicomps that can calculate another way out in any reasonable amount of time. They'll have to either talk or fight—they can't just run. If they do decide to light things up, you'll be ready to go?"

"Of course, Admiral," came the smooth voice of Jora Malli. "I think I'll take a Vector out myself, if it comes to that. I have Avar Kriss here on the *Ataraxia*—she can help link the Jedi together, as she did in the Hetzal system."

"Fantastic," the admiral said, and he meant it. The Jedi were always impressive, but what he'd seen in Hetzal during the *Legacy Run* disaster was remarkable. If Avar Kriss could apply that skill set to an actual battle, it could bring a decisive advantage.

Admiral Kronara clasped his hands at the small of his back. He gave the tactical display one last look, then gave the order.

"Open a comm channel," he said. "We'll see if these criminals want to talk."

"They're trying to talk to us," Dellex said.

"Don't answer," Kassav snapped.

"I wasn't going to," she snapped back. "But we need to do something. All this space dust from the nebula means we can't just jump from anywhere without blowing up. The Republic ships are blocking the closest clear access point to the hyperlane. We could get out with a Path, but the Eye didn't give us one."

"We gotta attack, right?" said Gravhan, at the gunner's station. "Battle fleet or not, if we don't kill these guys, no more Nihil."

"Just give me a second to think, will you?" Kassav snapped.

He turned to Dellex.

"Is there another one? An open spot to get to hyperspace without a Path, I mean."

The woman consulted her screens.

"Yeah. Not super close, but if we go for it full throttle, we can probably get there before the Republic ships catch us."

"Okay," Kassav said. "Give the order. All ships, head for that other exit point. From there, scatter, and wait until they hear from me before they do anything. *Anything,* you got it? No raids, no nothing. Just lie low until I give the word."

Gravhan spoke up. "I don't want to question you, boss, but—"

"Then don't," Kassav said, giving him a dark look.

His hand hurt. His head hurt. Everything hurt. He just wanted something *good* to happen. Gravhan didn't seem to get that, though. He swallowed. His throat felt dry as dust.

"Thing is, Kassav, Marchion Ro told me, Wet Bub, and Dellex about the orders he gave you, and he said that if you didn't do what he wanted, then—"

"Then *what*? What do you think you're going to do?" Kassav roared, pulling his blaster with his left hand and pointing it at his supposedly loyal Storm. Now Marchion Ro was telling his people what to do? Giving them instructions behind his back?

Wet Bub and Dellex drew their own weapons—well, Dellex just powered up her shoulder cannon, but he saw it light up and heard the little hum. The other Nihil on the bridge froze, unsure of what to do, waiting to see how it would all play out.

"We're supposed to kill you," Wet Bub said. "That's what the Eye told us to do, if you didn't do what he said. He said what you did at Eriadu put everyone in danger, and this is the only way to keep us all safe. Only way to make things good again."

What I did at Eriadu, you traitorous lizard? What I did? Like you weren't standing right there next to me, helping me run the whole job, Kassav thought.

He could maybe have taken all three . . . but not with his bad hand. He kept his blaster aimed at Gravhan and spoke, snarling out the words.

"You think Marchion Ro knew we'd end up with a Republic battle fleet on us? Look, this is one of two things—either he knew, and he sent us out here to die, or he didn't, in which case he'd want us to get out of here to live to fight another day. Whichever it is, we need to *go.* We can find another way to deal with the stupid flight recorder."

He saw his three Storms considering these possibilities.

"Wet Bub, get on the comm. Try to raise the Eye. Tell him what's happening, and ask him for a Path out of here."

The Gungan gave it a second or two, then holstered his blaster and turned to the communications console.

"Dellex, you give the order to the rest of the fleet. Tell them to run, get to the other transfer point as fast as they can. Gravhan, get back to the weapons grid, just in case these Republic bastards decide to start shooting."

"No answer from Marchion Ro," Wet Bub said. "But the Republic Cruiser is hailing us again."

Kassav gave his lieutenants a knowing look.

You see? that look conveyed. *We're on our own out here.*

Without another word, they put away their weapons and followed his orders.

He felt the *New Elite*'s engines kick into a higher gear as it prepared for its run to escape the trap he was increasingly sure Marchion Ro had led them into.

"Ugh," Dellex said, her voice uncharacteristically subdued.

"What now?" he asked.

"Another fleet just dropped in. From the other hyperspace transfer point. We're boxed in, Kassav."

"Tell me it's Nihil," he said. "Tell me it's Pan Eyta's Tempest."

"It's not. The ships all register as being from Eriadu."

"That's where we messed up the extortion job," Wet Bub said. "Where that moon got obliterated."

An entirely unnecessary clarification. Everyone on that bridge knew exactly what they had done at Eriadu.

What they might not know, though, was the reputation of the people who lived there. Kassav did. He had looked them up after his little visit to their system. What he'd learned had made him curse for a minute straight. Turned out that the Nihil weren't the only predators in the galaxy.

Eriadu was one of those warrior planets. A whole culture steeped in ideals of revenge and justice and blood and honor, easily slighted, always having duels and poisoning each other and whatever.

But for the moment, it seemed like they had stopped squabbling long enough to come together to hunt him.

"Guess we're not running after all," Kassav said. "Tell every ship. Time to fight. Let's kill 'em all."

Everyone on the bridge turned back to their stations, getting ready for battle. They seemed excited, even his idiot lieutenants, who should probably know better.

Kassav tapped a control on his command chair, and the music started. More wreckpunk, throbbing and pulsing and clanging. He set the volume to full.

"For the Nihil!" Kassav shouted, painfully closing his maimed hand into a fist and holding it above his head.

"For the storm!" came the answering cry, anticipatory and eager.

Kassav looked at his crew, his eyes flitting from face to face.

In the green light of the Kur Nebula, still pouring through the bridge viewports, they all looked like corpses, three days dead.

For the Nihil, Kassav thought. *For the storm.*

CHAPTER THIRTY-SEVEN

SPACE. ELPHRONA SYSTEM.

Loden Greatstorm pushed his Vector a bit harder, accelerating toward the wounded Nihil ship through the vacuum, the iron- and rust-colored orb of Elphrona receding behind them. He sensed Indeera doing the same in her own ship.

Not far now. He knew that a safe jump to lightspeed required a significant amount of distance from Elphrona. Like the world's surface, the space around the planet was a roiling mass of magnetic fields and gravity distortions. There was no way the Nihil would be able to escape before he and Indeera caught them.

And then . . . well, the Force would be his guide. He did not want the Nihil kidnappers to die. He did not want anyone to die, ever—but sometimes, he had found, people chose their own ends, and there was nothing he or even the Force seemed to be able to do about it.

Well, that was fatalistic. He'd do everything he could to save every life on that ship. But the innocents would have priority, and the line between innocent and guilty had been drawn very clearly when the Nihil chose to throw a young child out the air lock.

He keyed on his comm. "Bell, do you read me?"

"Master!" came the immediate response.

"Did you . . ."

"I did," Bell said. "I caught her, and we came down safely. Her name is Bee. She's afraid for her brother and father, but she's all right."

Loden grinned.

"I knew you could do it, kid," he said. "As far as I'm concerned, nothing the Council could come up with for your trials would beat what you just pulled off. I'm going to put you in for elevation to Jedi Knight as soon as this all gets wrapped up."

"Seriously?"

"Seriously. You heard me, right, Indeera?"

"Absolutely, Loden," came Indeera Stokes across the comm.

"See, Bell? All set," Loden said. "But you need to get Bee back to the outpost. Her mother's there, with Porter Engle. Tell her we'll have the rest of her family with her before she knows it. Have Porter give her some stew."

"I thought I'd introduce her to Ember, too," Bell said.

"Perfect. I'm going to sign off, Bell. Indeera and I have some work to do. I look forward to celebrating your elevation, Jedi Knight Zettifar."

"Master . . . thank you."

"I'm not your master anymore, Bell. You're a Jedi Knight."

"Not until the Council declares it, and I want you there when it happens. May the Force be with you."

"It is, Bell. Don't worry. See you soon."

Loden flipped off his comm and brought his focus back to the Nihil ship. They were within laser range, and sure enough a few bolts whipped back at them from the vessel's aft cannon.

He and Indeera each dodged to the side, their Vectors moving as one, easily avoiding the blasts. His comm crackled to life.

"How do we do this, Loden?" Indeera said.

"We both have room for one passenger, and there are two Blythes left on that ship. I'll slow them down, then you'll get the first one, and I'll get the second."

"That's it?"

"That's it. I don't want to overthink this."

"Fair enough. I'll follow your lead."

Loden accelerated, pushing his Vector to a speed that rapidly overtook the Nihil ship.

"Get ready," he said—both to Indeera and, at least to some extent, to himself.

He shoved his control sticks forward and to the side, simultaneously reaching out with the Force and taking the Vector's reactive control surfaces and *boosting* them, allowing him to perform a maneuver impossible for any pilot but a Jedi to pull off. Over the comm, he heard Indeera gasp, and despite himself, he found himself smiling.

The Vector spiraled up and *over* the Nihil ship, spinning like a drill, avoiding desperate shots from the vessel's cannons, and ending in a position where his own craft was nose-to-nose with the Nihil's but flying *backward,* matching the much larger ship's speed perfectly. He was close enough to the other ship that he was inside the effective range of its cannons, and as long as he stayed there, it couldn't hit him.

But more important, he had a clear view inside its cockpit, where a rather alarmed woman was flying the ship. She was a Nihil, the first he'd seen with her mask off, and she looked like . . . a person. A youngish human woman with ragged hair cut short, reddish dirt on her face from the sprint across the surface of Elphrona, and two jagged stripes painted down one cheek in blue. A child of the Force, like any other.

But the Force did not make your decisions for you, and this particular person had done many terrible things, whether by necessity or choice.

Her reckoning had come due.

Loden lifted a hand from his control sticks. He moved it gently to one side, locking eyes with the Nihil woman, and spoke.

"You will slow your ship and open your outer air lock hatch."

Through the transparisteel of the cockpit, he saw the woman mouth the words. Loden reserved the mind touch for times of extraordinary necessity—but this was that, if anything ever was. She didn't need to hear what he had said, either—the technique was aptly named. Mind-to-mind, that's all you needed.

Loden kept his eyes focused on the pilot, maintaining the connection in case he had to offer new instructions. He sensed the Nihil ship slowing, and then Indeera, pulling up and alongside it in her Vector. He knew she would have to leap through vacuum to get into the air lock—but it would be a matter of mere seconds, and the Jedi Order trained its members in techniques to withstand the harsh environment of space. These tricks only worked for a few moments—space was space, after all—but he knew Indeera could do what needed to be done.

In fact, his connection to the Force told him she had already begun. A sense of great alarm from inside the ship, quickly quieted. He didn't know if Indeera had also used the mind touch, or had been forced to kill the other Nihil inside—he knew several had survived the events on Elphrona.

This will be over soon, he thought.

Once Indeera finished her work and had retrieved the first Blythe, Loden could infiltrate the Nihil ship the same way. He would disable it, to allow any survivors from the raider crew to be collected by either Elphrona's security squads or perhaps a Republic vessel. And then he could bring his newly rescued passenger down to the surface to be reunited with their family. Not a bad day's work, all things—

From nowhere, appearing all around him—ships, *many* ships, leaping in from hyperspace, surrounding him and the Nihil vessel and Indeera's Vector. That should be all but impossible—so many vessels making such a coordinated jump, and so close to a planet—but the ships were there. Too many for him to count, of all different types. One large craft at the center, sleek and menacing, and around it, a swarm of others—but every last one had three glowing, jagged stripes painted on its hull. Once again, the lightning.

Once again, the Nihil.

The entire fore bulkhead of the *Lourna Dee*'s bridge was one large viewport, made of triple-hardened transparisteel inside a diamond-core matrix.

Through it, Lourna Dee could see what she had been sent to this forsaken planet to retrieve—a damaged Nihil Cloudship, which had brought Dent Margrona's crew to Elphrona so they could kidnap a family and ransom them off to their rich relatives on Alderaan. Near it, two of those annoying little Jedi vessels—Vectors.

One was right in front of the Cloudship, so close it was shocking the two ships hadn't collided—but she had heard Jedi pilots could do amazing things.

Much good it would do them now. It was two Vectors against an entire Nihil Tempest.

The first ship pulled away from the Cloudship's nose, trying either to flee or to get into some sort of attack position.

Lourna Dee snorted.

Good luck with that, she thought.

CHAPTER THIRTY-EIGHT

DEEP SPACE. THE KUR NEBULA.

Kassav looked at the battle display, frowning. Almost simultaneously with his order to his Tempest to move into an offensive position, to go on the attack, the Republic Cruisers had disgorged an unending stream of those arrowhead-shaped fighters they used—Skywings—along with a good number of the bigger workhorse ships, the Longbeams.

His people were fighting back, and mostly giving as good as they got in the small skirmishes, but the big guns on the Republic heavy cruiser and its five smaller companions were lashing out, almost every shot finding a Cloudship. The shields on the *New Elite* and some of the bigger Nihil ships could withstand those shots—for a while, at least—but the Cloudships? No way. They flashed into a cloud of flame and vaporized durasteel every time a shot found its target.

The numbers were still on their side, but it couldn't last—and the ships from Eriadu were getting closer with every second, creeping up on them, implacable. Either his Nihil punched a hole through the

Republic fleet and made it to the hyperlane access point, or they might all die right there.

There was another ship out there, too—the Jedi cruiser. So far, it hadn't done anything, but there was no way it didn't have some of those Vectors aboard. That was the last thing he needed.

"Anything from the Eye?" he called out.

"Nothing yet, boss," Wet Bub answered.

Kassav hadn't expected anything. He was pretty damn certain no miraculous escape route was going to be uploaded to their Path engine. If he wanted to get back to Marchion Ro and bury his blade in the smug bastard's creepy eye, he'd have to do it himself.

He looked at the tactical display, trying to figure out what orders to give. The Republic was chewing his people apart, their disciplined, coordinated attacks incredibly effective against his Tempest, where each pilot was their own master and fought however the hell they wanted. Most of his Nihil were engaging in dogfights, each trying to shoot down a Republic ship, make a big name for themselves, a good story to tell back at the Great Hall. But against trained military, they just couldn't—

That's it, he thought.

He keyed open a fleet-wide comm channel.

"My Nihil—this is the Tempest Runner. You're teaching these Republic fools one hell of a lesson. I'm impressed. But I want them to leave this battle knowing better than to go up against us again. Stop fighting them on their terms. They won't learn a thing.

"Fight like the Nihil," he said. "Fight *free.* Fight *dirty.*"

He grinned.

"Show them who we are. That's an order."

It took a moment or two for that instruction to sink in, but then one of the larger ships, a repurposed freighter only a little smaller than the *New Elite,* opened its cargo bay doors. Its engines kicked on and something spilled out, propelled by the momentum, a gelatinous gray goo. Kassav remembered that this particular ship was a hijack. Evidently the new Nihil owners had never emptied the cargo containers, and evidently the ship was originally some kind of waste carrier.

The sludge oozed out in a noxious flood, coating the Republic fighters pursuing the freighter. Two Skywings spun out and collided, causing an explosion . . . which ignited the whole load. Flame rippled out in a surging wave, catching every Republic ship that had been coated with the gunk when the Nihil freighter let fly. They all blew up, every one, in a chain reaction of explosions that was one of the most beautiful things Kassav had ever seen.

Fight dirty, indeed.

The rest of the Nihil saw it, too, and they got the message. Suddenly it wasn't about dogfights or head-on battles with your opponents. Kassav watched one of his ships land *on* one of the bigger Republic craft, then do a high-intensity engine burn right into the bridge viewport. He saw another crew use the harpoon trick that had worked so well in Ab Dalis, ripping apart one of the five cruisers.

It wasn't all good news, though—one of his bigger vessels, a light corvette, was under heavy attack from a squadron of Longbeams. Its engines flared out, and the vessel began to drift.

That's that, Kassav thought. *Blast it. Could've used that ship down the road.*

A number of escape pods jettisoned from the ailing Nihil corvette, and the Longbeams immediately broke off their attack and began collecting them with some sort of magnetic clamp apparatus. They towed them back to the nearest big Republic Cruiser, entering its docking bay with the pods trailing behind.

Kassav worried for a moment about what those prisoners might be able to tell the Republic about the Nihil and its operations, then realized it probably didn't matter. Things couldn't get much worse.

And then the Republic Cruiser blew up, in a massive explosion that also took out a number of smaller craft nearby. At the same time, the engines on the Nihil corvette, the one Kassav had written off, flared back into life, and the ship slewed around, its weapons firing at a nearby set of Skywings.

Kassav understood what had happened. The escape pods didn't have his people aboard—they'd been packed with explosives, and when the Republic idiots got all noble and tried to rescue them because . . .

"Heh," he said to himself. "We are all the Republic."

He keyed the comm back on.

"That's it!" he cried. "Smash a hole right through them! I'm with you all!"

He keyed off the comm system and lifted his hand to chew the edge of his thumb—a nervous habit—until he realized he no longer had a thumb on that hand.

"Any word from Marchion Ro?" he called over to Wet Bub.

In response, just a shake of the head, long, dangling ears flopping against Bub's skull.

Not that he had expected anything. It was Kassav against the galaxy. Just like always.

Admiral Kronara couldn't believe what he was seeing. He didn't expect a bunch of criminals to fight with anything resembling honor, but this was . . . despicable.

One of the larger Nihil vessels had just released a huge swath of reactor by-products from its engines, creating a tail of invisible, deeply toxic radiation that not only snarled sensors, but poisoned any pilot that happened to fly through it. They'd be condemning them to a slow, agonizing death unless they reached medical facilities immediately.

That will catch some of their own ships, too, he thought. *It has to. They're killing their own people.*

The Nihil didn't seem to care. About that, about anything, beyond causing as much damage as they possibly could.

That strategy was succeeding. He was down two of his *Pacifier*-class patrol cruisers, the *Marillion* of Alderaan and the *Yekkabird* from Corellia, along with their crews and a good number of the Longbeam attack ships and Skywing fighters.

He wouldn't say the Nihil were winning, exactly—their tactics were all offense, no defense, and they were taking hits, their numbers decreasing . . . but they weren't exactly losing, either. This had to end, and soon. It was time to escalate his response.

Admiral Kronara checked the displays again, looking at the position of the small Eriaduan flotilla moving inexorably toward the battle.

Not close enough yet, he thought.

"Get me the *Ataraxia,*" he said, calling over to his communications officer.

Master Jora Malli's voice came over the comm a few moments later. "Admiral," she said. "How can I help?"

"The Nihil are using unorthodox tactics, ugly moves. We can beat them, but RDC pilots don't train for things like this. It'll take time, and it'll cost lives. If you and your people are willing—"

The Jedi agreed before he finished the sentence. "We'll see what we can do, Admiral. The Force provides quite an edge in battle."

"We'd be grateful for the assist," he said.

"Of course," she said, and ended the transmission.

Jora Malli strode into the *Ataraxia*'s primary hangar, Sskeer at her side. She held a comlink in one hand.

"Avar, we're going to take out the Vector squadron. The Republic pilots need our help shutting the Nihil down before things get any worse out there. Can you establish your link to all of us, to help to make that task simpler?"

"I can," Avar Kriss responded. "I'm already hearing the song."

Jora knew that Avar interpreted the Force as music. She didn't see it that way. To her, the Force was . . . a force. But you couldn't deny the effectiveness of what Master Kriss could do.

All around her, Jedi ran toward waiting Vectors, the *Ataraxia*'s non-Jedi crew fueling and prepping the delicate ships for flight. She saw Elzar Mann and his friend Stellan Gios, Nib Assek and her Wookiee Padawan Burryaga, the Ithorian Mikkel Sutmani who had been part of the ill-fated mission during which the Order lost Te'Ami . . . all strong pilots. They'd need to be. She had reviewed the tactical data from the battle, and the Nihil ships seemed willing to go to any lengths to hurt or destroy their enemies.

"You ready, old friend?" she said to Sskeer as they approached their own Vectors.

"You should be on the Starlight Beacon," the Trandoshan Jedi hissed back. "You're supposed to be dealing with supply requisitions and unruly younglings, not leading an assault on a bunch of pirates. Let me go by myself—there's no need for you to fly."

"You can die in bed just as easily as in battle, Sskeer," she said, climbing into her ship's cockpit.

"That is certainly untrue," Sskeer called over, putting an oxygen mask over his broad snout and settling into his pilot's seat. "What if we both just agree not to die?"

"Deal," she said as the canopy closed.

Jora took her lightsaber—a golden cylinder with curved platinum guards swooping back down toward the hilt like wings—and placed it against the weapons activation panel on her Vector's console. The targeting systems lit up bright white, the color of her saber blade. She had retrieved its kyber crystal, then a bright blood-red, from an ancient Sith lightspear and healed it, purging the rage and pain instilled in it by its original owner. She performed the ritual mainly as an intellectual exercise, to see how it was done, but once the process was complete she found herself tightly bound to the crystal, and now used it as the core of her primary weapon.

She pushed her control sticks forward and shot out of the hangar into open space.

All around her, Vectors materialized, flashing out from the *Ataraxia.*

"On me, Jedi," Jora Malli said, and the ships came up around her, creating the tight formation that only the Jedi ships could achieve.

It was a Drift, perfectly composed, and the only thing more beautiful than seeing one was being part of one.

The battle lay ahead, and they would turn the tide.

The Eriaduan ships had advanced slow and steady, and were now in visual range, which meant they were in weapons range as well, but they hadn't started firing. Kassav thought he knew why. The hunters wanted to terrify their prey before they killed it.

A battle was one thing, but this waiting. It was agonizing.

The ships were all long, thin, bladelike craft. They looked like swords, edge-on, and they were headed straight for him.

"Divert a third of our ships to the Eriaduan cruisers," he ordered, shouting at Wet Bub. "We need them *gone.*"

"You got it, boss," Bub said.

He sounded dubious. Not surprising. Kassav was dubious, too. They had killed their fair share of Longbeams and Skywings, but the Jedi had finally joined the fight, sending out those blasted little Vectors. Still, whatever. Jedi could die, just like anyone. No one ever said they were immortal.

But the Nihil were running out of tricks to play, and the Republic was getting smarter, letting the big guns on their cruisers do more of the work. It was time to go. What Kassav really needed was a Path, but the odds of that were—

"Kassav!" it was Wet Bub, a new note in his voice—hope. "I've got Marchion Ro on the comm!"

"Put him through!" Kassav yelled. "Private channel!"

Marchion Ro's voice sounded in Kassav's mask.

"Hey, Kassav," he said. "You ran into some trouble out there?"

I think you know we did, Kassav thought.

"Yeah," he said. "Republic task force, a bunch of Jedi, even some ships from Eriadu. Like some sort of ambush. I know you want to get rid of that flight recorder, but we could really use a Path to get us out of here. We're getting hit pretty bad, Marchion. My whole Tempest is at risk."

"It was just supposed to be a few transports," Marchion Ro replied. "I don't know what happened. I'll get you a Path. Just keep fighting. I'll say something to your Tempest, too. As the Eye."

"Okay, great, but how long do you think it'll be until you can send a Path, because—"

The link went dead. Kassav wished he could race back along the transmission line, not to escape, but for the sole purpose of finding Marchion Ro and murdering him in the most savage manner he could dream up.

Wet Bub spoke again.

"Another transmission from the Eye," he said. "Every ship's getting it."

"Put it through," Kassav said.

The wreckpunk, still blaring through the bridge speakers, automatically reduced in volume as Marchion Ro's voice echoed out across the *New Elite* and all the other ships in the Nihil fleet.

"I am the Eye of the Nihil, and I see the battle you're fighting. I see the Republic, trying to take away your freedom, trying to take your hard-won credits, trying to take away your way of life . . . they want you *dead.* Just for living. Just for being. Just for walking a path they don't own.

"Who are *they* to tell us how to live? Who are *they* to come to our territory and try to kill us? The Republic. The *Jedi.* What gives them the *right?*"

Kassav looked across the bridge. Dellex, Gravhan, Wet Bub, and all the rest—all had stopped what they were doing and were very still, just listening to Marchion Ro's words.

He suddenly had a bad feeling. A very bad feeling.

"I will not allow this to happen," Marchion Ro said. "I have a responsibility to the Nihil, and the freedom we all believe in so deeply. I am the Eye, and I will give you what you need to defeat our enemies. These are the Battle Paths, my friends, and with them . . ."

A pause, a held breath, and Kassav knew every single one of his people was ready, waiting, desperate to hear what Marchion would say next.

". . . you cannot lose."

The *New Elite* thrummed, all its surfaces vibrating with a strange new energy, down to its very core. Dellex shouted, looking at her screens.

"Kassav . . . the Path engine . . . something's happening!"

Sskeer flew as part of the Drift, the connection to the Jedi all around him strengthened by whatever Avar Kriss was doing back on the *Ataraxia.* And the strongest connection of all was to Jora Malli, her ship just off to starboard, so close that their wingtips almost touched.

The Vectors had not yet engaged the enemy. The Nihil were still ahead, embroiled in battles with Longbeams and Skywings. He sensed anticipation, all around him, Jedi preparing themselves for the test of combat.

His own cockpit was bathed in blue light, the color of his lightsaber blade. Everything was ready. He would defend, he would protect, he would bring justice. He was a Jedi, and he—

Something happened.

The Nihil ships . . . moved. Shifted. All of them, at once, were in one place, and then they were in another. They didn't move as one, but in separate jolts and lunges, disappearing and reappearing in varying distances from their original positions.

It happened again, and there was no reason to it, no pattern. The Nihil just dropped from one place and then—

A momentary impression of something large, solid, too close to avoid, appearing right in the middle of the Drift, and then an impact so gigantic he could not truly comprehend it. A huge flash of light, and his sense of many of the Jedi around him vanished. Then something slammed into the canopy of his cockpit, and *through* it, some sharp chunk of metal that speared directly into his shoulder, through his body and well into his pilot's seat, severing his arm at the joint.

Through the shock, Sskeer thought he understood what had happened. Somehow, the Nihil were entering hyperspace, then dropping back out of it, impossibly short distances away. One had appeared from hyperspace directly in the middle of the Drift, and the ensuing collision had caused a spreading wave of destruction and chaos.

Sskeer howled, not so much at the pain or even the loss of his limb—he was Trandoshan, and so his arm would regrow in time—but at something worse.

One of the Jedi he could no longer sense . . . was Jora Malli.

CHAPTER THIRTY-NINE

ELPHRONA. LOW ORBIT.

Loden whipped his Vector up and away from the disabled Nihil ship, slamming his lightsaber against the control console, the weapons bank lighting up. He powered on his shields, knowing they wouldn't last for more than a few hits from the armada that had somehow appeared from nowhere.

The trick, then, was not to get hit.

"Indeera!" he called, scanning both the threat display on his console and everything the Force was telling him about the endless array of Nihil ships surrounding him.

A brief moment, a breath, as if the enemy fleet was considering the same collective decision, and then blasterfire. Everywhere, a cascade. Loden banked and wove and tried to be as challenging a target as possible, knowing that with this level of fire coming at him, he was just as likely to run into an off-target bolt as he was to be hit by a Nihil with exceptionally good aim.

So he stopped thinking about it at all and surrendered himself to the Force, letting it guide his movements. Overthinking the situation would only end up with him getting in his own way. While he wasn't certain—no one could ever be—he did not believe it was his time to die.

A blaster bolt sizzled off his front shields, and he reevaluated.

It is probably not my time to die, he thought.

"I'm here, Loden," Indeera said. "What's happening?"

"A Nihil fleet dropped in from hyperspace, and they don't seem particularly happy," he said.

"Here? That's not possible."

"Please let them know that."

"Are you all right?"

"For the moment. I'm just staying out of their way. But I can't do it forever. We need to resolve this now."

A brief pause, then Indeera spoke again.

"They aren't firing on this ship, or my Vector."

"I know. They must want to ensure the family survives," Loden said, sending out a few blasts from his own cannons, causing one of the smaller Nihil craft to explode.

"Who are these Blythes? Why are they so valuable?"

"Does it matter?"

"No . . . but I can only take one of them with me in my Vector, Loden. The father wants me to take his son first, if I can get him out—but I'm not sure how I get past the Nihil even if I can get back to my ship."

"Do that. Take the son. I'll cover your retreat, then I'll grab the father and follow you back to Elphrona. Planetary security might not want to do anything about a single marauder crew, but they'll have to respond to an entire invasion fleet."

"All right . . . but Loden . . . how will you do that?"

He put his Vector into a roll, shooting again. This time he missed, but at least he was alive, still fighting.

"Eh," he said. "I'll probably just trust in the Force or something."

Nothing from Indeera. Loden laughed.

"It'll be all right. Or it won't, but I'll do my best. Do me a favor and leave the outer air lock open when you go, Indeera."

"That sounds like you actually do have a plan."

"I wouldn't call it a plan. It's more like five impossible things in a row. I'm just going to hit them one at a time."

He flew straight at the largest Nihil ship, briefly evading fire from the nine or ten smaller craft on his tail while opening himself up to laser blasts from the cruiser. But better one attacker than ten.

"I'm running out of time, Indeera. We need to mix this up. You ready?"

"Ready," she said.

"Go!" Loden shouted.

Loden slowed his breathing, reaching out to the Force. He pulled his hands back from his control sticks, leaving just his fingertips touching their surfaces. Vectors were responsive craft as a rule—and this particular one was more attentive to its pilot's commands than most. He had once heard his Padawan—no, his *former* Padawan, Bell would soon be a fellow Jedi Knight—tell Ember the ship's name, when he thought no one was listening.

The *Nova.* Perhaps Bell kept it secret because he thought it was silly or childish. Loden thought it was beautiful. He wished he'd told Bell that. Next time they saw each other.

All right, Nova, *time to live up to your name,* Loden thought.

With his hands, he flew his ship, and with the Force, he triggered its weapons and moved through the battlespace in a way none of the Nihil had ever seen or could anticipate or, if Loden chose to go for kill-shots, could survive.

The *Nova* was a blossom of flame and laserfire, spiraling through the battle, every shot finding a target, every motion either an evasion or a retargeting.

The Nihil attackers moved from an attacking stance to something like a panicked retreat, the sphere of ships surrounding him expanding and becoming more diffuse, both from the increased distance between the vessels and from his own steady reduction of their numbers. Only the flagship didn't move, his lasers reflecting off its shields.

Dimly, his senses told him Indeera's Vector had taken the opportunity to move out of the shadow of the kidnappers' ship and speed through a gap in the enemy cordon. As he had suspected, the rest of the Nihil did not give chase. They undoubtedly were monitoring the communications between Loden and Indeera, or had access to cam feeds from inside their damaged vessel. Either way, they knew who Indeera had taken—the boy.

They didn't want him, though. They wanted the father, for some reason.

It was Loden's job to make sure they didn't get him.

He knew how he could get aboard the kidnappers' ship—but he didn't quite know what he would do after that. Getting through all of this intact seemed . . . improbable. At best.

But then, so was fighting off a massive marauder armada in a single Vector long enough for his colleague to escape, and he'd pulled that off. He'd figure it out.

Loden angled his ship to head straight for the damaged Nihil vessel containing the last Blythe.

He approached, then pulled back sharply on the control sticks, slowing his ship to almost zero velocity, feeling g-forces tug him forward.

In a series of rapid Force-assisted movements, he pulled his lightsaber hilt from the console—it was hot in his hand, almost burning—popped the emergency release on the Vector's canopy, released his safety harness, and shot forward, out of the ship and into open space.

Loden had aimed himself perfectly. Almost perfectly. He did indeed make it to the open air lock of the damaged Nihil ship, but one leg nicked the edge of the hatch as he passed, and at the speed he was traveling it was like taking a durasteel hammer to the limb. The bones of his lower leg snapped, and for a moment Loden felt nothing. But only a moment.

Then pain, white-hot.

He hit the inner air lock hatch, hard, though at least this he had been anticipating and was able to turn to soften the impact a bit. Loden slapped the control panel to one side of the hatch and the outer door slammed closed. The atmosphere began to cycle, oxygen rushing into the tiny chamber.

Loden took the moment to examine his broken leg—it was twisted at a bizarre angle, and it seemed like the bone had snapped clean through. Not good.

Outside the ship, through the air lock, he saw a flash of flame that he knew was his Vector being destroyed by Nihil laserfire.

Goodbye, Nova, he thought. *You were a wonderful ship.*

None of this was unexpected—well, perhaps the leg. That was not ideal.

Loden brought the pain-management exercises he knew to mind, and while he realized on some level that he was in agony, he was able to bottle it up and put it aside. The trick wouldn't last forever. You couldn't fool the body indefinitely. But hopefully, it would see him through whatever came next.

A soft chime as the air lock atmosphere equalized with that inside the ship, and the hatch opened. Loden pushed himself to his feet, favoring his good leg—no Jedi exercises were so powerful that he could put even a bit of weight on the other one—and pulled himself inside.

The first thing he saw were the corpses. Several, all Nihil, bearing telltale marks of death-by-lightsaber. All had blasters in their hands. Indeera had been forced to defend herself and the hostages, and these people had brought their deaths upon themselves. The pilot's body was here too, the unmasked woman Loden had influenced with the mind touch.

The second thing he saw was a man, his eyes wide, a blaster pistol in his hand. He did not look like a Nihil. He looked like a miner. The last Blythe.

"You're the other Jedi," the man said.

"You're the father," Loden said, his voice a little shaky.

"Ottoh Blythe," the man replied. "Before anything else, thank you for saving my family. If there is ever anything I can do for you, just—"

"I wouldn't mind a little help with this, now that you mention it," Loden said, gesturing to his leg.

Ottoh looked at the injured limb, realized what had happened, and nodded. He shoved the pistol in his belt and moved to a bulkhead, where a square metal container was bolted to the wall. He pulled it down, then opened it, revealing an emergency medpac.

From the kit, he pulled an injector and held it up. "This won't fix a broken leg, but it might let you forget it's broken. For a little while, at least."

"Yes please," Loden said.

Ottoh handed the injector to Loden, who promptly stuck it in his thigh and depressed the activator. A slight *whoosh,* and immediately the pain eased. He released the Force, saving his reserves for the challenges to come.

"Better?" Ottoh said.

"Better enough for us to get through this."

"They killed your ship," Ottoh said. "I saw it blow up through the viewport. How are we supposed to get away?"

"We're *on* a ship," Loden said. "And they aren't shooting at it. They don't want to kill you, which means we have an advantage. First thing we do, let's try to negotiate—I have some little tricks I can try on their commander, and if they work—"

A huge *thunk,* mind-crushingly loud, and in that instant something new appeared in the hold with them. It was the forward end of a torpedo of some kind, sharpened to pierce a hull, which was what it had done. Loden tried to shove it back out into space with the Force, then held back, realizing that he wasn't sure if the ship was still shielded against vacuum. Solving one problem might cause another, which honestly was all moot because the thing was going to explode, and how could he have miscalculated so badly, and at least they'd saved three of the family members, and Indeera and Bell and Porter had survived as well, and if it was his time, well, then—

Vents snapped open on the end of the torpedo, and gas hissed out, blue-gray like smoke or a thundercloud, filling the entire compartment in an instant. Jedi could hold their breath for a very long time, but this had happened so quickly that there was no time to *take* a breath.

Loden saw Ottoh Blythe sink to his knees, then topple over, his eyes rolling back and closing. He could feel his own head beginning to swim.

Loden reached for the Force, thinking again that perhaps if he just shoved the torpedo away, he could evacuate the air from the hold and the poison with it—yes, he and Ottoh Blythe would be in vacuum, but one problem at a time.

But the Force slipped out of his grasp. He could not think, could not focus.

He fell to one side, flaring agony in his shattered leg momentarily clearing his head. But only for that moment. He couldn't think. He felt stupid, dull.

The air lock hatch cycled open, causing eddies of air to whisk through the hold, but not enough to dissipate the gas. Only enough to stir it a bit, causing a clear area near the air lock, which meant Loden Greatstorm saw the monsters step into the ship.

The Nihil.

Lourna Dee walked into the hold, followed by a few of her best Storms. All were masked, the headgear doing triple duty as concealers of identity, inducers of terror, and, most important, filters of nerve toxin. The stuff was a special recipe she'd commissioned from a poisoner on Nar Shaddaa and had never shared with her fellow Tempest Runners—a girl had to have a few secrets, after all.

The gray fog swirled, breaking apart and re-forming, giving her glimpses of both the Jedi and the Blythe, collapsed on the deck, unconscious.

This should square me up with Marchion Ro, she thought. *Mission accomplished.*

Lourna Dee wondered how Kassav was doing, on his own assignment, if he'd redeem himself as well.

She hoped not.

"Take them both," she said.

CHAPTER FORTY

DEEP SPACE. THE KUR NEBULA.

"How are they doing this?" Admiral Kronara shouted, watching the green lights signifying his fighters blink out across the tactical display—blue lights, too, and those were Jedi.

The Nihil ships, all but the capital ship, were doing something unfathomable. They were disappearing and reappearing all across the battlespace, flickering in and out of existence. The Republic pilots couldn't keep up, and the Nihil were making the most of it, knocking his Longbeams and Skywings down one by one.

It didn't seem entirely controlled, however—the Nihil ships could and did appear directly in the path of Republic and Jedi ships . . . and even their own. The result was utter mayhem. Explosive, murderous mayhem.

"Cloaking fields?" he called out.

"Doesn't seem to be, Admiral," one of his bridge officers responded. "Scans suggest they're jumping in and out of hyperspace. Tiny little leaps, sometimes as short as a kilometer."

"That's not possible," Kronara said.

The officer did not respond, wisely enough. Obviously it was not impossible—the blasted ships were doing it there, right in front of his eyes.

Another Longbeam exploded—that was three good people lost, minimum. Some ships in that class held as many as twenty-four.

This was . . . how could you fight something like this? It was like battling chaos itself. Like trying to shoot down . . . a storm.

On the *Ataraxia,* Avar Kriss hovered in the air, listening to the song of the Force. She was attempting to focus only on the notes of the Nihil ships as they dipped in and out of hyperspace, using their bizarre tactic to deadly effect. The Nihil were just one thread in the great melody of the battle, however, and challenging to isolate. Choppy, staccato, disappearing and reappearing. Difficult to follow.

She frowned.

It did not help that her mind rang with the absence of the Jedi they had just lost. The great Jora Malli, but so many others. An accident, impossible to foresee, but that did not lessen the tragedy.

There.

There.

She had it. The Force had shown her the song of the Nihil, how they were flying and fighting. She could hear it clearly—and that meant she knew not just what was happening, but also, to some small degree, what would.

Avar reached out to the Jedi fighting in their Vectors through the net she created, giving them guidance, helping them hear what she heard, so they could anticipate where the Nihil ships would appear—and end this fight once and for all.

Elzar Mann flew his Vector, diving and weaving through the battle, moving from target to target, taking shots as they presented themselves. The Drift had disintegrated after the collision with the Nihil vessel took out more than ten of their ships, and now every Jedi found their own path through the fight.

Avar was there, of course, in the back of his mind, holding all the Jedi together, helping and guiding as she always did. He did not quite understand what she was doing—the information she was passing along was diffuse—but he was hitting his targets, every bolt finding a Nihil ship, often just as it fell from hyperspace.

It almost didn't matter what Avar was doing. He just liked having her in his head.

Less appealing was the feel of the Nihil. They seemed to be creatures composed entirely of rage and fear. Strange beasts crawling along the very bottom of the Force sea in which all things swam.

Elzar Mann dived deep, hunting them one by one. It was amazing. They were so easy to find. Their anger made them vulnerable. The thing they thought made them strong, dangerous . . . it made them weak.

He fired again, and another Nihil ship vanished. He flew through the debris cloud, already seeking his next target.

"Are we . . . winning?" Dellex said from her monitoring station, trying to track the incomprehensible activity of the battle raging in space around the *New Elite.*

Kassav had no idea how to answer her question. Marchion Ro's Battle Paths, whatever they were, seemed to have taken control of his Tempest's ships through their Path engines, whipping them in and out of hyperspace, a new leap every few seconds. It was making them almost impossible for the Republic ships to hit, but it was unclear whether it was giving them any real advantage, either. The few communications they'd received from Strikes and Clouds out in the battle suggested confusion, even terror.

"Another message from the Eye," Wet Bub called out. "Your private channel, Kassav."

Marchion Ro, Kassav thought. *Marchion blasted Ro.*

He activated his comm and didn't wait for Marchion to speak.

"What is this?" he said.

"Victory," Marchion Ro said. "A long time coming. The first of many."

"What the hell does that mean?"

"You killed my father, didn't you?"

Kassav hesitated. Not long, but probably long enough.

"What are you talking about, Marchion? We're dying out here!"

"I don't know for sure it was you," said the Eye of the Nihil, "but I'm choosing to believe it was. And if it wasn't, well, Lourna Dee and Pan Eyta . . . their time will come. Goodbye, Kassav, and thank you. You and your Tempest are about to save the Nihil. We thank you for your sacrifice."

The connection ended, and Kassav looked out the viewport at the battle. He saw what was happening, and so did everyone else on the bridge.

"What are they . . . doing?" Gravhan said.

The ships of Kassav's Tempest had changed tactics again. No longer just leaping from place to place through tiny hyperspace jumps, now they were actively targeting the Republic ships—leaping *into* them, colliding directly in the case of the smaller vessels and jumping inside the shield barriers of the larger cruisers and impacting against their hulls with massive blooms of fire and debris.

"Disconnect the Path engine!" Kassav shouted. "Right now!"

The *Third Horizon* shuddered as another Nihil craft exploded against its hull.

"Damage report!" Admiral Kronara called out.

This latest attacker had used the same trick a few others had managed—skipping out of lightspeed inside the *Third Horizon*'s shields.

"Breach on decks three and four, but it was a non-essential area, Admiral—we've got emergency crews on the way, but it won't affect any significant systems."

He'd never seen anything like this. The Nihil weren't fanatics, as far as he knew. They were just marauders. What would compel these people to kill themselves like this? They had to know the Republic would take them prisoner if at all possible. None of these people had to die.

"Send another transmission to the flagship," he ordered. "Reiterate that we will accept their surrender, and they will all be treated humanely. There's no need for this."

Whatever he had imagined this engagement would be, it was not this. This was . . . slaughter.

The song had become sad, and Avar Kriss no longer wanted to listen to it. From what she could sense, the Nihil had become like small, wild creatures trapped in a cage, desperate to escape, doing anything they could, even if it hurt them.

Even if it killed them.

Such a terrible waste.

They've gone mad, Kronara thought.

He truly believed himself to be a man of peace, despite his profession. The cliché of a military man, delusional in almost every case. But not in his. Kronara knew there was a time for war, but it was to be as brief as possible, and no more destructive than necessary.

These Nihil, though . . . they were fighting when they did not have to. Dying when they did not have to. Suicide attacks—it was hard to imagine what would drive thinking beings to such tactics. There were not many left now, compared to their original numbers. He had recalled most of his fighters to the capital ships. It was mostly just the Jedi out there on the Republic side. The Vectors, and their pilots, had the maneuverability and reflexes to stay ahead of the Nihil's hyperspace microjumps.

The area around the nebula was littered with slowly expanding debris clouds. A graveyard. The flagship was the only significant enemy vessel that remained, and so far it did not seem inclined to follow the smaller ships in a doomed ramming attack.

Mad beasts. They needed to be put down.

Kronara hated the thought. But he did not think he was wrong.

And as if on cue, a transmission came through to the bridge of the *Third Horizon.* A cold voice, but not emotionless. No, there was rage behind that tone, but controlled, focused like a diamond drill.

The commander of the Eriaduan phalanx. Governor Mural Veen.

"Admiral Kronara," the woman said. "We acknowledge that the Republic takes first position in this engagement, but we would request the courtesy of being allowed to take the Nihil flagship, considering the injustice these creatures visited upon our system."

"Fine, Governor," he agreed. "Be my guest."

He didn't even have to think about it. If the Eriaduan contingent wanted to attempt a boarding assault against the sort of enemy the Nihil had proven to be, more power to them. He suspected they would enjoy it, would find it a way to balance the scales.

And once they had the ship subdued, they could, perhaps, get some answers. There had to be a person in a position of power on the Nihil flagship. There was so much the Republic didn't know about this organization and desperately needed to.

The Eriaduan vessels did not hesitate. As soon as authorization was given, they began to dart in, stabbing inward toward the Nihil flagship like the spear tips they resembled.

Kronara had seen a reek hunt once, on Ylesia. It had been like this. It wasn't one big wound that killed the massive beast, but many small attacks, bleeding it out, until in the end, the huge creature had just lain down on the ground and died.

Every attack by the Eriaduans disabled one of the Nihil vessel's systems. Propulsion, weapons bays, shields . . . one by one, they fell. The ship was crippled, now just a hulk floating in the void.

Kronara watched as the largest of the Eriaduan ships approached the dead Nihil vessel, in preparation for docking and boarding.

He did not envy any Nihil left alive on that ship. Not even a little bit.

Kassav sat in his command chair on the bridge of his once-beautiful ship. The music had stopped—just static coming from the speaker systems now. The deck was full of smoke from fried systems, but his mask filtered it out and left him able to see.

For instance, he could see the battle display screen, which showed him that his strong, powerful fleet was all but gone. A few little ships here or there, still valiantly fighting to the last . . . but that was all. What was left was no Tempest, and certainly not a Blaze. Barely a Strike, really.

Marchion Ro and his father had given the Nihil the Paths. Every last ship was equipped with a Path engine, directly connected to the hyperdrive and control systems. That machine let them do incredible things—ride along hidden roads behind the fabric of space, perform feats no other ships could match.

The Paths made the Nihil strong. And, as Kassav had realized too late, far too late, the Path engines made them weak. Marchion had simply . . . taken control. Put the ships where he wanted them. He didn't know why—revenge, certainly, and some sort of power play, but there had to be more than that. The complexities were beyond him just then. Honestly, it didn't matter anymore.

He heard the sounds of combat behind him and realized that soon enough, the last of the thousand or so fools who had decided to follow his leadership would be dead. His Storms, Gravhan, Dellex, and Wet Bub . . . all gone.

Kassav decided to tell the Eriaduans everything he knew. He could make a deal. He was good at that. There was so much he could tell them—about Marchion Ro and the other Nihil. Things they'd want to know.

"You are in command of this ship?"

Kassav spun his command chair, to see the Eriaduans. They wore battle armor and stood ramrod-straight, and made Kassav wish very much that he had chosen a different system from which to extort fifty million credits.

At the front was a gray-haired, blade-thin woman, and Kassav now realized he had no chance of surviving this. Not because of her imposing physical presence, or the blaster in her hand, or the blood spattering her armor to which she paid absolutely no mind.

No, his time was up because Kassav thought he recognized the woman's voice, and if he was right, there was no deal to be made here. No way. But he had to try.

"I can help you," he said. "We should talk. Seriously. Let's make a deal."

"I know what your deals are worth, Kassav Milliko," replied Mural Veen, planetary governor of Eriadu, the very woman to whom he had made promises he had not fulfilled, and stolen from, and—

She shot him.

Admiral Kronara stood in silence on the bridge of the *Third Horizon.* None of the other crewmembers said a word, either.

They all just watched as the final Nihil ship, a small attack vessel of some kind, like a patched-together little freighter with no hope of doing any damage whatsoever to an *Emissary*-class Republic Cruiser, flew into the path of the *Third Horizon*'s laser batteries and exploded.

The green light of the Kur Nebula illuminated a scene of utter destruction. Pieces of starships of all sizes drifted free across the battlespace. Most were Nihil, but the RDC task force had taken horrifying losses, especially when they had expected to be facing no more than a skirmish against an undisciplined bunch of raiders. The remains of two *Pacifier*-class cruisers and all their crews floated out there, too, along with far too many Longbeams, Skywings, and Vectors. And of course, their pilots.

If there was any consolation—and it was small solace indeed—it was that Kronara was absolutely certain, without any doubt, that the Nihil was a threat that needed to come to an end. Now . . . it had.

Whatever the Nihil were doing here, whatever this group had been . . . it was over.

CHAPTER FORTY-ONE

NO-SPACE. THE *GAZE ELECTRIC*.

Lourna Dee looked at the Jedi's lightsaber. It was pretty, sort of, but it made her nervous to even hold the blasted thing. It was magic, they said.

I'm holding a magic sword, she thought. *What the hell is going on?*

"Give it to me," Marchion Ro said, holding out his hand.

She handed it over, happy to be rid of it. Marchion gave it his own look, then began to tap it against his mask, the eye right in the center.

Tap.

Tap.

"You sure you want to do that?" Lourna said. "I mean, if it turns on . . ."

"It won't."

Tap.

They were in a cargo hold on the *Gaze Electric,* where Lourna had brought the last Blythe as well as their captured Jedi. She hadn't caught either of their names. They were both still passed out from the gas, which made sense. She hadn't wanted to take any chances with Jedi magic, and had dosed them again on the journey back from Elphrona.

"They work like this," Marchion said, holding out the hilt.

He twitched his finger and the blade hissed into life, throwing the hold into golden relief.

He swung it a few times, like an experiment, seeing how it felt, listening to the humming, buzzing sound it made.

"I'm going to keep this," he said.

Lourna Dee took an involuntary step backward, hating herself a little for it. But Marchion Ro was no Jedi. She wasn't sure what he was these days, actually. He'd always had an edge, but he knew his place. He was the Eye, and nothing more.

Now . . . all that was gone. He seemed . . . confident, in some new and deeply unsettling way. Like he had changed, grown, become something greater than he previously was.

Or, as she was beginning to suspect, this was always what he'd been, and he'd just decided to hide it from her and the other Tempest Runners. But they'd all known it, hadn't they? Down on some instinctive level.

Marchion Ro was a predator.

He spun, swinging the lightsaber faster now, big, deadly sweeps. Lourna stepped back again. She didn't care if he thought she was a coward. If it slipped out of his hand, that thing could cut her in half with no trouble at all.

"Kassav's Tempest encountered a trap set by the Republic, Lourna Dee," Marchion Ro said. "A huge battle fleet. It was tragic. They all died. What do you think about that?"

"About Kassav?"

"Yes."

Swing. Swing.

Lourna Dee didn't respond, not for a long time.

"I think your spy in Senator Noor's office told you the Republic already had the location you sent Kassav to. I think you knew that battle fleet would be waiting, and sent him and his Tempest there to die. So what I think . . . is that you just killed a third of the Nihil."

Marchion Ro stopped swinging the lightsaber, ending its arc so it was pointing directly at her.

"Look at you, Lourna," he said, "Smarter than I would have guessed. The question is . . . what will you do now?"

Lourna Dee's attention was completely focused on the tip of the lightsaber, hovering and humming just a few centimeters from her face.

"You could leave, I guess," Marchion said, "but the Republic has all the specs for that beautiful ship of yours. Transponder signal and everything. You'd have to leave it behind, and you named it after yourself. That'd hurt, I bet."

It took her a moment to understand the meaning of the words he'd just used. She shifted her gaze to look at his masked face, at the swirling storm carved into it. She knew he was smiling behind it. She could hear it in his voice.

"The flight recorder mission," she said. "You gave the Republic the information on my ship. That's how they found me. How they were able to attack me."

"Technically, Jeni Wataro gave it to them—but I gave it to her."

"You wanted me to fail. Why, Marchion?"

"The Republic needed the flight recorder so they'd figure out where to send their fleet to look for us. If they didn't have it, I wouldn't have been able to sacrifice Kassav's Tempest. Now they'll think they destroyed us. They'll relax for a while. They'll stop hunting us."

Lourna Dee didn't care that Kassav was dead. Not in the slightest. But the audacity of what Marchion Ro had done, the casual way he had just sent a third of the organization to certain death . . . who was this man?

"You think that'll work?" she said, her eyes returning to the lightsaber blade. Maybe she could throw herself backward, get her blaster out in time. Maybe.

"It will, Lourna Dee. I've got it all figured out."

He deactivated the lightsaber, and she said a silent prayer of relief. Not that he couldn't just turn it on again. She knew she remained in extreme danger. What she was realizing was that she always had been, from the moment Marchion Ro—and his father, for that matter—had come to the Nihil.

"We are all the Republic," he said, spitting out the words. "Whether we like it or not, eh?"

He looked at her, the eye in his mask seeming to glow.

"I never told you much about my family, and I doubt I ever will—but I came from something I wanted to escape. This ship was part of it, actually, until it all went bad. My father and I both got out. We worked hard, and we had a plan . . . for the Paths, for the Nihil . . . for all sorts of things."

He gestured at his mask.

"It was always gonna be like this. Since the day I was born. I thought I escaped. I didn't, though. Not really."

Lourna Dee shook her head. She just . . .

"I don't understand why you sent me out there after the flight recorder, Marchion. If you wanted the Republic to have it, why did I have to go after the damn thing?"

"So your Tempest would see you fail, Lourna Dee, and start thinking about new leadership," Marchion said. "And so you'd have nowhere else to go. I'm going to need you, I think."

"For *what*?"

Marchion Ro tilted his head, and she knew he was smiling again.

"You'll find out," he said.

She had to get away, to think. It felt like Marchion had trapped her in a box, and she could barely understand its shape. It was like the Great Hall—the walls were invisible, but it didn't mean they weren't there.

"Look, Marchion," Lourna said. "I'm gonna get back to my people. They had some questions—like why you sent my whole Tempest to rescue a few Strikes and a Cloud. Kind of like overkill, you know?"

She pointed her thumb at the homesteader, the man they'd grabbed, the one remaining family member from the group Dent's Cloud had grabbed. He was still unconscious, ankles and wrists all lashed up in binder cuffs, propped up against a crate in the hold.

"My feeling is that it has something to do with that guy. Fine, whatever—you don't need to tell me why he's so valuable. You can even run the ransom, if you want. I don't care about the Rule of Three. You can have it all. Maybe just throw some of the proceeds back down my way so I can spread them around to my people."

Marchion Ro walked across the hold, the sound of his boots echoing off the durasteel walls.

"This guy?" he said, looking down at Ottoh Blythe.

He pulled the lightsaber from his belt again, igniting it and bringing it down in the same motion, a golden slash right across the man, dead in an instant, cut apart.

A weird smell filled the hold, and Lourna Dee wanted to get away from that particular odor as quickly as she could, but she was frozen.

Marchion's lost his mind, she thought. *His entire mind.*

"I don't care about that guy," he said. "Never did."

Marchion Ro shifted the lightsaber, pointing its blade a meter or so to the left, at the other person Lourna Dee had pulled from the ship above Elphrona. The owner of the weapon Marchion had just used to murder someone.

The dark-skinned Twi'lek Jedi.

He was bound even more thoroughly than the Blythe—triple-strength binders, chains, stun-packs, and a gag. She was glad, too, because the man's eyes were *not friendly.* She'd heard a lot of stories about Jedi; everyone had. She didn't know which were true, but she could now verify that at least one was false. Clearly, the Jedi could not shoot death-beams from their eyes, because if they could, then Marchion Ro would be stone-dead.

She couldn't believe Marchion had taken the man's weapon and used it to kill someone right in front of him. It seemed like tempting fate, even with the Jedi all tied up. You never knew what they could do.

"I didn't give your crew Paths to run that job on Elphrona to bring me a family of miners, Lourna Dee," Marchion Ro said. "I did it because that planet has a Jedi outpost. I figured there was at least a chance your crew might be able to bring me a Jedi. Why not try, right? Lo and behold, now I have one. Which is good, because a Jedi . . ."

He deactivated the lightsaber, and very ostentatiously hung it on his belt.

". . . is just what I need."

CHAPTER FORTY-TWO

CORUSCANT.

Chancellor Lina Soh considered whether the choice she was making felt right, after everything learned and lost in the past several weeks. She was in her office on Coruscant, with Matari and Voru at her side, all three looking out through the broad viewport behind her desk at the endless cityscape beyond. She had no idea what the targons thought about what they saw, but to her, the Coruscant skyline always felt like the Republic in miniature. Always moving, always changing and evolving, endlessly deep and strange and infinite. At that moment, the sun was setting, and the lights were coming up on the buildings. Stars in the heavens. Worlds in the Republic.

Yes. She was making the correct decision.

Lina turned away from the city-world to face the people she had called to her office, the group she had met in Monument Plaza when this all began. A senator, an admiral, a secretary, and, as always, Jedi. The Jedi were never anything less than helpful, solved every problem they were given and many they were not. Without their assistance, there was no question the mystery of the *Legacy Run* would not have been solved as quickly or decisively. Many of their number had died trying to help the Republic, including Master Jora Malli, whom she knew had been slated to run the Order's temple on the Starlight Beacon station. They had sacrificed and fought and triumphed, as they nearly always seemed to. She loved the Jedi.

But sometimes she wondered if they were *too* useful.

"I am reopening the Outer Rim," Chancellor Soh said.

She pointed at her aide, Norel Quo, his pale skin tinted orange in the light of the sunset.

"Put out a statement to that effect immediately. Hyperspace transit through the territories is once again authorized. I'll use executive orders to temporarily ease taxation on those trade routes as well, which will help repair any economic damage caused by the quarantine. Just for a month or so, though, which should incentivize merchants to get their goods out there quickly. That will ease the shortages."

A quick glance at her transportation secretary.

"Do you see any issues with that, Secretary Lorillia?"

"None," he said. "The only potential issue is a shortage of navidroids due to Keven Tarr's array on Hetzal, but I think we all agree that was well worth the expense. I've already asked manufacturers to ramp up production. Perhaps some sort of stimulus for them as well, just until the inventory levels come back?"

"We'll figure something out. That's good news, though. Speaking of Tarr, I know he generated a report on other potential uses for his array, before he headed off to work for the San Tekkas. Have you read it?"

"I have, Chancellor. Some brilliant ideas there. Could revolutionize hypertravel, and even has applications in realspace, if we can figure out how to do it in a way that doesn't require tens of thousands of rare, expensive droids."

"Keep me posted, Jeffo. Could be there's a Great Work in it, at some point. And of course, try to find a way to thank Keven Tarr. A medal or something. A high-level posting at one of the Republic universities, perhaps. A job, if you can find him one that would keep him interested. I hate to think of losing a mind like that to private industry when there's so much to be done in the Republic."

"I will consider," the secretary said.

She turned her attention to Senator Noor, whose face had lit up the moment she said she was going to open the Outer Rim, and had stayed that way all through her conversation with Secretary Lorillia.

"Izzet, on a personal note," Lina said, "I realize how trying this was for the worlds you represent. I appreciate your patience and theirs. I hope you will agree that everything we did was necessary for security and safety in the Republic."

He gave her a grave, dignified nod. "Of course, Chancellor. I never thought otherwise."

Lina Soh had learned to keep her emotions off her face decades before—she was a politician born and bred. Inwardly, though, her eyes rolled back so far she was once again looking out at the Coruscant sunset through the window behind her.

Noor turned to his aide, standing behind his seat with a datapad at the ready.

"I'll make a speech as well, Wataro. We'll need to thank the worlds for their patience and let them know that the Nihil threat has been eradicated. Schedule a tour, too. I think we start with Hetzal, Ab Dalis, and Eriadu, the worlds hit hardest by the Emergences, and then move to—"

"Senator, if I may."

Admiral Kronara lifted his hand. Senator Noor looked at him, not hiding his annoyance at a military man daring to interrupt him.

"Admiral," he said.

"We don't yet know if the Nihil are gone."

"I read your report, Kronara. Your task force destroyed hundreds of their ships in that engagement. You found their entire fleet, and you ended it. There hasn't been a single raid since. If that's not evidence, I don't know what is."

"Senator, respectfully, I think you saw what you wanted to see in that report. I can confirm that we destroyed a significant Nihil force. But at this point, we have very little intelligence about their operations. We know they had hyperspace capabilities we still don't understand, but we don't know how they got them, how many there were, where they're based, if they have goals beyond just simple raiding . . ."

He shrugged.

"Say whatever you want in your speech. It's not my problem. But if the Nihil aren't gone, and they start attacking worlds in the Outer Rim again, you'll look pretty foolish if you've already told your constituents they have nothing to worry about."

Chancellor Soh enjoyed that exchange very much. Senator Noor, perhaps less so. He turned back to his aide.

"Revise the phrasing. Let's just say that great strides have been taken toward making the Outer Rim Territories safe and secure, and we look forward to peace and prosperity in the months and years to come."

"You know what else you might mention, Senator?" Chancellor Soh said.

Senator Noor raised an eyebrow.

"The Starlight Beacon. It's going to open on time. I just got a report in from Shai Tennem. If the Nihil aren't in fact gone, or if anything else pops up out there, the Beacon will be a big part of handling it."

And the projection of Republic authority it represents will make it that much easier to negotiate the Quarren–Mon Calamari peace accords, she thought, *and the Beacon itself will serve as a communications relay that will increase the reliability of transmissions across the region and act as a linchpin for the rest of the new network, and once people see how effective it is, getting a vote through to authorize the other stations just like it will be simple.*

Her Great Works, falling into place one by one.

The Republic was not one world. It was many, each unique in ways large and small. Solving one problem inevitably caused others. There were intractable cultural, historical, economic, and military conflicts among inhabitants of worlds. There were warlords and agitators and malcontents and other less-easy-to-handle enemies—plagues and strange magical factions on hidden worlds who believed they should conquer the galaxy and, yes, even hyperspace anomalies.

But the key was this—and Chancellor Soh believed it to her very soul, and had made it the cornerstone of her entire government: You could not solve those problems individually. It was ridiculous to even try. What you could do, however, was make the various peoples of this high era of the Galactic Republic see one another *as* people. As brothers and sisters and cousins and friends, or if nothing else, just as colleagues in the shared goal of building a galaxy that welcomed all, heard all, and did its best to avoid hurting anyone. Truly tried its best.

If you could make that happen, then problems didn't have to be solved. Many would solve themselves, because people believed in the Republic more than they believed in their own goals, and would be open to that magical word—compromise.

That wonderful day had not yet come, not fully, and perhaps it never would. But she would work toward it with every hour and day she retained her office. All she wanted, truly, was for five words to live on past her term, even past her life. The words that had already become emblematic of her Great Works and so much more. Every time she heard them, her heart lifted. That was the goal. One idea. One sentiment.

She could do it. Everyone could do it.

Chancellor Soh knew it was true. Five words.

We are all the Republic.

CHAPTER FORTY-THREE

NO-SPACE. THE GREAT HALL OF THE NIHIL.

The Nihil stood assembled, a host of a few thousand people, masked and terrifying. They watched, silent.

The space above the Great Hall was a dome-shaped energy shield protecting the platform from the vacuum of No-Space. Ordinarily, it was invisible. But now images played across it, projected by hovering comms droids.

"For the Nihil!" came Kassav's voice, loud and fierce, and then a response, shouted from a thousand throats, all dead now. *"For the storm!"*

The Battle of Kur began, displayed in a series of images ranging from tactical displays to shipcam points-of-view to wider shots assembled by comms droid processing algorithms. The Nihil watched, as did Marchion Ro from the raised table at one end of the hall, with Lourna Dee and Pan Eyta beside him. One seat at the high table remained empty, for the one who was lost.

The Eye and the Tempest Runners wore their masks, but Marchion's was new. Ornate, with the suggestion of a crown, and the superstorm engraving subsumed within a circle of glowing red—the baleful gaze of a beast. Ro's clothing, too, had changed. He now wore a heavy fur cloak, worn and ragged in spots. But the wear conveyed a sense of history, of battles survived and won. As it should—it was the cloak of Asgar Ro.

"Kassav believed he was taking his crews to save us all, to protect us, to keep the Republic from learning our secrets," said the Eye of the Nihil. "It was a trap, a lie. You see how they came for him. The Republic and the Jedi hunted down Kassav's Tempest like vermin."

Murmurs through the crowd as the Nihil watched ship after ship destroyed by Republic attackers, all flying under the same banner they wore on their masks, their clothes, their bodies.

"But look," Marchion Ro said, pointing up at the battle raging above them. "Look what Kassav and his people did."

"Show them who we are!" came Kassav's voice again, and the next phase of the fight began as the Nihil began to use the new, aggressive tactics—radiation bombs and waste sludge and explosive escape pods.

"Our brothers and sisters refused to fight the way the Republic wanted them to," Marchion Ro said. "They fought like the *Nihil.*"

A roar of approval from the crowd. Not enough to shake the Great Hall, there was still too much uncertainty for that . . . but a start.

The Jedi entered the fight, and once again the tide began to turn against the Nihil, as the Vectors whipped through the battlespace, darting and firing their cannons.

Another voice echoed above the Great Hall, this time Marchion Ro's.

"I am the Eye, and I will give you what you need to defeat our enemies. These are the Battle Paths, my friends, and with them . . . you cannot lose."

The fight changed again. The ships of Kassav's Tempest began to leap from place to place, impossible to hit, taking down Skywings and Longbeams and Vectors. Excitement rippled through the watching Nihil. This was something new. Something powerful.

"Yes," Marchion Ro said. "The Paths make us strong—but Kassav's numbers were too few, and there was only so much he could do, even with the gifts I gave him. But look what he did. *Look what he and his people did.*"

The Nihil ships began to smash into the Republic vessels, exploding, causing horrendous damage even at the cost of their own lives. Now a sense of alarm from the watchers.

"I did not expect this," Marchion Ro said. "I don't know if Kassav ordered this, or our fellows just decided they had enough of their freedom being taken, enough of the Republic telling us what to do, thinking they can control our planets and kill our people and . . . well."

He gestured up at the display.

"There is a point where every being breaks, and chooses freedom over tyranny. Kassav's people did this for themselves. For each other. And for us."

The crowd had gone completely silent. Marchion gestured again and the battle froze.

"We are the Nihil," Marchion Ro said.

A few weak cheers, quickly fading into silence.

"I am the Eye, Marchion Ro," he continued. "I am the Nihil.

"And so . . ." he said, holding out his hands to his people, ". . . are all of you."

This is the moment, Marchion Ro thought. *Another step on the path.*

"Kassav and his people died, so we could stay free. But that fight isn't over. The Republic will come for us. And the Jedi. We are no longer Tempests, Storms, Clouds, Strikes. We are *one* thing."

Marchion Ro lifted his hands to his head and removed his mask. He stood there, looking out at the thousands of faces. His tool. His weapon. His *army.*

"We are all the Nihil," he said.

Throughout the hall, more masks came off, only a few at first, but then a flood, the heavy things dropping to the floor with rattling *thuds*.

Marchion Ro let his gaze wash across all of them, seeing the eagerness, the understanding.

He turned to look at Pan Eyta and Lourna Dee. Their masks were still on.

"Now," he said, quietly.

They glanced at each other. Marchion wondered if it would be knives, or if these two would get to live. He hoped for the latter. There was a great deal of work to do.

Slowly, the two remaining Tempest Runners took off their masks. Pan Eyta stood stiffly, his huge, tusked head expressionless—not that Marchion was very good at reading Dowutini emotions. Lourna Dee feigned nonchalance, shaking out her lekku.

Marchion Ro turned back to the waiting Nihil. With a flourish, he lifted his mask into the air.

"For Kassav!" he shouted, and this time there *was* an answering cheer, a torrent of sound, a release of tension and anxiety. They thought everything was going to be all right.

None of them had ever seen his face before. It didn't matter that they did now. None of them knew who he was. He wasn't Marchion Ro, either. His name was . . . it didn't matter. Where he came from was gone, other than the lessons it had taught him, and a few tools he had stolen from it when he left.

Marchion Ro lowered his mask, and as he did, a set of small servitor droids hovered up from behind the stage, each holding a metal bowl in its actuator arms.

They floated out above the assemblage, all but one, which stopped near Marchion.

"Kassav sacrificed himself to preserve the Nihil way of life, as did his Tempest," Marchion said. "He showed us the way. Whatever we have been, our wealth, our power . . . it's just beginning. Do you know why? Let me show you."

Another tap of a control on his belt, and the display being projected by the comms droids changed. No longer a frozen shot of the final moments of the Battle of Kur, it was now a beautiful, complex image of the galaxy in all its breadth and splendor, a slowly rotating spiral filled with countless worlds, countless riches, countless opportunities.

"The galaxy. But when I look at it, I do not see only stars and planets. I see . . . a storm."

The image began to spin faster, and now it did look like an enormous weather system, a hurricane rotating around a central eye.

"We are all the Nihil . . . we don't just ride the storm. We are the storm."

Understanding was beginning to dawn on their faces. Awe, even.

"Now we will *own* the storm," Marchion cried. "We've kept ourselves to the Outer Rim—didn't want to attract too much attention, didn't want to spoil a good thing. That is over. We are going to go as hard and as far as we can, and we are going to *take what we want.*"

Marchion gestured up toward the storm spinning above them all.

"The Nihil are going *galaxy-wide.*"

Now another cheer, no hesitation.

Marchion Ro began to pace back and forth across the stage, pointing at individual Nihil as he spoke, singling them out, watching them grin as he did, the looks of jealousy on their colleagues' faces.

"I have an archive of Paths that will take us all across the galaxy," Marchion said. "We can go anywhere we want, take anything we want. Lina Soh and her Republic and the Jedi tried to destroy us, but Kassav's sacrifice bought us time. Time to build, time to plan, time to grow our numbers. A day will come when we will teach the Republic that we cannot be destroyed. They will fear the Nihil. And if they try to take our freedom again, we will tear them apart."

Marchion reached out to the servitor droid hovering nearby and dipped his fingers in the bowl it was holding. They came out red.

"By the blood of the one who gave everything for us . . . Kassav."

Marchion took three fingers and drew them down his face in jagged lines. Lightning. Blood.

The servitor droids swooped down into the crowd, and he saw the Nihil repeating his gesture, taking the blood and swooping it down their faces, three jagged lines.

Marchion Ro didn't know if any of them were curious as to how one person could hold this much blood, or where he had gotten it if Kassav had died somewhere out in space . . . but it didn't matter. What mattered was that they would never ask those questions, because doubt could be perceived as weakness, and the Nihil stayed strong by removing what was weak.

Round and round it goes, he thought, looking up at the galaxy, gazing into the storm.

"Go," Marchion Ro said. "Bring me more Nihil, as many as you can . . ."

He grinned.

". . . and I will give you everything."

Mari San Tekka was asleep. She looked peaceful, wrapped in a cocoon of wires and actuator arms and monitoring systems—all the equipment her medical pod required to keep the ancient woman alive.

"Get your rest, my dear," Marchion Ro said, placing his palm flat on the pod, feeling the warmth emanating from the machine. "You have so much work to do."

She looked fetal—tiny and wizened, on her side, her hands curled up against her chest. The whole pod was like a womb in reverse—though he wasn't sure there was another human in the galaxy further from the womb than this woman.

Marchion had told the Nihil the truth. He did have an archive of Paths, thousands of them. Mari had spent the decades charting hidden routes all across the galaxy, and they were all stored in a database, able to be called upon at will. The Nihil could appear anywhere he wanted, even atop Chancellor Soh's palace, if he chose.

He wondered how long Mari would last. Long enough, he thought. He had found a supplier for the new miracle drug, bacta, which would probably help. It came from a world in the Hetzal system, which made Marchion laugh. He'd almost destroyed that planet.

Marchion Ro turned away from the sleeping Mari San Tekka. He left the chamber and descended three decks in his flagship. He walked through beautiful arched passageways, through large galleries, where once sermons were preached and dreams were built, and families worked and planned and considered a better way to live.

Until they didn't.

Now, the *Gaze Electric* was empty. Haunted.

At last, after a long trek through the huge vessel, Marchion Ro arrived in an area with a very different feel from the tranquil, subtly lit room where Mari San Tekka whiled away her endless years.

Here the lights were bright. The edges were sharp. Everything was reflective. There was nowhere to look to gain peace, and even closing your eyes could only do so much against the glare.

The walls were metal, as were the floors. Eight cells. Seven held prisoners delivered to him by Pan Eyta—nobodies, snatched from a passenger transport headed to Travnin. Ordinary people who certainly did not deserve imprisonment on the Eye of the Nihil's flagship.

Too bad. Life was rarely about what you deserved.

Seven of the occupied cells were wired to the ship's electrical system, and programmed to shock their prisoners at random intervals and intensity levels. Between the shocks and the lights, sleep was impossible. Being placed in a cell on the prison deck of the *Gaze Electric* meant anger, pain, fear, and, eventually, madness.

And all of it designed specifically for the man in the eighth cell.

The Jedi.

Marchion Ro walked down the hall, passing the poor wretches in the torture cells, coming to the last. The Jedi looked up, his face calm—but his eyes were tired. He could act as serene as he liked, but the emotional turmoil he must be sensing from the other prisoners was clearly achieving the intended effect. He had to be in pain, too—he had a badly broken leg, and Marchion had made exactly none of the high-tech medical facilities just a few decks up available to the man.

The Twi'lek moved quickly, lifting a hand with two fingers extended and speaking a single sentence.

"You will release us all," he said.

Marchion felt the pressure of the Jedi's intention washing across his mind. He *wanted* to do what the Twi'lek asked. Why wouldn't he?

Because he was Marchion Ro.

He smiled.

"It's not going to happen, Jedi," he said. "My family knew all about you people. They told me what you could do, and how to resist it."

He gestured vaguely toward the other cells.

"They're not getting out, either. If they die, I'll just bring in more. Their job is to fill this entire deck with pain and anger and fear. Makes it hard for you to think, doesn't it? Hard for you to call on the Force."

He leaned back against a nearby wall and crossed his arms.

"My grandmother told me how to do it; she learned from hers. You don't imprison Jedi behind bars. You do it with pain. I never had a chance to try it—but it seems like it works well enough."

One of the other prisoners moaned—not even enough energy left to scream, Marchion thought. The Jedi did not look. His eyes never left Marchion Ro's face.

"What's your name?" he asked. "I don't want to just keep calling you Jedi."

"Loden Greatstorm," the Jedi answered.

Marchion's eyes went wide. He pushed himself off the wall.

"Loden . . . *Greatstorm*?" he said. "By the Path, that's too perfect. It's truly a great pleasure to meet you, my friend. I think we will accomplish wonderful things together."

"What things?" Loden said. "Why are you doing this?"

Marchion laughed.

"You want my grand plan, Jedi? I don't do that. Plans can fail, at any step along the way. I have a goal, and goals can be achieved in any number of ways. As long as you get where you want to in the end, the roads you took don't matter. It's all the same path."

"Your goal, then," the Jedi said.

Marchion thought for a moment, considered his words.

"When my father died, I inherited a disorganized, broken organization. The Nihil had power, but it spent most of its time fighting within itself. It could never reach its full potential, and it had to, if it would ever become the weapon I need. My father tried to change things, but he failed, and then he was murdered."

Another moan from one of the torture cells. Marchion supposed the shock cycle had just triggered again.

"I almost didn't want to try at all. For a long time, I just carried on the same role he had—the Eye of the Nihil, keeper of the Paths. I got rich doing it. It was fine. And then . . . you came."

The Jedi's eyes narrowed. Marchion chuckled.

"Oh, not you specifically, Loden Greatstorm. I mean the Republic, building its Starlight Beacon out in my territory. Invading, taking over, with all its rules and laws and particular brand of freedom that isn't free at all. And you Jedi always just behind, absolutely convinced that every action you take is right and good. My family learned that to its cost, long ago."

"But we have met before," the Jedi said. "In a way."

His face was very, very cold, his dark-green skin seeming to absorb the bright lights of the prison deck.

"I recognize your voice," Loden said.

Marchion grinned. "There's a homesteader family, about thirty kilometers to the southwest of town," he said, his voice suddenly anxious, affected. "Two parents, two kids. You gotta go rescue them, Jedi, you just gotta!"

Marchion Ro slammed backward, hitting the bulkhead, hard. His head cracked against the durasteel. Nothing had touched him . . . but he knew it was the Jedi.

Loden slumped back—the effort to use the Force had clearly exhausted him.

"Not quite enough," Marchion said, gingerly touching the back of his skull. "Try that again and I'll kill one of the prisoners."

The Jedi did not respond.

"As I said, many paths, one goal. Hetzal was mine, too. I sent one of my ships to intercept the *Legacy Run.* A Stormship. They had no idea. I just needed an accident, a disaster, something to put the Nihil on the Republic's radar."

"Why would you do that?" Loden asked.

"Everything and everyone is a tool," Marchion Ro said, "I will use them however I need."

He smiled. A predator's smile . . . though this Jedi was dangerous, too, and he could not allow himself to forget it. His family had trusted the Jedi once, and it cost them everything.

"They will come for me," Loden Greatstorm said. "My Order. And if I am dead . . ."

He tilted his head, and a little smile played around his mouth.

". . . then they will come for you."

Marchion Ro reached inside his tunic and pulled out an object of stone and metal, a rod, three hands long, carved and incised with symbols -screaming faces, fire, chains. It looked as if it had been melted once and re-forged. As his hand touched the object, it began to glow, a sickly purple color that somehow overpowered the star-bright lighting of the prison deck.

This thing was almost as fully to blame for what happened to his ancestors as the Jedi—but that was an old story, and this was a new time. He could accomplish what they had not.

The rod grew warm under his hand. It felt almost alive, breathing. He showed it to Loden, whose eyes narrowed. In the purple light cast by the object, the Jedi's face looked strange. Dead.

"I'm not worried about your Order. If they think they can take me . . ."

He smiled at this Loden Greatstorm, so brave, the perfect Jedi Knight. So unafraid.

". . . let them come."

CHAPTER FORTY-FOUR

THE STARLIGHT BEACON.

The station was a wonder, gleaming in the void, an intricate gemstone sparkling in space, one of the largest offworld structures ever built. Its construction had taxed even the limitless resources of the Galactic Republic—but that was the point. Even the Outer Rim Territories deserved the best of the Republic.

We are all the Republic.

This was the Starlight Beacon, and it was, at last, complete. Not a day early, and not a day late. It was designed to serve many purposes, to attend to the diverse needs of the many citizens of the Republic in this region.

Perhaps two cultures required neutral ground upon which to negotiate a dispute—the Beacon would provide. Or if that dispute turned heated, and threatened to turn from words to war—the Beacon was a military base, with a strong contingent of peacekeepers staffed on a rotating basis from the worlds of the Republic Defense Coalition. Its superstructure was 19 percent triazurite, a rare mineral that boosted transmission signals, allowing it to serve as a massive relay point to facilitate better, faster communications among the peoples of the Outer Rim. It was a hospital, it was an observatory, it was a research station, it was a bustling market, trading in goods from across the Rim and beyond.

The Starlight Beacon was open to all citizens, built to allow them to experience the Republic in all its grand diversity. From subsonic whisper-fiber concerts by Chadra-Fan masters, to Mon Calamari ocean dancing, to modules demonstrating the flora and fauna of worlds from Kashyyyk to Kooriva . . . this *was* the Republic, the exhibits constantly changed and updated to provide a truly representative experience.

And of course, there was no Republic without Jedi. The Starlight Beacon housed the largest temple outside Coruscant, to serve as a hub for the Order's activities in the Outer Rim and beyond. Designed by renowned Jedi architect Palo Hidalla, and staffed by some of the most experienced members of the Order, the Starlight temple provided everything younglings, Padawans, Jedi Knights, and Jedi Masters might require to serve the people and the Force.

The Jedi quarter lacked a leader, after the tragic loss of Master Jora Malli at the battle against the Nihil . . . but perhaps that, too, might be addressed.

Luminaries from around the galaxy had arrived to mark the occasion of the station's dedication. The *Third Horizon*, hero vessel of so many recent events of galactic import, had already docked, its passengers released. And here, too, was the Jedi cruiser *Ataraxia,* permanently seconded to the Starlight Beacon as the Order's mode of transport to and fro. It had gathered Jedi from Coruscant and beyond, bringing them here to witness a great moment that would change the galaxy forever.

The visitors disembarked, all dressed for celebration and ceremony. The Jedi in their bright sashes of cerulean and vermillion and purple, draped across the gold and white of their tunics, with the symbol of the Order shining out, the rising light of the Force. The Republic diplomats and warriors and leaders of industry and culture, wearing whatever best reflected the occasion, a spectacle of chatter and enjoyable pomp.

The Beacon's staff took them in groups to demonstrate the station's many features, pride and optimism on every face, visitors and guides alike.

Bell Zettifar had come from Elphrona, along with Indeera Stokes and Porter Engle. The surviving members of the Blythe family were invited to this event, but declined, choosing instead to return to their relatives on Alderaan.

Bell was lost. He did not understand what had happened, how his master could be with him one moment and then . . . not. Indeera, who had taken him as her Padawan until some other arrangement might be made, believed Loden Greatstorm was dead. Bell did not. Technically, he could take the vows to become a Knight back on Coruscant, but he could not countenance doing such a thing. Loden Greatstorm was to preside over the ceremony, as was right and proper. But now . . . how?

Ember padded along at Bell's side. Perhaps unorthodox, but who would tell the Padawan he must be even more alone?

Porter Engle walked along with the group, quiet, and seemed to barely notice the wonders of the Starlight Beacon. He was remembering what it felt like to be the Blade of Bardotta, and remembering why he once chose to never be that person again.

Indeera thought about every decision she made during the rescue attempt on Elphrona, and wondered if some other path could have saved Loden and Ottoh Blythe. She did not know, and never would.

Led by another guide with a different group, Stellan Gios, Avar Kriss, and Elzar Mann walked through the station's bright corridors, together, as they often were whenever the business of the Order allowed it. There were rumors about who would lead the station's Jedi quarter now that Master Malli was gone, but the trio did not gossip. They were Jedi. All Masters now, too. The Council had finally indicated that they would allow Elzar Mann to take the vows; he would be able at last to see what awaited him in the depths of the endless sea that was the Force.

They passed the Trandoshan Jedi Sskeer, who had spent much time on the Beacon during its construction, and so did not require a tour. He stood at a viewport, looking out at space beyond. Avar offered a greeting, but Sskeer did not respond. He had survived the Battle of Kur, and his missing arm was slowly regrowing in the manner of his species, but the wound in his heart at the loss of Master Jora Malli was proving harder to repair.

In the huge assembly room at the heart of the Beacon, Nib Assek and Burryaga watched as Chancellor Lina Soh made her way to a dais in the center of the chamber. She walked side by side with Yarael Poof, a master on the Jedi Council. Every prominent Jedi in the galaxy was aboard the station, even Yoda, which surprised some. Ordinarily, the ancient master avoided non-essential social gatherings with determined glee, but here he was with the class of younglings he had taken under his tutelage in recent months. His reasons for attending the dedication of the Starlight Beacon were his own. Yoda kept his own counsel.

All around the chamber, many more people had gathered, the guides bringing their charges to the room as the tours ended for the primary event of the day. Mikkel Sutmani. Joss and Pikka Adren. Keven Tarr, Admiral Kronara, even Chief Innamin and Lieutenant Peeples. Jedi prodigy Vernestra Roh and her newly acquired Padawan, Imri Cantaros, just arrived from their own encounter with the Nihil at Wevo. Senators and ministers and presidents and more, people from stations low and high. Thousands of people had gone to extraordinary lengths to ensure this moment happened, and as many as possible were present today. Those who could not or chose not to attend were given access to a secure holochannel, to allow them to see and listen in real time.

Chancellor Soh reached the dais. Cam droids hovered, recording the moment. She spoke.

"You know I envision a galaxy of Great Works—connected and inspiring and filled with peace for all citizens. I believe this is possible, but not because of me, or any special ability of mine. I believe it is possible because of us. Because we can and will work together to achieve it. We are, every one of us, a great work. I see a galaxy where we use our strengths to shore up each other's weaknesses, where we understand and celebrate our differences and hold them up as valuable. We are a Republic where every voice matters, whether in the Core or on the farthest planet at the edge of the Rim."

She continued, addressing the sacrifices made to bring safety to the Outer Rim and allow the station to be completed. The deaths of Hedda Casset, Loden Greatstorm—Bell Zettifar blinked hard at this—Merven Getter, Vel Carann, Captain Finial Bright, and many more were acknowledged. A memorial was proposed, another Great Work, for all those killed in the *Legacy Run* disaster and the Emergences that followed. A multipiece sculpture, with works placed at the site of the Emergences in Hetzal, Eriadu, and Ab Dalis, containing the names of all who died.

Lina Soh spoke for precisely the right amount of time, and concluded with these words:

"This station will be a symbol of the Republic in the Outer Rim. A place where we will celebrate our union, and help each other to make it grow. It will send out a signal, for anyone in this sector to hear, at any time. The beacon. The Beacon of the Republic. The sound . . ."

Here she paused, and the cam droids captured sincere optimism on her face. This was not a politician. This was a woman who believed every word she was saying.

". . . of hope."

Across the atrium, against the stars, lightsabers ignited. Hundreds, in all the colors of the Jedi Order, a salute, held high.

In the space outside the station, anyone who looked would see a surging glow rush out from the beautiful, open space at its heart, pushing back the darkness.

The light of the Jedi.

The beacon activated, a signal, a sound, a chime, a tone that anyone with even the most rudimentary equipment could hear, for hundreds of parsecs around the station. Anyone who was lost, afraid, confused, hopeless . . . they could tune in. They could listen, and the sound would help them find their way.

The Starlight Beacon. The first of many.

All was well.

EPILOGUE

THE ENEMY.

"This is a beautiful place," Elzar Mann said.

Avar Kriss was at his side; they had left Stellan Gios behind at the dedication, deep in conversation with several Council members. Elzar and Avar walked along a path through one of the garden modules on the Starlight Beacon: a huge transparisteel bubble, through which a long spiraling walkway had been built. The base of the sphere was filled with the native soil of a world called Qualai, a small, low-gravity planet on the edge of the Outer Rim.

From that soil grew trees, tall and thin and elegant, reaching all the way from the module's base to its top, some three hundred meters above. Descending from the bright-blue branches of those trees, a drapery of vines, rippling ribbons stretching from crown to ground. These were varied shades of red and orange, graceful gradients running their lengths. Air currents stirred the vines, so they washed gently back and forth, their fragrance like incense.

The spiral path let one walk through these vines as they swirled and parted, tiny insects and birds bright with bioluminescence flitting between like sparks, each tree its own ecosystem.

At the center of the garden, with space looming beyond the transparisteel, the effect was something like standing inside a campfire, looking out at the night.

"Yes, it is," Avar said.

"And all ours," Elzar said. "No one else seems to have found it yet."

"It won't last," Avar said. "I'm sure people will leave the party and find their way here soon enough. Couples looking for quiet spots to be alone, probably."

"Then let's enjoy it while we've got it, eh?"

They kept ascending, the sound of the flame-ribbons washing through the chamber.

"Look at us, huh? Just a couple of Jedi Masters, taking a quiet moment together. Can you believe it? Sometimes I never thought it would happen."

Avar smiled at him.

"I knew the Council would promote you eventually," she said. "Was never a question."

"Easy for you to say. You made Master a few years ago."

"Hey, the Council knows talent when they see it. When will it happen?"

"Soon, probably. I'll need to stand before the Council, back on Coruscant. It feels like a formality, really. I can't imagine my life will change as much as it did at the last elevation."

"True. The jump from Padawan to Jedi Knight . . . that's where it all really sinks in. The choice of it . . ." Her voice trailed off.

Elzar suspected they were both thinking about the same thing. Shared moments as Padawans, tolerated and understood and even common—but things to be left behind once one ascended to become an adult in the Order.

They hadn't discussed those moments, not in a very long time, and never with more than an oblique reference, but they were never very far away from the other's mind, especially when they were together.

Those times, many years in the past, seemed very present just then.

Avar stopped. It took Elzar a step to realize she wasn't keeping pace, and he turned to look back at her.

He raised an eyebrow.

She held out her hand.

He took it. Held it up, looked at it, then looked at Avar Kriss, his friend.

The look she gave him was like that sea he found inside himself, the Force, deep and endless and impossible to fully comprehend.

You could drown in it.

"We are Jedi," he said.

"We are," she replied.

She looked away, and let go of his hand, and he was no longer drowning, but perhaps some part of him wished he was.

They kept walking.

"They gave me the station," Avar said.

"What?"

"I have command of the Jedi contingent on the Starlight Beacon. With Master Jora gone, they asked me to take over. I guess I impressed the Council after what happened in Hetzal, and everything after, and . . ."

"Yes. You are very impressive," Elzar said, his voice soft.

A little higher on the path, walking through the flames.

"I have work on Coruscant," Elzar said. "Research in the Archives . . . what we achieved in Hetzal has given me all sorts of ideas about new ways the light side might speak to us. I know the Council doesn't always understand the things I try to do, but I'm a Master now. I feel like this is my chance to really demonstrate how useful I can be to the Order."

"Yes," Avar said, her voice quiet as well.

"We won't be seeing each other as often," Elzar said. "Do you think we got too used to spending time together? Was that a mistake?"

"No," she said, her voice certain.

"I agree. And we'll stay in touch."

"Yes. We can speak whenever we want. Chancellor Soh's comm relay project will make that easier than ever."

"Of course," he said.

They had reached the top of the path, the end of the spiral, where an exit led back to the rest of the station. The sounds of celebration could be heard—dim and inviting.

"Sounds like it's ramping up. You want to put away a few glasses of whatever they've got? I wouldn't mind dancing, either. Should we go dance, Jedi Master Elzar Mann?"

He wondered what she thought of the look he was giving her just then. If she might be drowning a bit, too.

"I'll be along in a bit," he said. "It's nice here, and I don't know when I'll get to see this spot again."

"All right," she replied.

Avar hesitated, then smiled, full and open and honest, and walked away.

Elzar watched her go, then turned and looked out at the stars, at the emptiness of space, the deepest sea of all. Below him, the flame-trees churned, rustling and whipping—it was like standing atop an inferno. He let his consciousness roam out into the darkness beyond, looking, looking . . .

The Force seized his mind.

Awful visions flashed before his eyes, things he could not understand, cast in a sickly purple light. Jedi, many he knew, friends and colleagues, horribly mutilated, fighting battles they could not win against awful things that lived in the dark. Things that lived in the deep.

The Jedi, those who survived, were fleeing. Not retreating, but fleeing.

The visions spiked into his mind, the Force screaming some sort of warning or prophecy at him, shearing through his consciousness, and they would not stop.

Elzar fell to his knees, blood dripping from his nose. This did not feel like an unknowable, avoidable vision of the future.

This felt inevitable. Certain.

Evil, horror, sweeping across the galaxy like the tide.

He saw Jedi dying, screaming, and himself last of all, unable to escape what was coming.

Slowly, agonizingly, the vision receded. Elzar returned to himself. He gasped, and more blood spattered the deck.

What had he just seen? What had he seen?

The worst was not the chaos; the battles; the pain; the unknown, monstrous horrors surging out of the dark. It was what he had seen on the face of every single Jedi the Force had shown him.

The greatest enemy of all.

Fear.

Acknowledgments

Star Wars projects, of any type, are always a collective effort—from films to games to toys to this very novel . . . it takes a galaxy. That's particularly true of *Light of the Jedi*, which is the result of literally years of work by the group of people first introduced to the world as a collective of five writers working on the mysterious Project Luminous. I didn't know any of them personally when the project that would eventually become The High Republic began, though I knew their work. Now, though, it's rare that a day goes by that I don't talk to this incredibly talented group of writers: Claudia Gray, Justina Ireland, Daniel José Older, and Cavan Scott. They began as my colleagues and became my friends, and this book would not exist without their constant encouragement, vetting, and wonderful ideas.

Next, of course, the maestro who put Project Luminous together, and has sheltered his little group of writers from countless storms and kept us going since those first emails started circulating about what Luminous would become: Michael Siglain, creative director at Lucasfilm Publishing. He's the best, and I guarantee no one who's ever met him would tell you any different. He brought me in for this ride—brought all of us in—and I couldn't be more thankful.

The folks at Lucasfilm Story Group gave us endless time and focus as we were building The High Republic, and I'd like to particularly mention Pablo Hidalgo, whose notes were always additive and often came with instructive diagrams about the mysterious nature of hyperspace. James Waugh, for his constant, unflagging support, Matt

Martin and Robert Simpson, Brett Rector, Jen Heddle, Troy Alders . . . the list goes on. It's what I said at the beginning—*Star Wars* is a galaxy, and everyone contributes. It's wonderful to see.

Elizabeth Schaefer at Del Rey, for her editorial acumen and some really nice tweets after she finished reading an early draft of the novel. My agent, Seth Fishman, for whom no deal is impossible. Jordan D. White at Marvel Comics, who gave me my very first shot at writing *Star Wars* and from which all of the rest has come. Shawn DePasquale, my constant early reader. Tommy Stella, my constant assistant.

George Lucas and the many, many brilliant people he worked with to bring *Star Wars* to life (it takes a galaxy!). None of us would be doing this work without their efforts.

And, of course, my family—Rosemary and Amy, Hannah, Sam and Chris, Jay and Ann, Mary and Jim.

And finally, thank you. I hope you enjoyed the story.

We are all the Republic.

Charles Soule
Summer 2020

PHOTO: © MARC LEMOINE

CHARLES SOULE is a Brooklyn, New York–based novelist, comic book writer, musician, and attorney. His novels include *The Oracle Year* and *Anyone: A Novel.* While he has worked for DC and other publishers, he is best known for writing *Daredevil, She-Hulk, Death of Wolverine,* and various *Star Wars* comics from Marvel Comics (*Darth Vader, Poe Dameron, Lando,* and more), and his creator-owned series *Curse Words* (with Ryan Browne) and *Letter 44* (with Alberto Jimenez Albuquerque).

charlessoule.com
Twitter: @CharlesSoule
Instagram: @charlesdsoule

Read on for a sneak peek at

STAR WARS
THE HIGH REPUBLIC

THE RISING STORM

By Cavan Scott

Prologue

The Isle of Contemplation, Ashla.

The screams had never left Elzar Mann. Many months had passed since he stood on Starlight Beacon, dressed in his Temple finery, his collar itching and the memory of the dedication ceremony fresh in his mind. He had been standing alongside his fellow Jedi... alongside Avar Kriss... the eyes of the galaxy upon them. They had stood there, the light of distant stars streaming down from the ornate skylight, listening to the speeches and platitudes, first from Chancellor Lina Soh, leader of the Galactic Republic, and then from Avar. *His* Avar. The Hero of Hetzal.

The Beacon was their promise to the galaxy, Avar had said. It was their covenant. He could still hear her words.

Whenever you feel alone... whenever darkness closes in... know that the Force is with you. Know that we *are with you... For Light and Life.*

For Light and Life.

But that hadn't stopped the darkness from closing in later that day. A wave of pain and suffering, a vision of the future too terrible to comprehend. He had staggered, grabbing hold of a rail, blood gushing from his nose as the pressure in his head threatened to split his skull in two.

What he had seen had haunted him ever since. It had consumed him.

Jedi dying one by one, picked off by a twisting, unfathomable cloud. Stellan. Avar. Everyone he had ever known in the past and everyone he would meet in days to come. Faces both familiar and strange torn apart.

And the screams.

The screams were the worst.

He had made it through the rest of the evening in a daze, going through the motions, not quite present, the echo of what he had seen . . . what he had heard . . . burned onto his mind's eye. There had been mistakes, a few too many glasses of Kattadan rosé at the reception, Avar asking for that dance she'd mentioned, Elzar leaning in a little too eagerly, a little too publicly, his lips searching for hers.

He could still feel her hand on his chest, pushing him back.

"El. What are you doing?"

They had argued, privately, his head still spinning, Avar full of rebuke.

"We're not Padawans anymore."

It had been months since he saw her again, and when he did, the atmosphere was as frosty as a dawn on Vandor. Avar had changed toward him. She was more distant. Preoccupied with her new duties as marshal of Starlight Beacon.

Or maybe he was the one who was preoccupied. Elzar had meditated on the vision day and night since the dedication. He should have gone to Avar, to apologize and ask for her guidance, or if not her, then Stellan Gios, his oldest friend, but Stellan had duties of his own. He was a Council member now, responsible for guiding the Order as a whole. He would not have time. Besides, asking for help was hardly Elzar's style. Elzar Mann was the one who solved problems, not posed them. He found solutions. Answers. New ways of getting the job done.

So, Elzar did what he had always done: He tried to solve the problem alone.

First he had consulted the archives in the Great Temple, poring over every textfile and holocron in the collection, even going so far as to try to decipher the mysteries of the Ga'Garen Codex, the ancient grimoire whose text had confounded linguists for thousands of years.

Even then, sitting in the Archives, under the watchful gaze of the Lost, Elzar had heard the screams at the back of his mind, seen the faces of the slain in every reflective surface or passing Padawan.

He needed answers. He needed peace.

The Codex had brought him here, to the Isle of Contemplation on Tython's primary moon. He needed solitude if he was going to understand. He needed focus. The last straw had been receiving a message from Stellan's old Master, the esteemed Rana Kant, congratulating him on his elevation to Jedi Master. Furthermore, the Council had a posting for him; he was to be marshal of the Jedi outpost on Valo on the edge of the Rseik sector.

Him? A marshal? How could they be so blind? Couldn't they see he wasn't ready? Couldn't they see how troubled he was?

Elzar walked toward the ocean, feeling the warm sand beneath his feet, discarding his outer robes as he approached the water. Yes, this was better. This was where he would finally see the truth. Where he would finally understand. He didn't stop at the shore but strode out purposely into the waves. Up to his knees. Up to his waist. Soon he was swimming out to sea, stopping only when he could no longer see land. He spun slowly, treading water, surrounded only by the sea and the Force itself.

He was ready.

Elzar took a deep breath and pushed himself down beneath the waves, eyes closed, water rushing into his ears, blocking every other sound.

Show me.

Guide *me.*

Give me the answers I seek.

There was nothing. No revelation. No response.

He kicked back up, drawing air into his lungs before plunging back down again.

I am here.

I want to learn.

I need to understand.

Nothing changed.

Where were the answers he'd been promised? Where was the understanding?

He repeated the ritual, breaking for air, plunging back down, letting the ocean swallow him whole. Again, and again, and . . .

It was like hitting an air pocket. All at once he wasn't sinking, he was running, his fellow Jedi at his side as nightmares snapped at their heels. They weren't in water, but in fog. Thick. Acrid. Impenetrable. Nothing made sense. Not the chaos, not the panic.

Not the fear.

He opened his mouth to cry out, seawater rushing in from far away, from a different world, from a different time.

What is this?

Where *is this?*

Speak to me!

And the Force spoke with such strength that Elzar was thrown into a spin, images flashing past his stinging eyes like purple lightning.

Avar.

Stellan.

A Tholothian he had never seen before, one of her tendrils missing, face contorted in rage.

Bones splintering.

Skin cracking.

Eyes clouded, no longer able to see.

And the screams. The screams were louder than ever. Harsher than ever. And his scream was loudest of all.

Where?

Where?

WHERE?

Elzar's shoulders heaved, seawater spluttering from his lungs. He was back on Ashla, the salt drying on his skin, baked by the burning sun. He looked around, eyes still blurry, trying to focus on the golden sands that stretched out to either side of him, wingmaws circling in the sky above, ready to pick the flesh from his bones. But he wasn't dead yet. None of them were.

He pushed himself up and stumbled back toward his Vector, gathering his robes as he went. He needed to get off Ashla. Needed to leave the Core. The Force had spoken. It had answered his question. It had shown him where he needed to be. One name, a planet, where he would finally be able to put things right.

Valo.

Chapter One

The Rystan Badlands.

A comet plowed into the ice field, setting off a devastating chain reaction. Asteroids and space rocks bounced off one another like billiard balls. The only difference here was that most of the balls weighed millions of tons and could crush a ship like an egg. Those that weren't completely obliterated in the impacts were reduced into razor-sharp shards that only added to the wave of destruction.

No spacer entered the Rystan Badlands lightly. The ice field was filled with the twisted wreckage of cruisers that had attempted to run the gauntlet of colliding planetoids and failed. On a good day it was a dangerous, idiotic endeavor. On a bad day it was suicide.

Today was a *very* bad day.

The *Squall Spider* bucked as it wove through the spinning rocks. The craft was small, barely larger than a shuttle, but it was fast and as maneuverable as any of the Jedi's famed Vectors. In fact, anyone watching the strange arachnid-like craft could have been forgiven in thinking that a Jedi sat at the controls. Who else could have negotiated the ever-shifting starscape, weaving left and then right to avoid being pulverized by giant balls of ice? But the being in the pilot's seat couldn't have been further from a Jedi. The Jedi were the defenders of life and light the galaxy over. They lived for others, never for themselves, maintaining peace and harmony wherever they roamed. In short, they were heroes.

Udi Dis, on the other hand, had been born a Talortai but now only identified as a Nihil. As broad as he was tall, the avian had dedicated his life to piracy and plunder, taking what he wanted and decimating whatever was left. It wasn't a noble life, but it was the only one he knew and it had given him a place in the universe that had repeatedly spat in his face.

The only thing Dis had in common with the Jedi was his connection to the Force. Many if not all Talortai were sensitive to the energy field that bound the universe together, but few of his species ever made use of it, the cowards. They said it wasn't their right, that to do so was somehow immoral. Dis had never understood why. If you were lucky enough to have abilities, shouldn't you use them, hone them to gain an advantage over those who don't? This was why the majority of Talortai were doomed to remain where they were, scratching out a meager existence on Talor when he was out here in the stars. Sure, he had been let down many times, sometimes by others, most often by himself, but the Force had never betrayed him, not once. Life would have been better if he hadn't gotten himself addicted to reedug, but for now he was sober and had never felt so alive.

Dis clutched the controls with clawed hands, his muscled arms bunching as he slewed the *Spider* sharply to starboard, skillfully avoiding the debris that, with a lesser pilot at the helm, would have killed everyone on board. But Dis knew the badlands like the back of his feathered hand, even though he had never flown them before. All Talortai had an innate sense of direction, feeling the vibrations of the cosmos in their bones, but Dis's navigational skills were off the chart. Thanks to his talents, he could feel the location of every asteroid in the field. He didn't need maps or even a navidroid. All he needed was the Force.

Behind him, the door to the *Spider*'s cockpit slid open, stale air gushing from the planet-hopper's cramped corridors. Dis didn't turn to see who it was. There was no need. He heard the scrape of the boots on the deck plates, felt the swish of the cloak through the air, Dis's feathers ruffling in response to the presence of the man he had pledged to serve for the rest of his life.

Marchion Ro.

The Eye of the Nihil.

Had he been surprised when Ro approached him about this mission? Of course he had. He had no idea the Eye even knew his name, let alone what he could do in the pilot's seat. Dis had spent the last few years serving on the Cloudship of a saw-mouthed Crocin who went by the name of Scarspike, a thug who spent more time abusing his crew than planning raids. And it showed. Dis had killed Scarspike after a botched attack on Serenno's funeral moon. They had lost three Nihil that day, but Scarspike had lost more, Dis opening his scrawny throat with a slash of a wingblade. Dis had no idea if the Cloud's slaughter had first brought him to the Eye's attention. Maybe, maybe not. All Dis knew was that he suddenly found himself elevated beyond the Strikes and the Clouds and all the Nihil's ranks to join Ro's personal retinue. His aggrandizement didn't go unnoticed. The Nihil had a strict hierarchy. You started as a lowly Strike, working your way up to Cloud and eventually to Storm. The Nihil Horde itself was organized into three Tempests, each commanded by a Tempest Runner. There was Pan Eyta, a towering Dowutin with ideas above his station, the cold and efficient Twi'lek Lourna Dee, and the latest appointment, a scheming Talpini known as Zeetar. It was fair to say that the Talpini's promotion had put Pan's squashed nose out of joint. Dis's sudden promotion had only rankled him further. Pan and Dis had almost come to blows, the Dowutin claiming that Ro was undermining the Nihil's Rule of Three. Unlike the Tempest Runners, the Eye was supposed to have no crew of his own. Yes, he had the casting vote when making plans, and yes, he provided the navigational Paths that the Nihil used to avoid Republic entanglement (well, most of the time, at least). Dis suspected that if it weren't for the Paths, Pan would have sent Ro spinning out of an air lock long ago, but the navigational aids were too valuable. They gave the Nihil the edge, so Eyta's concerns fell on deaf ears. Dis was welcomed aboard Ro's vast flagship, the *Gaze Electric,* which was largely maintained by a crew of silent droids, its many chambers empty, like a palace with no occupants. It was here, in Ro's inner sanctum, that Dis had learned they were heading to Rystan on a private mission—not that they could have taken the *Gaze,* of course. The ship rarely left the Nihil's base in No-Space, and even then split itself into a smaller secondary craft that left the bulk of the *Gaze* behind, but even that would be too cumbersome to make it through the ice field in one piece. They needed something smaller. They needed the *Squall Spider.*

"How long until we clear the badlands?" Ro asked, resting a gauntleted palm on the back of Dis's seat.

"Just a few minutes, my . . ."

Dis swiveled in his chair to face his leader. "What should I call you, anyway? My Eye? *Sir?*"

Ro's thin lips curled at the obvious distaste in Dis's voice, his dark eyes glinting in the red light that streamed in through the viewport.

"You can call me . . . Marchion."

Dis's chest swelled. He had never been one for the chain of command, which was probably why he had stayed a Strike for so long—that and the fact he'd spent most of the last decade in a reedug stupor. But now look at him, on first-name terms with Ro himself. No one called the Eye Marchion, not even Pan.

"I still think it would've been easier to use a Path," Dis said, finally bringing the *Spider* out of the ice field to slingshot around Rystan's weak star.

Ro walked over to the vacant gunner's station to recover his mask, which had remained on the console ever since they had left the Great Hall.

"But then I wouldn't have seen a master at work," the Eye replied, wiping the mask's frosted visor with his sleeve. "You're every bit as impressive as your heritage suggested you would be, especially now that you're free from your . . . affliction."

Yeah, he was free all right. Ro had made Dis throw what little remained of his stash into a trash compactor back on board the *Gaze.* His mind was clear for the first time in years, his connection to the Force stronger than ever. There was no way he could have made it through the ice field when he was on reed. He owed Ro so much.

"And to think we had a Force-user in our midst all these years . . ." Ro continued, checking the filters of his mask. "Scarspike was a fool. I'm glad he's dead."

You're not the only one, Dis thought, but kept the thought to himself as the *Spider* dropped into Rystan's thin atmosphere.

"Have you ever been to a tidally locked world?" Ro asked.

Dis shook his head.

"They're fascinating," the Eye told him. "One face constantly angled toward the sun, its surface little more than charred desert."

"While the other's a frozen wilderness," Dis said, the blasted terrain not inspiring much confidence. "So where do we land?"

Ro pointed at a band of barely habitable land that ran between the two extremes. "There."

"Is there a spaceport?"

"Not exactly."

Ro directed them to a patch of barren ground, clumps of rollweed tumbling across the wasteland.

"Are you *sure* this is the place?" Dis asked as the landing gear deployed. "There's nothing here."

Ro merely smiled as he slipped his mask over his head. "Oh, you'll be surprised . . ."

Chapter Two

The Cyclor Shipyards.

Not long ago, Padawan Bell Zettifar would have been excited by the sight that stretched out beneath him. He was standing on an observation platform in the largest hangar he had ever experienced, just part of the vast shipyards that orbited Cyclor, a relatively small green-and-brown planet in the Mid Rim. Below, gleaming bright in the hangar's floodlights, was the vision in polished durasteel known as the *Innovator.* The starship, now hours from launch, was a technological marvel. Over 150 meters long and bristling with the latest scientific and medical equipment, the *Innovator* was quite simply the most sophisticated research vessel ever built, a fact its designer—the famed Aqualish engineer Vam Targes—had told Bell himself when he had arrived at the shipyards.

"It runs on a network of no fewer than forty-two intellex-grade droid brains, don't you know?" Targes had informed him as they strode through the ship's vast operations center on a whirlwind tour, the engineer's vocoder whirring excitedly as it translated Vam's native Aqualish to Basic.

"That's very . . . impressive," Bell had offered, only to be told in no uncertain terms that it was considerably more than that. It was outstanding!

"The entire network is supported by a multi-motion processor framework of my own design, one that rivals the Jedi Archives on Coruscant, if I do say so myself."

Bell didn't know if that was true, but he hadn't wanted to contradict the engineer. This was his moment, after all, or rather it would be when the *Innovator* arrived on Valo in a couple of days. The ship was to be a showpiece at the upcoming Republic Fair, the latest of Chancellor Lina Soh's Great Works. Soon millions of festival-goers would be marveling at Targes's achievement, and if they were anything like Bell, they would be dazzled. The *Innovator* boasted state-of-the-art cybernetic workshops alongside multiple bioengineering labs, analysis stations, research facilities, and a medical library second only to the Docha Institute on Dunnak.

But as extraordinary as the craft undoubtably was, it was still nothing compared with the beings who had constructed the ship rivet by rivet. The Cyclorrians were a wonder, unlike anything Bell had seen before. Insectoid in nature, they stood about a meter in height with a large bulbous head dominated by a pair of large compound eyes, much like the heat-flies that had buzzed through the halls of the Jedi outpost on Elphrona where Bell had received most of his training. He watched as they swarmed across the glistening hull, completing final checks, each Cyclorrian working in unison with their teammates without seeming to utter a single word. It was incredible. Each seemed to know instinctively exactly what job needed doing, none of them getting under one another's feet, each perfectly complementing the next. And the enthusiasm for their work was infectious. In the twenty-four hours since he had arrived, Bell hadn't seen a single Cyclorrian complain, despite Targes's reputation as a strict taskmaster. The insectoids just kept on working, hour after hour, antennae twitching happily as they buzzed from one task to the next. You couldn't help but smile in their presence. It was exactly what Bell needed, especially now.

Beside him, Ember stirred. The charhound had been sitting patiently at his feet, Bell's constant companion since they had left Elphrona. The dog had been a stray that had been adopted by the Elphronian Jedi, becoming something of a mascot at first and a loyal friend ever since. When Bell had left Elphrona, Ember had simply hopped into his Vector, her intention of staying by his side clear. She had been there ever since, his guardian and confidante. Now she was on her feet, looking expectantly at the door of the observation platform as it swished open to allow Indeera Stokes entry. The aging Jedi laughed as Ember bounded over, jumping up onto the Tholothian's legs to be rewarded by a tickle beneath the orange-flecked chin.

"Yes, yes," Indeera said. "I'm pleased to see you, too. Now down you get. That's it. Good girl. Good girl."

Ember obeyed, trotting back over to Bell where he had remained at the edge of the platform. Bell looked down at her and smiled, the charhound's excited tail thwacking against his boots.

"I'm sure she likes you more than she does me," he commented as Indeera joined him.

"I think we both know that's a lie," she said, joining him to gaze down at the majestic craft below. She leaned against the railing, shaking her head at the spectacle of the Cyclorrians hard at work. "Stars above, it takes your breath away, doesn't it?"

"Indeed it does, Master. The *Innovator* is as impressive as those who constructed it."

As always, Bell felt a pang as he addressed Indeera by her title. It was true, the Tholothian was his teacher now, having agreed to take on his training after his previous Master, Loden Greatstorm, had been lost in the Battle of Kur against the Nihil nearly a year ago. Their last conversation played regularly through his mind, Loden at the controls of his Vector.

"I'm not your Master anymore, Bell. You're a Jedi Knight."

"Not until the Council declares it, and I want you there when it happens."

Now that would never be. Loden had told him that he would see Bell soon and had never come back from the attack. No one knew what had happened, not really, only that his Vector . . . *their* Vector . . . had been reduced to atoms by a Nihil cannon. He was gone and even though Indeera constantly reminded Bell that Loden's final wishes had been for his Padawan to be Knighted, he knew he wasn't ready. How could he be, when he felt so empty inside, like someone was missing?

"Bell?"

He swallowed, suddenly aware that Indeera was studying him. His new teacher, no matter how weird that felt. And it shouldn't. He'd known her for years, even fought by her side, and respected her more than any Jedi alive, which, of course, was the problem. Loden Greatstorm was dead and no matter how much Bell admired Indeera, she could never replace him.

He offered a weak smile. "I was just thinking about how excited the crowd will be at the Republic Fair, seeing the *Innovator* for the first time."

"They will. And what about you?"

"What about me?"

"Are you looking forward to Valo?"

He shifted uncomfortably, careful not to kick Ember who was nuzzling against his legs, her pelt warm through his synthleather boots. "It will be good to see Mikkel and Nib. And Burry, too, of course." That was all true. He'd come to think of all three as friends, especially the Wookiee Burryaga, whom he had gotten to know after serving together at Hetzal.

"Of course," Indeera parroted, still regarding him with those warm eyes. "There will be much to experience together." She looked back at the ship. "Loden would have loved it. He would have loved this."

A lump formed in Bell's throat as Indeera continued. "I can imagine him standing here with us, watching the Cyclorrians work, appreciating their skill."

Bell's voice cracked as he tried to control his emotions. "And what do you think he would say? If he were here?"

The Tholothian pursed her lips. "I think he would compliment you on the shine of your holster buckle, tell you to smile more often, and point out that if you're *ever* going to master a lateral roll you're going to have to log at least two more hours a day in your Vector."

A grin broke out on Bell's face, despite himself. The last part of the sentence was pure Indeera, who always seemed happier in the sky than on her feet.

"He would also remind you how a Jedi faces the death of those they love," she continued, and Bell's smile immediately dropped away. "Because Jedi can love, Bell. We're not droids, nor should we ever be. We are living creatures rich in the Force, with everything that brings. Joy, affection, and, yes, grief. Experiencing such emotions is part of life. It is Light."

"But—"

"But while we experience such emotions, we should never let them rule us. A Jedi is the master of their emotions, never a slave. You miss what you might have shared with Loden if he were here. That is natural. I miss him, too. And so we acknowledge that hurt. We understand it, even embrace it, but eventually . . ."

"We let it go," Bell said, looking back at the *Innovator* so Indeera couldn't see the tears she must have known were in his eyes.

The Tholothian reached out, placing a comforting hand on Bell's forearm. "I didn't say it was easy. Just like a lateral roll."

That made him smile again, as did the slight squeeze she gave him before turning back toward the ship. "Besides, no one is ever really gone. No matter what happens, Loden will be with you, now and forever. He is a part of all of us now."

Again the tears pricked his eyes. "Through the Force."

"Through the Force," she agreed. "You believe that, don't you?"

He nodded, hoping that she was fooled while knowing full well that she wasn't. "Yes. Of course I do."

"I'm glad to hear it," she said, not sounding convinced. "Now, unless there's anything else . . ."

"We should get off this platform and actually do something with the day," he said, keen to bring the conversation to an end.

Indeera's comlink beeped before she could respond.

"Maybe the Force agrees with you, my not-so-young Padawan." Indeera fished the comlink from her tan-colored jacket and activated the channel.

"Stokes here."

"This is Stellan Gios," a voice crackled over the link, the Jedi Master's usually rich tones rendered tinny by the vast distance between them. While Starlight Beacon had improved communications on the frontier, the comm network was still stretched to the breaking point, even here in the Mid Rim. Chancellor Soh had promised a complete line of Beacons stretching from the Core to the farthest reaches of the Republic, but until that pledge became a reality, they would have to cope with bouts of static that frequently drowned out communications.

"Apologies, but can you repeat that?" Indeera was forced to say as the rest of Master Gios's greeting distorted beyond recognition.

"Of course," he complied. "I was just checking on your progress. Will the *Innovator* be ready to launch on time?"

"Ahead of schedule," Bell cut in, before blushing as he realized he had spoken when the question was directed at his Master. Indeera made a show of rolling her eyes, although the smile on her lips told him he wasn't in trouble. For all her wisdom, she wasn't one to stand on ceremony.

"I'm glad to hear it . . . Padawan Zettifar, isn't it?"

Bell nodded even though Stellan couldn't see him. "Yes, Master Gios. The Cyclorrians are a marvel, as is the *Innovator.*"

"Then I look forward to seeing it for myself, and to finally meeting you, of course. Nib Assek has been singing your praises."

Bell's blush deepened. "She is with you?"

"On our way to Valo, yes. She's looking forward to seeing you again."

"She is too kind," he stammered, not knowing what to do with himself.

"And my Padawan is too modest, even for a Jedi," Indeera cut in. "The Force has blessed him, as you will see for yourself, old friend."

Bell's eyebrows shot up. He had no idea that Indeera knew Gios, let alone that they were as close as her tone suggested.

"I don't doubt it," Stellan said. "Until Valo, then. I hear the pickled cushnip is to die for."

"Better than we ate on Theros Major? I'll be the judge of that."

Stellan chuckled on the other end of the line. "Why am I not surprised. Now, if you'll excuse me, I have an appointment with a cam droid."

It was Indeera's turn to laugh. "Well, if you will get yourself promoted to the High Council . . . People will be asking for your autograph next."

"I'll send them your way instead. Gios out."

"What's he like?" Bell asked as Stokes slipped the comlink back beneath her soft-leather jacket.

"Stellan? One of the finest Jedi I've ever met. We served together before he was stationed at Caragon-Viner. He's younger than me, of course, but—"

Indeera paused, her white tendrils shifting slightly on her shoulders. Bell didn't have to ask why. He had felt it, too, a cooling in the Force, its flame dimming just for a moment, before burning brighter than before.

"Something's wrong," he stated simply, Ember jumping up as the atmosphere between the two Jedi shifted, her hackles raised.

"That's an understatement," Indeera agreed, already making for the platform's doors. "Inform the *Innovator* we're on our way."

Chapter Three

Safrifa.

Will you help us?

Ty Yorrick had lost count of the times she had heard those words, usually delivered with a side order of pleading eyes and, more often than not, missing limbs. You had to be desperate to approach someone like Ty.

The swamp farmers of Safrifa were desperate.

They had found her repairing her ship on the edge of the bog fields, preparing to leave after a successful extraction operation where she had liberated the son of the local marsh-lord from a rival clan. There had been blood and screaming. Always blood and screaming. Some of the gore still caked her armor and the screams would linger when she finally fell into her cot that evening, even after taking keekon root to help her sleep. In all honesty she didn't mind the screams. They had been her companion for the best part of a decade, the one constant in her ever-changing life.

The novian ore she had received for the kid's safe return would come in handy. Her ship needed parts, and parts meant money. She knew an armorer on Keldooine who would take the novian off her hands, smelting it down to forge saw blades. Maybe she'd buy one herself. Less money for the ship, but her arsenal had been depleted after that botched job on Alzoc III. Kriffing Hoopaloo, stealing half her stash. Other mercs would have tracked down the traitorous parrot and ripped the smarmy beak clear from his face, but Ty wasn't any other merc. Bad things happened and you dealt with it. There was no point wasting time or effort on battles you didn't need to have, especially if no one was paying you.

She had sensed the swamp farmers long before she heard them slosh through the bog. Sensed and assessed. They were no threat to merc or beast. No threat to anyone. Most Safrifans were scrawny little creatures with skin the color of stagnant water and hair that hung like pondweed in front of large oval eyes. They were industrious, though. Ingenious, too. Ty had trudged through one of their floating beds—a long, narrow plot of thick soil raised from the marshwater by mud and decaying vegetation to stop the roots of their kru-kru crops becoming waterlogged. The farm had stretched on for kilometers, each plot framed by willow trestles and surrounded by a network of narrow canals. At first glance, you would be forgiven for thinking that nothing could be grown here, but the Safrifans had proved otherwise. Resourceful and resilient. Ty liked that. Admired it even. And now they were here, at her hatch. It could only mean one thing.

"Nice ship," the warbling voice asked in broken Basic. "What it name?"

"Doesn't have one," Ty replied in their native tongue, not turning around from her work. The damn stabilizer was hanging on by a thread.

"You speak our language?" the farmer asked, surprised.

"Enough to get by." She was lucky like that. It had always been the same. Ty picked up most languages quickly, a useful talent in her profession. Sometimes she let people know; at other times she kept quiet and listened. She had nothing to fear from these two, even as they dithered behind her, not knowing what to say now that their small talk had failed. She hadn't been lying, though. Her ship, a battered YT-750 freighter, didn't have a name, only a registry number logged in the Republic records. Several numbers actually, depending on the job or employer. She didn't see the point of giving anything a name—ship, weapon, or even the two droids that assisted her on missions, a sarcastic admin unit and an admittedly useful astromech. Like the ship, they were tools, nothing more. Why form attachments to something that could never be attached to you? Maybe it was a throwback to her training. Maybe not. Ty just thought it was common sense.

"What do you want?" She needed this conversation to be over. She had places to go, parts to buy.

"We have novian. Not much. But enough."

"Enough for what?"

Instead of answering, the farmers offered a simple statement: "It is killing our children."

Ty stopped working, the all-kit tool dropping down from the exposed stabilizer core.

"What is?" she asked, an air of resignation in her voice.

"A monster. A bad one."

Was there any other kind?

"How long has it been happening?"

"Three weeks. We have laid traps but it smashed them. It wrecks our plots, ruins the crops."

"How many?"

"Crops?"

"How many children?"

"Does it matter?"

Correct answer.

Finally she turned, taking in the pathetic sight in front of her. They were little more than walking skeletons, skin stretched over prominent bones. The taller of the two, relatively speaking, lifted a leather pouch. "We have novian," he repeated, his companion hunched behind him, leaning heavily on a staff.

Not much novian if the size of the bag was anything to go by. Hardly worth her time.

It is killing our children.

"Where?"

"In the Sorcan Swamp, three days' hike from here. One, if you have a skimmer."

"Do you have a skimmer?"

"No."

He looked at her and she looked at him. His companion looked at the marshwater. Exhausted. Without hope or expectation.

Back in the day, she would have used a set of Verazeen stones to make the decision, telling herself that she was leaving things to chance. To the will of the universe. One side of the stones was etched with moon symbols, the other suns. The process was simple enough. Throw them at the ground, decide whether you were banking on more suns or moons, and let fate guide your way. She'd been taking more of an active role recently, choosing her own path instead of relying on the stones, and right now she knew that the job wasn't worth it. She should get back in the ship and blast off for Keldooine. It was the sensible thing to do. Logical, even.

He needed to say the words.

"Will you help us?"

And there they were.

About the Type

This book was set in Hermann, a typeface created in 2019 by Chilean designers Diego Aravena and Salvador Rodriguez for W Type Foundry. Hermann was developed as a modern tribute to classic novels, taking its name from the author Hermann Hesse. It combines key legibility features from the typefaces Sabon and Garamond with more dynamic and bolder visual components.